Praise for the Fr...

"[A] witty, memorable st...

"Western aficionados will welcome a refreshing new voice in the subgenre." —RT Book Reviews

"This will appeal to those looking for not just a happy-ever-after romance for two deserving characters, but a credible account of challenging conditions during the settlement of the American West in 1849." —Historical Novel Society

"*Bound for Sin* was a sweet, fun historical Western that was exciting, romantic, and humorous, with a great couple." —The Reading Cafe

"I adored Tess LeSue's *Bound for Eden*! Her voice is brilliant, funny, and immediately draws you into the book." —*New York Times* bestselling author Jessica Clare

"I was blown away by the sparkling brilliance of [Tess's] writing. She has a real gift for historical atmosphere, compelling characters, sexual tension, and witty dialogue." —Anna Campbell

"[Tess's] writing is lively and taut and generates emotion. Her characters spring to life and her stories move at a fast pace." —Anne Gracie

"An accomplished mix of comedy and suspense. I found myself cheering with the heroine as she boldly navigates the journey to Oregon and, eventually, her freedom. I absolutely loved it." —Victoria Purman

Titles by Tess LeSue

BOUND FOR EDEN
BOUND FOR SIN
BOUND FOR TEMPTATION
BOUND FOR GLORY

BOUND
for
GLORY

———◆———

Tess LeSue

JOVE
New York

A JOVE BOOK
Published by Berkley
An imprint of Penguin Random House LLC
penguinrandomhouse.com

Copyright © 2019 by Tess LeSue
Excerpt from *Bound for Eden* copyright © 2018 by Tess LeSue
Penguin Random House supports copyright. Copyright fuels creativity, encourages
diverse voices, promotes free speech, and creates a vibrant culture. Thank you for buying
an authorized edition of this book and for complying with copyright laws by not
reproducing, scanning, or distributing any part of it in any form without permission.
You are supporting writers and allowing Penguin Random House to continue to
publish books for every reader.

A JOVE BOOK, BERKLEY, and the BERKLEY & B colophon
are registered trademarks of Penguin Random House LLC.

ISBN: 9780593098288

First Edition: December 2019

Printed in the United States of America
1   3   5   7   9   10   8   6   4   2

Cover art by Claudio Marinesco
Cover design by Judith Lagerman and Claudio Marinesco

For Lynn Ward.

Legend.

ACKNOWLEDGMENTS

It's so hard to come to the end of this series! It's been a rollicking adventure, and I've loved every minute. Thank you to all the readers out there who have enjoyed the Frontiers of the Heart series. Your letters and e-mails and messages on social media mean the world to me—thank you for reaching out.

Bound for Glory is dedicated to my Disco Queen, Lynn Ward. We have danced together, traveled together, quaffed margaritas together, planned books together, and generally been loud and annoying and had too much fun. My cat loves you, but not as much as I do. Here's to years more of doing what we love.

Once again, I'd like to thank my family, who supported me in a very real way as I wrote these books. Jonny, Kirby, and Isla: you are the reason for everything. Thanks for putting up with me. Thanks also to my parents, my bro, and my Zweck family. And my cat, who sat next to me while I wrote most of this book.

Thank you to Flinders University, particularly the creative and performing arts and English staff, and also the research support officers, Narmon and Elizabeth. Special shout-outs this time around to Patrick Allington, Tully Barnett, Kate Douglas, Amy Mead, Julian Meyrick, Sarah Peters, Alex Vickery-Howe, Elizabeth Weeks, and Sean Williams.

Thank you to Writers SA, where I have been proud to have been chair these last few years. Lots of love to my deputy chair, David Sefton. He knows why.

Thanks to the always fabulous women of SARA and RWA. Romance writers rock!

Thank you always to my agent, Clare Forster, and to Kristine Swartz and the amazing team at Berkley, who make the most beautiful books and who always give 110 percent. I deeply appreciate it.

I would like to acknowledge my reliance on Bob Drury and Tom Clavin's excellent book *The Heart of Everything That Is: The Untold Story of Red Cloud, An American Legend* for information about the Fort Laramie/Horse Creek Treaty of 1851. Drury and Clavin have written a riveting work of nonfiction, and I highly recommend it.

I would also like to acknowledge the First Nations people of California and the Great Plains, particularly the nations mentioned in this book; I would like to recognize their rich heritage and traditions and to pay my respect to their storytellers: past, present, and future.

✢ 1 ✢

Southern California, 1850

THERE WAS A naked man in the desert.

Ava Archer knew trouble when she saw it, and this was trouble with a capital T. She was alone in the desert, her horse was played out, her canteen was bone-dry, and she was out of bullets. This was no time to be running into natives. Even a solitary one. If she had any sense at all, she would turn right around and run in the other direction . . . but Kennedy Voss was in the other direction, and Kennedy Voss was a mean son of a bitch. Besides, she was desperate for water, and maybe this Indian had some.

She'd thought she'd known thirst before—but this was something else again. She felt made of grit and sand, her every pore a desert in miniature, her tongue thick and swollen in her cottony mouth; even her eyes and nose had dried out. And every thud of her horse's hooves on the ground made a drumbeat: *Water. Water. Water. Water.*

So Ava kept on toward the man, pulled by the hope of water. As she plodded closer, she reassured herself that at least there was only one of him, and from what she could see, he was in bad shape: he was squatting under the screamingly bright September sun, naked from the waist up, his body a patchwork of bruises, and both of his eyes swollen shut. Ava doubted he could see her. But he knew she was there, because he rose to his feet at the sound of her tired horse dragging his way.

Oh dear. He wasn't *mostly* naked, she saw as he stood: he was *completely* naked. He was also tall, wide, and terrifyingly powerful. A warrior. He was the color of rosewood, his muscles as hard as if he'd been carved from a tree. And he was covered in tattoos, including a sprawling, intricate pattern in the shape of a bird, which stretched its wings the breadth of his thickly muscled chest. His hair was long, loose, and coated in dust; it fell down his back in tangles to his shoulder blades. He was bruised all over, she realized as her gaze drifted down, wincing as she took in the black blotches on his legs. There was a particularly nasty one on his hip, right next to . . .

Ava tore her gaze away. Hell. *She was alone in the desert with a naked man.* A big, powerful, wounded naked man. And she was heat struck and ill with thirst, barely able to think straight.

She couldn't have stumbled onto a little old lady instead? Or a nice family, with a pack of kids? A pack of kids and an icy-cold barrel of water . . .

Ava rubbed her hand across her dry mouth. She felt skin flakes come away on her fingers and winced. She needed to get hold of herself. She was growing delirious. This here was just an injured man. Probably an Apache, considering she was somewhere near the Apacheria. Probably. Maybe. Who knew where the hell she was, to be honest. Purgatory seemed likely. Little old ladies and nice families didn't go wandering around Purgatory—this was the best she could hope for. She should have been grateful that he was just one beat-up Apache and not a whole party. And at least he wasn't Kennedy Voss. Without even realizing she was doing it, she glanced over her shoulder, as though thinking about Voss might summon him. That man gave her the willies. Voss was likely to be somewhere nearby (she hadn't had *that* much of a head start on him), and here she was about to die of thirst right in his path. She didn't have time to be distracted by naked strangers.

This Apache here might be big, and he might have more muscles than she'd ever seen on a man, but he didn't look too fearsome. Not as fearsome as Voss anyway. He wasn't charging at her or yelling at her or even looking angry. In fact, he stood quite calmly, head cocked, listening. And he was naked. That was just about as vulnerable as a man could get. Not to mention the fact that his eyes looked to be swollen all to hell.

Naked and blind. He was bound to be more scared of her than she was of him. . . .

Ava pulled her horse up a good few feet away from him. He held a rock loosely in his hand and seemed ready to peg it in her direction if she threatened him, but other than the rock, he wasn't armed. In fact, he didn't seem to have *anything*, she realized in shock as she took in the area around him. No weapons, no clothes, no horse, no baggage. *No water.*

Ava couldn't suppress her groan. He didn't have so much as a half-empty waterskin. Nothing. Her gaze flicked from him to the landscape around him, over and over again, compulsively hunting for water, as though she could will it into existence. She might well die out here, she realized, feeling light-headed with horror. After all of her years flirting with death, this might be it. And what a stupid way to die, running out of water in the desert. She'd survived gunslingers and gamblers, robbers and raiders, cold-blooded killers and the worst the west had to offer. Not one of those things had got the best of her. How could she be defeated now by something as simple as a lack of water?

This time her groan was splintered. And there was more than a touch of rage in it.

At the sound his hand tightened on his rock, and he

frowned. She'd just given away the fact that she was a woman, she realized. Oh well. It had to happen eventually. And what did it matter? She was the one on a horse. He could hardly catch her on foot. Especially in his condition.

"Do you speak English?" she called out to him. "Or Spanish?" She switched to Spanish, which she spoke badly. She hoped he spoke one of them, because she sure as hell couldn't speak Apache.

"Both," he replied. *"Ambos."* His voice was deep, smooth, startling.

"I don't suppose you have any water?" she asked, hoping against hope.

"Let me check my pockets," he said dryly. He seemed calm, but Ava could see his hand clenching and unclenching around the rock. Then something seemed to occur to him. "If you're asking me for water, that must mean *you* don't have any . . ."

She shifted irritably in the saddle. "And if *you're* that disappointed that I'm asking, that means *you* don't have any either."

"Looks like we're a matched pair."

He might be beat-up, but he seemed lively enough. His blindness and bruises looked painful, but he was standing tall and his wits were sharp. Ava didn't know yet if this was a good thing or not.

"You speak English well," she observed.

"So do you," he said, deadpan.

He was lively enough to be a regular clown, this Apache.

But lively or not, if he had no water, she had no call for him. She sighed. Poor guy. He wasn't going to last long out here, naked and alone, without water or a horse. And blind to boot.

"Well, although it's been a pleasure, albeit a brief one, I can't stay," she said, feeling a deep melancholy bloom at the thought of his fate. But what could she do? She didn't have any water to offer. All she had was some salty hardtack, and that was hardly likely to help; it would only make him *more* thirsty. She should know; she'd been gnawing on it all morning, and her thirst was out of control.

"I'm sorry I don't have anything to offer you," she apologized. "I wish I did. But since I don't . . . I'll have to be pressing on. Good luck out here, mister."

"You'll be *pressing on*?" He sounded astonished.

"Yeah," she said. "Unless you find water in your pockets." She hoped her horse could make it a bit farther. She hoped *she* could make it a bit farther. Oh God, think of all the water she'd wasted over the years; think of the washbowls she'd tipped out; think of the glasses gone unfinished, the streams and creeks passed by. . . . "I really need water," she said miserably, squinting at the parched desert, knowing every direction would lead her to more desert.

"*You* really need water?" Now there was a real edge to his voice. An edge she didn't like. She eyed him. He was a big one. Big enough that she didn't fancy a run-in with him, even if he was all beat-up.

"Mister, if I *had* any, I'd give you some. But I don't, so I can't." Ava gathered the reins into one fist and put her hand on the holster of her gun. Even though the weapon was without bullets, it reassured her to feel it under her palm. "There's no point in complaining. Facts are facts: my pockets are as empty as yours." Her gaze returned to his naked flanks. At least she *had* pockets. This poor bastard was deprived even of those.

"And you're just going to leave me here? In the desert? With no water?" His bruised and swollen face was trying to make her feel guilty, she could tell, even though it was hard for him to actually make an expression because of all the swelling.

"Oh no," she said, exasperated. "No, you don't. Don't you put the guilts on me. You are no concern of mine. I am not in any way responsible for your fate; I have enough on my plate looking after *me*."

"I have no horse. No food. No water." He was all but counting off on his fingers. "No clothing. How long do you think I'll last out here? You'd leave a man to die alone in the desert?"

Her ire was pricked. Wasn't she coping with enough? She didn't see why she should have to take responsibility for *him* on top of everything else. She had her own problems. Lots of them. Big ones, armed to the teeth. Not to mention that she was *dying of thirst*.

"*I* didn't put you here," she reminded him. "It's none of my business why you don't have so much as a stitch of clothing on. *I* didn't take your horse and your tack and your canteen. *I* didn't beat you black-and-blue. Besides, for all I know, you deserved it."

"I didn't." He was looking downright surly now.

Ava's head hurt. She was burning hot and cold with thirst fever, and she kept thinking senselessly about the posse of men riding north, away from her. Now she'd never catch up to them. Because she'd be dead. In the desert. She yanked at the brim of her hat. Goddamn it all to hell. She couldn't seem to catch a break.

"You can't leave me here. I can't even see," the Indian growled at her.

"Well, if you *could* see, you'd see that I ain't impressed, not by any of this nonsense." She used her sternest voice. *Men*. They were just so difficult. It didn't matter if they were white or Indian or blue in the face; they were more trouble than they were worth. Demanding, self-focused, bossy, needy. It was all *me me me*. No one looked after *her*; so she didn't see why she should look after *him*.

"I can't help you," she told him stiffly. "I'm in dire circumstances myself. I wish you all the best, but I'm no help to you. I'm sure someone else will come along directly who does have water and can offer you some assistance." She'd come over all formal. She was keenly aware of the ridiculousness of the whole thing, getting uppity with a battered Indian in the middle of nowhere. While they both died of thirst.

Her life was absurd.

But then it always had been.

He snorted. "Someone else will come along? It's some kind of miracle that *you* came along."

"Miracle? Curse is more accurate." She hadn't meant to say that aloud. She'd meant to bid him good day and ride off, but here she was, still having this insane conversation. It was only encouraging him.

"If you ride away, you'll have my death on your conscience," he warned her. "You'll be complicit. It's manslaughter."

Complicit. Manslaughter. Jesus wept, the man spoke like a lawyer. And he was out-uppitying her.

"Well, I won't feel bad about it for long," she retorted, "as I'm liable to die out here myself in the next couple of days." She paused as a thought struck her. "Maybe I'm already dead." This seemed a likely possibility now that she thought of it. She'd expired of thirst in the desert and was doomed to roam it for all eternity, looking for water. And to get stuck arguing with dead Indians. Because if she was dead, so was he. They were just a couple of cranky ghosts.

"If you go, I'm doomed," he said darkly, talking right over the top of her.

If he was a ghost, he was a yappy one—that was for sure. Where did he get the *energy*? It made her throbbing head hurt.

"It's tantamount to murder."

Tantamount. There he went, being all lawyerly again.

Did Indians have lawyers? Probably. They had laws and rules just like everyone else—someone had to be in charge of all that.

Trust her to find a lawyer in the middle of nowhere.

"If you leave me, I'll die slowly, in enormous pain," he continued. "And then I'll haunt you."

"You're already haunting me," she muttered. *Just ride away.* She didn't know this Apache ghost from Adam. She didn't owe him anything.

But *tantamount to murder . . .* Jesus wept. Now she had an image in her head. If she rode off, he'd return to squatting on the griddle-plate-hot ground, crisping in the hot sun. He'd die alone, with no one to talk lawyer talk to. The carrion birds would come, and eventually his bones would bleach and be blown by the winds. And no one would ever know what had happened to him.

God*damn.* This was all LeFoy's fault. If it wasn't for him and his Great Hunt, she wouldn't even *be* here. She'd be safe and sound in San Francisco, taking some rest and enjoying the cool sea breezes. She wouldn't be doing anything that was *tantamount to murder.*

"Fine," she said through clenched teeth, "but I'm only taking you as far as the next humans. I don't care if it's your tribe, or white people, or some old coot out hunting jackrabbits."

"It's unlikely to be my people."

She felt a chill. *Why* was it unlikely to be his people? Her gaze returned to his bruises. Someone had beaten him and left him out here to die in the desert. . . . Had it been *his own* people? Maybe he wasn't a lawyer; maybe he was just a common criminal. Maybe he'd committed some heinous sin and been driven out of his tribe. . . .

What would a man have to *do* to be punished like this? She couldn't think of a worse punishment than a slow, scorching, thirsty death. Well, she could. But this was still pretty bad.

Oh hell, what if she was about to go riding off with a rapist or a murderer?

Fantastic, she thought sourly. *Another one.* She'd just escaped from Kennedy Voss, the most infamous rapist in the west, only to get saddled with another one.

"Who left you like this?" she asked bluntly. There was no room for coyness in situations like these. Although, if he was a criminal, he wasn't likely to tell her the truth, was he? "I'm armed," she warned him darkly before he could even answer her. "And I'm a great shot." That was a flat-out lie, but with any luck, he wouldn't test it. Even if he did, what was she going to shoot him with? Air?

"I've got nothing but this rock," he countered, holding out the rock, which did seem pathetic in comparison to her iron Colt Baby Dragoon, bulletless though it might be. She supposed she could throw the gun at him. It was pretty heavy. It could do some damage as a missile.

"Drop the rock," she ordered.

He unfurled his fingers, and the rock dropped to the ground.

She considered her options. The man was a total wreck. Even though he was lively, his eyes were swollen shut and crusted with some nasty yellow stuff that had the flies swarming. "How are you even going to walk?" she asked, completely peeved by the whole situation. "Can you see anything at all?"

"No." He raised a tentative hand to touch the puffy skin around his eyes.

"How come they're not black?" she asked. "Usually when a man gets a black eye, the eye is, well, *black*."

"They're not black eyes. I got stinging nettle in them," he said shortly.

"How the hell did you get stinging nettle in your eyes?" She looked around—she couldn't spy a trace of nettles, stinging or otherwise. There was just chaparral and dirt.

"It was a few days ago." He paused. "I think it's gotten worse since then."

"It looks pretty bad."

"Thanks. That's very comforting."

"I ran out of comfort about the same time I ran out of water." She felt a bit queasy looking at his crusty eyes and forced herself to tear her gaze away. "I got poison ivy once as a kid. It was awful." That didn't come out as sympathetic as she had meant it to. But hell. He was probably an Apache-ghost-lawyer, so who wanted to give him sympathy? "How did you get nettles in your *eyes*?"

"I didn't. Someone did it for me."

"Someone did that *to* you?"

"Rubbed it right in."

What kind of crime *had* he committed? She was certain now there must have been one. No one treated a man like this unless he really deserved it. She felt a pull between sympathy and sheer aggravation.

"Now I'm blind." He stated the obvious for the millionth time. Definitely a lawyer.

"It might clear up." She said so only because it seemed polite. He'd be dead long before it cleared up. Unless a miracle happened, and it rained. She squinted at the merciless blue-white sky. No such luck.

"It won't clear up quick enough for me to walk out of here." He returned her pointedly to the issue at hand. "I can't walk if I can't see. I'll need to ride."

"Well, you're going to have to walk somehow, because you're not getting on my horse," she said. Goddamn it. She hadn't just agreed to walk him out of here, had she? Lawyer tricks. "If I let you on my horse, you'd be liable to just gallop off and leave me," she snapped. It was what she would have done if she were him.

"We could ride together," he suggested.

She gave a humorless laugh. "Do I look like a fool?"

"I don't know. I can't see you."

"You're naked," she reminded him. "And I'm not riding with a naked man." *Stop talking,* she screamed silently at herself. *You're getting yourself all tangled up with him. You're all but agreeing to* help *him.*

"You don't have anything I could wear?"

"No, I don't have anything you could wear."

"So you prefer me naked?" The bastard actually put his hands on his hips in pique, fingers splayed on the sharp V of his . . .

"I ain't going to be *looking* at you!" she shouted, exasperated. "Because I won't be *with* you."

The expression on his face—a silent, judgy expression that reminded her of her mother—sent her right over the edge. Her head gave a thick thud. Goddamn it! She wanted to throw things. How did she end up in these situations?

Fine. He was right. If he was coming with her—and somehow it looked like he was—he wasn't coming with her naked. She didn't want to look at his bits and pieces. Even if they were quite impressive bits and pieces.

She fumbled with her saddlebag. Damn it. She didn't *have* much. She was wearing her only riding culottes. She'd been traveling light and had only one dress and some underthings packed in her bags (because a lady never knew when she might need a dress). "You can have a petticoat," she snapped. She wasn't about to give him the dress. She tossed him the undergarment. Of course, he couldn't see to catch it; it flopped against his chest and fell to the hot ground. She sighed as she watched him bend down and feel for it. God, look at the bridge of muscles across his shoulders. Who even had that many muscles? He'd be awfully fearsome if he wasn't so battered.

"You're very trusting," she said crankily, mostly to distract herself as he struggled to get into the petticoat. There was too much naked flesh on display for comfort. "You could be riding to your doom, you know. I could be a killer."

"You *are* a killer," he said, "if you want to leave me here to die."

She rolled her eyes. "I *still* might leave you here, if you keep carping on."

He grimaced. Her stomach pinched at how painful his split lip looked. This was what she'd come to, feeling sorry for naked ghost-lawyer-rapists who were looking to hijack her.

"I can't guarantee we won't die together out there," she warned him. "Don't go expecting heroics. You might be better off staying here, without me."

"I'll take my chances." He wriggled into her petticoat and reached between his legs to pull the skirt through, blindly tying the petticoat into some sort of loose bloomer arrangement. It was actually quite a marvel, the way he did it without being able to see. And it didn't look half bad, like a very baggy pair of short pants. She got a bit distracted by the way the blazing white of the waistband contrasted with the bronzed ridges of his stomach.

"I can't walk without shoes," he said as soon as he was finished.

She glanced at his massive feet. "Well, I don't have a solution for that one in my saddlebag."

"The ground is too hot to walk on barefoot."

"Feel free to wait here, then."

"I won't make it walking. Or waiting."

There went the goddamn guilts again. She fought them as hard as she could, but she was hot and tired and thirsty as hell (*water water water*, rasped that endless voice at the back of her thoughts). She was too wrung out to keep sparring with him. Her head hurt.

"Fine." She unhooked a coil of rope from where it was tied to her saddle. "But the only way you're riding with me is if you're tied up."

"I beg your pardon?"

Where in the hell had this Apache learned his English? He'd be right at home in a Boston drawing room.

"Stop talking," she said curtly. "No more talking. I'm done with it. Let's get going." She slid off the horse. Her head was pounding fit to burst now. "We need water. You won't walk, and the only way you're getting on that horse is tied. So hush up and let me tie you."

Surprisingly, he obliged. Maybe he could tell she'd hit

her limit. And, let's face it, she was his only way out of here; it was in his best interests to do what she said.

"There's no point in trying to steal my horse out from under me either," she told him as she checked her knots and then led him to the horse. "You can't ride her blind—you need me. So behave yourself. You do what I say, or I dump you. Understand?" When he didn't answer, she gave him a poke in the shoulder, careful to avoid his bruises. "Well?" she demanded.

"I thought you told me not to speak?"

Impossible man. "Get on the horse."

She was expecting to have to help him up, but even blind and with his hands tied in front of him, he was surprisingly agile. He was on the horse in one fluid movement. She winced, hoping poor old Freckles, her horse, could bear his weight. And Jesus wept, how was the poor old girl going to manage *both* of them? The animal struggled enough with Ava on her own.

Ava had developed an affection for the hardy little horse. She didn't look like much, but she had some grit, and Ava had a lot of respect for grit.

"Wriggle forward," she ordered the Apache. There was no way she was sitting in front of him. First, because she didn't trust him not to assault her, and second, because she had no intention of letting him press his bits and pieces into her derriere. "And keep your hands on the pommel where I can see them," she said waspishly. "At all times."

Obediently, his hands found the pommel. She clambered up behind him, wishing she had a broader saddle as she found herself hard against his back. It wasn't comfortable in the slightest. Up close he was even taller and wider than he'd seemed on the ground. She couldn't really see around him. It looked like they'd both be traveling blind.

But at least Freckles was coping with carrying both of them. Grit. Ava gave her a pat on the rear. If they made it out of here, she was going to see this horse had the best a horse could want. Whatever that might be.

"Which way did you come from?" she asked the Apache, leaning to see around him. "Was there water back that way?"

"Head for the Colorado River," he told her shortly, ignoring her questions as he adjusted his position. His firm behind rubbed into her.

She gave him a shove between the shoulder blades. "Stop that."

"Head east," he said, continuing to ignore her.

"Surely we'll meet people before we find the Colorado."

"Let's hope so. But we may as well head toward water. Just in case."

"Mexico would be closer."

"No," he said.

"What do you mean, no? Of course it would. It's much closer than the Colorado River."

"We can't go to Mexico."

She gave him another shove. "There's no *we* about it. *I* can go to Mexico. And I'm not killing myself to get to the Colorado if there's a town right over the border in Mexico." She reached around him and took up the reins. "Whoever did this to you is in Mexico, huh?"

He didn't answer.

Well, that was a mess, wasn't it? Because Mexico was their only salvation. They were bound to find a village over the border in Sonora or at the very least some kind of creek or spring. So that was where they were headed. There was nothing westward that she knew of. And the Colorado, eastward, was so far . . . No. Mexico was the only choice.

But what if they rode straight into the people who'd done this to him? And what if those people thought she was the Apache's friend?

She swore. "I don't want to die because of you."

Silence.

"We're going to Mexico." There was no question about

it. Water was what they needed, and Mexico would have water.

"Are we? So there *is* a *we* now?" *Now* he talked.

He was such a pain in the ass.

"*I* am going to Mexico," she corrected. Damn finicky lawyers. "If you want to come, come. Or I can leave you here." She turned the horse and pointed them south. "Last chance to get off . . ."

Of course he didn't. She kicked her heels into her thirsty, tired animal. Freckles gave a halfhearted whicker and then plodded on, her load heavier than before.

"It might help if you tell me who did this to you," she suggested, "so I know who to watch out for."

He sighed. "It was more than just one incident," he admitted.

It took a minute for that to sink in. "You mean, more than one group of people did this to you?" She didn't doubt it had been done by groups. He was too big and too strong for a single person to do much damage. "How many *incidents* was it?"

"Three," he sighed. "First, it was the army—"

"The *army*? You mean the *United States* Army?"

"Turns out, they have a thing against Apaches."

"Are you telling me the *U.S. Army* rubbed stinging nettle in your eyes?"

"No, that was someone else."

"After the army?"

"After the army, it was the Chiricahua. It was the Chiricahua who took my horse. And my clothes. And my dog." He sounded regretful about the dog.

"And *then* someone came along and rubbed stinging nettles in your eyes? Why? What in hell did you do to *him*?"

"I got him in trouble with the army. And the Chiricahua."

"Was he the one who left you out here to die?"

"No. That was a man by the name of Pete Hamble."

She gasped.

"You've heard of him?"

Yes. Yes, she had. She'd had the misfortune of riding out of San Francisco with him a few weeks ago, when this whole nightmare had begun. When she'd been swept into the Great Hunt.

The Apache gave a disgusted grunt. "I'd never met him. But he seemed to think he knew me. And he didn't like me much."

She groaned. "Let me guess. He thought you were the Plague of the West? Deathrider? The most infamous Indian this side of the country? That man is a stone-cold fool. Everyone knows Bruno Ortiz caught Deathrider days ago."

"He did?" The Apache sounded shocked. Ava couldn't blame him. She'd never thought that anyone would catch Deathrider. And she was plenty upset that she hadn't been there to see it. Hell. *She* was the one who'd made Deathrider famous, and she should have been there to see his end. And if it hadn't been for Kennedy Voss, she *would* have been.

She must have written a dozen dime novels about the Plague of the West, but she'd never actually met him in person. Surely it wasn't too much to ask to see him in the flesh just once? Now she never would. If only Kennedy Voss hadn't up and kidnapped her from the Hunt . . .

"Bruno Ortiz caught *Deathrider*?" the Apache repeated as though he might have misheard.

"He did," Ava said glumly. "Didn't even have to kill him. I heard he's trussed him up to take back to San Francisco, alive and kicking." That was the only glimmer of hope. Maybe she could get there before they killed him . . . if she could ever get out of this desert alive.

"So Ortiz won the bet," the Apache said thoughtfully.

"You know about the bet?" Ava supposed that shouldn't have been a surprise. It was the story of the century. In these parts anyway.

"I know about the bet." The Apache sounded grim. She

guessed if Pete Hamble had mistaken him for the Plague of the West, then, of course, he knew about the bet. And had good reason to sound grim about it.

"How'd you get away from Pete?" she asked, curious. "He's a dangerous son of a bitch."

"The Hunt's over, then?" The Apache talked right over her. He had a nasty habit of doing that.

She frowned at his back but answered, "I suppose it's more of a race now than a hunt. The rest of them are trying to catch Ortiz before he gets to San Francisco to collect. I wouldn't be surprised if someone steals Deathrider off him before he gets there." And that would be the end of the Plague of the West, she thought disconsolately.

"*Someone* could steal him? Someone like Kennedy Voss?" the Apache asked.

"Someone exactly like Voss." And he could do it too, Ava thought. Kennedy Voss was smarter, meaner and more ruthless than anyone she'd ever met. He was liable to shoot Deathrider right off Ortiz's horse. Maybe he'd given up on chasing Ava and already turned around and started after Ortiz. Maybe if she could get to some water and dump the Apache, and get a fresh mount, she could catch up to the hunt before that happened. . . .

Maybe she could even get to Ortiz and Deathrider before anybody else did.

"How do you know about Voss?" she asked the Apache. "You seem to know an awful lot for a man who has been languishing out here in the desert."

"Pete Hamble has a big mouth," he said with a shrug.

Well, that was the truth.

"I guess we can all sleep easier, knowing that the Plague of the West has been caught," he said, and there was a sharp edge to his voice. "Now we just need to worry about the sadists who are out hunting him."

He wasn't wrong. Those men gave Ava nightmares.

They each fell into their own thoughts. Broody thoughts.

But the silence made Ava's thirst scream louder. At least talking was a distraction. Now she was painfully aware of her swollen tongue and stinging lips. And she felt strange. Not right. Even though the sun was fierce, she was barely sweating. There wasn't a drop left in her to sweat out. She was just a dry furnace, burning up.

"What's your name?" the Apache asked abruptly. From the thickness of his voice, she could tell he was suffering too.

"Cleopatra," she lied without missing a beat. She wasn't about to tell him the truth.

"Suits you." Was that sarcasm?

"Thanks." Two could do sarcasm.

They lapsed back into silence.

"Aren't you going to ask for my name?" he said after a few minutes.

"No." She licked her lips. It was like rasping with sandpaper. "I don't plan on knowing you long enough to need your name. As soon as we get to some water, we're saying adios."

He gave a parched laugh. "Fair enough."

This time the silence held, and they rode toward the shimmering horizon, each locked in their own broody thoughts and ravening thirst.

Later—much, much, much later—she could have kicked herself. Because if she *had* asked his name, he might well have told her. It was the kind of thing that would have amused him, the contrary ass. And knowing his name would have saved her a world of trouble.

❋ 2 ❋

One month earlier

SAN FRANCISCO UNFOLDED like a miracle as Ava crested the hill. There had been moments—such as when she'd lost the trail in the mountains, or when she'd stumbled into a nasty-looking brown bear, or when her horse went lame—when she'd genuinely wondered if she'd get to San Francisco at all. But here she was. Alive and kicking. If very, very tired. She'd barely been out of the saddle for the past year, and she was feeling it. She had the dust of seven states and territories on her heels, and a head full of stories as a result. She'd filled almost every page of her notebooks with research for new books, and completed two manuscripts already, both of which she'd painstakingly copied by camp-fire light so there would be duplicates to send back east. She had no need to travel again for a good long while, she thought with satisfaction as she took in the glitter of the bay. She was looking forward to finding a nice lodging house. One with a good cook, a comfortable bed and cozy armchairs, maybe even a rocking chair or two on the porch. She could sit in the sun and rest and write. Not that writing was restful. She pulled a face. But at least she could do it with her feet up, and with a cup of genuinely hot coffee beside her. And she wouldn't smell like horse anymore.

And when she wasn't writing, she could watch the world pass her by. Wouldn't that be fine. Maybe she wouldn't even budge from the porch for a month. What she needed was a boardinghouse with a view. Nowhere too quiet, somewhere she could just watch the bustle. Somewhere with a touch of luxury. She wasn't taking her rest in an uncomfortable bed, not after sleeping in a tent for months. She wanted cushions and white sheets, some fripperies and fancies; she wanted civilization.

And a town full of money, like this one was, should be able to provide that.

The harbor town undulated around the bay, a bustling sprawl with the scent of gold fever spicing the air. The sunshine was bright, and the air was fresh, and everything had that crystal clear sparkle that came with summer by the sea. The gold rush was in full swing, and the place was overrun with hopefuls from all corners of the globe: their high spirits made the whole town sing. The bay bristled with the masts of anchored ships, the docks were a hive of activity and the streets teemed with people speaking a dozen different tongues. It was a modern-day Babel. Ava felt her spirits lift. She inhaled the salt air and squinted against the light spangling off the surface of the water. Yes. Things would improve now. She could feel it.

Rejuvenated by the bustle, she set off into town. The boardinghouse could wait; there was business to take care of. It didn't matter how tired and travel sore she was; she never missed a deadline. Which was quite an accomplishment, considering she wrote miles from civilization, under the roughest circumstances imaginable. Ava Archer believed in getting her hands dirty. Unlike some of her colleagues, who stayed in their comfortable town houses back east and wrote a load of utter fantastical nonsense, Ava experienced her stories firsthand—at least as much as she could. She immersed herself in the west: she wanted to see it, breathe it, smell it. And she was convinced that *that* was why her books sold. People believed in her work—because it was *real*.

Well, mostly . . .

So she had dragged herself back and forth across the country, gathering up the legends of the frontier (and creating a few legends of her own in the process), working like a dog year after year, banking her money, saving for a future when she could pack her inkwell away and go home. In style. The adventuring had been fun for a good long while (although it was wearing thin of late), but she'd always been in it for the money. She'd wanted independence, and she'd got it—that and more. She hadn't just supported herself—she had *profited*. She was beholden to no one, and when she considered her past, the power of that was thrilling.

In order to get paid, though, she had to get the manuscripts to the publisher, which was no small feat when she was almost three thousand miles from New York. Over the years, she had found ways around the distance; which was why she headed for the newspaper office before she found a boardinghouse; her manuscripts would be bedded down long before she was. After all, books meant money, and money belonged in a bank. So she took her books straight to the "bank," handing the twine-wrapped sheaf of papers over to the local newspaper in exchange for a hefty check. Publishing on the frontier was rough and ready, and immediate. The newspaper would be cranking out her words before she'd crawled out of bed tomorrow.

The other set of copies she would send back east, for a much slower, but bigger, payoff. Her publisher would deposit the money into her account as soon as the manuscripts arrived on his desk in six months, and he paid much more than these frontier newssheets did. But the newssheets got the work out *fast*, in installments in their papers as well as in hastily slapped-together chapbooks. Her books were read a thousand times over on the frontier before the ship carrying the original manuscripts even made it halfway to New York.

It was that kind of thought that struck home: the sheer distance between herself and New York. Her birthplace was a lifetime away, not quick or easy to return to. The knowledge was as exhilarating as it was enervating. The frontier was wholly opposite to the world of her childhood: rougher, readier, less concerned with who your parents were than with who *you* were. So long as you were white anyway. Being nonwhite was a whole different thing. As she saw firsthand, because the frontier surely wasn't all white. It was a sea of difference: there were the myriad Indian nations (she couldn't even name a fraction of the tribes she'd spied on her travels); free black people seeking land and hope, the same as any white wagoner trundling west; Mexicans, some who had been in California since it was part of Mexico and some who'd come north for gold. And then there were the people pouring in from the ships: Chinese people, and others from farther-flung parts of Asia; Turks and travelers from the Far East; and an influx from the Southern American nations. For every blond German, there was a Filipino; for every Brit, a Chilean; for every white easterner, an African. The American frontier was the crossroads of the world, and nowhere was that true more than here in gold country. But even so, race mattered here as surely as it mattered in New York, perhaps more. She could see it in the way the man at the newspaper office fawned over her, even before he knew her name, while ignoring the black woman waiting patiently by the door. And she could see it in the way the woman deferred to her, keeping her gaze fixed on the floorboards.

Even on the frontier, the old rules won out. White people forced their way above other people; men forced their way above women; the rich forced their way above everyone. And her own freedom wouldn't last forever, she knew. The thought weighed heavily on her as she pocketed the check and left the newspaper office. She got away with being a woman alone because she was young and strong, quick and quick-witted. And armed. But one day she'd be old—like her mother—and the only protection against the powerlessness facing older women in this society was marriage. Or *money*. A moneyed woman could force her way through the world in ways poor women could only dream of. Unless they attached themselves to a man, which Ava Archer had no intention of ever doing.

No. Money was the answer. She held her saddlebag closer and forged ahead.

Her next port of call was usually the port itself. Most of the major shipping lines took post back east. But when she stepped from the newspaper office, she spied something better. Much, much better. An actual, honest-to-goodness sign of civilization: the United States post office. She hadn't seen an official post office in more than two thousand miles.

The gold rush had changed things, she realized as she took in the new buildings across the beaten-earth square. The post office was just a low-slung timber building, but it had grandiose white columns running the length of its street frontage, making it look respectable as hell compared to the buildings around it. A knot of people bunched at the postmaster's window, also making the place the busiest building on the street.

It was like a mirage in the desert. In the past, she'd had to fork out a ridiculous amount of money to get her package not only on a ship, but also hand-delivered to the recipient after the ship had docked.

A post office was progress. San Francisco was delivering on its promise of ease so far. Her spirits lifted again, like sails billowing in a trade wind.

"YOU'LL WANT TO be at the Palladium tonight, Miss Archer," the postmaster said eagerly, practically falling out of his window in his keenness to speak with her. He'd recognized her name, as everybody did; it was one of the most famous names in the west. And once he'd recognized her name, he tried to point her toward a story. Again, as everybody did. She tried to be nice about it; after all, sometimes the stories were really worth it.

"All of Frisco will be there. Including some very *interesting* types." He acted like he'd handed her a precious gift.

"Maybe tomorrow," she said, keeping a worried eye on her package as he handled it. The original copies of the manuscripts were at the newspaper already, which offered a measure of security, as they'd be in print by tomorrow night, but she still wouldn't relax until this package, with the copies, was safely processed and on its way to New York. The man was fumbling about with her livelihood—it made her nervy.

The postmaster realized she wasn't impressed with his hints. He deposited her package into his canvas sack and dropped the coyness. In a rush, he exploded: "Kennedy Voss is here!"

Ava kept her calm, but only because she'd had years to perfect her poker face. *Kennedy Voss . . .*

"And not just Kennedy Voss! Others too!"

And with that, the floodgates opened. The men in the queue behind her joined the explosive excitement. It became a mob in practically no time at all.

"It's like nothing Frisco has ever experienced before!" one man was babbling.

"They're pouring into town and heading straight for Le-Foy's dance hall!"

"There's some kind of to-do happening!"

"Everyone's there!"

"Any minute now even the Plague of the West himself might ride in!"

The Plague of the West . . . *Deathrider . . .*

Imagine . . .

A tingle shot straight through her.

But no, that was ridiculous. Deathrider was nowhere near these parts, not according to what she'd heard.

But *Kennedy Voss* was.

She tapped her fingers impatiently on the postmaster's windowsill. Perhaps she would go to LeFoy's after all. Kennedy Voss didn't sell as many books as the Plague of the West, but he was a good little earner. It seemed mad not to take the chance to make another few bucks—especially since he'd all but fallen in her lap.

Feeling magnanimous, she thanked the postmaster and promised the clamoring crowd that they'd see her later at LeFoy's Palladium.

"I wish you'd write a book about *you*," one man hollered as she walked away. "I wouldn't mind reading about what you get up to!" A chorus of catcalls and whistling followed that bit of charm.

Ava ignored them. She'd had practice at ignoring men.

"I can show you the way to LeFoy's," a very tall and stiff Englishman offered as she plowed across the street toward her horse. "I wouldn't waste time; I hear it's rapidly filling up."

She'd picked him up like a burr. He was overly eager and refused to take no for an answer. And that was how she got herself tangled up with Lord Whatsit, who was as garrulous as he was annoying and who, it turned out through the course of conversation, had it in his head to be the subject of her next book.

He had an icicle's chance in hell. But try telling him that.

"You're a *real* lord?" Ava couldn't keep the disbelief from her voice as they entered the main room of LeFoy's Palladium. Perhaps if she hadn't been sleep-deprived and soiled from the trail she might have been able to muster more courtesy, but she was, so she couldn't. Instead, she kept elbowing her way through the crowds in the hall, scanning faces for Voss. His lordship followed along like a puppy.

"In a line dating back to fifteen eighty-seven," his lordship insisted. He seemed to think she should be impressed. She wasn't. What good did a *lord* do her out here? She was much more interested in the knot of ruffians she spotted climbing the stairs to the gallery. She cricked her neck, trying to get a good look upstairs. The lamplight was dim, but she could make out a man—or, rather, *men*—who interested her far more than the Englishman trailing behind her.

Sweet Jesus.

Cactus Joe was there and Pete Hamble and, if she wasn't mistaken, that was Sweet Boy Beau! Kennedy Voss *was* there too, leaning back on the railing on his elbows, cocky as a bantam rooster in a yard full of hens.

It was a gallery full of legends. The kind that gave you nightmares.

But *why*? Why were they all here in the same place? And why weren't they killing one another? She never thought she would see the day when Kennedy Voss stopped to take a friendly drink with Sweet Boy Beau.

Something was brewing, and she meant to find out what. Even if she had to forgo her lovely boardinghouse bed and a good night's sleep. *Another* good night's sleep.

Well, she could sleep when she was dead. Until then she'd just feel like a limp bag of soiled linen. She'd survived worse.

"You can't turn your nose up at a lord!" Lord Whatsit protested.

Bah. The Englishman was a pinch-nosed streak of irritating, if she'd ever seen one. Who cared about him and his apple-in-the-mouth accent when *Kennedy Voss* was right there? She neatly sidestepped him and took the stairs at a clip.

"I've read your books," the Englishman called breathlessly as he hurried after her, "and I think you'd love to hear my story."

Of course he did. Men. They carried their egos on their backs like turtles lugged their shells. She paused at the top of the stairs and took in the clump of men by the railing. They were liquored up and had that charged air men got when they were thinking of violence. And that was *definitely* Kennedy Voss. And damn if that wasn't English George and Irish George over there with Pete Hamble. Every varmint on the frontier was here. And, unlike Lord Whatsit, each and every one of them *was* interesting enough for her to write about.

"Really, Miss—"

"Hush up," she snapped, elbowing Lord Whatsit in the belly as he huffed up behind her. "You can talk after you've bought me a drink."

Strangely, the gallery wasn't full; there was no one except for Voss and the other varmints. The bar against the far wall was deserted, the gambling tables quiet. She imagined this gallery was usually heaving on a Saturday night; it had a prime view of the stage, private nooks to carry on clandestine business, its own handy upstairs bar and all the gaming tables the establishment offered. Downstairs (where Voss *wasn't*) was certainly doing strong business: it was wall to wall with miners and fishermen; long-haul sailors fresh off the ship from the East Coast or Europe, South America or the antipodes; and merchants who'd closed up after another profitable week in a goldfield boomtown. The postmaster had told her the saloon–cum–dance hall–cum–theater was the hottest ticket in town, and when she walked in, she'd been impressed. It was something to see. There was a red-curtained stage at the northern end and a wide horseshoe bar at the southern end—a bar that was currently three men deep and doing a roaring trade. A sweeping staircase with curving balustrades led up to the gallery, which wrapped the three sides of the hall facing the stage. The place was as fancy as all get-out, with etched-glass lamps glowing like sunlit bubbles, gleaming brass trimmings and forest green flocked wallpaper above wood-paneled wainscots. Every inch of Californian oak (and there was a lot of it) was polished to a high shine. LeFoy's was classy for the frontier, classier than she'd seen since she'd left the east, and far classier than the sea of men who frequented it.

"You'll talk to me if I buy you a drink?" The Englishman was still breathless from her elbow in his stomach.

"This *is* a bar, and typically that's where people come to drink," she said dryly. "You do have bars in England?"

Ava kept a surreptitious eye on Voss as she led his lordship to the bar on the far wall of the gallery. Kennedy and Co. were clearly the reason upstairs was nearly deserted. She imagined on any other night the gallery would be as overstuffed as the floor below, but tonight the worst of the west were up here. And no one in their right mind would drink with Kennedy Voss and Company.

"Of course we have bars." His lordship sounded offended. "We invented them." Lord Whatsit might have been unwelcome, but he wasn't inconvenient, she thought as they took up residence at the bar. It was handy for a lady to have an escort in a place like this. It might give the varmints pause. At least for a moment or two, and especially when there was no one behind the bar to act as a buffer between her and the villains. She couldn't see anyone who looked like they worked here; if it hadn't been for Lord Whatsit, Ava would have been alone up here with the pack of wild dogs.

Voss noticed her before the rest of his companions did; she expected nothing less from a man with his reputation. Ava watched him in the brass-edged mirror that stretched the length of the bar. His gaze swept her from top to toe, and he smirked in that way men did when they liked what they saw. He wasn't a bad-looking man, Kennedy Voss. He had a shock of sandy brown hair and a broad, honest-looking face. He seemed for all the world like a good country boy—the type who split wood for his ma and went to church on a Sunday with his cap in hand. He had a wide

grin and a cowlick that stood straight up and bobbed when
he moved. Kennedy Voss was the type of young man you
might invite to come a-courting your daughter. But Ava had
seen enough of his handiwork over the years to have no il-
lusions about him. The man was surface charm and bone-
deep bad. She'd written about him in *The Bloodbath of Iron
Ridge* and *The Devil Came Calling.* She'd seen the bodies
he left behind. And her accounts were mostly accurate.

Mostly.

In the mirror she watched as Voss grinned, his gaze lingering on her rear end. She wondered if he knew who she
was. He might. She'd been around—and she stood out in a
crowd. She could thank her red hair for that. But then
again, he might just be grinning because he was Kennedy
Voss and she was a woman. Voss liked women. Or, rather,
he *didn't* like women. And he wanted them to know it.
Know it until they screamed for mercy.

"Well, then," the Englishman said happily, completely
unaware of the mortal danger they were in, "what can I get
you to drink, Miss—"

"Don't say my name," Ava said curtly, interrupting the
Englishman but not looking away from Voss. It would be
like looking away from a rabid dog. It was surely too loud
in here for Voss to hear the Englishman, but Ava had survived this long only by being careful; she didn't want Lord
Whatsit trumpeting to all and sundry that Ava Archer was
here watching their every move. Not until she had some
idea of what they were up to, at least.

"I beg your pardon?" His lordship struggled to take in
her meaning. At this rate he was unlikely to survive the
night, she thought ruefully.

"Don't say my name," she repeated. "Not unless you're
looking to get me killed." In the mirror Kennedy Voss said
something to his friends, and they all looked her way. Hell
and damnation. She rested her palm on the holster of her
weapon, mostly for comfort. She was a terrible shot. The

gun was for show more than anything; usually, she managed to talk her way out of a sticky situation. But it did help to be waving the gun as she talked.

She practically felt the greasy gazes sliding up and down her body as she stood at the bar with the Englishman. She hoped LeFoy would send his dancing girls out soon; she could use some help mopping up this male attention, and from what the postmaster had said, the dancing girls were the best this side of the country. Apparently they even indulged in some scandalous French dancing. She bet Voss and his slimy friends would enjoy the distraction to no end. And while they were distracted, she could get a good look at them.

"Pardon? What do you mean 'get you killed'?" Lord Whatsit, in pure greenhorn form, blinked in shock and turned to gawk at Voss and Co.

"I thought you said you'd read my books," she sighed, swatting him on the arm to snap his attention back to her. "Even if you just got off the boat, you should know not to go staring at men like Kennedy Voss." The last thing she needed was him bringing the wild dogs this way with all his openmouthed staring. They'd be over soon enough, but she'd rather it be on her terms.

"I certainly did *not* just get off the boat," he protested, realizing more than a little too late that he was staring at some heavily armed thugs. "I've been here for more than a week."

"I do beg your pardon," she said, rolling her eyes. She was glad to see Voss was now distracted by a barmaid who was huffing up the stairs with a crate of whiskey. "A whole week? You're practically a local. You can order me a dash of whiskey with water," she told his lordship. "And seriously just a dash. I need to stay sharp."

Lord Whatsit had returned to staring, rapt, at the varmints. "Do you know them?"

"I know *of* them." She realized she'd lost him. He was transfixed. Like a boy who'd stepped into a storybook.

Ava ordered the drinks herself as soon as the barmaid had dropped her crate behind the bar. "He'll pay," she told the girl.

"Give me a minute," the barmaid complained, putting her hands on the small of her back and stretching with a groan. Like the other women working here, she was very skimpily dressed. A starched white apron with frilled straps revealed more than it covered; the girl had wiry, muscular arms and the swell of pert breasts. Aside from the whimsical apron, she was otherwise clothed only in undergarments; she wore white pantalets and a chemise, with a blue satin corset pinching in her already thin waist, and her legs were clad in scarlet stockings.

"Goddamn, those stairs get worse every time I haul myself up them," she grumbled. "I told him to put in one of them dumbwaiter things. I told him till I was blue in the face, but do you think he'd listen?"

In the mirror, Ava could see that some of the varmints had transferred their attentions to the girl. But not Kennedy Voss: he had eyes only for Ava. Or, rather, Ava's derriere.

"Hey," the barmaid exclaimed, once she'd straightened up and caught sight of Ava, "I know you!"

Ava managed to keep her expression serene through sheer force of will. It was hard; she was tired. She really wanted to tell the silly girl to shut up and get the damn drinks.

"Hush," his lordship said in a far-too-loud conspiratorial whisper, finally tearing his gaze away from the men. "She's incognito."

"Oh no." The girl gave Ava a sympathetic look. "You want me to call for the doctor? It's no trouble at all. He's just downstairs."

God save her from fools. "He means I'm trying to go unnoticed," Ava told her impatiently.

"So you *are* you!"

"Last time I looked." Ava sighed. "Can we have those whiskeys now?"

"You wouldn't have a sherry, would you?" His lordship peered at the bar shelf. "These American spirits give me heartburn."

"I knew it!" The barmaid took no notice of him. She grinned at Ava. "You don't remember me, do you?" She clucked. "And fancy, I'm even almost in one of your books."

"Almost?" His lordship looked confused. But maybe that was just his face.

"We met back in Missouri," the girl trumpeted.

Luckily, someone downstairs chose that moment to start banging away at a piano. There was a ripple of excitement, and then a four-piece orchestra sent up a loud din. Voss and his crowd turned to peer over the railing at the stage below. Ava breathed a sigh of relief. Good. Maybe the show would keep them busy for long enough for her to have a drink and shake off Lord Whatsit and the bar girl.

"I'm Becky Sullivan," the girl said, leaning on the bar and beaming at Ava. "We met in the town square of Independence at one of them dances. You *must* remember. I was with Mrs. Smith? The lady in *The Notorious Widow Smith and Her Mail-Order Husband*." She laughed. "Lord, that was a night! I wore that beautiful pink dress Mrs. Smith lent me. *Gave* me. She never did want it back." Her expression turned dreamy. "It was too fancy for the likes of me and didn't I feel like Cinderella!" She sighed, the sparkle going out of her eyes. "I wish I still had that dress, but those little hellions cut it up for costumes."

Ava honestly couldn't remember Becky. She *did* remember the widow Smith; she'd made a wonderful subject, and the story had been syndicated around the country. The book had done very well too. Ava also remembered Matt Slater. Slater was big and bearish and possessed of a brother . . . and this brother of Slater's had many names: the Plague of the West, White Wolf, Rides with Death, the Ghost of the Trails . . .

Deathrider.

Some of the names Ava had invented for her stories, but most she hadn't; most of the tales about him she'd come by honestly. She'd hadn't made the man famous; he'd *already* been famous. Hell, *more* than famous: infamous. She'd just . . . spread the news of his fame a little farther than it might otherwise have reached. All the way to New York. And beyond . . . Her books were crossing oceans now, devoured as exotic fancies in European cities. But she certainly hadn't told people out west anything they hadn't known.

Everywhere you went, from Missouri across the Great Plains to the coasts of California, people knew of him. The stories were legion. She only followed along, gathering them up, publishing them in the western newssheets and sending them back to her publisher in the east. She didn't invent them.

Mostly.

It was only that sometimes a girl had to add some . . . flavor. A description here, a flourish there, a missing gap or two filled. Especially when she'd never even *seen* the man. How did you describe someone you'd never met? It took a little imagination, that was all. A touch of poetic license. Nothing too extreme, just enough to bring him to life on the page. People who *had* met him claimed the books were true to life, so she couldn't have strayed too far from the facts. . . .

It wasn't *ideal* that she'd never so much as glimpsed him from a distance. In fact, it felt downright amateurish. She'd spent years looking for him, and she hadn't seen him *once*. At least as far as she knew. Ava knew more about Death-rider than anyone in the west, but she wouldn't have known the Plague of the West if he was standing right here in front of her.

"There! Right there!" Becky exclaimed.

Ava's heart lodged in her chest, and she spun around, feeling like she'd conjured up a ghost.

"There! *That* used to be my pink dress!" Becky's finger jabbed at the stage.

Oh. Ava felt ridiculous. For a moment she'd thought. . . . Never mind what she'd thought. . . . She was jumping at shadows. On the stage below, she could see a little girl walking on her hands across the floorboards. The moppet was wearing a shaggy ballerina dress of pink satin and lace, and her mop of golden red curls flopped in her face.

"That too," Becky added glumly as the moppet was followed by another girl, this one cartwheeling merrily, her shaggy pink tutu glittering with spangles that caught the lamplight.

"And that." A smaller girl, with another set of golden red curls and another shaggy tutu appeared, this time turning aerial somersaults, flipping backward and forward like she could just about fly.

"I *loved* that dress," Becky said sourly, not at all impressed with the acrobatics.

Ava's memory stirred. She vaguely remembered the girls, standing on the steps of the Independence courthouse singing "The Rose of Alabama." Their voices had been incredible. Yes. That had been the night she'd learned of Deathrider's demise. *Saw him shot stone-cold dead,* Matt Slater had said. Shot by Saltbush Pete in Fort Kearney. *Buried him myself.* Ava had felt a chilly bolt through her heart at the hearing of it. It was a feeling too close to grief for comfort. Even though she'd never met the man, she'd *felt* like she'd known him. After all, she'd been writing about him since '42.

Down below on the main floor of LeFoy's, the crowd clapped in time with the music, and there were hoots as the titian-haired moppets climbed up one another to form a tower. Voss and the varmints were hollering and clapping along with the rest.

"Don't be fooled by those girls' sweet faces," Becky said in dire tones, "those three are demon hell spawn. They belong up here with the thieves and murderers."

"Aren't they a little young for a saloon?" Lord Whatsit asked dubiously.

Becky snorted. "Whiskey, you said?" She turned back to the task at hand.

"Sherry?" Lord Whatsit craned his neck hopefully.

"Sherry?" Becky sighed. "I'll have to go back downstairs. Do you want the Mexican or the Spanish?"

Lord Whatsit looked astonished that they even had sherry, let alone had a choice of vintages. But, again, perhaps that was just his face. "Erm . . . Spanish?"

Becky harrumphed and clomped over to the stairs. She only went halfway down, and then they heard her yell, "Frankie, get me the Spanish sticky stuff!"

At this rate, Ava would be waiting for her whiskey and water all night. Her impatience got the best of her, and she leaned over the bar and helped herself.

"Should you be doing that?" His lordship pulled nervously at his thin mustache.

Ava ignored him and poured herself a generous dash of whiskey. It was more than she'd planned to drink, but she was worn out and getting more irritable by the minute; she needed to take the edge off. "Look, mister, I've got plans for tonight," she told Lord Whatsit, "and I can't say they include talking to you. So, if you don't mind, I'd appreciate it if you could get your story out of your system so I can get along."

She heard him mutter under his breath, something about frontier manners. Well, he was welcome to go back to England. She saluted the idea and knocked back her drink.

"I thought you *liked* hearing people's stories," he said stiffly.

"Depends on the people." She refilled her glass, this time with plain old water.

"You don't think a lord is the right kind of people?" If he got any stiffer, he was liable to crack.

She sized him up. "You're a *real* lord?"

"I am." He gave her a slight bow. "Lord Justice Whent, at your service."

"Here's your sherry." Becky returned, slapping the bottle down on the bar and pulling out a tumbler. His lordship's eyes grew wide as she filled the tumbler to the brim. "Take it," Becky said. "On the damn house." She muttered to herself as she turned away, "Thinks he can tell me not to shout across the room. Should have put in that dumbwaiter like I said and then there'd be no call for shouting."

"Becky, was it?" Ava said, trying to get the barmaid's attention even as her gaze refocused on Kennedy Voss in the mirror. Onstage, the girls were singing now, and he was grinning from ear to ear like a farm boy. "You know anything about those men over there?"

Becky frowned, not happy to be interrupted. She'd clearly been settling into a long mutter. "Who? Them lot?" She shrugged. "They're here for the same reason you're here. Pete's little game."

Pete's little game. That sounded promising. Ava dug her notebook out.

"And who's Pete?" Ava asked, licking the tip of her pencil.

"Pete is *Pierre*," Becky said poisonously. "Pierre Le-Foy."

Ava brightened. She had a vague memory of meeting him in Independence as well; he'd been part of the knot of men standing with the widow Smith. He'd been there when she'd been talking to Slater about Deathrider. She wondered what LeFoy knew about Deathrider, and if she could get it out of him. Because after all this time, she knew with 100 percent certainty that Deathrider wasn't dead. He wasn't in some unmarked grave outside Kearney; he wasn't interred on his ancestral lands; he wasn't lying at the bottom of a ravine, the victim of either ambush or accident. He was riding the trails, a living, breathing man. A *dangerous* living, breathing man. As fearful an Indian as ever lived. Or . . . a *maybe* Indian . . . People described him as having pale eyes, the color of winter ice, so perhaps he wasn't quite as he appeared.

If only Ava could see him with her *own* eyes . . .

"Only his name ain't really Pierre LeFoy." Becky had gone back to grumbling as she clanked about in the bar. "His name is Pete Frick, and he's a no-count, lying, weaselly . . ."

"Gentlemen, welcome!" a voice boomed from the stairs.

"Speak of the devil," Becky muttered.

A trim man in a spotless suit stood at the head of the stairs. His mustache was waxed to perfection, and his eyes were twinkling. He looked thrilled to see the varmints.

"You're interrupting the show, LeFoy," Pete Hamble grumped, not looking away from the stage. The three moppets were singing as they twirled about, spangles flashing.

LeFoy laughed. "They are a marvel, aren't they? But they're just the opening act—wait until you see the French girls. Becky, send a bottle of our best whiskey over, compliments of the house!" He regarded the men in the gallery with a glittering smile, but Ava noticed the nervous bob of his Adam's apple. He wasn't a complete fool, then. He knew these were dangerous men to play with.

What exactly was he up to?

"If you want to wait until the end of the show to conduct business, all the better!" LeFoy said, his Adam's apple still bobbing nervously, belying his confident grin. "It will give the latecomers a fair chance to arrive."

"Our best whiskey, he says." Becky stomped out of the bar, bottle in one hand and a teetering stack of shot glasses in the other. "Why not just give them beer? They wouldn't know the difference."

"Smile," Ava heard LeFoy hiss at her as she passed him, but Becky did no such thing.

Ava took hasty notes as she watched LeFoy greet each of the varmints individually. She strained to catch the names. As well as Voss, Hamble, and English and Irish George, the group also included Bucket-eye Bob, Jim Holt and Sweet Boy Beau. They were a terrifying mix of men, and they were armed to the teeth. What on earth were they doing in the same room? What was LeFoy up to?

"There'll be violence tonight," Becky said darkly as she returned to the bar. "You mark my words. They'll shoot up the place, and we only just got it all finished." Absently, she topped up Lord Whatsit's glass of sherry. "You can pay this time," she told him.

"Becky!" LeFoy sailed their way, having caught sight of Ava and the Englishman. "You didn't tell me Miss Archer was here! I heard you rode into town this afternoon, Miss Archer. Welcome!" He reached for her hand as though they were old friends. She just about stabbed herself with the pencil as he crunched her hand in both of his. "We met back in Missouri!" He gave her a flirtatious smile. "I was devastated not to end up in your book."

"You need to *do* something for her to write about you," Ava heard Becky snort.

"Well, perhaps after tonight?" LeFoy gave Ava's hand another squeeze before he let it go. He gave her a look that was probably meant to be charming but wasn't.

She managed to smile, even though she'd taken an immediate dislike to him. Dealing with men like LeFoy was a hazard of the profession. "Perhaps I might," she agreed. "If you could illuminate me on the specifics of your . . . *game*?" She held up her notebook and pencil.

LeFoy just about split his skin with pride he got so swollen up. "*LeFoy's Game*—makes a good title for a novel, don't you think?"

"I say, I have to protest. You haven't heard *my* story yet," Lord Whatsit huffed, "and now you're going off listening to *him*." He was rather pink in the face from a tumbler and a half of good Spanish sherry. "You promised to listen if I bought you a drink."

"You didn't buy me a drink," Ava said. "I got my own." Lord Whatsit got all petulant at that. She really was sick to death of these men. They trailed about after her, yapping at her skirts, demanding her attention. Like they were entitled to it. Like she should devote herself to them, just because they wanted it. Like everyone would be *fascinated* by them and their little lives. They wanted her to drop everything for them. They didn't deserve it; they hadn't earned it; they didn't care a fig what *she* wanted. Well, they could go hang, because what *she* wanted had nothing to do with listening to men like Lord Whatsit and their silly stories; what *she* wanted was to find Deathrider, the Ghost of the Trails, the ice-eyed killer, the Plague of the West. She wasn't done writing about him yet. Not when there was a fortune to be made.

She just needed to *find* the Plague of the West . . . and survive him.

"I'll have you know that I'm a peer of the realm," his lordship protested hotly.

"You're a what?" Becky was pouring more sherry into his tumbler while clicking her fingers for payment.

Lord Whatsit fumbled for coin. "A *peer*. Of the realm."

"To each their own. But I reckon that's illegal round here. Isn't it, Pete?"

"Pierre," LeFoy said sharply.

"Sweet Jesus," Ava said, shocked, as she saw another group of men climbing the stairs. "Is that Bruno Ortiz? The Butcher of Borrego Springs?"

She heard Becky swear. "You're a madman," Becky whispered to LeFoy. "You're going to get us all killed."

"What on earth are you up to?" Ava asked. Her mouth had gone as dry as a cotton ball, and the pencil was unsteady in her hand. Any single one of these men would be enough to turn her blood cold, but now there were—she did a rough head count—more than a *dozen* of them here.

LeFoy heard the crackle of fear in her voice and grinned. "Just stay where you are, Miss Archer. You're going to have the best seat in the house."

"For what?"

But he was already gone, off to greet the new arrivals. And to Ava's horror, they weren't the last. By the time the moppets had finished their act and been replaced with the dancing girls, the gallery was getting crowded. And crowded with the kind of men who usually ended their lives on the wrong end of a rope.

"You might want to get back here behind the bar with me," Becky suggested as the gallery filled up. "At least then you'll have the bar between you and them."

There were a couple more skimpily clad girls back there with Becky now and two burly men, who were mostly there to keep the girls safe from the varmints.

Ava was tempted to take Becky up on her offer but . . . she was A.A. Archer. She couldn't be seen to show weakness. Even if they didn't know who she was right this minute, they would soon enough. One flinch and she'd be fair game—for the rest of her life. She knew the score. Your legend preceded you.

"I'll be fine." She'd been through worse than this. Although . . . taking in the crowd and the atmosphere of simmering violence, she wasn't quite sure that was true. The varmints howled and cheered at the dancing girls, who were smiling brightly but starting to look a little skittish. The crowd downstairs had caught the mood, and the whole place had the feel of a tinderbox. It could go up at any moment.

The upstairs bar was snarled with men looking to get liquored up, and Ava didn't like the way they were looking at her. His lordship was sobered by it too, despite the tumblers of sherry he'd knocked back.

"Is there another staircase? Or is the one I came up the only way out?" Ava asked Becky as the gallery filled to bursting.

Becky was looking skittish herself. "Over there, behind the curtain. There's a stairway down to the kitchens, and one up to the bedrooms. You know, for later." She flushed. "When the dancing girls are working late."

"Come on, your lordship." Ava snagged his arm and half-dragged him to the curtain. She didn't know why she bothered, except he seemed so inept. It would be coldhearted to leave him to the mercies of the crowd. "We'll just stand here," she said, positioning them directly in front of the curtain. "So we have an escape route . . . should we need it." She felt better knowing she could run for it if she wanted to. "Are you armed?" she asked him.

"Of course." He sounded offended again. "You don't have any idea whom you're dealing with. I'm no milky fop."

"Hush, something is happening."

The show below had drawn to a close with cymbal-clashing fanfare, and LeFoy had claimed everyone's attention. He stood at the head of the stairs, arms spread, grinning like the cat that had got the cream. From where he stood, he could see every man in the building: in the gallery and on the floor below.

"Welcome one and all!" he said, his showman's voice filling the hall. "Tonight, LeFoy's Palladium is host to the best, and the *worst*, of the west!"

There were cheers and the sound of a breaking glass. Ava heard Becky's groan even through the cacophony. "Not another one! We're not going to have any glasses left at this rate."

Whispers swept the floor below as people spotted the men on the gallery. Ava saw Voss puff up; once again his preening put her in mind of a bantam rooster.

"Tonight," LeFoy proclaimed, "we gather to launch *the great hunt*!"

A lusty cheer went up.

The great hunt. Ava felt a chill run down her spine.

"What's he talking about?" Lord Whatsit asked.

Ava wasn't sure, but she had a sinking feeling in her stomach.

There was a staccato drumroll from the orchestra pit and LeFoy pointed dramatically to the stage. The heavy velvet curtains pulled back to reveal a chalkboard, a table and two bespectacled men. Heavily armed thugs advanced to guard them, standing on the lip of the stage and watching the crowd carefully.

Hell. She couldn't see properly. Ava grabbed hold of a brass wall sconce and hauled herself up by the strength of her arms so she could see over the ocean of heads. She braced her feet against the wall to keep herself up and strained to see. The chalkboard contained lists of names and numbers; Kennedy Voss was listed, as was Bruno Ortiz . . . as were all of the other bloodcurdling varmints.

Oh my God. Odds. She was looking at *odds*.

"In a moment we will invite you to lay your bets, gentlemen!" LeFoy trumpeted. "Come daybreak, the hunt for the Plague of the West begins!"

The hunt for . . . Oh. My. God.

"Which of these men can kill the Ghost of the Trails?" LeFoy's voice sent shivers down her spine. "Who will be the man to bring *death* to the Deathrider?" LeFoy now flung a hand in the direction of the gallery. Heads turned, and there was a chilly hush as everyone looked up at the gallery. Ava knew what they were seeing: rapists and kidnappers, butchers and gunslingers, thieves and child killers. The very worst the west had to offer, lined up like horses at auction. LeFoy began listing them, reciting a litany of evil. Ava heard him bellow nicknames that she herself had invented. The hair stood up on the back of her neck.

"And who are they hunting?" LeFoy dropped his voice, a seasoned showman in full flight.

"Deathrider!" the crowd roared.

"The man who kidnapped Susannah Fuller!" LeFoy raged. The crowd hissed.

Only Matt Slater said that was a lie. . . .

Ava shook her head. This was no time for her conscience to nag at her.

"The man who shot up Birchville!" Hissing became booing.

Lie . . .

No. It wasn't. She'd heard it from Fordham Fuller himself.

There's no such place as Birchville, Slater had insisted. But there *was.* There had to be. Fuller had said so.

"We have word our quarry is in the goldfields of Mariposa," LeFoy told his captive audience, "just a couple of days southeast of here."

Mariposa. So *that* was where he was. As awful as this farce was, at least tonight was tangible proof Deathrider was *alive.*

For now . . .

"Tomorrow at dawn," LeFoy announced, "the starting pistol will fire, and hell will be *unleashed*!"

Ava's arms were trembling from the effort of holding her weight, but she held on to the sconce, unable to look away. She'd come looking for a story—and she'd found one. She was ice-cold and prickling with a thrill that was equal parts curiosity and terror. She'd seen bad things in her life, things that could curdle your blood, but this . . . this was something else again.

It would make a sensational book. . . . Maybe even a series . . .

LeFoy's barking voice continued, hammering away at the seething crowd below, describing the possibilities ahead: all the ways Deathrider might be captured and killed. In some versions Voss was triumphant; in others it was a fight to the death among two or more of them, and all for the pleasure of ending the Plague of the West. "But"—LeFoy paused for effect, his eyes sparkling—"there's a twist in the tale!"

What more could there *be*?

"If they manage to bring the Plague of the West in *alive*, there will be a two-hundred-and-fifty-dollar bonus!"

Alive . . .

"No one's dumb enough to keep him alive!" Kennedy Voss hollered, and the room erupted in laughter.

LeFoy gave a rueful shrug. "I just hoped you'd give the rest of us a chance to meet the legendary Deathrider . . ."

"You can meet him when he's dead."

More laughter.

LeFoy was losing them, and he knew it. Because once again he upped the ante. "There's more!"

"What now? A bonus if we bring him in a gilded carriage?" Irish George joined in the heckling. He was a loudmouth who couldn't stand sharing the attention with Voss.

LeFoy laughed, but Ava could see his eyes darting around the room. "Riding with the killers will be none other than"—LeFoy paused for effect again, and then his voice soared—"A.A. Archer herself!"

Ava lost her breath. *What?*

The crowd made a noise like the ocean rushing to shore.

"Who better to witness the death of a legend than the woman who *made him*!" LeFoy turned in her direction, his eyes gleaming. Relishing every minute, he snapped his fingers at the bartenders in the gallery bar. One of the burly men leapt the bar, and she flinched. A rumble ran through the crowd as the bartender lifted her bodily from the sconce and up onto the bar. Ava slapped his hands away, her face burning. How dared they! She wasn't a piece of meat to be put on display.

And there was no way in hell she had agreed to be any part of this.

"A.A. Archer," LeFoy continued, "the author of *Blood Moon*, *The Trail of the Dead*, and *The Wolf of the West*."

Ava kept her head high, even as her knees went weak. Oh, hell. What had she stumbled into? The faces blurred, a nightmarish smear of eyes and leers. The ground telescoped away from her as she heard a bizarre rumbling noise. *Don't faint. Please don't let me faint and fall face-first off the bar.* Through sheer force of will, she managed to steady herself.

"A.A. Archer: the woman who coined the name *the Plague of the West!*"

The rumble swelled, and she realized that the men downstairs were stamping their feet on the floorboards. It was more visceral than applause; it sounded like a stampede. She put her hand on her Colt, but it didn't reassure her. The varmints were all staring at her with greedy eyes. Dear God.

Show no fear.

It took every ounce of courage she had to stare them down. She lifted her chin and threw her shoulders back. She hoped her expression showed frosty disdain and gave no hint of the fear sweat that was rolling down her spine.

LeFoy was still talking, as fervent as a preacher in the pulpit. "Whoever kills the legendary Wolf of the West will be immortalized in Miss Archer's next work . . . *LeFoy's Great Hunt!*"

How *dared* he? Rage bloomed. That manipulative, opportunistic *bastard.* Rage was better than fear, although it made her tremble with its force.

"That shit," Becky gasped. She'd moved to stand behind Ava. She must have seen the tremble in Ava's legs because she reached out and pressed a hand against her calf in a show of comfort.

"What are the rules?" someone shouted.

"What are the rules?" LeFoy was proving to be an expert in whipping up the crowd. The air was crackling, as though a lightning storm was gathering energy. "The rules of the game, gentlemen, are *there are no rules!*"

The crowd erupted. Ava watched wide-eyed as the hall roiled with bloodlust. The atmosphere was feral.

"Be in the street outside at dawn tomorrow, and watch the Hunt begin!"

The cheers were deafening. And then a cacophony of shouts, all variations on the same theme: "How will you prove the winner?" "They're all a pack of liars!" "How do you trust they've done what they claim?"

LeFoy laughed, genuinely amused. "How does any hunter prove his prowess? They'll bring back his head!"

Ava's stomach lurched. But only for a moment, until she remembered who their quarry was. There would be no head brought to LeFoy's Palladium, and there would be no accounting of bets. Because this was *Deathrider* they were talking about. The man was unkillable. He should have died a thousand times over by now, and yet he was still roaming the west, his long shadow falling from prairie to coast.

But . . . oh my God, the bloodlust . . . the butchers arrayed before her . . .

Surely no man could survive this . . . not even the Plague of the West . . .

Someone needs to warn him. The thought came unbidden. Warn him? *She* was the one who had documented his crimes; of all the people in this room, she knew best that his victims deserved justice. He was a killer, no different from these other butchers and villains. *But* had *he really committed all those crimes?* There was that flicker again, the one that had been bothering her of late. Now and again a tremulous whisper tried to interrupt her when she wrote. *What if he hadn't done* everything *she'd accused him of?*

Enough. He *had.* She had reliable sources; she'd traced his steps and done her research as well as was humanly possible; everything else had simply been embroidering existing facts. He *had* done it all . . .

Mostly.

But . . . sometimes, maybe, *perhaps* . . . she had taken a few liberties. For the sake of the story, or when the facts ran out. It was no more than any writer did. Her conscience was bothering her only because this sick circus was anathema to her humanity, that was all. *No* man deserved this. Not even the Plague of the West.

"At dawn tomorrow the Hunt begins! But *now*," LeFoy was bellowing, confident his Hunt was already a roaring success, "now we take an accounting! Gentlemen: the betting is *open*!"

As Ava watched, the sea of men rushed the stage, waving their hard-earned cash. The bookmakers worked in tandem, adjusting numbers, tabling bets, accumulating a fortune on the desk. The guards had their weapons drawn and kicked the crowd back whenever it roiled too close to the stage.

Kennedy Voss watched as his odds grew shorter. When he led the field, he turned to grin over his shoulder at Ava. His gaze swept her body. And then he had the gall to wink at her.

Oh my *God*. What on earth had she gotten herself mixed up in? And how the hell was she going to get *out* of it?

✳ 3 ✳

I'M COMING WITH you." Becky had squirmed her way through the half-open door and set herself stubbornly in the middle of Ava's room before Ava quite registered what had happened. In her defense, she'd been pulled from her bed and wasn't at her sharpest. She blinked, thickheaded, trying to work out what was going on.

The girl had changed out of her skimpy work clothes and into sensible traveling wear. She was carrying saddlebags and had a huge straw hat rammed on her head. She wore a mutinous expression, and it was clear that she meant business.

Ava knew she shouldn't have opened the door. If it had been anyone but Becky, she wouldn't have; she'd had restless nightmares about Kennedy Voss and the others coming for her in the night, and she'd all but barricaded herself in the attic room.

Pierre LeFoy had been ostentatious in his hospitality; he wanted people to see him leading her away upstairs. She was his trump card, there to immortalize the whole event, there to immortalize *him*. She grew increasingly furious—he acted like he owned her. On the surface he was solicitous, but in actuality he was all but holding her prisoner. Because of LeFoy, every man and his dog in San Francisco knew she was closeted up here. She'd felt their hot gazes on her back as she'd left the bar.

She was being led even deeper into a trap, she'd thought grimly as she allowed herself to be escorted up to a room. But what choice did she have? She couldn't leave on her own—it was too unsafe. She could hardly parade out of LeFoy's and walk San Francisco's dark streets looking for accommodation, could she? One of those varmints would be sure to follow hard on her heels. There was Kennedy Voss to worry about for starters; he had been giving her looks like he was a hungry dog and she was a package of fresh sausages. But being led upstairs wasn't a much better alternative to roaming the dark streets alone. She was a prisoner until dawn. And she was locked in the building with the very men she wanted to avoid.

LeFoy led her to one of the rooms reserved for the dancing girls. It was in the eaves, like a servant's room, but fancily decorated. It was a bit like stepping into a highly ornamental jewelry box; it was all sloping ceilings, plush velvets and glittering mirrors. Wherever Ava looked, she could see fragments of her own reflection. It was a room for debauchery, she thought dryly. The bed was thick with pillows and bracketed by mirrors. She caught her reflection and pulled a face. So much for her luxurious boardinghouse.

"There will be no charge for the room," LeFoy said graciously as he left. "You're our guest." He closed the door before she could respond. Clever man. Because he'd been about to get an earful.

"You might want to lock yourself in," a red-faced Becky suggested when she'd come by soon after with a sandwich and a glass of milk. A sandwich was apparently the best this fancy place could offer her for supper. It wasn't even a very good sandwich. And *milk*? She could have stomached something a little stronger.

"Is this free of charge too?" Ava asked dryly as she poked at the stale bread and stingily cut ham.

"You'd hope so, wouldn't you?" Becky's nose wrinkled as she considered Ava's supper. "You know what *he* had for supper? Prime rib." She sighed. "I'd best get back to work. And I mean it about locking yourself in. Pete's ordered a couple of the boys to guard the stairs but . . ." The girl shrugged.

But indeed. If Kennedy Voss and Co. decided to come up here after her, LeFoy's men were hardly going to stop them.

It was only once Becky had clomped back downstairs and Ava was alone in the mirrored treasure box that she had time to really ponder how much trouble she was in, and the more she pondered, the more ominous it seemed. But what to do about it?

As far as she could see, she had three options. One: she could get the story of her career by traveling along with the Hunters, while also putting herself at hourly risk of rape, assault or worse. Two: she could take her chances braving the gauntlet below, then running like hell until she'd got as far away as she could, losing the story but keeping herself alive and unharmed. Three: she could watch the Hunt start tomorrow and *then* run like hell, thereby getting some of the story firsthand, whilst minimizing her exposure to the killers.

The first option was the riskiest, but it would give her enough material for a whole slew of books. The second option was also risky—she was liable to be caught midflight by Voss or one of the others—and even if she *did* escape, she'd be left not knowing the outcome of the Hunt and having to scrounge for the crumbs of the story after the fact.

The third option was the only sensible one. It was a logical balance of risk and reward. A sane person would obviously take it. . . .

Ava pushed the sandwich away, overcome by revulsion. Oh, but how *could* she?

The mere thought of missing the action sent a bolt of

angst through her. She'd be running away from the biggest story of her career. It would be like Cinderella missing the ball.

She *hated* the thought of missing the action. How on earth could she hide away from a story like this one? After everything she'd been through, after all she'd risked and all she'd achieved. To miss out on the big story *now* . . .

Ava met her own gaze in the mirror. No. She might be a storyteller by trade, but she had one cast-iron rule: she never lied to herself. This was about more than a story. This was about *Deathrider.*

Most people were disappointing when you met them, legends more so than most. Like Jim Bridger, for example. He was the most famous mountain man in the west—but in person he was just a grump who didn't wash very often. Deathrider was liable to be the same. He was probably short, plain and thick as a plank. Maybe he didn't even have pale eyes, like everyone said he did, because she hadn't ever met an Indian with blue eyes. And he definitely couldn't turn himself into a wolf at will—*that* was pure fantasy.

In the telling, Deathrider was mythical: tall, bronzed, with quicksilver speed and the stealth of a hunter; he was as strong as a buffalo, as fast as an antelope and as deadly as a rattlesnake. She knew Deathrider the man could never live up to the story version of him she'd helped to construct . . . *but what she wouldn't give to find out.* . . .

What if she never could?

Because those men down there were out to kill him. And while deep down she didn't really think they'd succeed—because this was *Deathrider*—what if they did? If she didn't go along on the Hunt, she might never get the chance to see him alive. . . .

Her stomach twisted into complex knots as she contemplated traveling with the villains downstairs. English George and Irish George; Pete Hamble; the Butcher of Borrego Springs . . . *Kennedy Voss* . . .

But *Deathrider*. Imagine seeing him in person. Finding out if he really did have eyes the color of ice. If he traveled with a wolf. If he exuded the dark majesty and aura of threat that people said he did . . .

God help her. She was really going to do this. . . .

She didn't see how she *couldn't* do this. Their destinies were intertwined, hers and Deathrider's. He'd shadowed her for almost a decade, a flickering presence on the edge of her life. Everywhere she went, there were traces of him. And, she admitted, while she had made his name legendary, *he* had also made *her*. Because of him she had managed to escape; she could turn her back on the money her mother offered—money that Ava had once needed, but which came with so many compromises. She could walk away from being her father's mistake and her mother's last great hope. Because of Deathrider, Ava had her *own* money. She was free. Her future was her own.

Her feelings for the Plague of the West were colored by these facts, she knew. Deathrider was doubtless even more terrifying than the men downstairs. His name struck fear into the hearts of travelers and homesteaders from here to Missouri, and going to find him was objectively insane. The man made Kennedy Voss look like a saint. And yet in her secret heart, Deathrider remained her savior, the man who had enabled her to forge her independence, on the back of the books she wrote about him.

Maybe she'd live to regret it, but she was going on this ugly hunt. If anyone was going to find Deathrider, it was *her*. Come dawn, she'd be saddled up, down there on the street with the rest of them, waiting for LeFoy to fire his pistol in the air and declare the Hunt open. If she didn't fall off her horse from exhaustion, that was.

Decision made, and realizing she needed rest, she'd checked the door was locked, then double- and triple-checked it, and then propped a chair under the handle and then she'd climbed onto the bed fully clothed, boots still on, her gun close to hand. It wasn't the most soothing way to rest, and sleep was hard-won that night. She woke at every noise, which meant she was awake more than she was asleep, because the Palladium below was still doing a roaring trade. It was impossible to sleep, knowing those killers were directly beneath her, especially remembering the look in Kennedy Voss's eye as he'd stared at her, and knowing what she knew about his past victims. Every noise made her heart leap into her throat.

As she jerked in and out of sleep, the night became both endless and slippery. She lost track of time. When Becky came knocking, Ava was thickheaded with exhaustion and she'd thought vaguely that Becky was there to wake her up for the Hunt.

But it seemed Becky was here on her own business. Her small frame was rigid with determination, and her chin had a stubborn set as she shoved past Ava into the room.

"I'm coming with you," she repeated mulishly.

Ava had a sinking feeling that this wasn't any kind of wake-up visit she wanted. She reached over and lifted the heavy curtain away from the window. It was still full night, although the street below teemed with revelers who had decided to wait out the hours until the Hunt, drinking rather than sleeping. She could see some wobbly drunk trying to paint a starting line in the dirt and some of the "Hunters" were out there too, cheering him on. Then she spied Kennedy Voss and pulled away from the window so sharply that she whacked her head on the sloping roof.

That was another thing to hold against him, she thought sourly as she rubbed her head.

"I'm coming with you," Becky repeated more forcefully. "On the Hunt."

Becky was glaring at Ava like they were arguing about it. Which they weren't. Yet. But only because Ava was still rubbing her head and gathering her overtired wits.

"I can help you," the girl insisted.

"Help me do what?" Ava gave the rumpled bed a longing look. She was so tired. She'd come into town last night simply looking for a place to post off her books, and then to get a solid month of rest. She remembered her fantasy of a plush boardinghouse, with rocking chairs on the porch and a view of the sparkling water and bustling streets. She hadn't wanted to find any chatty English lords, or gunslingers, or a skinny bar girl who wanted to run away from home. She'd just wanted a *bed*. When all this chasing ghosts across the west was done, and her bank accounts were healthy enough for her to quit writing about these jackals, she was going to buy herself an enormous feather bed and sleep for at least a year. Maybe even hire a servant to bring her coffee when she called for it. She could have a rope pull installed right next to the bed, she thought dreamily. She could yank on it without ever lifting her head from the pillow.

"I can help you with the Hunt." Becky's eyes were gleaming. She looked mighty pleased with herself. Too pleased, considering the hour, Ava thought grumpily.

"You didn't bring a pot of coffee up with you, by any chance?" Ava dropped into an overstuffed armchair. It was close enough to dawn to abandon all hope of sleep. She could add tonight to her tally of sleepless nights, she thought crankily. She doubted she'd slept a night through for the past month. It was a damn poor way to be starting out on a dangerous journey: she wasn't provisioned, and her horse was run into the ground. The fact was, she'd have to stay back in San Francisco once the Hunt had galloped off, whether she wanted to or not. She couldn't be riding a horse that would drop dead beneath her, or be running out of food and water in the middle of nowhere. She sighed and dropped her head to rest her forehead on her knees. She didn't have the energy for any of it. Why couldn't LeFoy have planned for this nonsense to start a week from now? After she'd slept and eaten and recovered her zest.

"We can get coffee from the kitchen on our way out, and I've packed food for us already," Becky told her. "I've been planning to get out of here for a while. I hate it here. I hate working my fingers to the bone for that no-good liar; I hate that bar; I hate those men who drink in it; and, God have mercy, I hate those three little hellions. I've tried my Christian best to be the closest thing to a mother to them, but those three don't need a mother. They need a horse breaker. Or a dog trainer. Or a lion tamer." The words were bursting from her, like water overflowing from a river after the snows had melted. "I'm done. That soft-bellied no-count snake ain't never going to marry me; Mrs. Tilly was right: he's all talk. I ain't wasting any more of my best years on him. I'm all ready to go: I've got us provisions and fresh horses, including spares. I've done enough traveling to know we'll need us some spares."

Ava wearily lifted her forehead from her knees and squinted up at Becky. "Us? There is no us." The last thing she needed was Becky in the mix. Things were difficult enough as it was. Lord, imagine trying to keep *both* of them safe in the midst of that pack of jackals . . . because Ava *was* planning to be in their midst, right in the thick of it. That was where the story was. And there was no room there for Becky. The girl would only get herself killed.

"There's no *us*, Becky. There's no *we*. And there's no way in hell you're coming along," she said firmly. The story of Becky's rape and murder was not one she planned to write. The girl was staying put, and that was all there was to it.

"Oh, yes, there is." Becky crossed her arms, and she got an obstinate look on her face. "I want out of here and this is my ticket. I've entered the competition."

"You *what*?" Ava was horrified.

"I've got the longest odds," Becky said proudly, as though that were a good thing. "I'm going to make a fortune. And you can have a front row seat to write about it."

The girl had most definitely lost her wits.

Ava tried to keep her patience and took a deep breath.

"I figure we head to Mariposa behind the rest of the group," Becky told her quickly before she could interrupt, "and work out what to do from there. Maybe we'll get lucky."

No. There was no chance Ava could keep her patience. "That's the dumbest thing I've ever heard," Ava said crisply. "It's dumber than a bag of hammers."

"I *know* him," Becky interrupted before Ava could get into the swing of her scolding. "I know Tom Slater! The Plague of the West. I traveled with him for a piece, when he was with his brother Matt. I didn't know it was *him* at the time—everyone thought he was dead. I mean, everyone thought that Deathrider was dead. We didn't know then that he was Tom Slater! I only knew it was him afterward, when I read your book."

Ava's head cleared in an instant. It was like having ice-cold water splashed in her face. She was on her feet and had seized Becky's arm before the girl had even finished speaking, as though she needed to hold fast to her before she could disappear.

"You *know* him? You could recognize him—even in a crowd?"

"I know exactly what he looks like," Becky said in an eager rush. "I know his voice. I know his horse. I know his dog. I even know his favorite food: it's fresh-caught walleye, fried in butter."

Ava took note of the specificity.

"And better yet, *he* knows *me*." Becky's grin was getting wider by the second. "He *trusts* me. I reckon we could get right up close to him, talk to him even, without him getting suspicious. He'd never think a couple of *women* would be out for him."

Ava felt a thrill. *Deathrider.* Becky knew *Deathrider.*

"And once you're up close, you honestly think you're

capable of killing him?" Ava asked dubiously, evaluating the scrap of a girl. She already knew the answer: of course she wasn't capable of killing him. It was an absurd proposition.

"I don't know," Becky admitted. "But I'd rather be going on this Hunt than scrubbing the floors here. Besides, according to your books, it sounds like he's in need of killing." She bit her lip, her eyes troubled. "Did he really rape that little Fuller girl?"

"That's the story I was told," Ava said, her mind whirling. There was definitely a book in this. It didn't even matter if Becky was a real contender or not—the story had spark. *The Killer Barmaid? Deathrider Meets His Match?*

Even without the story of her hunting Deathrider, just talking to Becky would be worth its weight in gold, considering the details the girl knew about him (*fresh-caught walleye, fried in butter*). Just imagine what Ava could learn, simply by riding along with the girl, plundering her memory.

While Ava was bursting with questions about Deathrider, this wasn't the time. She pulled her watch out of her vest pocket. Dawn was inching closer. No, this definitely wasn't the time. She felt a familiar fizz of excitement. Her exhaustion had evaporated. "You've got fresh horses, you said? And provisions?"

Becky nodded vigorously, grinning now that she realized Ava was going along with her. "Yes. Good ones too. I didn't skimp. His lordship is waiting with the horses, to make sure no one steals any of our stuff."

"His lordship?" Ava frowned.

"His odds are almost as bad as mine," Becky said cheerfully.

Ava groaned, remembering how the irritating Englishman had dogged her steps from the post office. "Don't tell me he signed up for the Hunt too?"

"*Everyone* signed up. Didn't you see how much money is involved? Why wouldn't you have a try?" She cocked her head. "I thought you must have forgotten to add your name, so I did it for you."

"You *what*?"

"I put your name down. Your odds are surprisingly good."

Ava felt the urge to shake the girl. "Are you mad? I don't want to compete with those cretins! They're liable to kill us just to get rid of the competition!"

A cloud crossed Becky's face. "Oh. I didn't think of that."

"Obviously. You have no idea who you're dealing with, and neither does Lord Whatsit."

"Whent."

"What?"

"No, Whent."

"Stop talking now," Ava ordered. "I need to think." Good God. She wasn't just writing about this grotesque Hunt; now she was *competing* in it. Which led her to a worrying thought . . . "Becky? Why would you want to travel with me and Lord Whatsit—"

"Whent."

Ava pressed her hand over the girl's mouth. "Stop talking."

"His name's Whent." Becky's muffled voice came though Ava's fingers.

"Why do you want to travel with us if you're competing *against* us? Surely *you* want to find Deathrider before we do?" Ava removed her hand so the girl could talk.

"You're very bossy," Becky observed. "Fancy telling people when they can and can't talk. Last I heard this was a free country."

"Becky . . ."

"Well, we're hardly going to *win*, are we?" Becky said, exasperated. "I'm not *stupid*. I know why my odds are so long. I'm not likely to actually have to decide whether to kill him or not, or how to beat you and his lordship. I mean, have you *seen* who's down there?" She gave Ava a frustrated look. "I know this is a wild-goose chase. I'm not a ninny. But I also know that life is a game of chance. We might as well have roll of the dice, don't you think? And I figure we're likely to do better if we stick together. And it's worth having a man along—his lordship can protect us from the other Hunters while we travel."

Remembering the limp Englishman, Ava was far from reassured.

Becky shrugged. "It'll be an adventure. And who knows? Maybe they'll all get food poisoning and die, and we'll be the last ones left."

"Even if we were the last ones left, we'd still have to find Deathrider," Ava reminded her.

"Yes." Becky seemed undaunted. In fact, she seemed to get cheerier by the minute.

"And kill him," Ava said.

"We'll cross that bridge when we come to it." The girl grinned again. "And anything's better than working here."

* 4 *

Mariposa, three days later

NATHANIEL RIDES WITH Death, known to friends and foes alike as Deathrider, had been through hell more than a few times before, so word of LeFoy's Hunt wasn't entirely unexpected. It was just a total pain in the ass.

Inconvenient too, as he had other problems to deal with. Problems that currently involved trying to cram one of his oldest friends into a whore's pink dress.

"How do I let you talk me into these things?" the friend in question complained, swearing vigorously as the corset pinched off his circulation.

"I don't know," Deathrider admitted. He could honestly say that he wouldn't have done it himself.

Micah was dressed head to toe in screaming pink satin. In order to get the whore's dress buttoned up over his broad back they'd had to cinch the corset so tight, he could barely breathe. His long hair was crammed up under an ugly pink silk rose-laden bonnet, and Seline's chopped-off orange locks were dangling from it in a hastily fashioned wig.

The whole ordeal was in order to save Seline from capture, so sacrificing her hair to the cause was the least she could do. She'd turned up in town in a flap, fleeing a man who was trying to keep her as his own private sex slave. Deathrider had known Seline a long time and couldn't leave her to fend for herself. Besides, he thought he'd found a way to solve both their problems at once: getting him away from LeFoy's Hunters, and her away from Hec Boehm, the man who was out to kidnap her. And that way just happened to involve dressing Micah up as Seline.

"You look mighty fetching," Deathrider reassured him. Although he didn't. He made the ugliest woman Deathrider had ever seen.

"Go to hell."

Deathrider gave him a smack on the rear, and Micah kicked out at him like a cranky mule. He wasn't happy with Deathrider's escape plan. Or with the plan to rescue Seline.

"No one is going to believe this," Micah said, regarding himself in the mirror with pure disgust. "Forget looking like *her*," he sniped. "I don't even look like a woman. This is never going to work."

"No," Deathrider agreed, tossing Micah a pair of pink satin elbow-length gloves, "probably not. But it can't hurt to try."

"It can," Micah grumbled. "It can hurt to try." He pulled at the bodice of the dress. "In fact, it *does* hurt to try. Quite a lot."

They were upstairs at the La Noche whorehouse in the gold town of Mariposa, locked in the madam's private office, planning their escape from LeFoy's Hunt. It was two in the morning, and the whorehouse was bedlam. That was mostly Seline's fault. She'd got the clientele all riled up by parading around in nothing but that ugly pink bonnet, so half the town would see her in the flesh—*all* the flesh. He'd been shocked to hell when she'd appeared in the main saloon buck naked. That part hadn't been Deathrider's idea . . . but he grudgingly admitted that it was a good one. Who wasn't going to remember a naked redhead strutting around in a big pink hat? Despite his shock, he'd played his part by throwing her over his shoulder and carrying her off upstairs. *The Outlaw and the Whore.*

"I think we were memorable," Seline said happily as soon as they'd locked themselves away upstairs, ostensibly for a night of passion, but in actuality to get Micah disguised as the whore.

Their performance certainly guaranteed they'd be the gossip of town, and *everyone* would recognize the pink bonnet and the shock of orange hair in the morning, when Deathrider and Micah rode out. Seline hadn't been thrilled about losing her hair, but it was better than losing her life. At this stage, she'd have been willing to do just about anything to escape Hec Boehm, the man who'd taken a shine to the idea of owning her.

Deathrider was going to make a circus of leaving Mariposa in the morning, dragging Micah-dressed-as-Seline ostentatiously along with him. He was counting on witnesses telling both Hec Boehm and the Great Hunters that the Plague of the West and the whore had left town. Together. He and Micah would draw Hec Boehm after them, allowing Seline time to escape. And they'd draw the Hunters too. . . .

The goddamn Hunters.

They've got a bet running in Frisco, Tom Slater had told him, still breathless and shiny with sweat after riding hard from San Francisco to warn Deathrider about LeFoy's scheme. *People all through the goldfields are gambling on who will shoot you first; there's big money in it.* Tom had come into Mariposa like some spirit of doom, his usually serious face more serious than ever. Tom's distress had startled Deathrider. Tom was the calmest man Deathrider had ever met; if *he* was worried, then things were bad. Very bad.

You've got to get out of the territory . . . , Tom had insisted. And then he'd started listing the names of the men hunting Deathrider: English George and Irish George, Cactus Joe and Kennedy Voss.

Kennedy goddamn Voss. It beggared belief. The man was an utter sadist. A woman killer. What in hell was he doing chasing down *Deathrider?*

You got less'n a day on them. Tom had been relentless, pushing Deathrider and Micah to move fast. His anxiety was palpable. *Less than a day.* And it would be a hard-riding day.

The thought made Deathrider tired. These past few years he had felt increasingly like a rabbit being run down by wolves. No matter where he went, the predators followed. Someone was always getting it into their head to shoot him. There seemed no end to the idiot gunslingers or the random drunks made brave by cheap beer or the wet-behind-the ears *kids.* They lurched from the shadows on the trail, reared up at him in saloons, ambushed him in the middle of the street in broad daylight. . . .

Each and every one of them looking to kill him.

Hell, even men he'd known for years were tempted to shoot him clean through. All for the sake of imagined rewards. Or, worse, for fame. The temptation of money Deathrider could almost understand, but fame? Imagine killing a man in order to be *famous?*

Hunger for that kind of renown showed a shallowness of character. A starvation of spirit.

Half the country seemed to be starving, though. And they looked at him and saw a solution to their hunger.

And it was all that *woman's* fault. Because of that Archer woman he had to watch his back wherever he went. It was obnoxious. And now there was Kennedy goddamn Voss to be worried about. Drunks and kids dreaming of being gunslingers were bad enough . . . but *Kennedy goddamn Voss?* What had he done to deserve *that?*

Nothing, that was what. He was a simple man. He lived a quiet life. He roamed the trails, relishing the great spread of country stretched out wild before him, enjoying the peace, the silence, the sense of being completely and totally at ease. When he stopped moving, his mind grew choppy with thoughts, like a rushing river. At home with Two Bears and his people, he spent his days keenly feeling his difference, his gaze drifting to the horizon. He couldn't help it. He didn't *fit*. And in his mother's world . . . well, just look what had happened to him out here. Everyone was trying to kill him.

When he was younger, his difference had eaten him up inside: was he white? Was he *Hinono'eino*? He was both, and he was neither. . . . At home his father, Two Bears, was always pressuring him to marry and settle into life with his people, to take up his responsibilities as a warrior, to turn his back on his mother's white history, to be fully *Hinono'eino*. But there was a deep restlessness in Deathrider's spirit. He couldn't stay. Not anywhere. He moved through the world like the ghost that Archer woman accused him of being: unsettled, lost.

He wasn't lonely exactly—he had friends along the trails: mountain men and settlers, farmers and nomads, Arapaho and Cheyenne and Pawnee, wagoners and gold miners, whores and fortune hunters. And he *did* have family—his wandering always led him back to Two Bears and his extended family, the way a river always found its way to the sea. But just like a river, he had no capacity for stillness.

It wasn't that he was unhappy. He just moved along, keeping ahead of his own restlessness. He belonged to the plains and the sky; he belonged in the saddle, with the sun in his face and the wind at his back. He was never alone; his dog ran alongside him and kept his feet warm on cold nights, and Micah fell in beside him for months at a time, talking enough for both of them.

Deathrider counted himself a lucky man. Or he *had* until that Archer woman had started writing about him. *Lying* about him.

And now there was this damn Hunt.

It was irksome. That had been his first response, as he'd listened to Tom's increasingly dire warnings. He'd been so-bered by Tom's evident disquiet, but mostly he found the whole thing a wretched bore.

These Hunters and their posses were just more of the same. It was annoying rather than frightening, like finding your bed full of fleas. He'd been dealing with people trying to kill him for years now. He and Micah would just pick up and move along, as they always did. Hell, he was just as likely to be shot here in Mariposa by some drunk kid as he was to be shot by Kennedy Voss or English George.

But then Tom threw another name in the mix. A name that *did* change everything.

Guess who's with them, Tom had snapped when Death-rider and Micah hadn't seemed concerned enough. *A.A. Archer herself.*

That had made Deathrider sit up. *A.A. Archer.*

Of course she was involved. Everything bad that hap-pened to Deathrider happened because of that woman. He wouldn't be surprised if she'd engineered the whole stupid Hunt.

She's writing a book about it, Tom had snarled.

Of course she was. Deathrider's thoughts were racing as Tom described the scene he'd witnessed in San Francisco. The killers pouring into town; the packed house at the dance hall; the bookmakers tallying odds; and Ava Archer herself, on display as an enticement—offering fame to the man who brought Deathrider's head to San Francisco.

It would make a great book, he thought. The best one yet—and he'd read a few. When Tom rode up, Micah had actually been reading the latest one: *The Notorious Widow Smith and Her Mail-Order Husband.* It was loosely based on reality and included the time Deathrider had rescued Mrs. Smith's son, Wilby. It was also the book that had con-fused him with Tom Slater. That was Matt Slater's fault—it had been his idea to pass Deathrider off as his brother after Deathrider had been shot in Fort Kearney.

The problem Deathrider had with Miss Archer's version wasn't that she mistook him for Tom Slater, however; the problem he had was that in her version Deathrider wasn't *rescuing* the kid; he was *kidnapping* him. And then threatening to drink his blood. It was thoroughly ridiculous.

Just imagine what she'd come up with this time. She'd probably have him laying siege to Mariposa. Kennedy Voss would be transformed into an avenging hero, while Deathrider would be the stuff of nightmares.

As he fell into grimness, an idea flickered and then flared.

She was making it all up anyway . . . so why not lend her a hand . . . ?

"If she wants a book, let's give her a book," Deathrider had said to Micah and Tom, his mind racing with possibilities.

Tom had scowled, and Micah had laughed. It was only when Seline turned up and Deathrider's plan had started to solidify that Micah had stopped laughing. Tom didn't know about the worst of it yet—they needed him to be in the dark about Seline's identity for the plan to work. Because, as usual, things had got complicated fast.

Seline had turned up in Mariposa not long after Tom Slater. The sassy whore had been dressed like a nun, of all things. She had one of her girls in tow—also dressed like a nun.

"I'm in hiding," she'd said sourly. She was as full to the brim of grim news as Tom had been. It seemed to be one of those days.

Seline was on the run from Hec Boehm, a man who ruled the goldfields with his petty tyranny. She'd fled to the whorehouse in Mariposa, which she owned shares in, but Boehm was hot on her tail, and she couldn't stop for long.

"He's going to catch up to me," she sighed. She and

Deathrider were old friends. They'd traveled across the plains together after he'd been shot in Kearney, when she'd been striking west to start up her own business. Seline was good company. He liked her. And he didn't like that many people.

When she'd come riding into Mariposa and heard Deathrider was in town too, she'd wasted no time in finding him, looking for help. And, of course, that meant he'd been dragged right into her problems. He couldn't seem to help himself.

"What is it with men?" she'd complained to him, looking strikingly odd in the heavy black nun's habit. "Why do they think a woman is like a gold claim? You can't *claim* a woman."

"Some men think they can claim everything," Deathrider said with a shrug. He helped her find a wagon and get provisioned for a long piece of traveling. The girl with her was Mexican, and he'd convinced Seline to go south with her to Mexico, to hide out until Boehm had run out of puff. Which he was bound to do eventually.

Tom was headed south too. It seemed logical he should escort them. So long as he thought they were nuns, he was hardly likely to refuse, was he? Who wouldn't help out a couple of desperate nuns? Deathrider wished he could be there when Tom finally realized they weren't nuns at all, and he was actually escorting a couple of whores. . . .

"Leave Boehm to me," Deathrider told Seline. He cursed himself for volunteering, but what else was he supposed to do? Leave Seline to Hec Boehm's mercies? Not likely.

And besides, as he'd listened to Seline's problems, an idea had blossomed. Why not kill two birds with one stone? Why not give Miss Archer a story too good to pass by?

"I reckon there's a nice little tale in *The Outlaw and the Whore*," he'd said mildly as he and Micah were loading up her wagon, not wanting to give away his rising excitement. He'd given Seline a sideways look. "I always did like redheads."

She laughed. "Too bad mine ain't entirely natural." Then she caught up. "What are you yapping about?"

An idea had been brewing ever since Tom had mentioned that Archer woman's name, an idea that cracked his boredom with the whole situation wide open.

Why not turn things on their head?

What if he decided he didn't want to be hunted anymore? What if he decided he'd rather be the hunter?

Which brought them to Micah in the dress. Deathrider was going to make sure the whore and the outlaw came to a bad end—an end that Miss Archer would be compelled to write about. She was going to put the nails in the coffin of his legend by writing about his demise. His *and* Seline's.

Which would leave both of them free as birds.

"Why do you always have to play at being a white knight?" Micah grumped once Seline had ridden off into the night with Tom Slater, headed for Mexico under cover of darkness, disguised as a nun. Micah was suffering in the tight corset, and he was souring on the idea by the second. And he'd been plenty sour to begin with. "You're always off saving people. I wish you'd think about *me* once in a while."

Deathrider didn't dignify that with a response. *White knight.* It was the stupidest thing he'd ever heard. If he was anything, he was a lone wolf, not a white knight. Hell, he wasn't even *white*.

Micah didn't take the hint. As usual, he kept on bitching. "Last time we were in Utopia, I had to sit through hours of those women swooning over you. You rescued Alex Slater from some crazy varmint who was out to rape her, blah blah blah, and saved the other one's kid from death, blah blah blah. And when we're camping with the Cheyenne, Yellow Bird always twitters on about how you saved her from a witch."

"She made that up," Deathrider said shortly. "She was always hoping I'd dress up and sit outside her tent and act the suitor. If her father thought I'd saved her from a witch, he might have let her marry me."

"There was also that white girl you pulled from the river last winter, even though she was screaming fit to bust because she'd never seen an Indian before. You can't seem to help but get mixed up in other people's business."

"That's ridiculous. I don't even like people," Deathrider grunted.

"You like 'em just fine. *They* just don't always like *you*." Micah looked down at the pink dress Deathrider had slapped on him. "I can't imagine why."

"I certainly didn't agree to be *your* white knight, so quit your complaining."

"You sure didn't," Micah grumbled, yanking at the collar of the dress. "Why I agreed to this, I'll never know."

"You can leave anytime you want."

"And miss all the fun?"

Deathrider rolled his eyes.

"NOW WHAT?"

The next morning found them miles from Mariposa after hours of hard riding. They'd put on a ridiculous display as they'd left. Deathrider had waited until the town was awake and businesses were opening on the main street, to ensure they'd have a receptive audience. There'd still been drunken miners lolling about the whorehouse and a couple more sleeping it off on the porch. Enough people to bear witness to their nonsense.

Micah had crept out to the stable before dawn, to get the horses ready. He'd gone out the back entrance, down the outside stairs off the whores' washroom. He didn't pass for a woman on close inspection, and they couldn't risk him going down the main stairs. His part would have to be played at a distance—letting the costume do the work. The first bit of the performance was left entirely to Deathrider. And Deathrider took his performance seriously.

He'd removed his shirt, revealing his tattoos, and knotted his hair with his eagle feather; he'd even slapped on some war paint—not in any design he would have used in real life, something much blunter and sillier. All of it was in aid of looking the way whites imagined Indians to look. Frightening. He slung his saddlebags over his shoulder and carried his ax.

People were scared of him when he wasn't even trying; now that he was trying, they just about fainted on sight. He didn't need to whoop and holler as he left La Noche. As soon as he appeared at the head of the stairs, the room below fell silent. A few of the whores had been milling about over morning coffee; as they spied him, they hushed. The hush disturbed the leftover miners, who grew wide-eyed at the sight of him and rose shakily to their feet. Deathrider kept close watch on them. None of them was armed, but who knew what they'd do, as spooked as they were?

He swaggered down the stairs, keeping his ax visible. The miners and the whores watched him warily, as though he were some kind of wild animal that had wandered in from the hills. It never ceased to amaze him how jumpy whites were around him. As he reached the front door, he called over to them in his native Algonquin. They all flinched. They might not have looked so scared if they'd known he'd just told them they looked like they'd found a bug in their coffee. But then again, maybe they would have.

It was only once he got outside that things got interesting. He could see Dog standing at the mouth of the stables, ears cocked. Deathrider caught a flicker at the edge of his vision and turned to see the group from inside the whorehouse all but pressed up against the windows, gawking at him. Good. He gave a sharp whistle and Dog barked. The snoozing drunks on the porch startled awake. Once he had their attention, Deathrider threw his head back and gave voice to a war cry. Again, not one he'd ever use in real life, but it was guaranteed to strike terror into anyone who heard it, so it served its purpose.

At the sound of Deathrider's cry, Micah came tearing

out of the stable, pink satin blazing in the sun. He had a fist-ful of reins, leading Deathrider's horse and the packhorses. He kept his head down as he rode, hiding his face from view. It wasn't a bad disguise, Deathrider thought apprecia-tively, as Micah reached him and dropped the reins to Deathrider's horse. All you saw was pink. And that telltale orange hair.

Deathrider leapt smoothly onto his horse, dropping his saddlebags in front of him. He'd cinch them on later, once they were safely away. The two miners on the porch were scrambling for cover, and he was wary of them reaching for their weapons. He shook his ax at them, whooping, and tore after Micah down Main Street before anyone could shoot at him. He had a hard time not laughing as he saw the looks of horror on the townspeople's faces. Not to be outdone by all the whooping, Micah had pulled his Colt and was taking random shots at the signs swinging from the shop fronts. There were screams at the sound of shattering glass. People ran for cover.

It worked perfectly. No one would forget them. When Hec Boehm, Kennedy Voss and that Archer woman rode into town, all they'd hear about was how Deathrider and the whore had shot up the place. The citizens of Mariposa would be rehashing this tale for a good long while.

And now Deathrider and Micah were hours away, with no one on their trail that they could see, and Micah wanted to know what they were up to next.

"Now we head to the Apacheria," Deathdrider told him calmly.

"But that's so far away!"

He ignored Micah's groan. "I told you: we're going to stage our deaths."

Micah snorted. "And how are we doing that?"

"We're going to get ourselves killed by Apaches."

"I assume you mean *pretend* to get ourselves killed by the Apaches?"

Deathrider didn't dignify that with an answer. "We'll follow their plunder trails, find the remains of one of their raids and dress it up to look like us. No one will mistake that pink dress."

"You mean I can take it off?"

"Not yet. We need to make a few more appearances as we head south—we need to lay a trail for those Hunters: we want everyone between here and Mexico talking about us."

"You're the only man I know who wants to *let* a posse find him."

"And you're the only man I know who'd let me dress him up like a whore and *then* let a posse find him."

That shut Micah up. But only for a minute or two. "Can we at least go to Mexico after? There's a pretty señorita I promised to visit next time I was back this way."

Deathrider sighed. If only *his* life was that simple.

✦ 5 ✦

Two days earlier

THERE'D BEEN NO question of not traveling with the pack. Ava had seen the way it was going to play out the minute she'd descended from her mirrored bedroom to the gallery of the Palladium to find Kennedy Voss waiting for her. Voss had his eye on her, and he wasn't letting her out of his sight. He'd been waiting in the gallery, watching the doorway for her to come down the stairs from her room in the eaves. He was the only one there. The rest of the jackals were presumably saddling up for the Hunt. But not Voss. No, he was set up at a table in the deserted gallery, with a napkin tucked into the collar of his shirt, eyeing a plateful of steaming biscuits. She felt an icy curl of terror at the sight of him. For all of his farm boy good looks, there was something . . . *off* about him. He had flat eyes. Empty eyes. It was like looking into the gaze of a rattlesnake.

"Miss Archer," he said cordially, rising from his chair. He looked for all the world like an awkward suitor. He was completely out of place in the fancy surroundings of the Palladium. His rumpled, dusty clothes jarred with the polished oak and etched-glass lamps. He seemed painfully aware of the juxtaposition, brushing at the crumbs on his pants. His pose was that of a hick boy courting a girl far above his station.

He seemed innocuous. He had dimples. And a shy way of looking up through his eyelashes. But those eyes . . . they put the sheer fear of God into her. Maybe if she hadn't known about all the things he'd done, she might have been fooled. But she did, so she wasn't.

"I've done the courtesy of ordering us some breakfast," Voss told her, beaming proudly. His cowlick bobbed. The eyes, though, the *eyes* looked her up and down, lingering where they had no right to linger.

Never trust a charming man. Or a powerful man. Or any damn man at all. That was what Ava had learned from watching her mother's mistakes. Ava's father had been— *was*—a powerful man. And he'd brought her mother nothing but gilded servitude. Not even all that gilded now that she'd grown old. That was what happened when you let a man make you his mistress. You had no rights to even the gilt on your cage.

Ava had learned that lesson many times over.

"I didn't know if you took coffee or tea," Voss said, stumbling charmingly over his words, as though he'd had a fit of nerves at talking to a pretty woman, "so I ordered you both."

Hell. She didn't want coffee *or* tea, not if she had to have it with him. Ava considered her options. There weren't many. She could sit and eat with him, or she could beg off. Which would be more dangerous?

It was hard to say.

"Eat," he said. He didn't seem to blink. "I insist." As he pushed the plate of biscuits toward her, she saw the gleam of lamplight on his bandolier. It was mighty well stocked with bullets.

Yes. Well. Begging off might not be an option.

Oh well. At least it meant she could take accurate notes. She resigned herself to the situation and joined him at the table. Besides, two could play this game.

"How dreadfully kind of you, Mr. Voss," she sighed, wilting into the chair like a fatuous belle. "Coffee would be delightful. I didn't sleep a *wink*."

"Too excited?" The farm boy pose slipped slightly; now his voice had a lascivious edge. "I hear you like a bit of action."

Wonderful. He wasn't going to waste any time, was he? Hell. How was she going to manage him . . . ?

"I've read those books you wrote about me."

Ah. He had, had he? Well, that shouldn't come as a surprise. But what did he *think* of them? That was the real question. Ava kept her expression lightly flirtatious and tried to look as unthreatening as possible. "They sold very well. You're quite popular."

That got him. He got all puffed up like a bantam again. Vanity was the downfall of so many men. Ava leaned in for the kill. "You have no idea how the readers clamor for more."

The first flicker of feeling sparked in those rattlesnake-flat eyes. "I can give you more," he suggested. Greed, that was what was in his eyes. Greed, hunger, the desire for *fame*.

She heard a gasp and turned to see Becky in the doorway. The girl couldn't contain her horror at the sight of Ava sitting with Voss.

Amateurs. Ava gave her a sharp look. "I'm just having coffee before we ride out," she said calmly. "It's so horrifically early. I'll never survive without coffee." That, at least, was true.

Becky's traveling gear was already looking rumpled, despite the fact that they hadn't gone anywhere yet, and her giant straw hat was hanging from her neck by its cord. "We can't stop *here*," Becky blurted, her gaze darting over Kennedy Voss. "I just gave my notice! And I told Pete I've left him." She pulled at the cord until she was almost strangling herself. "I can't stay here for *breakfast*!"

"Of course you can," Ava said calmly, turning back to the table, where Kennedy Voss was pouring her coffee. "You're a paying customer now. What's he going to do?"

She heard Becky make a despairing noise. "And his lordship is waiting for us . . ."

"His lordship?" Voss sounded lazily curious, but Ava could see the sharpness in his gaze.

"He's nobody," Ava said swiftly. "Just a burr we picked up. Sit down, Becky. We have time enough for coffee." She had no idea if they had time enough at all, but she was going to need coffee to face the ordeal ahead. She was glad Kennedy Voss had already poured it for her because her hands were trembling; she would have spilled it all over herself. *I can give you more.* He gave her the holy terrors.

"This lord fella, is he the tall one what was at the bar with you last night?" Voss asked. He was spooning sugar into his tea: one, two, three, four teaspoons. And a hefty dose of cream. The spoon clanked against the cup as he stirred. It got on Ava's nerves.

"There really isn't time for this," Becky said anxiously. "Everyone's down in the street already."

"They're not going to start without us; we're the star attractions." Voss didn't look up from the biscuit he was eviscerating but reached over and yanked a chair out for Becky. "Sit."

Becky sat. "He *might* start without you," she muttered under her breath. "You don't know him." Ava kicked her under the table. Kennedy Voss wasn't a man to get mouthy with.

"Do you mind if I ask you some questions, Mr. Voss?" Ava asked, stealing his move and looking up at him though her eyelashes.

"Ask me anything." His eyes still had that spark. He liked talking about himself; that much was clear.

This wasn't an easily managed man, but his self-absorption might be the way to do it. "How do you plan to catch the

Plague of the West?" she asked, glad her voice betrayed no trace of her unease.

A slow smile broke across Voss's wide freckled face. "You'll see for yourself," he drawled. "Firsthand."

"She will?" Becky asked weakly.

Voss didn't spare her a glance. His rattlesnake gaze was fixed on Ava. "You can ride with me the whole way." He was still grinning. "I insist."

"HOW ARE WE going to get away from him?" Becky hissed when they'd finished breakfast and were following Voss down the stairs.

"We're not."

Becky tripped and almost went head over heels down the staircase. Ava caught her by the elbow and yanked her back to her feet.

"Are you out of your mind?" Becky whispered, appalled.

"Honey, you're the one who signed us up for the Hunt."

"Yes, *the Hunt*. Not cavorting with Kennedy Voss!"

Ava gave a harsh laugh. "What did you think the Hunt was?" She settled her hat on her head and yanked it to a rakish angle. "And it's not just cavorting with Kennedy Voss. There's the rest of them too."

"The rest of them" were already saddled up and milling around in the street, loosely keeping behind the crooked line—the very line Ava had watched the drunk painting on the hard-packed dirt the night before. Cactus Joe was already on his horse, chewing on a wad of tobacco and glaring at anyone who dared to come close; Irish George was red-faced drunk and gabbing away with Pete Hamble (both of them could talk the hind leg off a mule); and Sweet Boy Beau was flirting madly with Skipper Wallace, who looked half-besotted already. Who could blame him? Beau was beautiful.

She and Becky looked to be the only women in the pack.

Ava was intensely aware of the attention they drew as they descended from the porch of the Palladium. A hush met them, and ripples of gossip followed them. The pack of jackals had been joined by untold numbers of joyriders, most of them drunk and trigger-happy and whooping up a storm. They were far more uncontrolled than the actual killers and villains. The street had the feeling of a lynch mob—only without a victim. Ava imagined they'd remedy that before long.

As she and Becky wound through the pack, dawn was splitting the sky: a bloodred wound. Banks of clouds were soaked with lurid color, and even the dust in the air was ruddy, swirling in russet clouds in the sea breezes. Ava could smell the brine of the harbor. She'd never even managed to get to the shore, she realized regretfully.

She was so mighty sick of traveling. Her saddle sores had saddle sores.

"His lordship has our horses," Becky said. She'd lost some of the zest she'd shown previously, when she'd come barging into Ava's room. Breakfast with a killer would do that to you. She was more than a little slump shouldered as she led Ava toward Lord Whatsit, who seemed entranced by the killers around him. He was standing near the back of the field, close by the porch of the bakery, holding the reins of half a dozen horses. None of them was Ava's, which was probably for the best. Her horse had been worn out by the last journey, and the hostler was welcome to keep her. After a good feed and a rest, he'd be able to sell her. Ava felt a pang about losing the money she'd bring, but only a small one and only for a moment. After all, by the looks of it, she was gaining *two* horses. And my, a couple of them were prime horseflesh.

"Is that an *Arab*?" she asked, stunned by the beauty of the animal standing immediately to Lord Whatsit's right.

"Indeed, she is." Lord Whatsit tore his gaze from the killers and beamed at Ava. "A beauty, isn't she? I brought her all the way from England with me." He gave the horse a vigorous slap on the neck, and she danced sideways. "High-spirited, the way a lass should be."

"These are yours," Becky said sullenly, untangling a couple of sets of reins from Lord Whatsit's gloved hand and holding them out to Ava. "You owe me eighty dollars."

Ava stared at the horses at the end of the reins in disbelief. God*damn*. She'd been so dazzled by the Arab, she hadn't noticed these fleabags. "There's no way *those* animals are worth eighty dollars!"

"The packhorse only cost twenty-five," Becky admitted, "but the other one was fifty-five dollars."

"Which one's the packhorse?" It was impossible to tell. They were both solid little things, built for pulling wagons. Neither of them looked in their prime.

"The roan. The speckled one is for riding."

Ava and the speckled horse eyed each other. "I might stop by and pick up my old nag on the way out," Ava said dryly, refusing to take the reins from Becky. "I hate to waste a good horse."

"There's no time." Becky's limpness had turned to crankiness. Ava followed her gaze and saw why. Pierre Le-Foy had emerged on the balcony of the Palladium, flanked by his daughters, the redheaded moppets from the night before, who were again attired in their spangly stage clothes (which had apparently once been Becky's nice pink dress). LeFoy was holding a bottle of champagne and a pistol. The moppets were climbing the railings, their sequins blazing in the bloodred dawn.

"I can go and get your horse for you," Lord Whatsit offered, oblivious of both LeFoy and his moppets and to Becky's pique.

"Then *you'll* miss the start." Becky was turning into a regular thundercloud. Ava guessed she'd had a stressful morning—after all, she'd broken up with her lover *and* quit her job. And now she was out eighty dollars (because there

was no way Ava was paying for these wretched animals—
Becky was welcome to use them as packhorses).

"I'm sure they'll wait for us," Lord Whatsit said.

"Said like a true gentleman," Ava observed as he
mounted his high-stepping Arab and picked his way through
the crowds.

Once Lord Whatsit was directly in LeFoy's sight he
called up to him, "I say, LeFoy! Miss Archer needs to collect her animal—would you mind holding off on the start
of this hoo-ha while I go rustle it up?"

"Hoo-ha?" Ava echoed. The man was too much.

Meanwhile, the crowd set to with a mighty booing. Le-
Foy laughed and hushed them. "Now, now, you wouldn't
want Miss Archer to miss all the fun, would you?"

"She don't need no horse. She can ride with me," a voice
called. Ava jumped a mile. It was Kennedy Voss, and he
was right behind her. Or, rather, above her, as he was already mounted on a horse that must have stood sixteen
hands high. She shrieked as he went from being behind and
above her to being all over her. He had the sheer gall to yank
her bodily off her feet and across his saddle. The crowd
cheered at the spectacle. They loved watching her cowed.

Ava felt the blood rush to her head. She could hear her
pulse thudding in her ears. Goddamn it. They hadn't even
started the damn race, and she'd lost control.

"I am not a piece of meat!" she yelled, writhing on the
saddle until her elbow found Kennedy Voss's tender parts.
He squawked in pain, and the crowd started laughing. At
him. She much preferred that to them cheering her humiliation. That was until it occurred to her that there would be
a price for humiliating Kennedy Voss. In public.

Not that he'd cared about publicly humiliating *her*. He
wasn't afraid of *her*, was he? The thought had her elbowing
him again. He swore and clamped a hand on the back of her
neck. Goddamn, he was strong. Ava had a sudden fear he
would choke her right here, in front of the whole street.

But then there was a blast of gunfire, and his hand flew off her.

"Damnation!" Voss yelled. He shoved Ava off his saddle, and she went sprawling onto the hard-packed dirt of the street. It took her a minute to regain her wits. The world was a mess of dust and hooves, and her ears were ringing from the gunfire.

Coughing from the dust, she managed to get to her feet in time to register that Lord Whatsit had apparently shot Kennedy Voss's hat plum off his head.

"You, sir, are a *rascal*," Lord Whatsit bellowed, still aiming his weapon at Voss. "One does not lay hands on a lady."

He was far stupider than she'd given him credit for. Ava speedily assessed the situation. They were blocked in by a solid circle of heavily armed men, trapped in the center of it with Kennedy Voss—who had lost all trace of the innocent farm boy and now just looked like a hot-blooded killer. Dear God, that was the face his victims must have seen right before he silenced them forever.

"Good thing she ain't no lady, then," Voss snarled. As he and Lord Whatsit continued to stare each other down, Ava unpinned her fob watch from the pocket of her vest. This was probably even stupider than Lord Whatsit's heroics, but she had to do *something*. Lord Whatsit was about to get himself shot through. She took a deep breath, and with absurd daintiness, she stuck the pin into Kennedy Voss's horse's ass.

The horse screamed and reared, and Voss went ass over teakettle into the dirt at her boots. He rolled several times and leapt straight to his feet. Shame. She'd half-hoped he might have broken an ankle and would have to sit out the Hunt.

Now the crowd was laughing in earnest, and Voss was the color of a ripe beet.

Ava took a step back. He wasn't to know she'd stuck his

horse . . . but she had a feeling he was just rodent smart enough to guess.

"Enough!" A pistol fired from the balcony of the Palladium. LeFoy recaptured the crowd's attention. He was looking amused but only just. There was an edge of impatience in his voice. "Are you forgetting why we're here? No more delays! This is a Hunt, not a circus!"

He was more than a little undercut by his moppets, who were climbing all over the railings, looking for all the world like they *did* belong in a circus.

"No! We're not starting until Miss Archer has received an apology from this ape!" Lord Whatsit shouted. He had an authoritarian air, like he thought he was the president himself. That wasn't going to serve him well in these parts.

Luckily, he backed it up by being a crack shot, she thought dryly, remembering how Voss's hat had gone flying into the dirt. But then again, maybe he'd been aiming for Voss's head and missed. In which case, his days were certainly numbered. But he had gumption; Ava had to give him that. He hadn't lowered his rifle; it was aimed straight at Voss's head. And he was still issuing orders.

"And then I insist she be allowed to collect her animal!"

"Shut up, you flouncy Yankee!" someone shouted. And then abruptly Lord Whatsit found himself at the wrong end of two dozen drawn pistols. The crowd was sick of the circus apparently.

"Yankee!" Lord Whatsit was outraged. "I'm an *Englishman*!"

Ava stepped in before he could get himself shot through. "Thank you, Your Majesty!" she interjected loudly, stepping between him and at least half the drawn weapons. "I appreciate your chivalry. But we should let these, uh, *gentlemen*"—here she stole a glance at Kennedy Voss, who was giving her his rattlesnake stare—"get on with their Hunt."

"Not until you have your horse!"

"She's got horses already," Becky snapped, completely out of patience. She brandished the reins of the two pack-horses. "And they're already packed with her gear. I did it myself."

"Problem solved!" LeFoy called from his balcony. Ava saw Becky flinch at the sound of his cheery voice. "There you are, Miss Archer—you're well mounted after all!"

There were snickers at that. Filthy bastards. Ava kept her head high and refused to look at Kennedy Voss—she had no doubt that he'd be smirking.

"Saddle up, gentlemen!" LeFoy called. He was escalating into full-blown-showman mode again. "Day is breaking!"

As if on cue, the sun cracked the clouds, sending shafts of brassy light over the street. Now Ava had a clearer view of the crowd and, Jesus wept, there were a lot of people. All of them armed to the teeth.

The residents of San Francisco had turned out to watch the show. The porches and balconies and sidewalks were crammed with spectators, and even more people clustered at the junctions. *Wonderful,* Ava thought as she took the reins of the fleabags from Becky, *more witnesses to Kennedy Voss's humiliation.* He was going to kill her for sure.

Oh God, here he came again.

He'd remounted his monstrously tall horse and was towering over her. He leaned on the pommel of his saddle and fixed her with his flat stare. "Lucky for you, I'm not one to hold a grudge," he told her.

"Lucky for you, I'm not either." Her mouth ran away with her. She could have kicked herself as she saw him blink in surprise. She kept losing her poker face lately—it made her nervy. She'd get herself killed if she didn't get it back in place permanently. She had the holy horrors that she was losing her edge. But maybe it was just exhaustion. She'd been on the trail for a very long time, and she wasn't as young as she'd once been.

"You know what, Miss Archer?" Kennedy Voss drawled, leaning in even closer. "I like you."

Oh dear.

"So, I'll still let you ride with me."

"Really, there's no need."

"I insist." He sat back and gave her a smile that could only be described as terrifying. "Once you've saddled up, come and join me up front."

"Don't feel you have to wait," she said. "I wouldn't want to slow you down."

"Oh, you won't." He tipped his hat at her and then shoved his way through the crowd. Not that he had to shove. The people parted for him. Because he was Kennedy Voss and he turned grown men into sniveling children.

"Hey, Horse," she sighed, resigning herself to her fate and confronting the speckled horse. It lowered its head.

It looked tired. Standing still.

"Her name is Freckles," Becky told her stiffly.

Ava felt again the loss of her poker face.

"And *you're welcome*," Becky continued. "You're welcome for the horses, *and* for the food and water I packed, *and* for saddling the animals, *and* for hauling your saddlebags down and cinching them on. *You're most welcome.*"

Ava pursed her lips. She hadn't asked Becky to do *any* of those things. The girl had done them all off her own back. Not only that, but *she* was the one foisting herself on Ava, not the other way around.

But Ava heard the hurt in the girl's voice. And she *was* benefiting from all of Becky's labor—even if the horses left something to be desired. And she could see how leaving LeFoy was stinging Becky. Mostly because he didn't seem to care in the least.

Well, she was better off without him. Even though it might take her a while to feel the truth of it.

Becky had her back to her. Ava thought she heard her sniff. She put a hand on Becky's shoulder and felt her flinch. "Thank you," Ava said softly. There was no reply. "I mean it, Becky. Thank you very much. I'm sorry I was so ungracious."

"It's fine," Becky sighed gustily. "I reckon I'd be ungracious too if I were in your boots. Stuck with me like this."

"I'm not *stuck* with you," Ava protested. "I can get rid of you whenever I want. All I'd have to do is ride off." *Although perhaps not on this horse,* she thought as she put her boot in the stirrup. Poor Freckles didn't look fast enough to outride Becky, even if the girl was on foot.

"Thanks," Becky said sourly.

"You're most welcome." Ava gave her a sunny smile. Becky remained stone-faced. Jesus wept, this was going to be a long journey. "That was a joke."

"Was it?"

Ava settled into the saddle. She could have sworn the horse's legs shook beneath her. She hoped they weren't going to give out. They hadn't even left yet. "Come on, Miss Sullivan," Ava cajoled, "once you're in the saddle, things won't be so grim. Well, they will. But you'll at least be off your feet. You look like a girl with sore feet."

"Not anymore. My feet got used to hard work years ago. It's other bits of me that are sore." She shot LeFoy a hangdog look.

Ava had a hard time not losing her temper. God save her from lovelorn women. She'd grown up in a house with one, and she had no patience with it. How did women find it so *surprising* when men scorned them? It was what men *did*. The history of the world was full of the proof of it. The shock would be if they *didn't* behave like liars and cheats. Abandonment was the only logical end to a relationship, and that was all there was to it.

"Up you hop, or I really will ride off and leave you," Ava said sternly. "And that would be a shame. You've the makings of a good book."

"I do?" Becky brightened at that.

"Miss Archer!" It was Lord Whatsit again.

"Oh, Your Majesty! I was wondering where you'd got to."

"You may address me as 'sir,' not 'Your Majesty.'"

"I beg your pardon?"

"The Queen is addressed as 'Your Majesty,' and I am many things, but I'm no Queen. A simple 'sir' will suffice for me."

Ava looked at him askance, unsure if he was joking or not. He didn't seem to be.

"But in fact, when one does meet the Queen, one addresses her as 'ma'am,' as a rule."

"Does one?" Ava paused and then couldn't quite resist needling him. "I mean, does one, *sir*?"

"That's it!" He looked pleased as punch.

"Have you *met* the Queen?" Becky asked. She seemed utterly captivated.

Ava took the opportunity to leave them to it, urging poor Freckles to drag her feet through the crowd. Not quite to the front—she wasn't delusional enough to think Freckles could keep up with the pack once the firing pistol sounded. Best to be off to the side somewhere where they wouldn't get trampled. Vaguely she could hear Lord Whatsit jabbering on about the Queen of England, although what use or relevance that had to the current moment was beyond her.

"Good luck, Miss Archer! I put a bet on you!" a woman called from a window above.

Ava gave her a wave.

"Give them hell!"

Yes. Hell.

Ava felt her pulse quicken as the pack moved forward to clump behind the wonky starting line. The air crackled with anticipation as the reddish gold rising sun cut long shadows across the street. Ahead of her, Ava could see English George and Irish George, their mean rat faces frozen in intense focus. The buoyant cheer had evaporated, and in its place, expectation seethed. The gates of hell were about to open, and the worst of its dominion were going to be loosed on the west.

Deathrider had better be ready for this, she thought, wrapping the reins tightly around her fist, *because hell is headed his way.*

Consummate showman that he was, LeFoy didn't cheapen the moment with words. Instead, he waited until the sun broke the roofline opposite, hitting him full in the face with its bloody light. He was chased with gold as he thrust his arm toward the sky.

Boom. The sound of the starting pistol was followed by the seismic force of a hundred horses surging forward. Ava felt like she'd been caught in a flood. There was no hope of doing more than holding on for dear life as the stampede stormed down Main Street.

The Hunt was on.

❖ 6 ❖

THEY FOUND THE bodies close to the border of Mexico. Deathrider felt a heaviness settle on him as he took in the devastation. The bodies belonged to a couple of travelers who had made the mistake of camping in the heart of the Apache plunder trails. As soon as Deathrider and Micah had seen the oily black smear of smoke on the horizon, Deathrider had known exactly what they were looking at. What else would it have been out here? Micah swore when Deathrider kicked his horse in the direction of the carnage.

"Where are you going?" Micah squawked.

"It's what we've been looking for!" Deathrider called back over his shoulder. "We need it to look like Apaches killed us."

"But they might still be there!"

"Probably not."

"*Probably* not? Every time I think you can't get crazier, you do," Micah moaned. But he followed, as Deathrider had known he would. They'd been friends for too long to let a few rampaging Apaches get between them.

Deathrider had been stalking the Apache raiding party for a couple of days, following them right into the heartland of their plunder trail, knowing eventually he'd find something he and Micah could turn to their advantage. They needed a way

out of the mess they were in, and the misfortune of these travelers might well save their lives. He pushed away the revulsion he felt at the idea. Sometimes you needed to do things
you didn't like in order to survive.

"We'll pass their victims off as us," he told Micah for
the fifteenth time. "We'll make sure some of my buckskin
and some of your gown are left unburned so the Hunters
have something to find. They'll put two and two together."

"What if they put two and two together and come up
with five?"

"We'll spell it out plain enough for a fool to do the
math."

"This gets worse by the minute. You're trusting our fate
to whether or not killers can do *math*." Micah was still all
rigged up in the whore's dress, but he was looking ragged
after a few days of traveling in the heat. The big pink bonnet, with its swatches of orange hair stitched to it, sat high
on his head. He looked ridiculous, and he was hot and
sweaty and sick of the whole business. He'd been bitching
Deathrider's ear off for miles.

Deathrider was starting to regret the whole thing himself. It had been an absurd act of charity, and he was suffering for it. As the days passed, he felt increasingly
oppressed. He couldn't stop thinking about the Hunt or
about *her*. "Brooding" was probably a better word for it
than "thinking." He'd been *brooding* about it. About *her*.
That damn woman.

A.A. Archer. He'd never once met her, but she'd made
his life an unholy misery. Here they were, in the searing
heat, darting about the desert, playacting a bunch of nonsense, and for what? Because some twit of a woman told a
bunch of lunatic stories about him. What kind of woman
went riding about the west making up lies about a man anyway? She was devoid of sense or reason. And it wasn't like
it was a brief loss of her senses, because she'd been doing it
for almost a decade now. Why in hell did she keep going?

One year she was in Missouri, the next in California. No matter how far he roamed, she always seemed to follow. Why hadn't she behaved like a regular woman and found herself a husband and settled down by now? Surely she was long overdue for it? Why was she so damn *persistent*? And what was so goddamn appealing about tearing around the west, making up utter nonsense about a complete stranger?

He didn't care what it took; he wanted her out of his life. Preferably somewhere on the other side of the country. With her pen locked away in a box.

But in order to do that, he had to give her something better than the lies she was making up. A story so packed with drama, she'd write it even if it meant that it was the last story she'd ever write about him. A story so good she wouldn't be able to resist it.

And this was the story he'd concocted for her: hunted by the most glorified killers in the west, Deathrider would find himself holed up in the Apacheria, fighting for his life down to the last bitter bullet. Or, rather, arrow. And then he'd find himself surrounded by Apaches, who would take the prize right out from under the noses of all those Hunters. It would be goodbye to the Plague of the West, and also goodbye to his redheaded whore, Seline (forget the fact that he and Seline had only ever had a platonic friendship—in this version they'd be lovers). A.A. Archer wasn't the only one who could make up a compelling fabrication.

With one deft move, Deathrider could free himself from infamy, get Seline clear of that swollen hog Hec Boehm and frustrate those bastards on his trail. Oh, A.A. Archer would have something to write about all right. He'd make sure of it. Best of all, the glory for killing the Plague of the West would go to the Apaches and not to any of those blood-hungry whites. Those Hunters could damn well go home empty-handed.

To leave a clear trail, Deathrider and Micah had kept themselves visible, and they headed toward the Apacheria, streaking through towns and villages and past trading posts, making sure that Seline's pink dress and orange hair were on full display. So long as Micah kept his head down, he was passable enough. He moved so fast that he was just a blur anyway. Deathrider, on the other hand, made sure that people saw his face wherever they went. He struck dramatic poses, giving the townsfolk and ranchers time to take note. He threw in a bloodcurdling war cry or two, shaking his bow in the air. It was a ridiculous display, but people had ideas about Indians, and sometimes it was useful to play into them. Just like the folks of Mariposa, they'd sure have something to tell the Hunters when they came riding through.

"It *is* a good plan," Deathrider reassured Micah now, as they reached the source of the oily smoke. "It will work." In truth, he wasn't sure if he was reassuring Micah or himself as he took in the charred remains of the two travelers who had fallen foul of the Apaches. None of their belongings remained, so it was impossible to tell who they'd been.

"A *good plan*? The hell it is!" Micah's horse became skittish at the smell of smoke, and he struggled to control it. "*Look* at those poor bastards." He was chalky with horror. "This is the work of the Chiricahua. It's got to be."

The Chiricahua were the deadliest Apaches west of the Rio Grande. While some Apache bands were farmers, the Chiricahua were nomadic: they traded and raided and struck fear into every traveler in the southwest.

But the Chiricahua couldn't kill him any deader than a single bullet from one of those Hunters, and Deathrider was long used to living under the shadow of death. It took a lot to worry him. And as far as he could see, this didn't look too dangerous. There wasn't anyone alive to pose a threat to them.

"Chiricahua or not, they've already gone." Deathrider swung down from his horse. As he did, Dog jogged into the remains of the camp, breathing hard. Deathrider opened his

canteen and pulled a tin bowl from his saddlebag while Dog
nosed through the charred timbers of what had once been a
wagon. By the time Dog had sated his curiosity, Deathrider
had filled the bowl, and Dog collapsed next to it, vigorously
lapping up the water. "See? Dog doesn't see any danger."

Micah snorted. "This place ain't nothing *but* danger.
And we've been hip deep in danger for so long that his nose
probably can't smell it anymore."

Deathrider gave Dog a brisk rub on the back of his neck.
"Good thing you don't bitch as much as Micah does, or I'd
never get a moment's peace."

Dog looked up and gave a low *woof.*

Deathrider tossed the canteen to Micah. "Come on, get
that dress off. We've got a scene to stage, and the quicker
we move, the quicker we can be out of here."

"It ain't right." After he'd taken a drink, Micah set to
complaining again, but he dismounted as he did it, and
yanked the bonnet from his head. His own jet-black hair
came tumbling down. Micah stared miserably at the victims
of the Chiricahua. "I bet their ghosts will haunt us."

"Their ghosts will be too busy haunting the Chiricahua."
Deathrider grabbed Micah by the shoulders and turned him.
He started undoing the fancy buttons down the back of the
dress. A couple had already popped off, and the rest were
straining. It was amazing they'd managed to cram him into
the dress in the first place; he was far bigger than Seline. As
the back of the dress gaped open, Deathrider turned his attention to unknotting the corset laces. The knot had just
about solidified, as the cord had swollen from absorbing Micah's sweat.

"You smell terrible," Deathrider said.

"You try wearing one of those contraptions for weeks in
the middle of summer. It's hotter than a clay oven." Micah
wasted no time stripping down to his trousers. "I ain't never
doing anything like that for you again. Not even if they
have you cornered."

"They *did* have me cornered." Deathrider held the pink dress up. It was damp from Micah's body and stained from the dust they'd kicked up. He was glad Seline couldn't see it. It was her favorite dress.

Deathrider ripped the gown down the front. *Sorry, Seline.*

"They *do*, you mean," Micah corrected cheerfully. "They *do* have you cornered. Last I looked, the Hunt was still on." He watched as Deathrider considered the scraps of pink dress in his hands and the smoldering remains of the fire. He scowled at Deathrider. "You're a ghoul. I don't want any part of this."

"You'll thank me when we're free."

"*I'm* already free. In fact, I could shoot you myself and collect the money."

"Go ahead. Put me out of my misery."

Micah snorted. "Yeah, right. And then I ride into Frisco to collect, and they shoot me for a lying Indian. I know how that story goes."

Deathrider shucked off his buckskins and tossed them to Micah. "Make it look good," he told his friend, as he pulled his "white" clothes out of his saddlebags.

"My pleasure." Micah took his hunting knife and hacked at the buckskins. "Those Chiricahua have taken an extreme dislike to you, my friend. They're about to leave no bit of you unstabbed." Micah made a show of dismembering Deathrider's clothes.

"You're enjoying that too much."

"I have a lot of pent-up anger toward you."

Deathrider hadn't worn his white clothes in a good long while. The shirt was so crumpled, he doubted it could ever be ironed straight again, and the trousers were still stained from the last time he'd worn them. It didn't matter. He'd only wear them as far as the plains, and then he'd go home and shuck them off. Two Bears had been wanting him to stay with the camp, to stop his wandering ways and make a life for himself with his father's people. Maybe this time, he would. Even if it meant he'd have to put up with his father's endless matchmaking.

Once the gown and the buckskins looked convincingly assaulted, and he and Micah were dressed like whites, they stood over the smoldering fire. Deathrider was struck with soul-deep melancholy as he regarded the dying embers. He felt the phantom presence of the people who had fallen prey to the raiders. Whoever they might have been . . . People just like his mother, perhaps. Hopeful. Heading for a new life. Running headlong into heartbreak.

Was he really going to add to the tragedy by hijacking the site of their deaths for his plan?

Damn it. He didn't know these people or the quality of their characters. And their suffering was done, while his went on.

They would never know, and it would save his life. . . .

But . . . The vulgar pink satin of Seline's dress shone in the harsh sun.

He met Micah's gaze.

Damn it. It wasn't right, and they both felt it.

"Hell," Deathrider growled. "I can't do it." These people had suffered enough; they didn't need some stranger violating the place of their deaths. "We'll have to think of something else."

"Good," Micah said. "I wouldn't have liked you anymore if you'd done it."

No. He wouldn't have liked himself. He balled the remains of the gown in his fists. Goddamn it. This whole business was turning him into someone he barely recognized. He felt soiled. How in the hell had he ended up here?

"We need to give them a decent burial."

Micah nodded in agreement.

"You think we have time?" Deathrider squinted at the horizon. "You think we still have good distance on them?"

"Enough to do what needs to be done. Then I vote we go to Mexico."

"We can't," Deathrider sighed, dropping the gown and heading back to his saddlebags. "We don't want to put Tom and Seline in danger. They're headed to Mexico. We'll just have to head up into Apache lands. We can skirt the Coyotero and Mimbreño and hope Voss and his friends get picked off by raiders."

Micah didn't look happy at that, but for once he didn't start up with his bitching. When Deathrider began digging a grave, he set to finding rocks to lay a cairn on top. They worked in silence, dousing the fire and watching somberly as the steam billowed in blue-gray clouds.

"If they're nearby, the sight of that's going to bring them," Micah observed grimly.

Without doubt. They'd have to move faster.

"You should say a few words," Micah suggested, once they'd laid the unfortunate travelers to rest.

"Me? Why not you?"

"I don't know who they are."

Deathrider gave him a sour look.

"We're here because of you," Micah reminded him.

Deathrider sighed. He regarded the graves, piled with rocks and marked by boards from the charred wagon. The sun was slanting west, sending the shadows jutting accusingly at the smoking remains of the fire. He didn't know what to say. Unconsciously, he lapsed into his father's tongue, even though he was hundreds of miles from Arapaho lands. "We don't know who you are, strangers. Whoever you are, we hope you followed the rising smoke to the afterlife and are not locked in suffering to this place."

"Tell them not to haunt us," Micah said. He couldn't understand a word of Deathrider's eulogy; he wasn't Arapaho or from any of the Algonquin-speaking tribes.

"I'm not telling them what to do," Deathrider protested,

switching back to English. "After everything they've been through, they've got the right to do whatever they want."

"At least tell them to haunt the Chiricahua, not us."

"You tell them. They wouldn't understand me anyway. My people live a long way from here; I doubt these people speak Algonquin."

"Dead people speak all languages," Micah said sagely.

"So, you tell them." Deathrider took his leave of the graveside and left Micah to say whatever the hell he wanted. He threw the slashed gown and buckskins over the wagon remains. He was sore that he'd ruined his clothes for nothing.

Dog gave a sharp bark.

"Hell. Micah, say goodbye to those dead people. We've got company!"

Not just company. A *lot* of company. A lot of *armed* company.

❧ 7 ❧

AVA DIDN'T KNOW what was worse: Kennedy Voss's silence or Lord Whatsit's chatter. Both made her head ache. Voss's silence had a menace to it. He had a way of looking at a girl that was downright frightful. He'd not said a word to her since they'd ridden out of San Francisco. Her nags couldn't keep up with the pack, and they'd fallen rapidly behind. The dust cloud around the Hunters ballooned as they tore away over the horizon. Soon all that was visible was a ruddy smudge against the bleached sky.

As they dropped farther and farther behind, Ava had assumed they'd fall behind Voss too—but no such luck. He was fixed on riding with Ava, and he'd pulled in beside her and reined his horses in to match her pace, never once saying a word. He didn't hurry her or harry her; he was just there. Watching her.

Some of the other men got nervy when they saw Voss dropping back. A couple followed suit, shooting him anxious looks. They thought he knew something they didn't. And when they saw the way Voss watched *her*, they thought *she* knew something they didn't.

Like where Deathrider was.

If only. She had no more information that they did, and Ava was crawling out of her skin at the thought of the pack galloping into Mariposa so far ahead of them. What if they caught him and she wasn't there? What if they *killed* him?

She jammed her heels into poor old Freckles, but the horse was already giving it all she could.

Lord Whatsit was endlessly appalled at the pace. His mighty Arab was champing at the bit to join the rush, and he was too. Becky was caught in the middle, seesawing between fear of missing out on the Hunt and being relieved that they weren't in the thick of it with the hot-eyed killers.

"It'll all be over by the time we get there," Becky fretted. Ava couldn't tell if she was happy about that or not.

Lord Whatsit wasn't happy. "I don't see the point of this goose chase unless we actually chase the goose!"

"You can let me ride one of your horses if you want me to go faster," she said sharply.

Of course he didn't. He had no intention of sharing his magnificent animals; he just wanted to complain. And complain. And complain.

If he said one more thing about goose chasing she was going to scream.

"Maybe this will give the goose a chance to thin the field," she suggested waspishly. "This *is* the Plague of the West we're talking about. By the time we reach Mariposa, he'll probably have shot half a dozen of them. And then you'll be glad you weren't caught in the carnage."

"He couldn't shoot *me*," Lord Whatsit said disdainfully.

"No? Lords can't be shot?" She wondered if she should give it a try.

"I'd have him before he could draw his weapon." The man's arrogance was astonishing.

"You would, would you?"

"I'm a crack shot; he wouldn't stand a chance."

Kennedy Voss stayed silent, but he was clearly taking it all in. Ava thought Lord Whatsit's chances of survival were looking slimmer by the minute. Voss was probably having the same thoughts she was.

"But I can't shoot the goose from back *here*," his lordship said in disgust.

"Feel free to go on ahead, Your Majesty," she said stiffly. *Or loan me one of your damn horses.* That seemed like it would be a perfect solution. If he'd be willing to share, they could all go at a fair clip. But no, he kept his prime horseflesh to himself and made her ride the nag. Ava was beginning to suspect poor Freckles might be a depressive animal. Or a sick one. She had droopy ears, and she hung her head as she walked. Now and then she let out an existential whicker.

Not that Ava could blame her. She felt more than a little droopy too. And don't even get her started on existential despair. She was feeling a fair whack of it herself.

There was something about the desert: the endless chaparral and the faded sky, the whirls of dust kicked up by the devil winds, the bleached skeletons of dead trees; it all contributed to an overwhelming sense of being at the edge of the world. The sun had a mean bite, and the flying sand got in your eyes.

It really made you question the point of it all.

She was getting too old for this, that was all. She'd loved it once . . . all of it: the hours in the saddle, the outdoor life, the camping, facing the unknown, the ride between exhilaration and terror. She had thrilled at the chase and at the sheer wildness of the frontier. She'd loved every inch of it: the seemingly endless prairie, with its rippling grasses and wild storms, its deep and relentless snows in winter and its jewel brightness in spring. She'd loved the soaring mountains with their stark peaks and thick woods; she'd loved the raw mining towns and bleached deserts. Everything west of Missouri was brighter and louder and rougher than in the east—an unbridled pleasure.

Or it used to be.

Nowadays the color seemed to have leached out of things, like the sun had gone behind the clouds. The trail made her tired, the camping hurt her back, building a campfire made her surly and the sight of the vast empty land made her . . . *afraid*. She couldn't say why.

Maybe it was simply ennui. Or saddle weariness.

If you're honest, you have enough in your bank account already. You could stop. Just climb down off the horse and stop.

It was true. If she wanted to, she could probably quit today. It would always be good to have just a little bit more money—but did you ever feel like you had enough? Her bank accounts were healthy enough. . . . She could go back east and live off the fruits of her labor; she didn't have to be dragging along on this nag, feeling her skin crawl from a rapist's gaze and listening to some mad Englishman brag about his capacity for killing people. She could leave them all to it and get on with her life.

But the thought didn't fill her with the sense of pleasure she'd thought it would. If anything, it only increased her weariness.

What would she *do* back east?

Enjoy herself.

Yes. But doing *what*? Needlepoint?

"I reckon we should camp when we find water. There's a creek about an hour ahead." The sound of Kennedy Voss's voice made her jump. It was the first thing he'd said since they'd left San Francisco. "There ain't a lot of water out this way. We'd be fools to pass it by."

Camp. With Kennedy Voss. Ava let that sink in.

It sank right to the pit of her stomach.

"It's too early to camp!" Lord Whatsit kicked up when he heard Voss's suggestion. "Absolutely not! There are hours of good riding time ahead! Egad, you people are determined to fail! Well, we Whents are no also-rans! We *win*."

"So, get riding," Voss sneered. He didn't have much use for a lord either, apparently.

"We will!" Becky joined in now. "Won't we, Miss Archer?"

She was pulling faces at Ava, clearly thinking she was being subtle. It was painfully obvious she wanted to get Ava away from Voss. Ava bet she was a terrible poker player.

"You ain't catching up to those boys. They'll be in Mariposa before you've so much as scratched yourselves." Kennedy Voss was unperturbed. He just rode along, his sweet farm boy face as deceptively mellow as ever. "But by all means, y'all go chasing shadows all you want. I'll take good care of Miss Archer for you."

"I'm not leaving the lady at your mercy." Lord Whatsit looked set to get all outraged again. It was a flat-out waste of energy.

"I'm not at anyone's mercy," Ava corrected him. She was feeling prickly from the heat and from the tension. "And no one takes care of me. I take care of myself." At that point, she would have liked to kick her horse into a trot to pull ahead of them, but no matter how hard she dug her heels into Freckles, there was no trotting. Which quite ruined the effect of her haughtiness. She kept her nose in the air anyway. Sometimes a girl had to act like she had dignity, even when it was falling from her in flakes, like old paint.

BY THE TIME they got to Mariposa it was all over. There were no Deathrider, no other Hunters, no mayhem. There was just a community left more than a touch high-strung by events. Events that Ava had clearly missed by a mile.

Damn it.

The ride to Mariposa had been agonizingly slow, and camping with Kennedy Voss had been an exercise in sleep deprivation. Of course she couldn't sleep with that maniac outside the tent. She and Becky had spent every night with their weapons loaded and cocked, jumping every time a lick of wind flapped at the canvas of their tent. Voss hadn't done anything more inappropriate than stare at her over the campfire with his flat snake stare, but Ava felt she was simply waiting for the ax to fall. . . . He might be holding back now, but he wouldn't forever. That wasn't how he worked. And she shuddered to think what fantasies and plans were passing through the mind behind that flat gaze.

And it wasn't just him. The other couple of Hunters who'd stuck to them like grime were almost as bad. Rowley and Hicks were a half-witted pair of trail hounds who fancied themselves gunslingers, but who were actually just failed miners–cum–two-bit thieves. They'd brought a jug of moonshine along and spent most days falling-down drunk. How they kept in the saddle was a mystery. Both were in awe of Voss and fell over themselves trying to impress him, although no one doubted their plan was to shoot Voss as soon as there was competition over capturing the Plague of the West. By falling in with them, Rowley and Hicks had bet on Ava and Voss finding Deathrider first; they thought that Ava had some insider knowledge and that while the Hunters were tearing off after a shadow, they'd follow her right to the prey. They thought they were being crafty.

They weren't. It was a plan hatched by stone-cold idiots. Firstly, because neither Ava nor Voss had any information on Deathrider; secondly, because the large pack of Hunters was liable to find Deathrider long before they did; and thirdly, because there was no way a couple of drunken hustlers like those two could shoot a man like Kennedy Voss. Voss would have them eviscerated before they'd so much as twitched a finger toward their weapons. In no small part because they were *blind drunk*.

For his part, Voss ignored them. They were flies he couldn't be bothered swatting. Yet.

By the time they reached Mariposa, Ava was sandy eyed with exhaustion. She knew if she kept on this way, she was headed for disaster. She'd fall off her horse and break her neck, or shoot herself in the night when she nodded off with her gun in hand, or get so addled that Voss would easily overpower her. She figured that was his plan—to wear her down until she had no fight in her, to get her so tired she'd be utterly at his mercy. Although it was possible that he was also dumb enough to think she knew where Death-rider was. And why kill her before she'd led him to the Plague of the West? Or before she'd immortalized him in another book, this time for killing the only man she'd made more famous than him?

Mile by mile, her memory threw up stories of Kennedy Voss's crimes: the Pettifrew girls, for example, up there in the mountains, or when he had ripped through a whore-house in Bellevue. On a Sunday, no less, while the rest of the town was in church. Which was why no one had been there to rescue the whores—he'd had the place to himself. Ava had ridden into town after the fact, quite a long time after the fact, but she'd seen the bloodstains for herself—they'd still been stark even so many months later. No matter how hard the proprietor scrubbed the floorboards, he couldn't get the stains out. It wasn't a whorehouse anymore by that stage; no one fancied whoring there anymore, not after what had happened. Even if they could have found a whore to work there, she wouldn't have been able to coax a customer over the threshold. Some places have a history so burdensome, it eclipses their future. When Ava reached Bellevue, months after Voss had left, the building had been taken over by the local pastor, who'd planned to turn it into a school. They were in the process of painting over the stains when Ava had come to see it. She'd written about those stains in *Kennedy Voss and the Belles of Bellevue*. It sold well. People liked a bit of horror.

But it was the horror that was fraying her nerves now that she was riding along with the man who was the cause of it all.

Hell, traveling was hard enough without adding a mur-derous rapist into the mix. It was a relief to get to Mariposa and no longer be in desert country with him. It was a small measure of comfort, but comfort nevertheless.

Ava took in the dirt pit of Mariposa. As they rode in, people scattered like pigeons. Anxious faces peered out of windows, blinds were pulled and doors were locked. Ava noted the bullet holes in some of the shop signs down Main Street.

The place looked like the seventh level of hell, just like every other mining town she'd seen. Every tree for miles had been torn down, and the earth had been blasted and burrowed until all you could see was churned muck. Civilization was a thin veneer. The stumps of felled trees still jutted from the earth, even in the middle of the street, so you had to pick your way around them. The clapboard buildings rose from the mud like crooked toadstools; they were splattered with dirt, and their windows were opaque with dust. The fanciest by far were the whorehouses, which didn't surprise Ava in the least. Whores did a roaring trade in these towns. There were a hundred men for every woman, and the nature of the town meant that almost every woman was a soiled dove. Regular women didn't stop in these places; it wasn't safe or congenial.

Unless you were traveling with Kennedy Voss, Ava thought dryly. Then a mining town looked like a veritable *refuge*.

She made for the general store and hitched her horses to the post.

"We're not stopping!" Lord Whatsit looked ready to pitch a fit.

"All the best, then," Ava said, giving him a faux-cheery wave. She dug her notebook and pencil out of her bag and headed for the store. She didn't bother to see if anyone followed her. She didn't need to. Voss was close enough by that he might as well have been her shadow.

The store door was locked. The wax blinds had been pulled, covering the windows as well as the panes in the door.

"Guess they don't want us here," Voss said. He was so close, she could feel his breath on her neck. *Show no fear.*

Ava gave a lighthearted knock on the door. It wasn't easy trying to seem this cheerful when her blood was cold with fear. She had more of an urge to pound impatiently at the panes. Maybe smash one or two of them.

But she'd need to put the occupants at ease if she was going to get any information out of them, so lighthearted was the order of the day. Something had badly scared the citizens of Mariposa. Ava doubted the Hunters had been gentle as they'd come tearing into town, but she wondered if it was more than that. . . . She wondered if their fear had anything to do with the Plague of the West.

"Hello?" she called, injecting a chirpiness into her voice that she most certainly didn't feel. When there was no answer, she rapped with a little bit more force.

"You need something in there?" Voss asked curiously. He leaned against the doorframe, so close he was brushing her elbow. All he needed was a thread of straw between his teeth, and he'd look like a perfect hick.

"Yes, Mr. Voss, I do." She tucked her pencil behind her ear and prepared to talk her way in.

"Yeah? And what are you needing? A shovel? Some feed for that bag of bones you're riding."

She gave him a disdainful look. "No, Mr. Voss, what I need is much more vital. What I need is *information*."

"Information, eh?" He scratched his chin. "About that Plague of the West fella and whether those Hunters got him?"

She snorted. "They didn't get him. If they'd caught him, these people wouldn't be locked behind their doors."

Voss nodded in satisfaction. "So, you want to know which way they went?"

"I want to know the details, Mr. Voss. I want to know what *happened* here. In vivid *detail*."

For a moment the flatness left Kennedy Voss's gaze and he looked at her with something akin to admiration. "You like details? I like details too. I notice everything. It's why I'm good at what I do."

Ava kept her expression serene, even though he was making her toes curl. *Why I'm good at what I do.* He made murder sound like a job.

"Stand back," Voss said, pulling his gun. "I'll get the door open for you."

And with that, Ava lost every last hope of putting the citizens of Mariposa at their ease. All thought of talking to them faded, replaced with a simple desire to keep them *alive*. Because Kennedy Voss was about to show Mariposa that they hadn't seen anything yet.

❧ 8 ❧

THERE WAS NO point in running. They were surrounded. A great ring of men on horseback, rifles drawn, was advancing at a measured pace. The lazy tightening of their noose showed their power—these men were in no rush because they knew they'd already won.

Even from a distance, it was clear to Deathrider that this was something worse than Hunters or Apaches.

This was the United States Army.

"How in hell did they manage to get this close without us noticing?" Micah complained. He'd drawn his weapons.

Deathrider didn't know.

The *army*. The goddamn *army*.

"Since when do we get outmaneuvered by white men?" Micah asked, sounding more than a little shocked.

"Since today."

Dog growled and stood protectively in front of Deathrider. Deathrider gave him a scratch. "Relax," he told Micah. "Try to look confident."

"Are you mad?" Micah couldn't seem to tear his gaze away from the approaching blue-clad army. "What am I saying? Or course you are. You're insane. Loco. Out. Of. Your. Mind."

"Put your hands in the air, Micah. Keep them where

they can see them." Deathrider's mind was racing. How in hell did they get out of this one?

"You're *giving up*?"

"No. I'm just doing this the smart way."

"Why start now?" Micah muttered, but he lifted his hands in the air and turned a slow circle to show the army he was no threat.

"You too, Dog." Deathrider pulled on his ears. "Drop. Play nice."

Keeping a wary eye on both Deathrider and the approaching men, Dog dropped on his belly in the dirt. He put his chin down and his ears lay flat to his head. He let out a reproving whine.

Deathrider lifted his own hands in the air and cursed the fact that he and Micah still had their hair down. If they'd had hats on already, they might have passed for white. At a distance anyway. But it was too late now. Hair down, they would never pass. But at least they spoke English and could play the part of being "civilized." That usually kept men like these happy. Happy enough to ask questions first and shoot later anyway.

"Howdy," he called once the men had drawn to a halt. They stopped a good five yards out, their noose drawn tight. Deathrider turned full circle, searching for the leader. "We speak English," he said amiably. He kept his voice calm as his eyes skipped over the soldiers. They were a rag-tag bunch who had clearly been on patrol a good long while. Their blue jackets were crusted with dust, and their faces were sunburned above their whiskers.

"Drop your weapons!" Ah, there was the leader. He was a square brick of a man, with muttonchop whiskers and a hell of a lot of gleaming buttons. The fabric of his coat was as dusty as the other men's, but he'd clearly taken the time to keep his buttons polished. His boots too. His whiskers were trimmed, and his tack was freshly oiled. This was a man who kept to the rules, Deathrider intuited. Which might play in their favor.

"Have we broken a law?" Micah called. He was shifting nervously from foot to foot, his hands turning in the air. He looked like he was warming up to dance.

"Sir."

"What?" Micah looked confused, and Deathrider's feeling of dread intensified.

"'Have we broken a law, *sir*?' I don't know what kind of manners you use amongst your own people, but *we* address people respectfully. Especially when speaking to a man of my rank." The man turned his body to show his decorations so they could appreciate his rank.

"Have we broken a law, *sir*?" Micah parroted. Deathrider was glad to see he refrained from rolling his eyes. Just.

"Just by *being here*, you broke the law, son," he said. His voice was like a pistol crack. "It's illegal for Apaches to cross the border." His sharp gaze drifted to the remains of the fire and to the wagon. "But it looks like you've broken more than just one law here today."

"We're not over the border," Deathrider pointed out.

"And that wagon wasn't us," Micah said hastily. "That was the Chiricahua. We think. We just stopped to bury the poor bastards." He pointed at the cairn.

"That's a clear lie, sir. It ain't normal for them to bury their kill, Captain," one of the soldiers said authoritatively. "They usually leave them for the vultures."

The captain nodded at the man who'd spoken. "That seems to fit with what we've seen in these parts."

"I can examine the scene, if you wish?"

"By all means, Walker. That's why we brought you."

Deathrider caught Micah's eye. What was to examine?

The man called Walker dismounted, while the rest of the soldiers kept their rifles trained on Deathrider and Micah.

"You two throw your weapons down," the captain ordered. "There's nothing to be gained by fighting—you're outnumbered ten to one."

Still holding Micah's gaze, Deathrider nodded. "We might as well do it."

Micah scowled at him. Deathrider imagined he'd be bitching about this for weeks.

As they carefully unholstered their weapons and laid them in the dirt, Deathrider watched Walker examine the graves and then the burned-out wagon, where the remains of Seline's pink dress caught the breeze and fluttered like a pennant.

"What do you see, Walker?" the captain rumbled.

"A lady has been murdered here," Walker said grimly. "A gentlewoman by the look of this gown. The material is of fine quality."

"They've massacred a white woman!" There was outrage among the men, and the sound of rifles bracing.

"Don't shoot!" the captain said sternly. "Not until Walker has discerned the cause of events."

This man Walker must have been their tracker. Of sorts.

"Yes, there was definitely a woman murdered here," Walker said solemnly, finding Seline's hacked-up pink bonnet. A chunk of orange hair was tangled in the silk roses. With great sadness, Walker untangled the hair and examined it. "Sir," he called to the captain, his voice grave, "it looks like they scalped her!"

There was a rolling sound of disgust from the soldiers. Micah gave Deathrider a filthy look.

Deathrider watched in disbelief as Walker took the hank of hair over to the captain. The man took it and, following Walker's lead, examined it closely. What they were hoping to find was beyond Deathrider. It was just a hank of hair. Glaringly orange from the henna dyes Seline used, but unremarkable otherwise. There was no sign of scalping in that hank of hair. If it was proof of anything, it was proof of a haircut.

The captain looked up from the hank of orange hair and addressed his men. "It is true. The lady was most definitely scalped."

The rolling dismay became a low growl of rage.

White people. They beggared belief. The irony of the situation hit Deathrider hard. He'd been planning to stage this scene so everyone would think Seline had been attacked, scalped and killed by Apaches. And that was exactly what was happening here—only he hadn't staged it yet. And they thought *he* was the Apache who'd done it. When he wasn't even a damn Apache! He didn't look anything like an Apache: not like a Chiricahua, not like a Jicarilla, not like a Mescalero. He looked as much like an Apache as he looked like a Spaniard.

"They're going to lynch us," Micah hissed.

It was fifty-fifty, in Deathrider's opinion. It would all depend on this captain. And whether his men respected, or feared, him enough to follow his orders. Deathrider was hoping a man who shined his buttons even in the wilderness, and one who put heavy stock in the rank on his uniform, might be too "civilized" to lynch them. He might be more inclined to drag them to a jail somewhere for a trial. Which would give Deathrider and Micah time to get away.

But then again, when had being "civilized" ever stopped whites from shooting Indians?

"You want to run now or see how this pans out?" he asked Micah quietly.

"You're not to confer with your compatriot!" the captain bellowed. "You are in the custody of the United States Army, and the United States Army is to be obeyed!"

Deathrider met the captain's gaze. He kept his expression amiable, even though dread was spreading through him like a winter frost. "We understand." The captain seemed a man who liked obedience, so Deathrider would give him obedience. For now. "We speak English. We can answer any questions you have."

"In good time! You will have opportunity to answer the charges once they've been brought."

Deathrider took a moment to digest that. Charges. *Once they've been brought.* Which meant they weren't going to be shot on the spot . . . That was heartening, wasn't it?

The captain turned impatiently to his man. "Walker! What is your official report of the crime? We need to level the appropriate charges against these villains."

"Yes, sir. It's very clear. Cut-and-dried. A party of white travelers was set upon by Indians and killed, presumably by these two here, as we caught them in the act red-handed. The travelers' wagon has been looted, their animals stolen, and it looks as though their bodies were burned."

This Walker man stated the obvious as though it was a great pronouncement. He looked proud of himself and his assessment, and the soldiers made a low noise of appreciation, while the captain nodded sagely. Deathrider could see Micah's eyes growing wide. He hoped his friend could hold his tongue. Deathrider thought he could get them out of this—but only if Micah kept his composure. If Micah started mouthing off, he was liable to get shot before Deathrider could save him.

"You have the wrong men," Deathrider interjected, drawing the attention to himself. He kept his voice low and calm so as not to startle the soldiers. Whites could be like buffalo—prone to startling. And once they startled all hell tended to break loose. "Look around: we don't have their horses or stock; we don't have *any* of their belongings. We're not Apache. We're just traveling through. We found them and stopped to give them burial." He kept his hands in the air and looked from face to face. No one was listening to him.

"Why would they bury them *after* they burned them?" the captain asked with a frown, his attention still completely on Walker. "That seems an unlikely thing for savages to do."

"That's a very good question." Walker had been squatting by the blackened remains of the fire. Now he rose, his forehead knotted with concentration as he moved back to the cairn. "Perhaps these are old graves . . ." He scratched his chin. "But if they didn't bury them, where are the bodies now?"

"Do something," Micah hissed at Deathrider. "These idiots are talking themselves into a lynching."

"I'm trying. I'm just trying to do it in a way that doesn't end up with us used for shooting practice. Haven't you ever heard of diplomacy?"

"The bodies of the victims were thrown on the fire," the captain declared with bluff authority. "They've clearly burned the poor beggars."

Walker shook his head. "There's no trace of their remains in the ashes." He looked disappointed. Deathrider got the impression he would have enjoyed finding an especially gory crime scene. And pinning it on him and Micah.

"They probably ate them!" one of the soldiers shouted. His finger had tightened on the trigger of his rifle.

"Now, hang on a minute!" Micah protested. He shot Deathrider a warning look. "I don't like where this is heading . . ."

Neither did Deathrider. This wasn't going well at all. "We didn't eat them," Deathrider said, exasperated. "We didn't kill them. We didn't attack them. We *found* them." Deathrider was still managing to sound reasonable. Just. But he inched toward where his weapons lay in the dirt. His gut told him words weren't going to work, but he had to try. "And after we found them, we gave them a decent burial."

"Cannibalism," Walker mused, staring thoughtfully into the middle distance. "Yes, perhaps."

"No!" Deathrider and Micah spoke simultaneously. Damn it! These people were ghouls.

"But then we still have the problem of the graves . . . ," Walker said thoughtfully.

The captain swore. "Just once I'd like a simple situation. Every time we come upon one of these scenes, it's the same story: Indians run amok."

Deathrider had an idea why they always discovered bizarre scenarios, and it had nothing at all to do with Indians run amok.

Dog picked up on Deathrider's body language and rose from his crouch. He backed against Deathrider's leg, his hackles up. Deathrider put a calming hand on the back of his neck. The last thing he wanted was for his dog to get shot.

"This *is* a simple situation," Deathrider reassured the captain, still striving for calmness in the hopes he could salvage things. "We found them. We buried them. You came along."

But the soldiers weren't listening. They didn't so much as look at him when he spoke. Goddamn it. If people would just *listen* . . .

And use their common sense.

"These *must* be old graves," Walker pronounced. "As you say, savages don't usually bury their victims."

These blue-clad idiots actually enjoyed conjecturing about the possibilities. It was like a game. One they seemed to take very seriously.

Walker considered the cairns Deathrider and Micah had built not half an hour before. "They're a red herring. They just happen to be here . . . but they have nothing to do with the current events."

"Sir?" another soldier called out excitedly. He was a keen-faced boy wriggling in his saddle with barely suppressed glee.

"Not now, son." The captain flapped his hand at the boy. "Now isn't the time to go distracting Walker. He's getting to the heart of the matter."

A chaparral bush would have had a better chance of getting to the heart of the matter, in Deathrider's opinion. It looked like he and Micah would have to fight their way out of this mess. The odds weren't in their favor . . . but then they never were.

"But, sir!" the boy protested. "I think your answer might be right there." The boy jabbed his finger vigorously in the direction of Deathrider's shredded buckskins. "Look! One of *them* got killed in the melee too!"

"By God! He's right!" Walker found the buckskins and held them aloft. "There we have it! Mystery solved. A couple of their number were fatally wounded, and they buried them here. That explains the graves."

"Incredible," the captain rumbled. "Just incredible what you can tell from a few small clues."

Yes. It was incredible. Deathrider and the captain could agree on that.

This stupidity had gone too far. Daeathrider had lost patience with it. "*I* can tell you exactly what happened," he said irritably. "And it doesn't include Apaches burying their own."

"I thought you said to keep calm," Micah said under his breath. He sounded plenty amused, but he also took a sensible step back as he spoke. You didn't want to get too close to Deathrider when he'd decided enough was enough.

"We know exactly what happened, you savage." The captain fixed Deathrider with a baleful look. "You Apaches set upon these poor travelers. Clearly, they fought like lions, as evidenced by these graves. They managed to bring down two of your mighty warriors. But they were no match for your superior numbers, and you killed them. Man, woman and child."

Child? What child? There wasn't the slightest sign this party had had any children in their numbers. Deathrider took a deep breath. He was still prepared to try reason, although he didn't think he'd get far with it. Not with these idiots.

"Firstly," he said, striving for equilibrium, "we're not Apaches. I'm Arapaho, and he's a mix of Shoshone and Ute."

"With a bit of Pawnee thrown in," Micah added helpfully. "My grandmother was Pawnee."

"We're as foreign to this place as you are and just as liable to be set on by Apaches. Secondly, *what* superior numbers? There are *two* of us—"

Walker interrupted him. "*Now* there are two of you." He pointed at the graves. "Now that your friends are dead."

It was like arguing with the wind. "This is absurd."

"*I'll* be the judge of that," the captain told Deathrider sternly. "And believe me, I'm taking note of your lack of remorse."

"We found the remains of these people, and we stopped to give them a decent burial," Deathrider insisted mulishly. "That's *all*. There are no bodily remains of the travelers because we *buried* them."

"You're lucky we found you this year and not last," the captain said, unimpressed. "If we'd found you last year, you'd have been shot by now. But this year we have procedures: we'll be taking you to face formal charges."

The captain's men didn't look thrilled about that. Deathrider bet that it wasn't the norm. They'd just happened to be caught by a man who was a stickler for rules.

"Where are you taking us?" Micah asked, looking more appalled at the thought of being in custody than he was at the thought of being shot.

"The fort."

Fort? What fort?

"Are you really going to let this happen?" Micah demanded of Deathrider.

"No," he sighed. "I guess not." Why did life have to be so damn difficult all the time?

"Good." Micah had lost his sense of humor. "I'm ready when you are."

"Captain," Deathrider called as he made a snap decision about how to proceed, "I have a confession to make . . ."

From the corner of his eye, he saw Micah's head whip around.

"Oh no," Micah moaned.

Oh yes. If he was going to do this, he might as well save Seline in the process.

"You want to know who killed the woman who wore that dress?" he called, raising his voice.

The soldiers took the bait. He didn't miss the prurient gleam in their eyes.

Deathrider smiled.

"Oh no." Micah scrambled for cover.

It was time for the U.S. Army to meet the Plague of the West—and if he was smiling, they didn't stand a chance.

❧ 9 ❧

"**Y**OU'RE A LUNATIC!" At some point Ava's rage had out-paced her fear. She had no compunction about railing at Kennedy Voss as they charged along, following the trail the Hunters had left many hours before. A trail that, frankly, a half-wit could have followed, as it looked like it had been made by a herd of elephants.

The madman had *kidnapped* her. Right from her own damn bed. In the end, it was her exhaustion that had brought her down. When they'd decided to spend the night in Mariposa (because there was no way in hell they were catching the other Hunters before nightfall anyway), she'd succumbed to the pleasures of a feather bed. She and Lord Whatsit and Becky had found rooms in a quiet boarding-house, paying an exorbitant sum because the proprietor mistrusted strangers—particularly after Kennedy Voss had terrorized the town.

The sight of the brass bed had filled Ava with heady anticipation. An actual *bed*. She'd sat down on it just to feel the pillowy give of the mattress . . . and that was the last thing she remembered. She hadn't barricaded the door or cocked her weapon or even pulled the blind. It was a mistake worthy of a greenhorn. The mattress had proven so comfortable, she'd thought she'd stretch out, just to test the pillow too. Just for a minute. But she passed out stone-cold asleep the minute her head hit the pillow. There hadn't been anything she could do about it. Her body just couldn't stay awake for another moment; her eyes slid closed of their own accord. *I'll just rest them for a minute,* she'd thought. And that was the last thing she thought for a good long while.

When she finally woke up, she was miles from camp, jolting along in front of Kennedy Voss, slack in his arms, gathered close to him, like they were sweethearts and he was riding her home. Her head was pounding like a blacksmith's hammer, and she felt sick to her stomach. Dawn had broken; it had been the glare of the sun that had woken her. She came to slowly, feeling disoriented, nausea rolling though her in waves. She'd been dreaming about being on a ship in high seas, mistaking the gait of his horse for the swells of the waves. But then she opened her eyes. And once she realized who was holding her, she started screaming. She realized in horror that he didn't look startled by her shrieks at all. In fact, he looked amused. Somehow that was even more terrifying.

"Why didn't I wake up?" she shrieked, writhing in his arms. "How did you get me here without me waking up?"

She realized she was still armed and reached for her gun. He didn't try to stop her, which was bizarre. She shoved the muzzle of the gun under his chin and pulled the hammer back.

"That's liable to go off by accident," he said cheerfully. "This ain't terribly even ground." He didn't seem even the slightest bit perturbed that she might shoot his head off.

"You took the bullets out, didn't you?" she guessed. Her tongue was thick in her mouth.

He grinned. "Yeah," he said sheepishly. "But I'll give 'em back as soon as you've simmered down."

She didn't lower the gun. In fact, she shoved it harder into his skin, which was senseless, since the gun didn't have bullets, but it made her feel better. "How did you kidnap me without me waking up?"

"I'm good at what I do," he told her, grinning even wider. "You should know. You wrote about it."

It wasn't natural, his ability to haul a grown woman out of a boardinghouse without waking her up. Getting her downstairs, getting her on a horse, cantering out of town in the dead of night—without her so much as stirring. He'd ridden for miles, and she'd slept through the whole thing?

"You drugged me," she guessed.

"You're pretty good at this." He was as breezy as though they were going courting on a lazy Sunday afternoon.

"But *how*? We didn't eat together."

"It weren't in nothing you ate." He was enjoying the whole guessing game thing.

"Did you chloroform me after I was already asleep?" He must have. Somehow he'd gotten in her room and drugged her. Goddamn it. Why hadn't she locked the door?

"A boy has to keep some secrets," he told her with a coy wink.

Ava's mind was racing. She went over his old crimes, and a number of nagging problems were resolved. He'd *drugged* them. That was how he managed it. She'd always wondered how he'd gotten the girls without a fight. At least the most recent ones. Looking like a charming farm boy took you only so far . . . especially once your name was out there as a murderous maniac.

She had to get away. She considered her options, taking in Freckles and the packhorses, and the wild country around them. She didn't even know where they were. A long way from Mariposa already, by the looks of it. How long had she been asleep? She'd stretched out on that feather bed in the late afternoon . . . and it was now past dawn. Theoretically he could have taken her miles and miles from Mariposa. If she got away from him, how would she ever get her bearings? She checked to see if he'd strapped her saddlebags to her horse. Hell. He hadn't brought her packhorse, just Freckles. All the packhorses were his. So she had only one lot of saddlebags. She hoped her compass was in there. . . . She'd need it once she got away from him.

"You're welcome to ride your own horse now that you're awake." He gave her a sly look, like he'd been reading her thoughts. They both knew she'd never outride him on Freckles, so of course it was safe enough for him to offer.

If she was going to run, it had to be done with stealth. Because Freckles couldn't outpace a turtle. *Thank you, Becky, for buying the slowest horse in California.*

"What did you do to Becky and Lord Whatsit?" she asked abruptly. Now that Becky had leapt to mind, she was worried about her. Her stomach gave a weird twist. She felt responsible for the girl and Lord Whatsit—God knew why, since they were grown adults and seemed plenty good at getting in and out of trouble without her. But if Kennedy Voss had hurt them, it would be her fault. There was no way he would ever bother with them in the normal course of events; they were only at risk because they'd been with *her.* Ava had a sudden image of Becky in bed in the boarding-house, with Voss looming over her.

Voss gave a horsey laugh. "Lord Whatsit: that's good. You should use that in a book. When you write the story of how the Plague of the West cut him down."

How the Plague of the West cut him down . . . "So, he's still alive, then?"

"I've got no trouble with either of them. Nor with those two idiots who were dogging us."

"But you have trouble with *me*?" The nausea was rising again, and she didn't know if it was the thought of what happened to people Voss had a problem with or if it was the residue of the drug.

"Of course not. You ain't the prey. *You*, Miss Archer, are the prize."

The prize. Goddamn it all to hell!

"Stop the horse." She gave him a shove. "Right now. I want off."

He merely watched as she tumbled down from his saddle. Her foot got all tangled up as she pushed herself out of his arms, and she almost landed on her face. He didn't try to help. He just watched in that disconcerting flat-eyed, genial-smiling way he had as she fumbled for Freckles' reins, which were hitched to his packhorses.

"Careful there. You look a little unsteady on your feet," he drawled as she missed the stirrup on her first try.

Her vision wasn't as clear as it should have been, and her head felt stuffed with straw.

"I wonder why," she muttered under her breath. She was sluggish and sickly from the drug. "Prize, my ass."

"It's true. You're the prize. Everything hinges on you." Kennedy Voss leaned back in his saddle and watched her trying to mount her horse. "You see, what I've been thinking is: if they catch old Rides with Death and you're not there to witness it . . . did it really happen?"

"Did you chloroform yourself too?" she snapped. "Because you're talking nonsense."

"The way I see it, you're as important as he is. The story you write will be the one that people remember."

"Not if Pete Hamble or Cactus Joe goes riding into San Francisco with his head. They'll remember that just fine." Oh, she felt like she was going to be sick. It was the thought of the head that did it. She'd never in her life get used to that kind of violence, no matter how many times she witnessed it. It made you doubt everything. What was *wrong* with people?

"You might feel better if you eat something." Kennedy Voss tossed her a hunk of hardtack. If she hadn't already felt like vomiting, she would have at the sight of the hardtack. It had clearly been in his saddlebags a good long while.

"The thing is, how are they going to verify it's *his* head?" Voss said with enormous satisfaction. He'd clearly thought about it a great deal. "Who's to know that they got the right Indian?"

"He's got blue eyes," she reminded him. "Ice blue. So pale they look almost colorless. They can't just go killing any Indian and claiming it's him."

"According to your books, you mean?"

She didn't respond. Yes, according to her books. And according to everyone she'd spoken to who'd actually met him. It was part of the legend.

Voss shrugged. "But he'll be dead. So they won't be able to tell what color his eyes are."

"Stop! I don't want to hear any more about dead people's eyes." Ava felt queasy enough as it was.

"They'll need someone who knows him, to verify it's him. There's no way in hell LeFoy is handing over a fortune without proof of identity. I guarantee you there'll be fifty men trying to claim the prize before the month is out—and LeFoy is going to need someone like you, someone who knows Deathrider, to verify it's him."

Oh God, she hadn't thought of that. Some of those vile Hunters wouldn't bother looking for the *actual* Deathrider; they'd be perfectly happy passing anyone off as him, in the chance of tricking LeFoy out of his money. All those innocent men, pulled into this nightmare, murdered, so some greedy trailhound could claim the money.

Ava kept her mouth shut. She knew two things that wrecked Voss's logic, but neither of them helped keep her safe right now. The first was that she *didn't* know Deathrider; the second was that LeFoy *did*. He'd traveled in the same wagon train as Becky and met Deathrider when he was traveling as Tom Slater. Becky had regaled Ava with the details back in the treasure box room above the Palladium. LeFoy would know at a glance if they'd caught the right man or not; he didn't need Ava's help or anyone else's. But if Ava told Voss that, he might realize he didn't need her—and then he might kill her.

Voss grinned. He was looking smug. "They can't do anything without *you*," he said happily. "And *I* got you. Which gives me the upper hand. Nothing can happen till *we* get there."

"Of course it can. I'm not the *only* person who knows the man." Now she was agreeing that she knew him. Jesus wept. "I'm going back to Mariposa," she said tightly.

"Nah, you ain't. You know why you ain't?"

She ignored him and turned Freckles around, hoping she was facing the right way. She wouldn't travel alone with Voss if her life depended on it.

"You ain't going back there, because if you do, I'll kill that girl you were traveling with. That skinny little Becky girl."

Ava pulled Freckles up short. Hell.

"You know I ain't bluffing. And let me tell you, honey, I'm pent-up. Traveling with a woman such as yourself takes a toll. Hell, you been jouncing up and down my thigh all night, and that does things to a man."

Terror went through her like a cold snap. She felt like her insides had turned to ice. Out of habit, she chose to thaw her fear with anger. At least anger was hot. It kept her alive when sheer terror wanted to freeze her to the spot.

"A jouncing woman makes a man want to kill?" she snapped. She couldn't bite the words back. She was infuriated. Because she was stuck. She *knew* he was capable of killing Becky—and not just killing her, but enjoying it.

"Nah. Not most men. Just me. But I ain't like most men." His voice had dropped and become greasily seductive. "I'm something special."

"Special like a two-headed goat?" Her mouth was unbuttoned good and proper now.

He laughed. "You know, I like you. And I don't like many people."

She threw the hunk of hardtack at him. It hit him in the chest and fell to the ground with a thud. "You're an unholy bastard—you know that?"

He gave another horsey laugh. "You say it like I should be insulted. Now, come along, we're wasting daylight. We're going to track that posse and see what they've found. With any luck they've done all our work for us and found our prey. Thanks to the way I helped you back there in Mariposa, we know Deathrider and his whore ain't that far ahead of us."

"Your *help*," she grumped. "I could have got exactly the same information by *asking nicely*."

"Asking nicely didn't even get the door open. Not at the store, not at the saloon and sure as hell not at the whorehouse."

The angrier she got, the more cheerful Voss got.

"They barely spoke to me!" Ava fumed. "Do you have any idea how much I could have learned if you'd shut up and kept out of it?"

He shrugged. "We'll never know now, I guess."

Damn straight. Voss had terrorized every last creature in Mariposa. And each and every one of them had told the exact same story: tales of Deathrider and the redheaded whore's outrageous display in the whorehouse—with her buck naked, no less—and their wild ride out the next morning; and then the descent of the Hunters, who were responsible for more than a fair few bullet holes and broken windows in Mariposa. The whores were still incandescent with fury at the way they'd been treated by the posse as it rode through looking for answers.

Ava knew she could have got more out of them if it hadn't been for Voss. Oh, she had the bare bones of the story, but none of the *substance*. Had Deathrider met the whore there? Or had they arrived together? How long had they known each other? Did he love her, or were they just having fun? Why *her* and not another?

Ava felt a disconcerting pang at the thought of Deathrider with a woman but batted it away. She'd never found a trace of women in Deathrider's past before, but that didn't mean he didn't have them. He was a man like any other. He must have had a mistress or two. Or a wife. Or both.

How likely was it that a man of his age had entirely escaped lust, love or even matrimony? Maybe he had a wife back in his village and a pack of plump children. When he disappeared for months at a time, maybe he was at home, playing happy families.

The pang became a pain, like a muscle cramp.

"I'll tell you what," Voss said, breaking into her thoughts like an ice ax shattering the surface of a January pond. "When we catch old Rides with Death, I'll keep him alive long enough for you to ask him for all the *details*. That's what you really want, isn't it? To get your notebook out and pepper him with questions, just like you did to all those people back in Mariposa? I'll make sure he's amenable to answering your questions, have no doubt about that. And you can get all of those lovely details out of him."

Humph. Voss had said he liked details, but he wouldn't have known a detail if he sat on it. He'd ridden roughshod over her interviews and then had the nerve to kidnap her, right out from under everyone's noses. And now he thought offering her a beaten and terrorized Deathrider was what she wanted. The last thing she wanted was to see Rides with Death captured and constrained, answering her questions under sufferance. But men like Kennedy Voss would never understand that.

It didn't matter, because she wasn't going to be around long enough for his ghoulish scenario to play out. In a day or two at most, she'd escape from Voss. She'd wait to give Becky and Lord Whatsit time to get clear of Mariposa. He was using Becky as a bargaining chip, but once she was on the trail, she'd be harder to find. For one thing, Ava was sure Becky and his lordship would get themselves royally lost, which would probably protect them from Voss finding them.

"C'mon, Miss Archer, we're wasting daylight." Voss

reached over and clipped a rope to Freckles' reins. "I'll lead you till you're feeling better."

"I feel just fine," she said waspishly. But she wasn't. A wave of nausea rolled over her as they started moving. She broke out in clammy sweats, and her brain felt like it was swelling up in her head.

Chloroform. That sneak.

It gave her an idea though, one that she kept coming back to over the course of the day, as she suffered through her headache and stomach pains. She had a tincture of laudanum in the leather pouch that held her notebook—it was a luxury in many remote towns and could buy her more information than hard cash could, so she always carried a few bottles with her. Homesteaders always needed medicines. After the last trip she was down to her final bottle—but there was enough to get even with Kennedy Voss. Laudanum had a bitter taste and was hard to slip into people's food, but she was a terrible cook. She'd have no trouble disguising the bitterness in a charred salt beef stew. And then, while he dreamed his salubrious opium dreams, she'd get the hell out of here.

While she still could.

❧ 10 ❧

T HIS IS GETTING US *out* of trouble?" Micah was bitching again. He sounded marginally more chipper than he had when they were back with the army, but only marginally.

They were lost. And they had only one horse. But no saddle. And no food.

They didn't even have a canteen.

All Deathrider and Micah had were the clothes on their backs and a single saddleless horse. It wasn't even one of their horses. It had been roped to one of the soldier's pack-horses, and they soon found out why. It was as wild as all hell. It kept trying to throw them or scrape them off against the prickly pears. Dog snapped at it when it tried to kick him, but it kept kicking nevertheless.

"We'd be better off walking," Micah said after he'd ended up on his ass in the dirt one too many times.

"Feel free."

"I will." Mulishly, Micah continued on foot. "This is the worst thing you've ever done to me."

"I didn't do anything. Blame the army, not me."

"The army didn't dress me up like a whore and go dragging me into the Apacheria. The army didn't get me lost in the middle of a wasteland."

"Well, they did. We're only lost because their stupid horse went tearing off in the wrong direction. I'm not wearing the blame for being lost when it's the army horse who did it."

"Even their horses are idiots."

Deathrider was relieved that Micah was bitching—it meant they were still talking, at least.

"You should have shot them in the first place, and not wasted time talking to them. If you'd dealt with it straightaway, we'd still have our own horses."

"Or we'd be dead."

"You're always such a damn peacemaker."

"I thought I was a white knight?"

"Same thing. You have to go trying to *talk* to people when it's clear they just want you dead."

"A white knight is not the same thing as a peacemaker." Deathrider was starting to relax now. The rush of battle was subsiding; his heart rate had slowed, his breath had returned and his thoughts were regaining order.

"If you want to help people, you should help *me* instead of getting me tangled up in these stupid situations. Do you know how many times I've almost died because of you?"

"Not because of me. Because of the crazy people trying to kill me. It's not my fault people want me dead."

"*Us* dead. It's not just about you, you know. People shoot at me too now. And Tom Slater. And now Seline—because of you she's going to be in those books too. *The Outlaw and the Whore.* I bet they'll start hunting her too."

"No, they won't. The army think she's in one of those graves back there—the news will be all over the territories soon."

"All over the territories that *we* killed her, thanks to you. Now it's not just those Hunters after us. It's the damn *army*."

"I told you I'll make it up to you."

"In Sonora." Micah got a stubborn look. He was determined they should head south, over the border.

"*Not* in Sonora," Deathrider said firmly. "The army thinks we're headed to Mexico, so we can't go to Sonora; they'll be waiting for us at the border."

"Those idiots think we're already *in* Mexico." Micah lapsed into a tirade in Shoshoni, which Deathrider didn't speak. He got the gist of it from Micah's pissy tone though. And by the way he kicked at the dirt as he walked, sending up explosive puffs of dust.

Deathrider was wary of upsetting him further, which was why he didn't tell him about the riders. At first they were shadowy flickers at the edge of his vision, far in the distance. Dog noticed them too. He gave a yip. Oh yes, they definitely had company. And this time it wasn't the army. This time it was something much worse.

"Uh, Micah?" Deathrider dropped back to ride next to his friend. "Get up on the horse now."

"That devil animal? No, thank you. I'd rather ride Dog."

"Micah," Deathrider said warningly, "get on the horse."

Micah groaned as he recognized Deathrider's tone. "What now? Let me guess. We're surrounded by the Chiricahua?" His voice dripped sarcasm.

"Not surrounded. Not yet."

"What! I was *joking*."

Deathrider gave an apologetic shrug and held a hand out to haul his friend up onto the horse.

"I hope it rains on you for a year," Micah shouted as the horse surged beneath them. He grabbed hold of Deathrider, hanging on for dear life. "I hope the only women who let you touch them are crones!" Deathrider urged the wild horse into a gallop, with Micah still hollering in his ear. "I hope your crops get bugs!"

"What crops?"

"One day you'll have crops, and I hope they get bugs. Lots of them! Big ones!"

They tore across land woolly with chaparral and spotted with cacti. They heard whooping behind them as the Chiricahua broke cover and came hard in pursuit.

"They're going to torture us," Micah shouted. "And it's all your fault."

"Stop being such a doomsayer. I got us away from the army, didn't I?"

"You got us *hunted* by the army!" Micah yipped as an arrow skipped off the ground close beside them. The horse startled and suddenly changed direction. Dog barked madly, chasing them. "The army didn't even know who I was before—now I'm a wanted man!"

"They still don't know who you are," Deathrider shouted back impatiently. "They think you're an Apache. Stop being melodramatic."

"This horse is going to kill us!" Micah thumped him in the shoulder with a fist as the mad horse went running at a prickly pear.

"Better the horse than the Chiricahua!" Deathrider said, right as the stupid animal reared and sent them flying headfirst into the cactus.

Deathrider wasn't sure what hurt most: the landing, which was sure to leave him covered in bruises, or the cactus prickles, which were sticking him right in the ass.

Actually, maybe his right ear hurt the most, from Micah screeching in it. It was ringing like a mission bell.

They were still sitting in the smashed flesh of the prickly pear, covered in slime and spiked with thorns, when the Chiricahua bunched around them. There were a lot of them. They had dusty yellow-orange bandannas tied around their foreheads and were attired in white peasant shirts with vests and leggings. And they were armed to the teeth.

Micah said some kind of prayer in Shoshoni. He was preparing for death.

"I don't suppose you speak English?" Deathrider asked the Chiricahua ruefully, slipping on the goo oozing from the smashed cactus as he tried to gain enough purchase to stand.

"Today, you are a lucky man," one of the Chiricahua replied in heavily accented English.

"Funny, I don't feel lucky." Deathrider winced as his feet slid out from under him and he went down hard on his ass. He yelped. The movement had shoved the cactus spines even deeper into his flesh.

"Trust me, he's not lucky. He's about to get shot by his friend." Micah was tentatively more hopeful now that he realized they weren't facing an immediate death. He had a few prickles stuck in the side of his face and looked like a porcupine.

Deathrider hadn't heard of the Chiricahua talking much to their victims, so Micah's hope might have been well-placed. "Who said you were my friend?" Deathrider reached over and plucked one of the prickles out of his face.

Micah slapped his hand away. "Rub salt into the wound, why don't you?"

There was a pause as Micah took in the bandoliers hanging across the Chiricahua warriors' chests and the sheer number of their unholstered weapons. "We're doomed."

The leader of the Apache band—at least Deathrider assumed he was the leader, as he had the most gravitas—unleashed a torrent of words at the English-speaking warrior. Deathrider wished he spoke even a smattering of Chiricahua. The leader was frowning, but the English speaker seemed kind of amused.

"I reckon he's telling them to get ready for a torture party," Micah said glumly.

"No," the English-speaking warrior said, a slight smile on his broad face, "he's telling me you look too intelligent to be white men, but too dumb to be Apache."

"You can tell him he's right about that."

"I told him you might be dumb, but you're very lucky. So, you might be white after all."

"He's part white," Micah admitted, nodding in Death-rider's direction. "But neither of us is very lucky."

Deathrider squinted up the English-speaking warrior. The Chiricahua were standing between him and the sun, so it was hard to see their faces clearly, but they didn't seem overly aggressive.

"I think you've got your words confused," Micah continued helpfully. "Lucky means of good fortune. You know, blessed. The only thing we're blessed with is a bunch of cactus pins in our cushions."

"That horse sent you through the air—you could have broken your necks, and you didn't," the warrior pointed out.

"That's true," Deathrider conceded, finally managing to get to his feet. "We didn't break our necks."

"That prickly pear has many prickles," the Chiricahua continued.

"You're telling me." Micah groaned as he slid an extra-long cactus spike from the webbing between his thumb and his finger. "I think I've got most of them in me." He hadn't bothered to get up but stayed sprawled in the cactus juices.

"But for all those prickles," the Chiricahua observed, "you didn't get a single one in your eye. A cactus prickle could have blinded you, but didn't."

Deathrider blinked. A talkative, *philosophical* Chiricahua was the last thing he had been expecting. The Chiricahua were the most fearsome of all the Apache—legendary throughout the territories and into Mexico. Their plunder trails extended further every year. He'd expected violence and torture. At the least. But not this kind of lazy conversation.

Maybe they started by lulling you into a false sense of security?

"And now look," the Chiricahua said brightly. "Here you meet the great Loco and his warriors."

Loco. Deathrider and Micah exchanged a look. Of all the Apache warriors to stumble into out here, they'd bumbled into *Loco*? It was hard to believe they could be so unlucky. Sure, they hadn't broken their necks or had their eyes spiked out by a cactus but . . . *damn. Loco.*

Deathrider examined the severe, dignified warrior who sat silently beside the talkative Chiricahua. He must have been Loco. He wore his hair in two loose braids, his bandanna bisecting his broad forehead. He was staring at Deathrider, his eyebrows drawn together. He didn't look pleased.

"This plunder trail is Loco's," the chatty warrior said cheerfully. "You have blundered where you don't belong. If you were smart, you would have known better."

"We would, wouldn't we?" Micah agreed. "But as you said, my friend here is as dumb as they come. If he was any dumber, he'd be a block of wood."

The Chiricahua grinned. "But here again, you are lucky."

"Why? Are you going to skip the torture and kill us quickly?" Micah asked hopefully.

"Micah, shut up." Deathrider kicked dirt at his friend. Micah was still on the ground and the puff of dust hit him square in the face. Not in the mood to take it, he reached up and sharply yanked a cactus spine from Deathrider's thigh. Deathrider swore at the pain.

"You are lucky for many reasons." The Chiricahua warrior went on blithely, as though they weren't bickering right in front of him. "Firstly, because we have been raiding for many days and have won many prizes."

"Congratulations," Micah said sourly.

"You have no prizes," the Chiricahua observed, taking in their sorry state.

"No," Deathrider agreed. "We don't even have our *own* belongings. Not so much as a saddle."

"And we have no time," the Chiricahua said regretfully. "We were on our way home to the mountains when we saw you."

"Lucky us." Micah grimaced.

"Yes, lucky you. Loco has decided not to bother with you."

"He couldn't have done that *before* you chased us into a prickly pear?"

"Shut *up*, Micah. I think he's telling us they're going to let us live." Deathrider couldn't quite believe it was true, but there it was.

Micah blinked, surprised.

"Live, yes. For now," the Chiricahua warrior agreed.

"What do you mean, *for now*?" Micah turned a black look on Deathrider. "What does he mean, *for now*? You got my hopes up."

The Chiricahua shrugged. "Who knows how long you'll last on foot, without food or water?"

"Without . . . ?" Micah groaned and flopped back on the squashed cactus. "Of course. Of course this is what happens next."

"We'll take your horse." The wild horse had come to rest not far away. It was giving them all evil looks. Deathrider figured they were welcome to it.

"We'll also take your weapons and your clothes. Your shoes too. And your hats. Everything." The Chiricahua's gaze drifted to Dog. "Including him."

"No." Deathrider drew the line at Dog. He loved that animal.

The Chiricahua trained his weapon on Dog. "You'd rather I shot him?"

Deathrider struggled to contain himself. He wanted to throw things and curse and tear this Apache from his horse. "No," he said tightly. "Don't shoot."

Deathrider took a deep breath. This month could just go to hell.

"Take your clothes off," the Chiricahua instructed cheerfully.

Micah was smart enough to stay silent as they were stripped of their belongings, and smarter still to continue his silence when the Chiricahua rode off with Dog. Deathrider couldn't quite keep his emotions hidden as he watched

his dog go, roped and dragged until he fell in line. The confused look in Dog's eyes was his undoing. Deathrider stood
frozen to the spot until the Chiricahua and his dog were
specks on the horizon and then gone. The memory of Dog's
whines lingered in his ears long after he had disappeared.
Losing the dog opened an old well of sadness, one Deathrider always kept tightly capped. Inside was all the grief he
never let himself feel. Enough for a man to drown in.

Micah didn't say a word as Deathrider got himself in
check and they began trudging away from the broken
prickly pear, silently pulling prickles from their tender
skin. Step by step, Deathrider's mood blackened.

That goddamn Archer woman and her goddamn books.
If it weren't for her, he'd be relaxing in the shade back in
Mariposa, waiting out the worst of the summer's heat before moving along. If it weren't for her, he'd have his horse
and his saddlebags; he wouldn't be stuck full of prickles
and black-and-blue from a horse fall. If it weren't for her,
he'd have his *dog*.

That goddamn woman. He was going to make her pay.
Even if he died out here in the desert, he'd come back to
haunt her. One way or another, he was going to make her
pay for this.

145

❖ 11 ❖

I T'S GOOD THAT we're *lucky*, isn't it?" Micah sniped at him as they huddled naked in the pitiable shade of a cactus, waiting out the worst of the day's heat. It was impossible to walk barefoot on the scorching ground; they'd given up hours before. They were both already sunburned in places so tender they usually didn't see the sun. With burned feet and blistering skin, they'd admitted defeat and hunkered down to wait until nightfall, both in filthy moods.

"Just imagine what would happen if we weren't so *lucky*." Micah wasn't going to drop it.

Deathrider clenched his teeth. Micah's complaining was getting under his skin. It was bad enough being stranded naked in the desert, without being stuck with a fishwife to boot. "Shut up, Micah."

"Oh look, it talks. The statue has a tongue."

"Hold yours," Deathrider snapped. "It's running away from you."

That did it. What little restraint Micah had been exercising (and Deathrider hadn't really thought he *had* been exercising any) snapped. With a growl, Micah launched himself at Deathrider. It was like having an adolescent bear land on him. Deathrider went sprawling under his weight.

"Damn you and your stupid plans." Micah went to punch

him, but Deathrider dodged his fist. That only made him madder. "Damn you and that pink dress." *Punch.* "Damn you and that idiotic attempt to talk your way out of being arrested by the army." *Punch.*

"Stop hitting me, Micah, or you'll regret it." Deathrider rolled away, but Micah came after him.

"I can't regret it as much as I regret ever meeting you." *Punch.*

"Last warning, Micah." Deathrider's temper was strained to breaking point.

"Last warning?" Micah hooted with barely concealed hysteria. "Or *what*? Or you'll strip me naked and steal my horse and leave me in the middle of nowhere? Screw you." *Punch.*

"Enough!" Deathrider held him off, but it took every last ounce of strength that he had.

"*Not* enough!" Micah jackknifed, and they went rolling together into a chaparral bush. Deathrider felt his sunburned skin getting shredded by the twigs. He clenched his teeth against the pain and managed to keep tight hold of Micah's wrists so his friend couldn't punch him again. But Micah simply started kicking instead. And his knee was dangerously close to Deathrider's tender parts.

"Stop!" Deathrider growled. "I've got a solution!"

Micah froze. "You've got a *solution*? To *what*? To my nakedness? What are you going to do? Clothe me in cactus? Have you got a solution to our lack of horse too? Why don't we weave a horse out of chaparral sticks!"

Deathrider grunted as Micah landed another well-aimed kick. "No," he hissed, "I meant I've got a solution to your anger."

"So do I!" *Punch.*

"Stop that!"

"No!" *Punch.*

Deathrider wrenched away and managed to get to his feet. His bruises were going to have bruises, he'd taken such a beating. If it had been anyone else, he would have fought back, but this was Micah. And Micah had a point. He wouldn't have been here without Deathrider. He'd have been lazing around the yard of the whorehouse, reading dime novels and taking long afternoon naps. He'd be drinking a beer as evening fell and maybe flirting with a girl or two. He was a fine old flirt.

What he wouldn't be doing was dying slowly of thirst in the desert, his skin blistering in the fierce sun.

Deathrider had brought ill luck to his friend.

That was his way. *Rides with Death,* his father had called him. *Your mother brought death with her, and you ride beside her in the memory of the people. When they look at you, they will remember the days of death.* His father had always known the legacy of loving Deathrider would be grief, but he had loved him just the same. Even though Deathrider carried the seeds of sadness in him.

Now Micah suffered because of him too. He brought nothing but destruction to those who loved him. He should have known better than to let Micah travel with him. Or Dog.

Don't think about Dog. He was too low in spirit to think about his dog; the wound was too fresh.

"I'll let you hit me," Deathrider suggested to Micah. Once they'd settled their differences, he would find a way to get Micah out of here alive—after that, they would have to part ways. Otherwise, he would bring further misery to his friend.

He was no good for people. He should have known that by now.

Micah was crouched on the ground, looking disgusted. "You don't have to *let* me hit you. I just hit you half a dozen times, and I'll hit you half a dozen more if I want to."

"I won't fight back," Deathrider reassured him. "You can hit me once for the pink dress, once for the army, and once for the Chiricahua. And then we're even," he said firmly. He figured he could bear three hits, but his body couldn't take more. He was looking like a patchwork quilt, and *everything* hurt.

Micah was still looking disgusted.

"It's fair," Deathrider coaxed. "You're right. I got you into this. You have cause to be angry."

"You're such an idiot!" Micah exploded, throwing a handful of dust at him.

"Do it."

"No! It's not the same!" Micah slumped back, sitting in the dirt with a childish pout. "You ruin everything. I can't even be mad at you now."

Deathrider rolled his eyes. "You're never happy."

"I'll hit you when we get out of this mess. But you're not allowed to *ask* for it." He scowled. "And you have to fight back."

"And you call *me* an idiot," Deathrider grumbled. He held out a hand to help Micah to his feet. His friend took it. They stared at each other.

"You think we'll get out alive this time?" Micah asked soberly. His gaze showed more than a flicker of fear.

"Yes." Deathrider was certain. He wouldn't let Micah die. He'd walk through hell first. Besides, he wasn't dying until he'd settled his score with that Archer woman.

His certainty steadied Micah, who took a shaky breath and nodded. "You know we're liable to run into those Hunters now, right? Because we're cursed." He went back to crouching in the thin shade of the cactus.

"Since when are we cursed?"

"Since you wanted to meddle with those people's graves. I told you they'd curse us."

Deathrider didn't know about curses, but they'd certainly had a terrible streak of bad luck. And it continued the next morning, when they stumbled upon a cold campsite. It was only an hour past dawn, when the ground was still cool enough for them to walk. They'd jogged for miles through the starlit darkness and were both weary.

"It's them," Micah had said grimly when they found the campsite. "It's those Hunters."

"Only one of them." Deathrider studied the traces of the camp. "They're all competing against one another; they would have split up by now. There was only one man here."

Micah was looking nervy again. "We need to lift this curse. It just keeps going from bad to worse, and I don't fancy running into one of those Hunters while I'm buck naked."

"How do you lift a curse?" Deathrider asked, figuring it was easier to humor him. It kept his mind off their raging thirst.

"Human sacrifice?" Micah turned a speculative look on Deathrider.

"Me? You might as well wait for the Hunters to do it for you." Whoever had camped here was a seasoned traveler, Deathrider noted as he examined the site. And they might not be too far away. "His tracks lead this way." Deathrider gestured and then started walking.

"Where the hell are you going?" Micah asked, exasperated. "If *he's* that way, surely we want to go in the opposite direction?"

"He'll have water." Deathrider kept walking. "And clothes. And we need both."

"You can't be serious . . ."

Deathrider didn't wait to see if Micah was following.

"What in hell are you going to do? We've got no weapons! Are you just walk up to him and say 'Howdy, pard. Got some water?' He'll take one look at those eyes of yours and know exactly who you are!"

Deathrider stopped in his tracks. Hell. That was true. Not for the first time, he wished he'd been born with his father's brown eyes, instead of his mother's distinctive pale blue. Too pale to even really be called blue. Eyes that marked him wherever he went.

"You're right," he admitted, frustrated. "You'll have to do it."

Micah laughed. "No way in hell. He'll just shoot me."

"The alternative is dying of thirst out here."

Micah swore. He glared at the ground for a moment and then brightened. "No. You know what? There's another alternative."

Deathrider doubted it.

Micah went stalking off into the nearby chaparral.

"What are you doing?"

Micah ducked out of sight.

Deathrider sighed. He wanted to go home. The feeling hit so suddenly that it knocked the breath out of him. More than anything he wanted to see his father. To go riding into the summer camp to see Two Bears lighting up with joy at the sight of him; to settle into the summer rhythm of his people; to watch the long days cast dusty shadows; to eat with family and to see the stars wink to life above the glowing teepees. To follow the buffalo through the hazy summer, wandering until the chill bit the air, when they would set up their winter village and prepare to wait out the snows.

"Here!" Micah reemerged from the brush, shattering Deathrider's idyllic vision. He was carrying a handful of some kind of plant. Deathrider didn't like the look on his face.

"What's that?"

"A solution!"

BY THE TIME they caught up to the Hunter, who turned out to be Pete Hamble, Deathrider's eyes had swollen closed, and he felt like he had a severe head cold. His throat was swelling, and the palms of his hands and the soles of his feet were itching madly. Micah hadn't asked for permission to "solve" the problem of Deathrider's pale eyes—he'd just grabbed Deathrider by the hair and rubbed the stinging nettle into his face.

That was when Deathrider had punched Micah. But the damage had already been done.

The stinging nettle got in his eyes and mouth and nose. His nostrils got so swollen, they closed over and he had to breathe through his mouth; his lips puffed up to three times their normal size, and his skin was itching like mad. It was like he'd been stung by a swarm of wasps. But it was his eyes that worried him the most. Within minutes he couldn't see.

He called Micah every name under the sun. "I'm trapped out here, in the middle of nowhere, naked, with no water, being hunted down by the most murderous men in the whole west, and you've *blinded me!*"

"No one is going to know you have blue eyes now," Micah said. He easily kept out of reach, because Deathrider couldn't *see* him to hit him.

"What if I'm blind? For good?" He felt panicked at the thought. His eyes burned like someone had shoved hot coals into them; first his vision had blurred, like he was seeing the world through oilcloth, and then his eyes had closed over completely until he couldn't see *anything*. He felt a surge of pure black terror.

For the first time he really felt he was going to die out here.

"No one will know your eyes are blue if they're swollen shut," Micah said. The idiot sounded *proud* of himself. "And *I'm* here. You'll be fine. I'll make sure of it. I can lead you."

"What if something happens to *you*?" The terror intensified. Hell. He was in the worst trouble he'd been in since that time he'd been shot in Kearney.

"Nothing's going to happen to me," Micah scoffed. He went silent for a minute. Deathrider imagined he might have been considering his own position: the nakedness, the lack of water or food, the fact that they were *lost*. "It's this or die of thirst," Micah said eventually, throwing Death-rider's own words back at him.

"How am I going to walk?" Deathrider asked. He took a couple of steps. It was like being on the edge of a cliff—he felt like he might fall. The ground was uneven, treacherous. "Hell, Micah. I'm *blind*."

"Oh, calm down, you baby. It's only stinging nettle. My sister got it in her eyes once—"

"You did it to *her* too?"

"No, she just rubbed her eyes after touching some. And she was fine. It's nothing to worry about."

"This is completely different. You rubbed a whole *plant* in my eyes."

"She didn't go blind," Micah told him. "She just got all swollen up like that for a day or so. It went away."

"It hurts like a bitch."

"Yeah, she did cry a lot." Micah sounded more cheerful again. "This can count as me punching you, if that makes you feel any better."

It didn't.

Micah had to lead him like he was a child. Even then Deathrider stumbled a lot, once hitting his hip so badly on a boulder that he almost gave up and sat down and refused to move again. He felt his bare skin burning in the sun and the lack of water was starting to tell. His confidence was shaken, and he felt like death.

"I can see that Hunter up ahead," Micah told him, completely unsympathetic to his plight. He was stupidly confident that Deathrider would get his sight back. Deathrider wasn't feeling at all the same way. The burning had given way to searing pain; his eyes were streaming tears, and it was hard to breathe. He was exhausted by the past few days, and his mood was maybe the lowest it had ever been.

"I'm going to tell him the Chiricahua attacked us." Micah paused. "Which is true. If he asks who we are, I'm going to say we're vaqueros. I can say they ambushed us for our cows."

"It would take more than two men to drive a herd of cattle," Deathrider told him.

"So, I'll say the Apaches killed the other cowboys. We managed to get away . . . We both look pretty beat-up . . . you more than me . . . so it's believable." Another pause. "If I had a gun, I wouldn't bother with all this talking, but because of you, I don't have a gun."

Deathrider didn't dignify that with a response.

"I'll feed him that story you told the army too, if you want. About how you killed the whore. Not *you*, because you're not supposed to *be* you right now. I mean, I'll tell him the story about how the Plague of the West killed the whore. I'll say we heard it from the army."

"But you were telling him the *Chiricahua* attacked us, not the army."

"Stop picking holes!" Micah gave his arm a yank and dragged him on.

"What are our names going to be?" Deathrider asked, wincing at the stones underfoot. "He's going to ask, and you can hardly tell him the truth."

"I'm Trevor and you're Nesbitt."

"I don't look anything like a Nesbitt."

"Yes, you do. Now shut up, Nesbitt, and let me do the talking. You're not only blind. You're mute."

"I am?"

"Yes. It's simpler that way. No one is going to think you're the Plague of the West looking the way you do right now; you can be my blind, mute little brother."

"We don't look anything alike."

"Who can tell with all these bruises? And your face looks like an overfull water bladder. Now, shut up or I'll make you eat nettles so you you're actually mute, and not just pretending."

"You already made me eat them," Deathrider grunted. It was hard to talk with his swollen lips and tongue.

In the end, Micah did a better job than Deathrider would have given him credit for. He let out a piercing whistle to get the Hunter's attention and then, before the man could so much as greet them, launched into a monologue about being set on by Apaches and robbed; they were just two poor Mexican vaqueros and *Look what they did to my brother. . . .*

It was quite a performance. And Deathrider had the feeling that Micah was rather enjoying himself.

Luckily for both of them, Pete Hamble was a sociable man. Crazy as a fox but sociable. He could talk the hind leg off a mule, they discovered, as he invited them to camp with him for the night. Deathrider wished he could see what the man looked like. But he was trapped in miserable darkness.

Worse, he was in *pain* in miserable darkness.

Hamble tossed them each a horse blanket to cover themselves with but didn't have spare clothes for them. Even if he'd had them, he said, he wouldn't lend them to a couple of strangers. Deathrider didn't see the blanket coming, and it hit him hard in the shoulder, right where he was bruised and tender from falling off the horse.

"I'll want them blankets back in the morning," Hamble said. He had a gravelly voice. The voice of a man who'd been out in the wind and dust a long time; the voice of a man who'd drunk a lot of pure corn liquor. "I'll be needing them to get the animals through winter."

Deathrider let Micah push him into place by the campfire and arrange the blanket over him, but then he was left to his silent darkness. All he could do was take the mug of bad coffee pressed into his hand and listen to Micah and Pete Hamble gab. The horse blanket was rough against his sunburn. If he hadn't been so battered and blind, he'd have taught Pete Hamble to show a little respect.

Although he was a bigot, Hamble seemed glad they'd stumbled into his camp. Trailhounds were used to strangers, and they relished a chance at conversation after long hours on their own, and Hamble proved to like conversation more than most. Once he opened his mouth, he never closed it again. Their nakedness didn't upset Hamble, nor did their tattoos or long hair. He obviously thought they looked the way vagabonds should look. He wasn't the first white person Deathrider had met who couldn't tell the difference between a Plains Indian and a Mexican. Even though they looked nothing alike.

Over the crackle of the fire, Hamble's voice rose and fell through the night. He told them about the to-do in San Francisco when LeFoy had announced the Hunt, describing the crowd, mentioning at least a dozen cold-blooded killers by name. He was a man who liked to take his time with a tale; as he named each of the Hunters, he went into their entire life histories. He droned on into the night, his voice becoming a low lullaby.

The burning in his eyes began to subside, and Deathrider found himself dozing. But then Pete Hamble got onto a topic that snapped him awake. *Ava Archer.*

Deathrider jumped like he'd been shot with an arrow at the sound of her name.

"She was there," Hamble enthused. "I saw her myself. Standing up on the bar." Hamble gave a low whistle. "And, boy, was she a looker. Did you know she was a looker? Because I sure didn't. Tall, you know? Must have legs like you wouldn't believe under those clothes. And she has lips like a bee stung them. And a redhead. God, I love a redhead. She's not pretty, not in the least. Pretty suggests a kind of gentleness, which that woman sure don't have. She's got something else. If pretty is a kitten, this woman is a jaguar. I saw her all but scratch Kennedy Voss's eyes out. Can you imagine? I bet she'd be a wildcat between the sheets."

Hamble's words painted a picture in Deathrider's head. He imagined a redheaded vixen standing on a bar. Brazen. Mean eyed. Haughty.

Pete Hamble was describing the woman who'd ruined Deathrider's life.

"She and Kennedy Voss have teamed up." Pete Hamble sounded glum as he said it. "Voss was always going to be hard to beat, but the two of them together . . ." He let out a low whistle.

Deathrider coughed. He was supposed to be mute, so he couldn't ask any questions, but he desperately wanted to know more about the Archer woman. When Micah didn't follow up with any questions about her, Deathrider coughed again. And again. Damn Micah and his wool-headedness.

"Your friend sounds in a bad way," Hamble observed.

"He always sounds like that." Micah was clearly still enjoying needling Deathrider.

"He contagious?"

"No."

"'Cause I had a cousin had a cough like that, and he killed his whole family with it."

Later, Deathrider realized the coughing had probably saved him. And doomed Micah. Although maybe Hamble had already decided Micah was the one who'd made a better trophy. Because, as Micah had observed earlier, no one would ever believe that the beat-up blind man was the Plague of the West. He looked too bedraggled, too pitiful. Too weak.

He *was* too weak. There was next to nothing he could do to save Micah when the trouble started. Hamble waited until they were good and relaxed, full of food (not good food, but anything was welcome after the miles they'd walked on empty stomachs), dozy from the campfire and Hamble's endless tales. Deathrider and Micah were exhausted, drained from a series of ridiculous events, battered and bruised and just plain tired; they were easy marks.

Deathrider was asleep when it happened. Usually he was a light sleeper, and usually he also had Dog to warn him when something was wrong. But tonight he was so bone weary, and his body so desperately needed the rest, that he'd fallen into sleep like a stone dropped to the bottom of a lake. When he woke, he woke suddenly. The world was black. He was disoriented and couldn't remember where he was, could barely remember *who* he was. There was the sound of grunting and scuffling. A *thud*. And then silence.

He rolled over, able to feel the roughness of the thirsty earth beneath his hands and knees—but he couldn't see anything.

Blind. I'm blind.

Nettles.

Micah!

He'd never felt so vulnerable in his life—not even when he'd been shot and bleeding in Kearney and Matt Slater had thought he was going to die. Blindness was infinitely worse. It was difficult to tell where the sounds were coming from in the darkness. He could hear breathing, the sound of something being dragged, grunting. . . .

"Don't you move from where you're at, you blind bastard." Hamble's raspy voice came out of the darkness. "I got no trouble with you, and you ain't worth a bullet. You're half-dead as it is, so there ain't any point. Firing a bullet into you would be a flat-out waste of money. Nature will finish you off quick enough."

Deathrider rose to his knees. He felt a lick of fury. "Micah?" he called. His voice was still thick from his swollen tongue and throat.

"Mute, my ass . . . although you might as well be. You don't sound like you got two wits to rub together." Hamble lifted his voice and started talking to Deathrider like he was impaired. "Get off my blanket, you bastard. And you stay down. I don't want to waste a good rope tying you up or a good bullet putting you out of your misery, but I *will* if you make me. It'll just piss me off to do it." Deathrider felt the cold touch of iron as Hamble held a gun to his head.

"What about Micah?" Deathrider wasn't used to the hot

shameful feeling of impotence that flooded him. It was poisonous.

"Your friend's a notorious criminal—did you know that?"

"He's not."

The gun pressed harder into Deathrider's forehead.

"Yeah, buddy, he is. He's Deathrider. Rides with Death. The Plague of the West. And he's going to make me a very rich man."

"His name's Trevor," Deathrider said flatly. His mind raced. If he reached out, he could probably grab Hamble by the legs and topple him.

"It's Deathrider now. No one'll pay me a cent for a man named *Trevor.*" And then Hamble had been true to his word and not wasted a single bullet. Instead he'd *thwack*ed the barrel of the gun into Deathrider's head. And left him for dead in the middle of the desert.

✣ 12 ✣

T HEY'D *CAUGHT* HIM. Ava reeled at the news. She and Voss
had found a bunch of the straggling Hunters as night
was falling. They'd been on the trail for weeks when they'd
seen the smoke from their campfire and gone to investigate.
The evening was lushly purple, the angles of the cacti in-
digo against the deep plum-colored sky. Their campfire
was a sharp flicker of orange in the clear desert air and the
Hunters' voices carried in the stillness.

"They might have some news about where old Deathrider is," Voss had said, pulling Ava's horse by the lead,
which he refused to relinquish, even though Ava could
manage her horse just fine without him.

And he was right. The straggling Hunters *did* have some
news. News that Ava had been dreading.

Deathrider had been caught. . . .

Her stomach felt like it had turned itself upside down
and inside out at the news.

She didn't know any of the stragglers—they were just a
bunch of cowboys who'd joined the Hunt for a lark. They
were dusty and sunburned and too cheerful about Deathrider's capture for Ava's taste. They'd been at their moonshine as they were skinning rabbits for their evening meal
and, by the time Voss and Ava had found them, they were

well and truly in their cups. They were also downright glee-ful that the Plague of the West had been defeated so quickly.

The cowboys had fallen into a stunned silence when Kennedy Voss and Ava Archer had ridden into their midst, and then they set up a-howling and a-hollering, all laughing fit to bust. They were thigh slapping and red-faced at the hilarity of *Kennedy Voss* finding out he'd lost from *them*.

"You missed out, Voss. It's over already!"

Ava's heart thundered in her ears. Over? What did that mean? Was the Plague of the West *dead*? The thought made her head spin.

Kennedy Voss took the news in his stride. He dismounted and then offered to help Ava down. She ignored him and got herself down.

"We thought for sure you'd get him, but looks like Ortiz beat you to it." One of the cowboys held out a jug of moon-shine to Voss, grinning like a fool.

"Poor old Carson here bet on you too!"

That set them all off, poking fun at Carson, who frankly didn't seem too upset. The moonshine had clearly dulled his pain.

Voss took the jug and downed a swig. "Ortiz, eh? He was always going to be stiff competition. Did he take the bastard alive or dead?"

"Alive, if you can believe it."

"Not sure if I can," Voss said cheerfully.

"There were witnesses. Everyone's talking about it. A bunch of 'em went tearing after him, hoping to swipe the Indian right off him."

"How . . ." Ava's voice cracked, and she took a minute to collect herself. Painfully aware of how closely Kennedy Voss was watching her, she cleared her throat and tried again: "How did it happen?"

"Don't forget your notebook," Voss suggested. He of-fered her the moonshine jug, but she refused it. "You'll want all the details." He handed the jug back to the cowboys and turned his attention to settling his animals for the night. "Make sure you give her the details, boys. She likes details."

The cowboys were happy to oblige. Ava's pencil was a blur as she tried to keep up. They were so drunk, they repeated themselves often and got into fights when they contradicted one another. But they told quite a tale. About Ortiz coming upon Deathrider as he camped with the Apaches; about how he fought it out with more than a dozen seasoned warriors; about how he took the Plague of the West alive and immediately rode hell for leather for San Francisco, determined to claim the bet.

"The bet," Voss murmured to Ava, "but not the prize." He winked at her.

Ava shuddered. Kennedy Voss sober was frightening enough, but Kennedy Voss drunk on moonshine was something else again. Something unspeakable.

She was starting to have serious doubts that he'd keep his hands to himself for much longer.

"Reckon we're headed for San Francisco, then," Voss told her, his gaze beginning to roam her body.

"You think Ortiz really has him?"

"Yeah, I think he does." Voss betrayed his annoyance. "You heard them; there was too much detail for them to have made it up."

"But he might not have the right man . . ." Ava hoped so anyway. "You said there was nothing stopping a man trying to make a false claim . . ." This whole thing was such a nightmare. How was she even here? Look at these cretins. What had she come to, sharing a campfire with men like these, a prisoner of Kennedy Voss . . . ?

And how on earth was she talking about *Deathrider* being captured?

"Ortiz might not have the right man?" Voss looked disappointed in her as he shook his head. "This is *Ortiz*. If he's got someone, it'll be Deathrider. Ortiz is no fool." Voss leaned back to look at the stars. "Lucky for me, I have *you*."

He yawned. "We'll catch up to him, and *you* can tell me for sure if he has the right man."

Like hell she would. She wasn't planning on being with him for more than another couple of hours. She'd managed to slip the laudanum into the second jug of moonshine they'd popped the cork on. The lot of them were starting to nod now. Voss was heavy eyed and slurring. He was stretched out on his back, blinking long, slow blinks, his expression slackening.

Ava helped herself to a second helping of the rabbit and a hunk of corn bread. She felt easier now they were all falling quiet. The ribald talk and rowdiness over dinner had been a chore to listen to. She was always tense around large groups of men anyway. They were unpredictable at best, and downright life-threatening at worst.

The low murmurs faded away, and soon all she could hear was the sound of her own chewing. This had been easier than she had anticipated. The moonshine had such a pungent fragrance (she bet it had tasted even worse than it smelled) that none of them had suspected that it had been spiked. They'd glugged down the laudanum happily enough, and slipped into their opium dreams without so much as a single protest.

The campfire crackled and popped, the flames leaping at the stars, which were flickering to life above the glow of the fire. She sighed as she mopped up the rabbit juices with the last of the bread. She was in for a long night of riding. She didn't doubt Voss would be on her tail the minute his head cleared, so she'd have to get moving. He had a good night's sleep ahead though, full of some very vivid dreams. It should give her enough of a head start. . . .

She considered stealing his horse, but horse theft was a hanging offense. Whereas rescuing one's self from kidnapping wasn't a crime. As far as she knew. She also resisted giving Voss a hefty kick as she passed him. Only because she didn't want to wake him.

She did borrow his canteen. Borrowing wasn't a crime, was it? She didn't fancy his hardtack though, so she helped herself to some of the cowboys' supplies. They had an awful lot of jerky. And how was anyone going to prove she'd taken it? She would have eaten it by the time anyone found her. It was the perfect crime.

"C'mon, Freckles, looks like it's just you and me now." Ava swung into the saddle. She gazed down at the dreaming outlaws. She envied them their rest. She didn't think she'd be sleeping for the foreseeable future—she'd be too busy looking over her shoulder to see if Voss was chasing her down.

Freckles plodded off into the darkness. She wasn't a quick horse, but she was a steady one. She picked her way carefully over the uneven ground, sensibly avoiding the dark humps of the chaparral and the deeply pooled shadows that suggested potholes. Ava gave her a scratch behind the ear. She was developing an affection for the old girl.

"If you could just go a little faster," Ava suggested, "we'd get along even better."

Freckles whickered but didn't quicken her pace, not a jot.

Ava glanced back over her shoulder. The campfire was still visible as a red-gold shimmer in the distance. Maybe she should have risked the hanging and stolen Voss's horse. . . .

SHE GOT LOST almost immediately and ran out of water by the end of the first day. She also found that jerky gave her a horrid stomachache when there was no water to wash it down with. After two days she was burning up with heat stroke and dehydration. She had no idea how she'd kept ahead of Voss for that long. She could surmise only that the laudanum had knocked him out for longer than she'd expected. It was possible she'd even killed him. . . . After the water had run out and her brains had started to cook in her

head in the beating summer heat, she had waking nightmares that she'd killed the whole lot of them. They'd tumbled off into their opium haze and never climbed back
out. . . . Forget hanging for horse theft, she'd be up for mass
murder. . . .

But then, she thought philosophically, she was about to
die of thirst in the desert, so who the hell cared about hanging? If they offered her a glass of water first, she might even
climb up on the scaffold of her own free will.

Those were the thoughts she was having when she came
upon the naked Apache. The blind, naked, stubborn-as-all-
hell Apache. The one who spoke like a lawyer and hounded
her until she roped him up and let him sit in front of her on
Freckles. Poor Freckles, who now plodded along even slower
under their combined weight.

How was her *luck*? She felt buried under the weight of her
misfortune. LeFoy's stupid Hunt; Voss kidnapping her;
Deathrider being captured by Ortiz before she could get anywhere near him; getting lost in the desert; and now getting
lumped with a dying Apache! Curse her dumb conscience. It
was sheer madness to drag a dying warrior with her.

She'd thought *she* was pretty wrecked when she found
him, but he put her to shame. He'd seemed lively enough
when she found him, but that faded mighty fast once they
were traveling. He was near delirious from thirst and hunger, and when he wasn't being an irksome lawyer, he was
prone to dizziness. A few times he almost slid right off the
horse. Ava rapped him sharply on the back of the head.

"Apache!" she snapped. "If you fall off, you'll break a
leg. And I'll be damned if I'm nursing you out here."

"I have a name," he mumbled. He was barely conscious
by then.

"I don't care," she reminded him. She tried to hide her
concern behind a sharp tongue. She didn't like the look of
the way he held his head; it was heavy on his neck, his chin
bouncing along on his chest. Riding behind him, she had a

good view of his bruises, and she wouldn't have been sur-prised if he was sporting a broken rib or two. His skin was peeling from severe sunburn as well; the burns were bad enough that he was suffering from chills, bone-shuddering shivers that made his teeth clack together. Although maybe that was caused by severe dehydration.

And that was just the fresh stuff. He had some terrify-ingly serious old scars too; nets of silver cobwebbed his back, and there were slashes that were still recent enough to be angry red, not to mention the chips out of his flesh, which she assumed were old bullet holes.

"You sure you're not a ghost?" she asked as she grabbed hold of him the next time he keeled sideways. "'Cause you look like you've been killed at least a dozen times over." She struggled to keep him upright. In the end she had to wrap both arms hard around him and grip his legs with her thighs to keep him steady. He moaned in pain as she squeezed his sore spots.

"Don't you go getting any ideas," she told him snap-pishly, but she couldn't quite keep the worry from her voice. "This isn't any kind of come-on. This is just pure Christian charity."

She spread her hands flat against his chest to hold him back against her. She could feel the heat of his skin. He was sure running some soaring fever. She could feel his heart skipping and skidding under her palm; it worried her greatly. She hadn't asked to be saddled with him, but she sure didn't want him dying right in front of her. Essentially *on* her.

"Apache!" she snapped. "Sit up and stop carrying on. We're not far from Mexico. I didn't take you on just to have to dig your grave."

"I'm fine," he slurred.

"Good. Because I don't even have a shovel. And I'm not digging a grave with my bare hands."

"Can't die," he whispered.

"No, that's right. You can't. I won't allow you to."

"Can't die until I find her."

"Her? Her who?"

But he'd lapsed into a half-world by then, too fevered to make much sense or hear her when she spoke. He muttered in his own language, sounding like he was arguing with someone.

"Hush," she said. She gave him a pat right over his heart. "Settle down now."

She managed to keep hold of him as they plodded on through the blazing afternoon, but it wasn't easy. Her arms and back were killing her. He was just so *heavy.* She couldn't have picked up a skinny Apache? She had to find one who was the size of a small mountain? She cursed herself. She was too soft. She should have left him there. It was utter madness expending so much energy over a man who was clearly dying.

"Cleopatra?" he rasped as the cactus shadows grew long on the ground and the light blazed orange around them. The sky was a lurid splash of red and gold, all swirled violently together.

"Yes, Apache?"

He drew a shuddery breath that was too close to a death rattle for her liking.

"Thank you."

Jesus wept. What was a girl supposed to say to that?

"You're welcome. Now shut up and stop dying."

❧ 13 ❧

SHE THOUGHT SHE was hallucinating at first. It was deep in the night, and she had only skipped in and out of sleep for the past few days. The more tired she got, the thinner reality seemed. Her arms were locked around the Apache, who had long ago fallen silent—she would have thought he was dead if she hadn't still been able to feel his heartbeat under her palm. The night grew dense around them, heightening the sense of intimacy. *Her* sense of intimacy; he wasn't feeling anything except pain. It began to feel like they had always been together, here on this horse, in the middle of nowhere. It was just them and the darkness and the uncompromising fury of her thirst. Now and then she pressed her forehead into his hot back and let her eyelids droop. It didn't seem unusual anymore to be pressed up hard against his naked skin. In fact, it was strangely comforting.

She dreamed about water as she rode. Waterfalls and fountains and cascades of rain, puddles and ponds and splashing spigots. At one point she imagined she was working the handle of a pump—up and down, up and down, up and down—but nothing came out. She felt like crying from the sheer frustration of it, but she couldn't. She had no moisture left in her to make tears.

So when she *smelled* water, she thought she must be dreaming. But no, she was awake, still rocking along on the horse, with a naked Apache in her arms. She'd never really thought about the smell of water before, but now the heavy perfume saturated the air around her, filling her with hope. It was a luscious, cool, fresh smell that made the hair stand up on the back of her neck.

"Apache!" She gave him a few sharp slaps on the chest. "Wake up!"

He mumbled but didn't wake.

How was she going to find the water in the dark? It was here somewhere; she *knew* it was. The fragrance was overwhelming. It made her think of grass and leaves and rain.

She pulled Freckles to a halt. The Apache moaned.

"Hush up," she told him. "I'm listening for water." She cocked her head. If there *was* water, it sure wasn't anything big like a river; there was no rushing or gurgling to be heard. But then faintly, a musical kind of slapping noise. *Babble.* Isn't that what they said? *A babbling brook . . .* Only they didn't have brooks in the west. Brooks belonged back home, in the green woods. But that was definitely a babble. Very soft.

"Freckles, find the water," she ordered.

The horse whickered.

"If you've got any brains at all, horse, you'll find that water," she said sternly, "because I don't reckon our friend here can make it much longer."

The scent of the brook, or whatever it was, enveloped her as she urged Freckles on. The babbling grew louder. It was joined by *sloshing* and *lapping.* There was definitely running water ahead. Freckles whickered again, her ears flicking, and she picked up the pace.

"That's right, girl. *Water.* I'll let you drink as much as you want, so long as you leave some for me."

It was either a very small river or a substantial creek. Freckles broke into a trot and went surging into the narrow waterway. Ava felt the spray fly over her boots, wetting her ankles. Freckles stopped dead in the middle of the water and lowered her head. Ava could hear her drinking noisily.

"Hey," she protested, "back up. How am I supposed to get him down in the middle of the creek? If I drop him, he'll drown." She kicked Freckles, but the thirsty horse was having none of it. It didn't matter how much she kicked or sawed at the reins or cursed a blue streak; the horse refused to move until she'd drunk her fill. Which took roughly *forever*.

Eventually, the animal lifted her head and shook it, sending horse spit and drops of water flinging back into Ava's face. Then the horse gave a healthy-sounding neigh and plodded out of the creek.

"That was incredibly selfish," Ava told her. The horse gave an unladylike snort.

Ava tried to work out how to get down without sending the Apache spilling off. She tried to push him forward so he was draped over Freckles' neck.

"Apache! Hold on to the horse." She took his arms and tried to wrap them around the horse's neck, but he was as limp as hell. There was no way he was gripping anything. He was barely holding on to life. Damn it.

She kept her hand pressed into his back as she swung her leg over the saddle. Even that almost unseated him. She tried to keep him dangling on Freckles' neck as she slid down, but no luck. He went sliding with her, and next thing she knew, she'd slammed into the hard ground, with him landing on top of her with a meaty *thud*.

God, he was heavy. He probably weighed more than the horse did.

The stupid horse that didn't give a toss that she was being squashed to death by an Apache. Now that she was free of riders, Freckles took a couple of steps and then lay down. She gave a horsey sigh and went straight to sleep, not even caring that she was lying on the saddle.

The Apache groaned right in Ava's ear. She clenched her teeth and shoved him off her; it took all her strength. He went rolling off her and straight down the slope toward the creek. Ava yelped and scrambled to arrest his descent before he drowned. It wasn't a deep creek, but you could drown in a puddle if you were as incapacitated as he was. She threw her body across him to pin him still.

Her breathing was labored, like she'd been sprinting. Bright spots swirled in front of her, and the world tilted. She was in terrible shape. Not quite as bad as him, but she was only a shade away from passing out.

Water. That was what she needed.

Vaguely, she realized the night was fading. She could just make out the shapes of the bushes and the banks of the creek in the gloom. She could also make out the swirling surface of the slick, dark creek.

"You wait here," she told the unconscious Apache. "I'm just going to buy a drink from the saloon. I'll bring you one back." She crawled to the creek. And, oh my, the water might have been muddy as hell, but it sure tasted good. She crammed cupped handfuls into her mouth. It wasn't quick enough, so she stretched out on her belly and drank like a horse, submerging her face to take big gulps.

When she was done, her belly felt stretched and painfully full. Was it possible to get drunk on water? Because she felt positively giddy. The perfume of the creek was utterly intoxicating, and the coldness of the water slid down into her like a starburst. The sweetness on her tongue was beyond pleasure. How had she ever taken water for granted? It was miraculous.

She crawled over to Freckles and unbuckled the nearest saddlebag. The horse lifted her head, snorted and then went back to sleep. Ava ignored her and took out a tin mug. She filled it up for the Apache and shuffled back to him on her knees, careful not to spill so much as a drop.

He wasn't alert enough to drink, so she tore a strip off

the petticoat he'd tied around himself and dipped the strip into the mug. Then she lifted his head and squeezed the sodden strip of cloth against his lips. The night had become a sage gray predawn half-light, and she could just make out his eyebrows pulling together. His eyes were still swollen and crusted closed. He made a soft, helpless noise and opened his mouth. She squeezed water onto his lips and managed to get some into him. She jumped when his hand reached up and grabbed her wrist, bringing the cloth hard against his mouth.

"No need to be grabby," she said. "If you're awake, you might as well drink from the mug." She helped prop him up and held the mug to his lips. He gulped the water down gratefully.

"More," he growled.

"More, *please*," she suggested sniffily as she went to refill the mug. He grabbed hold of her wrist again as she held the mug to his mouth.

"Thank you," he whispered when he was done. He sure had some pretty manners. They jarred with his lawyerliness.

By then day was threatening to break; an iridescent green sheen was glossing the thin dark line of the horizon.

"I think we should probably stay here through the heat today," she said. Even though she was worried about Kennedy Voss finding her, she was thoroughly played out and couldn't find an ounce of energy left in her to face another day of riding in the blazing heat. Besides, she couldn't bring herself to leave the water. Not yet. She was going to drink until she leaked. The Apache didn't look capable of getting back on the horse anyway. Hell. Forget the Apache. The *horse* didn't look capable of anything but sleeping.

"Seems wise," the Apache rasped. She didn't like the look of him. He was like wax.

Please don't let him die. She didn't want to be stuck out here with a dead man.

"No *seems* about it." As the first pale spill of sunrise pearled the green horizon gold, she took in the creek and the scraggly bushes that grew in clumps. "I'm going to drag you under one of those bushes," she told him. "It's probably going to hurt like hell, because you're one big bruise. But it's best if we keep you out of the sun today. You're already burned to a crisp."

He didn't respond, which she took as an assent. She untied her blanket, which was rolled up and strapped behind her saddle, and made them a nest under a bush. Then she got her gown out of her saddlebags (she figured she wasn't going to need it anytime soon) and hung it over the bush to give them extra shade.

"I'm going to haul you toward a bush that's uphill on the right," she told him as she returned.

He was as still as death. She put her hand over his heart. Still alive. But maybe only barely.

"You ready?" she asked sharply.

"Yes," he said, his voice slow and thick.

She grabbed the Apache under his armpits and started to drag. She saw his swollen face twist in pain, but he didn't protest. God, he weighed a *ton*. She put her back into it. It was like carrying an anvil up a hill. He made a deep groove in the sandy soil. And then, just when she thought she might break her back, she got him there.

"Can you move at all?" she asked. "Get yourself comfortable. It's shady."

He curled himself into a miserable ball under the bush, his back to her. Now that it was light, she could see his bruises had darkened even further, into enormous black and purple splotches. And his sunburn was blistering something awful. He'd really been through the wringer.

"I'm just going to fill the canteens, and then I'll be back," she told him.

She crawled out of the bush to find that Freckles had

finished her nap and was once again face-first in the water, drinking like she was a camel and needed to fill her hump.

"Here," Ava said tiredly, "let me get that saddle off you."

Freckles didn't stop drinking as Ava uncinched the saddlebags and then the saddle. She left the reins on and roped the horse loosely to a nearby bush, giving her enough lead to move between the creek and her sleeping spot. Then she filled the canteens.

By the time she was done with the chores, the sun was blazing, casting fat shadows over the parched earth. She didn't care about Kennedy Voss, the rest of the horrid Hunters, murderous raiding Apaches or even getting bit by scorpions (which she'd always been afraid of). She just wanted to sleep.

She crawled under the shade offered by her gown and the scrappy bush, and joined the Apache on the blanket. It was already hot under there, made worse by the baking heat radiating off his fevered body. Ava flopped down beside him, feeling like pitching a fit. She just wanted to *sleep*. But here he was all *sick*. Damn having a conscience. Why couldn't she be a heartless monster like Kennedy Voss?

Feeling like she was made of lead, she ripped another strip off the petticoat and soaked it; then she rolled it up and rested it against the back of the Apache's neck. He moaned.

"Feels good, huh?" She leaned over him. Oh Lord, his face. It was a total mess. She took the damp cloth off his neck and set to work cleaning him up. Gently, she wiped his eyes clear of the crusty buildup. They were still swollen shut, but they didn't look as bad as they had the day before. "You sure must put people off," she observed as she ran the damp cloth over his sunburn, "if you make them want to beat you up this bad and rub nettles in your eyes." He shivered at the feel of the moist cloth. "I put people off too." She sighed and refreshed the cloth with fresh water, before placing it on his neck again. "I always have. My mother finds me too brassy, and my father . . . well, the less said about that, the better." She pulled a face.

The Apache took up most of the space under the bush, even when he was curled into a ball. He was a tall one, all right. She was tall herself, but he made her feel downright dainty next to his length. Ava struggled to find a comfortable position next to him. The only way she could find that didn't involve a great big branch in her side, or a face full of twigs, was pressed close to the Apache's hot, sweaty back. Her nose was just about squashed against those great knots of muscle.

"You really need a bath," she told him. Then a thought occurred to her, and she dipped her head to smell under her arms. She wrinkled her nose. "Or it might be me."

He stirred.

"I'll bathe tomorrow," she assured him. As she closed her eyes, she heard the jangle of the horse's bit, the soothing sound of running water and the steady tide of the Apache's breath.

❖ 14 ❖

Ava slept most of the day. A few times she half-surfaced, but the somnolent warmth of the sun on the makeshift canopy over the branches and the rhythm of the Apache's breathing lulled her back to sleep. She was too exhausted to struggle; she just sank down into slow-moving dreams. She dreamed she was walking around the edge of a vast freshwater lake, climbing slick gray rocks, wading through carpets of emerald grass but never quite able to reach the shore—or the water. Eventually she sat on a hill, looking down at the wind riffling the surface of the vast lake. Gazing at it, she felt a welling sense of peace. A warm summer rain began to fall, and all she had to do to slake her thirst was tilt her head skyward and open her mouth.

When she finally woke, the world seemed sharper edged, brighter, zinging with color. She hadn't realized how much exhaustion had dulled her senses. And her mood . . .

Now she felt positively buoyant with hope. *Of course* she'd get out of this situation. She'd survived worse than this. With full canteens, they'd get to Mexico easily.

Canteens. The thought made her reach for one. She took a deep draft. Then another. Then another. Until she'd completely drained it. It tasted like a crisp winter morning.

God. How had she never realized that water was so *wonderful*?

Now that her thirst was slaked, and her exhaustion extinguished, she felt near indestructible. She *was* still hungry though. She could probably stomach that salty jerky in her saddlebags now. Especially if she soaked it in the creek to soften it up first.

In the late-afternoon light, the creek bed looked positively pretty. Buttery shafts of light slanted across the water and gilded the olive green leaves of the scrappy bushes. In the daylight, Ava could see that the water itself was the color of red mud; it was like a slow-moving mudslide. But even that looked almost pretty in the brassy light.

Hell, even Freckles looked better. The horse had lost her depressed air and was standing midstream, letting the creek wash around her legs. Her ears were swiveling merrily, and she was bright eyed and perky looking. She'd also worked her rope free from the bush Ava had tied her to. *Best remedy that quick smart.*

When she saw Ava, the horse gave a zesty whicker. Ava only just managed to get hold of the rope before the frolicsome animal pranced away.

"No, you don't. I got no plans to walk to Mexico." Ava tied the rope more securely this time, around the trunk of a thin-leafed tree. She double-checked her knots. Freckles gave a philosophical whicker and then headed straight back into the stream. Ava made sure she had enough rope to move about. She wasn't going to deprive Freckles of a paddle in the cool water after everything they'd been through.

"That looks like a good idea," Ava observed as she watched the horse enjoy the water. "Let me just get the Apache a drink, and then I'll join you. It's a perfect day for a swim." She found herself whistling as she filled the mug and headed back to rouse the Apache. They weren't out of the woods by any means, but she sure felt they *would* be. Eventually.

Only the Apache couldn't be roused in order to drink. He was shiny and red and searing hot to the touch.

"You men sure know how to milk an illness," she scolded, giving him a shake. He didn't even moan. He was as listless as hell again. It gave Ava an awfully bad feeling.

"Freckles," Ava said frantically as she crawled back out of the bushes, "what do I do? He looks terrible." Goddamn it! She *knew* she should have left him to fend for himself. Now she was *responsible*. And she hated being responsible for people. She'd spent her entire life *avoiding* being responsible for people.

"What do I *do*?" she wailed again.

Freckles huffed but didn't move from the water.

"I should cool him down, shouldn't I?"

According to her nanny, fevers could cook your brain. *I knew a girl once who got so fevered that steam came out of her ears; she was never the same again after that,* Nanny said every time Ava had so much as sniffled. A sneeze led to confinement in bed when Ava was growing up, as did headaches, nosebleeds, coughs, shivers and pretty much everything else.

It probably wasn't true about the steam coming out of the girl's ears; her nanny had been prone to exaggerating. And she was a hypochondriac to boot. According to Nanny, everything could kill you or maim you or cause irreparable harm to your system.

But she *might* have been right about fevers. How was Ava to know? She wasn't a doctor.

So maybe she *should* cool him down to prevent him from steaming and cooking. . . . But how in the hell was she going to do that? It had to be more than one hundred degrees today.

Ava looked down at the mug of water. It was a start. She mopped at his face with the damp cloth. And even poured some water on his head. It didn't blunt his fever in the least. And the mug was so pitifully small that she could barely bathe his face with the contents of it, and he needed cooling down quicker than she could carry water back and forth. What she needed was a bucket. Or a bathtub.

He needed submerging. . . .

"You owe me," she told the Apache grimly as she grabbed him under the arms and started hauling him to the stream. "You owe me for the ride; you owe me for the clothing, even if it was just a petticoat; you owe me for the water; and now you owe me for saving your brains from steaming." She took a moment's rest and gulped in deep breaths. Lord, he was *heavy*. It was like dragging a dead horse. Or a buffalo. "You also owe me for dragging your heavy ass all over the desert. Between last night and today, I think I've hurt my back." Not just her back. Her *everything*. He was a dead weight. "You had better not be actually dead," she huffed, dragging him over the bumpy banks toward the ruddy waters. "I didn't put in all this effort for you to die now. You have to live forever, just to show some damn appreciation." Once they were close to the water, she paused to gather her strength. The next bit was going to *hurt*. The banks didn't look steep until you had to negotiate them carrying an Apache who weighed roughly the same as a bull buffalo.

She didn't bother stripping the petticoat from his hips; she figured wetting it would keep him cool later. She hopped on one foot as she struggled to get one of her boots off, and then the other. The rest of her could take a dousing, but these boots were too important to her survival to risk them. Once she had her boots off, she resumed pulling the buffalo of an Apache down the banks.

"I have no idea how I'm going to get you back up again," Ava admitted. The stream was shallow and flowing fast; it had clearly been higher and was receding, because half the streambed was just a glug of mud. She fell headlong into it as the Apache tumbled down the ragged edge of the bank and onto the muddy flat below, bowling her over in the process.

The river mud squelched between her fingers and up her nose, a thick red clay that tasted weirdly chalky. The only positive thing about the whole situation was how cool the mud felt against her skin. She'd been sweating something fierce, and now she was in a chilled cocoon. She struggled upright, groaning at the sight of her only clothes. She looked like she'd been carved of mud. "Now I'll have to wash them."

Freckles whickered. Ava threw a spatter of mud at her. "Don't you go laughing, or I'll make you do it."

The horse didn't look remorseful in the slightest.

"This is your fault, Apache." Ava slopped on her knees back to the Apache, who had barely registered their fall. His swollen face was covered in great whacks of red mud, and his body was slick with it.

"Mud: another thing I can add to the tally of misery you've brought me."

He was struggling to lift his head. Ava slid her hand under the nape of his neck to support him; her touch was gentle. "Hush, Apache. Don't struggle. We're just going to take a dip in the water to get your fever down."

His lips opened, but he couldn't seem to speak. Ava stroked his head until he calmed. He was as hot as a furnace. Jesus wept. She hoped he didn't have some nasty disease. Because by now she probably had it too.

Not much she could do about it now, she supposed.

"My nanny might have been right," she muttered as she considered how to get him safely into the water without drowning them both. "And not just about brain steaming. She said I'd meet a bad end, and I just might have met it. But who knew a bad end would be so *heavy*?"

At least the mud was slippery, so she could drag him more easily. She managed to launch him into the shallow, rapid-running water and sit herself in the thick mud. She kept him between her legs, with his head on her collarbone and her arms clasped tight around his chest so the water couldn't tug him away. She had to dig her heels in deep, but the mud was accommodating and wrapped itself around her, anchoring her. She half-wondered if she'd be able to drag herself out of it again, it held on to her so tightly.

After a few moments, she'd caught her breath, and when she realized he wasn't about to be yanked out of her arms and drowned, she managed to relax a little. He was completely limp. Freckles ambled over to them, stretching out her rope to its full capacity, and snorted.

"Don't be ridiculous," Ava told her. It was comforting to talk to the animal like she was a person. Ava felt in need of comfort. She usually had ironclad nerves, but these past few weeks had done her in. "He's not going to die," she told the horse firmly.

Somehow over the past blurry hours, it had become vitally important that the Apache survive. Maybe it was because his death would be a dark omen for her own future.

She'd only just regained her spirits, and she didn't want them sinking again. Despair was a precursor to death, and she'd be damned if she was going to die such a small and miserable death. If she had to die, she'd rather go out in a blaze of glory.

"Look at all his scars," she instructed the horse, craning her neck to take another look at the Apache's old battle scars. "He's survived worse than a fever. This man looks like he's survived several *wars*. Nothing as petty as a fever will kill him. I'm certain of it." She hugged the Apache tighter as the creek pulled at him.

Freckles whickered and lowered her head to nudge Ava's arm.

"I know," Ava sighed. "I did say he could be a rapist and a murderer. And maybe he is. But maybe he's also *not*. I mean, look at me. I'm not what I seem."

The horse snorted.

"Fine. I am what I seem. But only until you get to know me *well*. I'm not all thorns. My mother always said I had a tender heart." She paused. "Actually, that wasn't my mother. That was the nanny. Mother said I was determined to do things the hard way." She shrugged. "But Nanny liked me well enough. The first one anyway. The second one said I was demon hell spawn and took away my spider collection. And let's not even talk about the *third* nanny, who took up with my father and just about ruined Mother's life."

Why was she thinking about her mother again? She hadn't seen her or thought of her in years. She wrote the obligatory letter home now and then but never left a forwarding address to receive return mail, so she hadn't heard back. For all she knew, Mother was dead by now.

Except she wasn't. Ava knew for a fact she wasn't. Her mother wouldn't die until she saw Ava again so she could scold her daughter until her ears bled. *You ruined everything.* That was the old refrain. And if her mother ever *did* die, she'd probably come back from the dead to haunt Ava, because she'd have no intention of resting until Ava was locked into some loveless match with a man just like her father. Yvonne had spent her life as a rich man's mistress, and she thought her daughter should do the same. And it didn't matter how many arguments they had; she was unshakable in her belief.

"It's a good life," her mother had told her a million times, usually as she soaked her hands in lemon water to keep them soft and white, or rouged her cheeks to keep them looking bright and young, or put cucumbers on her puffy eyes to get rid of the signs of tears after Ava's father had neglected her yet again for a younger woman.

Good life, my ass, Ava thought sourly, bracing against the tide of water rushing over her as she held tight to the Apache. It was a terrible way to live, surrendering all your power to a man who could toss you aside at any moment. Sure, she got an income—but only as long as she *pleased* him. And who wanted to please a man all the time? Sometimes you just wanted to tell them to go to hell.

At least a wife had some law on her side—not much, admittedly, but *some*, certainly more than a mistress had. A mistress couldn't even be publicly acknowledged; she was kept in the shadows, in the margins, on the edges of a respectable life. It was like a whole secret society, one that Ava had grown up in. Her father and his friends had their wives and public lives, but they also had their mistresses and private fun. There were separate dinners and dances and whole social calendars for the kept women of men as wealthy as Ava's father. As a kid, Ava had taken it all in her stride. Her father came in and out of her life, in a perfumed cloud of cigar smoke and brandy. Usually he came at night, and she associated him with lamplight and the hastily eaten chocolates that he slipped her when the nanny wasn't watching. He and Mother existed in a golden bubble of their own, all flickering candlelight and hushed voices, giggles and whispers. When Ava was very young, she'd spy on them, feeling a warmth deep inside at the sight of them together. At their happiness. At the way they curled around each other, at the way her mother's eyes shone when she looked at him, at the way Mother could always make Father smile. When her parents were together, Ava felt safe and happy and *whole*.

But then, when she was twelve, she had learned that her father wasn't hers. Not to keep. He flitted in and out like a moth, arriving once the candles were lit, disappearing into the shadows once day broke. And it turned out that not all fathers were like hers. Most fathers *stayed*. That became clearer to her as she aged. And the reason *her* father never stayed was because he *wasn't* hers, not really. He didn't belong to her or to her mother. Because, Ava learned (thanks to a spiteful school friend), her father had another family. His *real* family.

It was like a curtain being ripped aside, revealing the machinations of backstage behind the players. Her life was a total lie. Mother wasn't Father's wife. Father had a *real wife*. A woman who might not have even known Mother existed, but if she did, she didn't care, so long as Mother kept discreetly to the edges of Father's life.

Father had a wife who lived with him, who had him every single day, not just here and there, after dark, on random days that broke like Christmas, full of cheer. Father's wife was an everyday woman: a wife who went with him to balls and operas and luncheons, who bore his heirs, who was more than mere adornment. Father's wife was central to his life while Ava's mother was a decoration.

But it wasn't the wife who bothered Ava. Well, she did. But not as much as the children did. The *daughters*. The half sisters she'd never met. The tall, beautifully dressed willowy blondes who were so similar to Ava and yet so different. Those girls and Ava shared a father, but not a history; they shared a resemblance, but not a name; they shared an inheritance of secrecy, but not the implications of it. Arthur Addison's daughters were *all* tall; they were *all* striking, Ava included; but while the Addison heirs were blondes in shades from strawberry to moonlight, Ava's hair was an indecent red; where their figures were elegant and slender, she was overly tall and rude with health; where their manners were sweet and their smiles coy, her charm bordered on boldness. Certainly according to Nanny Number Two. And Ava's mother.

Her father's daughters were girls slightly older and slightly younger than Ava; they led lives parallel to hers, separated from her by a yawning chasm. They didn't even know she existed. While she went to a modest school and walked home to a silent social calendar, her father's daughters had dancing lessons and painting lessons, piano lessons and singing lessons. They debuted to glittering seasons, belles of every ball. While Ava spent the summer sweltering in the city, her father's daughters spent their summers by the sea and, later, taking tours of the Continent and even being introduced to the Queen of England. While Ava's mother introduced her to older men who were hunting for fresh young mistresses, her father's daughters had spectacular society weddings to powerful men. Her father walked publicly with them, beaming his pride, while Ava was closeted at home with her clingy mother. Those girls made her feel like she was nothing but cheap costume jewelry while they were diamonds and pearls.

Not a single one of them would ever be sitting here in the mud, struggling to keep a rapist-lawyer-Apache alive. They were all living in luxury, spitting out heirs to the fortune.

Well, screw them. And screw their luxury. Screw their blondness, their white skin, their easy smiles. She had something better than fancy jewelry and boxes at the opera and thin-nosed, uptight husbands. She had *freedom*.

It was just a shame it was so full of mud.

❖ 15 ❖

THE RIVER DIDN'T do much to assuage the Apache's fever. It just made them both wet and filthy. Ava tried to nurse him as best she could, but after a full day and night she had to admit defeat. She couldn't rouse him from his delirium, and no amount of cooling water reduced his fever. Touching him was like touching a brick oven in full burn.

"Right, Freckles, there's no point in sitting around and waiting for him to die," Ava announced. "We're going to have to get moving. The last thing we want is for Kennedy Voss to find us. And we're nearly out of food. If you can call jerky food." She looked around at the scrappy trees and bushes. "I guess we'll need to find a way to move him . . ."

A travois was the logical solution, the kind she'd seen Indian tribes use. She looked down at her bare hands and sighed. Why did everything always have to be so *hard*? She wished she had her packhorse. Her ax and all her useful tools were on it. Without them, fashioning a travois was damn hard work. Sweating through the heat of the day, she wrestled with fallen branches, which she gathered from where they'd tangled at the bend in the creek. She used a sharp-edged rock to hack at the dry limbs, getting a hand full of splinters in the process. She did her best, but her best wasn't terribly good. The two main poles of the travois were different shapes and sizes, and the hammock was just a complete mess, a badly worked combination of her gown and what rope she had. He'd be lucky if he didn't drag his ass on the ground the whole way.

She'd been forced to sacrifice more clothing in order to create makeshift ropes to bind the thing together, once she'd run out of actual rope, and she figured at this rate they'd both be naked soon. Why she was so doggone set on saving the Apache was beyond her now; her sheer stubbornness had kicked in, and her entire focus was on getting him out of here. She wasn't losing him to death, and she wasn't leaving him behind, and that was that.

By the time she was done with her toil, the Apache was slung across a badly made and clearly fragile contraption that only vaguely resembled a travois. If you squinted. Somehow she managed to harness the thing to Freckles, despite the horse's disgust. Now she just had to hope it would hold together once they started dragging it.

"I'll walk," Ava told the horse. "That way I can keep him from falling off."

It was a wretched way to travel, on foot, trying to lead the horse and watch the Apache all at once. And it was made worse by the heat of the day. They couldn't travel through the cool of the night because it would be impossible to navigate the rough terrain with the travois. This way they could see, but the sun was cooking them alive.

Ava had soaked the blanket in the creek and draped it over the Apache before they set off, hoping the moisture would keep him cool as it evaporated.

"I wouldn't be adverse to a reward if we get out of this mess," she told him as she struggled to keep on through the worst of the day. She kept looking over her shoulder to check he was still safe. "I'm hoping you Apache lawyers are the wealthy kind?"

Freckles whickered.

"She's right. You should probably factor in a reward for her too. After all, she's doing all of the work."

Freckles whickered again, and Ava noticed that she was looking skittish. Her ears had pricked right up, and her eyes were rolling. There was danger about.

"What now?" Ava's heart rate spiked. She couldn't take much more.

Freckles let out an alarmed neigh, and that was when Ava heard the barking. A high, staccato barking, getting closer. Freckles reared up, and Ava fought to hang on to her. "Don't do that," she scolded. "You'll knock the Apache off!"

Freckles didn't care. She was spooked by the sound of the dog. Or coyote. Or whatever it was. Did coyotes bark? Probably not. It was definitely a dog.

Oh hell, maybe it belonged to one of the Hunters?

A gray and black blur came exploding out of the chaparral. Jesus wept, it was a *wolf*!

Freckles reared and Ava screamed. The damn thing was launching itself at the Apache! It was going to kill him!

"Get off him, you horrid thing!" Ava wasn't in her right mind. Obviously. Because no *sane* person would get between a wolf-dog and its prey. But she was damned if she was going to let the Apache get mauled, not when she'd worked so hard to keep him alive.

It was only once she'd reached the travois (which was no mean feat, the way Freckles was jumping about) that she realized the wolf-dog wasn't trying to kill the Apache at all. It was . . . *kissing* him? The animal was whining and shivering and licking the Apache's face in a fit of pure joy. It kept nuzzling him and letting out the most pitiful noises. Now that she was up close, she could see that it was an Indian dog and not a wolf at all.

The Apache stirred and spoke for the first time in more than a day. "Dog?" His voice was cracking and parched.

The dog nuzzled into his hand, and the Apache gave him a limp pat. "Dog! Good boy." Then he said something in a language Ava didn't recognize.

It was his dog. . . . Didn't that beat all.

The Apache struggled to sit up and wrap his arms around the animal.

So he was feeling better, then. . . . Well, he had better give credit where credit was due, and not go thinking the miraculous return of his dog had made him recover. *She* was the one who'd dragged him for miles, and nursed him through the fever, and fed him drops of water and walked hellish miles in the hot sun to save him. This dog hadn't done anything but *lick* him.

"Freckles," Ava said sharply, stepping closer to the skittish horse and putting a solid hand on her side. "Stop that. It's not a wolf. It's his *dog*." It took her forever to settle the horse. "He's not trying to bite you. Look: he's too busy having a cuddle. He's just a big, cuddly puppy." Albeit one that looked like it could tear your throat clear out.

The Apache had said that someone had stolen his dog. She couldn't remember who now, whether it had been Pete Hamble or the army, or another Apache tribe, or his friend. . . . Not that it mattered. Someone had stolen his dog—and now here it was.

She groaned, as a thought struck her. *Another mouth to feed.* "We'd best be getting to some kind of settlement, quick smart, before we run out of food and water."

There was another problem too. The dog wouldn't let her get close to the Apache. The stupid man had overexerted himself and gone limp again. Ava needed to see to him, but the dog growled if she so much as took a step toward him.

"Look, dog, I get that you're worried about him," Ava said, when she found herself in a face-off with the animal. "I'm worried about him too. But who do you think made the travois? Who do you think is trying to drag him to safety? I could have left him, you know. I *should* have. But I didn't. So how about you quit pointing those scary fangs at me and let me *keep* helping him?"

The dog was crouched between Ava and the Apache, teeth bared, growling low in its chest, its eyes an eerie shade of yellow.

"Dog," the Apache rasped, and his hand managed to lift an inch so his fingers could curl through the dog's hair. The dog glanced back, confused, gave a short whine and then resumed growling at Ava. The Apache spoke in that language again, the one Ava couldn't place. It sounded vaguely familiar, even though she didn't understand a word of it.

The dog understood though. It clearly didn't like what he was saying, but it understood. It gave Ava one last threatening growl, its black lips drawing back from some truly terrifying teeth, and then it turned and plonked itself on the Apache's feet. It rested its head on its paws, its yellow eyes fixed warningly on Ava.

"I'm sorry about Dog," the Apache rasped. "He's protective."

"You two seem temperamentally suited," she observed.

"I'll take that as a compliment, Cleopatra." He was definitely feeling better, even if he was as limp as a wet sheet.

"Can you make sure the dog doesn't eat me if I come check on you?" she asked.

"He won't eat you."

Ava wasn't entirely sure about that. The dog lifted his head and watched every move she made. She felt like it could all go horribly wrong at any moment, and clearly so did Freckles, as she was prancing from foot to foot like a nervy Thoroughbred.

"I knew I should have left you in the desert," she told the Apache as she inched closer to him and the wolf-dog.

"You would never have left me," the Apache said in that dry, scratchy voice that had her worried.

"Sure I would." Ava kept a close eye on the dog as she

reached out to touch the Apache's forehead. He was clammy and cold. His fever had broken. She saw goose bumps break out on his arms when she touched him.

"No, you wouldn't," he disagreed. "You're too soft-hearted to leave a man to die."

"I'm just going to take this wet blanket off you, all right?" She eased it off. The dog gave a sharp bark, but the Apache lifted a hand, and he stilled. "And I'm about as softhearted as a viper. Don't you go thinking otherwise. I'd just as soon shoot you as look at you."

"If you say so."

"I do." She folded the blanket. "Now, we should get going again. I assume your animal is coming with us?"

The dog barked again, answering for himself.

"Fine. But tell him he can get off that travois and walk on his own four legs. My horse is tired enough as it is."

They reached the one-horse town two days later. By then they were running low on water again, and Ava was feeling that whispery panic: *water-water-water.* At first a pale bluish blur on the far horizon, the town emerged like an answered prayer. She watched it suspiciously for a while before telling the Apache about it.

"It might be a mirage," he warned. "Is it shimmering?"

"Everything is shimmering," she snapped, not appreciating his negativity. She needed the town to be real. She was at the end of her rope, and she wasn't sure she could keep going. "It's *hot*. Everything shimmers in the heat."

"Don't get your hopes up," he counseled.

"I liked you better when you were fevered," she muttered under breath. What did he know anyway? He was *blind*. She was the one who could see it, and it was definitely a town. Although it didn't seem to get any closer, no matter how many steps she took . . .

They certainly seemed no closer by the time dusk fell, and she had a mood-plummeting moment as they staked camp, when she faced the reality of their dwindling water and hardtack. If it *was* a mirage, they were right back to where they had started, lost in the middle of nowhere with no supplies. She found herself overcome with tears as she tried to get a fire lit. Her throat swelled up, and her chest felt tight. She wasn't one to cry, but this seemed like as good a time as any.

Sometimes she just wished she wasn't so alone. It was so hard to keep going day after day, knowing that there was no one to lean on when things got hard. And they got hard so *often*. She rubbed the heels of her palms into her eyes. Damn it. She didn't want to be weak like her mother. She *wasn't* weak like her mother. She could do this. She'd done worse.

But wouldn't it be nice if someone else could make the fire tonight . . . if someone else could worry about finding food and water . . . if someone else could just shoulder some of the burden . . . even just for a few hours?

The hot tears tumbled as she piled up the dry horse dung she'd gathered the day before, trying to make a decent campfire. There was so little wood out here that manure made a better source of fuel. It was just one more way that Freckles had come to their rescue. As Ava indulged in a silent self-pitying cry, she got the fire lit, mostly for the sake of cheer, as they had nothing to cook and it was too hot to sit close to it. At least she could boil some of their last water and make a pot of weak tea, using the tea leaves she'd used at least a dozen times before.

"Cleopatra?" The Apache's tentative voice came out of the rising purple dusk. He was still stuck on the travois, too weak to move. The travois itself had half fallen apart the moment they'd stopped, and he was mostly sprawled on the ground. "It's not like you to be quiet. What's wrong?"

"Nothing." Ava swiped the tears from her face and poured the tea from the tin into their single mug. "Here, I made tea."

"Are you crying?"

"No." As if she'd tell him if she was. When she stood, she caught a flicker on the horizon. A tiny glow. She squinted. The flicker became a steady yellow light. It was joined by another. "It *is* a town! I can see light! It's the firelight through their windows!" Relief swept through her like a spring rain. She laughed and rubbed the tears from her face with more vigor. "Thank God! I thought we were going to die out here." She crouched next to him and offered him the tea. He tried to hold the mug, but she had to help him. The firelight edged his swollen face with amber light. He winced in pain as he lifted his head.

"We won't die," he told her calmly after he'd had a couple of sips. He pushed the mug toward her, encouraging her to drink the rest. "You're too stubborn to let that happen."

"I'm not stubborn." The tea tasted god-awful. Like river water. She wished there was coffee. She hadn't had coffee in so long. . . .

"I meant it as a compliment." He sounded drowsy. Before she'd even finished the river-water tea, he'd slipped back into sleep. Possibly unconsciousness. She leaned forward to check, resting a hand on his forehead. No fever. Not for the first time, she wondered what he looked like without the swelling. It was hard to even tell how old he was when he was all misshapen like this. She hoped for his sake the swelling went down and there was no permanent damage. Especially to his eyes . . . What would he do, if he were blind? He'd lose his warrior status.

Still . . . he could always fall back on being a lawyer.

She heard a rustling in the bushes and jumped a mile. Stupidly, she reached for her gun, even though she didn't have a single bullet left.

But it was only Dog. He came slinking out of the shadows, his yellow eyes gleaming. He had something in his mouth.

"I didn't even know you'd gone," she said nervously. She tried to stand her ground, as she remembered her father telling her that dogs could smell fear. That had been one of the few fatherly things he'd ever done. And he'd told her *that* only because he'd bought her mother a dog, and it had scared the life out of Ava. Her father had turned up at the town house with an enormous Afghan, a hugely tall dog that towered over little Ava. Father couldn't have bought Mother a Pomeranian or a bichon friese, could he? Something small and fluffy and cute? No. Her mother had wanted a regal dog, one she that she could promenade with. The Afghan hadn't been an affectionate animal; it had been aloof and stubborn and prone to growling at Ava. It had scared the wits out of her.

You need to show the animal who's boss, Father had told her. *Just like with a woman.* He'd winked at Ava's mother then, and the two of them had disappeared upstairs, trailing her mother's giggles, and leaving Ava alone with the imperious-looking dog. It didn't matter how little fear she showed; the dog knew very well who was boss—and it wasn't Ava.

She tried again with Dog, but Dog also knew who was boss—and, again, it wasn't Ava. He prowled into the campsite and dropped his mouthful next to the fire. Then he sat down and fixed her with an expectant look.

"What have you got there?" she asked, inching closer. It was a dead animal. A rabbit. Oh my, the blessed dog had brought them *dinner.* She lit up, even though it meant she'd have to skin the thing, which was one of her least favorite jobs in the world. "Good dog!" she exclaimed, taking a step forward. Dog leapt up at her movement, and she froze. He was enormous, and she was conscious that if he chose to her attack her, she would be helpless. But he merely wagged his tail and then dashed off again into the night.

She'd barely started skinning the rabbit when he came bounding back. He dropped a groundhog at her side, barked and ran off again. Before she'd managed to get the first animal ready for the cook fire, he'd made a nice little pile at her side, adding a quail and a couple of small birds.

"That's enough," she laughed, when he dropped another quail on the pile, his tail thumping madly. He looked ridiculously pleased with himself. "Enough! We'll never eat it all!" She cut off a hunk of the raw rabbit and tossed it to him. He barked and snapped it up. "Shame you can't pluck those birds for me." Plucking birds was almost worse than skinning rabbits. Almost.

As she sat working, Dog crept close beside her. He rested his head on his paws and watched the food, and she could have sworn his eyes gleamed with anticipation. Ava wasn't the best cook in the world, but even she could roast up some small game over a cook fire. She might have burned it, but it sure tasted good after so many days of hardtack. She gave Dog the groundhog and two of the birds, and he ate with glee.

"Father should have told me the way to a dog's heart was through its stomach," she said wryly as she passed him on the way to the travois. He seemed to grin at her.

She tried to rouse the Apache to eat. He managed a couple of mouthfuls and then pushed the food away, shaking his head. He was looking peaky again.

"Suit yourself," she said. She smoothed his hair off his poor face. "More for me, then."

So when morning came, and the town had gone back to being a bluish smudge on the horizon, and when she had a resurgent fear that it *was* just a mirage, she knew it wasn't hunger causing her to hallucinate. She'd eaten enough to feed a small army. Not just last night but also again this morning, when she and Dog had split the leftovers.

Could sore feet cause hallucinations? Because she'd never known feet could hurt this much. She was *desperate* to stop walking. It wasn't outside the bounds of possibility that she'd conjured up a town to get her out of walking any farther. Trust her to conjure one that looked so desolate. She couldn't have pictured one with a lake and a bunch of trees? Maybe whitewashed buildings and a nice, big, fancy hotel?

No, she fantasized about a skeleton of a town on the edge of nowhere. . . .

It made her feel better about herself when she realized that it *wasn't* a fantasy. It was an actual place, one that grew steadily clearer and more solid, the closer they came. It wasn't so much a town as a handful of bleached adobe buildings, but it looked like paradise after the past few days. As they came dragging in, a woman emerged from the central building, shading her eyes with her hand to get a good look at them. She was a big woman, with enormous round cheeks and a delicate rosebud mouth.

Ava was painfully aware of her bedraggled appearance and the fact that she was coated in dried mud. She straightened her waistcoat as they approached the woman, brushing a thick crust of mud from the edge. "Good morning," she said brightly.

"Where did you all drag in from?" the woman asked in Spanish as soon as they'd scraped to a halt in front of her.

"Hell," Ava replied, also in Spanish. "Hot, endless, deserty hell." She wasn't an elegant speaker of the language, but she could make do. She noticed a couple of men had crept out of adjoining buildings to get a look at the curious arrivals.

"What happened to your friend?" the woman asked.

"What *didn't* happen to him? He's been beaten and blinded and burned, and then he got sick with fever."

"If he's got fever, we don't want him."

Ava's stomach sank. She had been hoping to leave the Apache here. Because she had things to do. Namely, catching up with Ortiz before anything too final happened to the Plague of the West.

"His fever broke two days ago," Ava told the woman reassuringly. "He's definitely over the worst of it."

The woman gave the Apache a dubious look. It didn't help that he looked a complete mess.

Ava sighed. This was going to take some work. She wasn't likely to convince the woman immediately. She'd have to get the Apache fixed up first. Hopefully she could clean him up and have him looking decent by the tomorrow. . . . "Could we stay in your stable for a day or so? We need to get our strength back."

"He looks like he needs more than strength."

"He does," Ava agreed, cheerfully enough. "He looks a fright. But he's a scrappy one. Nothing's killed him yet. And, as I said, the fever broke a couple of days ago. He's over the worst of it and on the mend."

The woman nodded. "The barn is over there." And that was about all they heard from her. She wasn't a talker. Neither were the two men. Other than the three of them, the town seemed to consist of an old woman with no teeth, a milk cow, three goats and a bunch of dusty-looking chickens who'd gathered around the well, scratching in the dirt.

Before she did anything else, Ava went to the well to fill their canteens with fresh water. If there was one thing she'd learned in all of this, it was to always keep stocked with water. She took a drink while she was there, and also made the Apache take a mouthful, and led the animals to the trough at the base of the well. For the rest of her life, she imagined she'd take a drink whenever she had the opportunity. Because thirst was a raw hell she never wanted to experience again.

They entered the barn to find it was blessedly cool. Ava figured if she couldn't have a luxury hotel, this would do just fine. She gazed longingly at the hay. It would do in place of a feather bed, and she couldn't wait to avail herself of it. Once she'd taken care of the Apache and the animals anyway . . . Ugh. This was why she avoided responsibility like the plague. It was just endless *work*. She unhooked Freckles from the travois, which promptly fell to the ground in bits, as it did every night, bumping the Apache against the ground.

"I thought you fixed that thing," he said, as he said every time.

"I did. And I'll fix it again tomorrow," she said tartly. Then she caught herself. No, she wouldn't. Because she wasn't planning on ever fixing the travois again. She was going to leave the travois—and the Apache and his dog—well behind her when she rode out of this place. She had to catch up to Ortiz and Deathrider, and she couldn't afford to be wasting time here with a sick Apache. Although she was so far behind now, what were the chances Deathrider was still alive?

No. He *had* to be. She refused to believe anything else.

"You need someone who's not white to show you how to make a proper travois," the Apache said in his raspy way as he blindly tried to extricate himself from the jumbled branches that made up her rustic travois.

"You're making a lot of assumptions," she sniffed. "How do you even know that I'm white? You can't see me."

"Intuition," he said dryly. *"Cleopatra."* He was trying to stand but not having much luck.

She took his big hands in hers and hauled him to his feet. He was definitely well enough to leave behind. Look at him. Yesterday he wouldn't have been able to stand; today he was on his own two feet. Shaking like a baby foal but standing nevertheless. She helped him steady himself. "I'm going to lead you over to the hay. You can lie there while I get Freckles sorted."

"I want to stay on my feet for a bit," he rasped. "The longer I'm on my back, the weaker I'll be."

He couldn't be serious? The man looked like he was going to keel over sideways at any moment. "You're too sick."

"Just stay there, in case I need support." He stepped away from her grip and sought his balance. He wobbled a bit and went quite pale, but he managed it.

"Here." She reached out and grabbed his arms. "Walk." She led him to a post and put his hands on it. "Hold on to this. I've got things to do. I can't be propping you up."

She left him there and went to unsaddle Freckles and give her a brush down. She kept a wary eye on the Apache as she worked. "Don't you go falling and whacking your head on that post. I'm sick of nursing you."

He was doing some very distracting movements, lifting one arm, then the other, then one leg, then the other. Was he *exercising*? Every time he moved a chain of muscles rippled down his body.

She needed to find him some clothes.

Luckily he wore himself out pretty quickly, or she'd never have finished her chores. She kept finding herself staring at him, wondering what he'd look like unswollen and unbruised. *Pretty damn fine,* she imagined.

But maybe not. Maybe he had beady little eyes.

Would it matter, with a body like that?

Jesus wept. Listen to her. What did she care? She wasn't in the market for a man, muscled or not. *Why not? It's been a long time* . . . She snorted. *Her* brain had clearly been cooked if she was thinking about a warrior-lawyer-Apache as a romantic prospect.

Not romance . . . just . . .

Shut up. Clearly she wasn't just cooked; she was *fried.* He was a complete stranger. A possible rapist, probable lawyer, and certain disaster. He was also practically *bedridden.* Any feelings she was having about him were merely caused by the forced intimacy of almost dying together. It was a reaction resulting from nervous exhaustion and . . . well, *more* nervous exhaustion. The threat of almost dying made a person aware of their body, that was all. It made water sweeter, food richer, the air fresher and perhaps caused a body to be prone to some animal feelings of lustiness. That was all. It was just the body's way of exclaiming that it was still alive.

Even if the only man her body had to focus on had a face like a cauliflower and a way of wily talking like a lawyer ...

It wasn't his *face* that was causing her heart to trip though. ....

"That's enough," she snapped at him when he stretched his arms over his head, showing off a long torso with clearly defined stomach muscles. The tattoos pulled tight over his hard-packed physique, and the badly fashioned loincloth he'd made from her petticoat slid down his hips, revealing sharp hip bones and the shadow of dark hair.

"Neither of us is up for this," she grumbled, escorting him roughly from the center of the barn toward the hay. "You were dying of fever not twenty-four hours ago. Have some decency and act sick."

He didn't protest. He merely let her make him a bed of hay. He relaxed into it, and she realized that things weren't much better now than when he was stretching. His muscled thighs were spread as he tucked his left foot under his right leg, and oh my, they were quite some thighs. Long lines of muscle, shining rosewood skin, with white scars gleaming amid the hair. How did you even *get* muscles that defined?

Ava backed away. Maybe she'd caught fever too. It might explain why she was having such mad thoughts. Who cared about his thighs? Or his stomach, which was hard as rock ... or his dusky nipples, which were circled by the wing tips of the giant bird tattooed across his chest ...

Hell. It was hot in here. She splashed herself with some of the cold water from the canteen. Maybe it wasn't fever; maybe it was heatstroke. .... Definitely heatstroke. Or maybe both.

The village woman was kind enough to interrupt at that point to deliver some beans and tortillas. Dusk was falling, and a lush violet sky was heavy beyond the open barn doors.

"Leave them open tonight," the woman told her as she put two plates of food down for them. "It will give you air. It's very hot."

"Yes," Ava agreed fervently. "It is. Hot. Very, very hot."
She handed a plate of beans to the Apache. He couldn't see
what he was doing of course. "Food," she told him shortly,
pushing the plate against his hand until he opened it and
took clumsy possession of his dinner.

The woman was giving a bucketful of oats to Freckles.
Then she ducked back outside, returning a few minutes
later with a pail of water, a washbowl, a washcloth and a
hunk of soap. "Anything more and you have to pay," she
said over her shoulder as she left them to it.

"Wait," Ava protested, darting after her. "I need to ask
you something . . ."

The woman paused in the yard in front of the barn. Ava
joined her, trying to look as ingratiating as possible. "Thank
you for the food and the soap . . ." Jesus wept. How was she
going to raise the topic of leaving the Apache here . . . ?

The woman gave her a suspicious look. Ava smiled weakly.

"Uh . . . I don't suppose you have any clothes he could
wear?" she asked in her childish Spanish, chickening out at
the last minute from saying what she really meant. *Tomorrow* she would ask if the Apache could stay. First, she'd better clean him up and dress him and make him look less like
a man on a wanted poster and more like a man this woman
would want to keep.

The woman stared at her, then gave a sharp nod and
walked off.

"Not much of a talker, is she?" Ava said to Dog, who'd
joined her outside the barn. "I guess if you choose to live
out here, you like your own company."

The door to the house closed behind the woman with a
brisk bang.

"Maybe she just doesn't want to talk to *us*," the Apache
called from inside the barn.

"That shows plain poor taste," she retorted. "Eat your
beans and stop eavesdropping on other people's conversations."

"I thought you were talking to me."

"Well, I wasn't. I was talking to your dog." She braved giving Dog a scratch on the back of the neck. He looked up at her, his tongue lolling out of the side of his mouth.

Ava returned to the barn. The lantern the woman had hung on one of the poles cast a soft golden light. Night drew in around them, making it feel like they were in a magic circle of light.

Ugh. Listen to her. She was falling into romantic nonsense now. That was what a toxic combination of sunstroke and fever would do to you.

Ava considered the Apache as he ate. It looked like he had his appetite back. That was a good sign. The better he was, the easier it would be to leave him.

Dog trotted over and waited patiently next to the Apache, ready to catch any falling food. The Apache gave his dog a scratch, and Dog's tail thumped against the hard-packed earth floor of the barn. It was reassuring to see he was kind to animals. It made it less likely he was a villain. Maybe.

Well, villain or not, if he could stomach food again, then he could stomach the news she had for him. She cleared her throat. "I'll be heading out in the morning," she told him, picking up her plate and keeping her gaze fixed firmly on her beans. Not that he could see her. He was blind.

While she'd been outside with the woman, he'd gone and bandaged his swollen eyes with a strip of petticoat; it covered up the worst of the swelling and gave her some idea of what he'd look like when the swelling went down. He had a very square jaw, with hollows under his cheekbones, and long lips in the shape of an archer's bow. When had the swelling around his lips gone down? Jesus wept, he had a pretty mouth.

Oh God, the quicker she got out of here, the better.

"Tomorrow I'll be heading out *without you*," she clarified. "I said I'd get you to people, and I got you to people." She risked a glance. He didn't argue—yet. He was too busy fumbling with his food.

She sighed. "Here, I'll help you." She moved to sit beside him. The hay sank underneath her until she was cocooned with him in a scratchy nest. Their thighs were touching, and hell if it didn't seem even hotter than ever in this damn stuffy barn. She took the plate and spoon off him. "Lucky we didn't put you in any clothes already, or they'd be covered in stains." She flicked a bean off his chest. That had been a mistake. Best not to touch him . . .

She shoved a spoonful of beans into his mouth.

It was honestly hard to read his expression, between the swelling and the bandaged eyes, but she had the distinct impression that he wasn't pleased with being fed like a child.

"You should count yourself lucky there *is* someone to feed you," she said tartly, even though he hadn't complained, "or you'd have starved to death long ago."

"There won't be anyone to feed me tomorrow, though, will there? If you abandon me here."

She scowled and shoved another spoonful of beans in his mouth. "You're not my responsibility, Apache. I got you to people like I said I would. And that's that."

He radiated disapproval. Jesus wept, he was just like her mother. She was the master of using silence to make Ava feel two inches tall.

She kept the Apache's mouth full of beans so he couldn't keep heaping on the guilt. While she was feeding him, the village woman returned with a stack of clothing.

"There's something there for you too," the woman said, looking over Ava's muddy clothing. "He's not the only one who needs new clothes." She paused before she left. "You tie that dog up before you sleep," she said sternly. "I don't want him eating my chickens."

Remembering the pile of animals Dog had caught, Ava thought that was probably wise.

"*Buenas noches,*" the woman said. "I'll bring you more tortillas in the morning before you go."

Before you go . . . Not the subtlest of hints. Damn it.

She'd have to use all her charm in the morning to get the woman to agree to keep the Apache. It wouldn't be for long. . . . He'd be fighting fit in no time and heading off on his own. If he wasn't permanently blind . . .

"How are your eyes?" she asked abruptly, pressing the last tortilla into his hand and struggling to climb out of the hay.

"Not sore anymore," he said shortly.

"Can you see anything?"

"Blurs," he admitted. "But the light hurts."

"That's why you bandaged them?" *Of course* that was why he'd bandaged them. She was just blathering now. She was acutely aware of him over there in the hay, the whole long, burnished, near-naked mass of him. She didn't wait for him to respond but kept talking. "I'll bring you the water and soap, and you can try to clean yourself up. We can move you to fresh hay afterward." She wasn't about to bathe him, not with the thoughts she was having. She dumped the pail next to him and dropped the washcloth and soap in his lap. "I'll eat outside to give you privacy," she said primly, all but running for the door. She was sweating profusely.

"It's nothing you haven't seen before," he said dryly.

"I have no desire to see it again!"

Which was a total and complete lie, because she couldn't resist stealing a peek when he was scrubbing himself. Maybe even more than one . . .

If she'd been fevered before, she was liable to burst into flames now.

❧ 16 ❧

H E COULD SEE much better than he let on. And Cleopatra didn't look at all the way he'd imagined. For some
reason, he'd pictured someone smaller, more wizened.
Much older.

She sounded like one of the hardy homesteaders you met
on the plains—practical women with cynical edges. He'd
pictured someone stringy and seasoned, a tough old boot of
a woman. But now that he had limited vision back—oily,
indistinct, but *there* at least—"Cleopatra" upended all of his
assumptions about her. For one thing, she was tall. And she
wasn't wiry. She was built like someone who spent a lot of
time on a horse: she was muscular and athletic. And she was
certainly vigorous; she was a crackling ball of energy, strid-
ing this way and that, never still. He couldn't see her very
clearly; she was just a chalky red-gray blur in a misshapen
hat, but even just that blur suggested that she wasn't at all
what he'd been picturing.

Deathrider's vision had started to return only the day
before, and it was mostly just a smear of blurred light and
shadow, but it was enough to reassure him that he probably
wouldn't be blind forever. *Lucky for Micah, or he'd be a
dead man.*

If he wasn't already . . .

Hell. Deathrider didn't have time to be blind. Or sick. While he sat around here, unable to even feed himself, Micah was being dragged straight into the mouth of hell. Who knew what Pete Hamble had done to him by now . . . ?

Deathrider wasn't used to being impotent, and he didn't like it, not one bit. When he'd gone down with the fever, he'd fallen into a surreal swirl of dreams, most of which included Micah: Micah in the pink dress, hauled across the desert, always just out of Deathrider's reach, a pink flicker ahead; Deathrider could hear Pete Hamble's voice echoing, repeating, over and over and over, *Stay down. Staydownstaydownstaydownstaydown.*

It was his fault, all his fault. And he was powerless to stop any of it.

And then *she* broke into his dreams. Cleopatra. The woman who'd found him in the desert. The one who had more prickles than a prickly pear. He'd been stone-cold blind when she'd found him, so he had no idea what she actually looked like. All he knew was that her voice broke into his fever dreams like rain falling in the desert. Her voice meant water. Her voice meant life. Her voice led him safely out of the desert and out of his fever.

Fortunately for him, she talked a lot. She never left him alone in the darkness for long. She talked to him, to her horse, to Dog and most of all to herself. He'd seen it before in people who spent a lot of time alone on the trail: they talked incessantly, whether there was anyone to talk to or not, because solitude could be overwhelming, particularly when you were out in the wilderness. The vastness made you feel small, and all you could do to exert your selfhood was *talk*. Which was why Micah bitched all the time and why Pete Hamble had been such a yapper.

Deathrider's savior—Cleopatra—was one of their ilk. She didn't let silence take root, not for a minute. Even as he scrubbed the mud from himself in the barn, he could hear her chattering away to Dog outside, telling him that if he so much as *looked* at those chickens, she'd cook *him* for supper.

Deathrider had no idea how he'd ended up covered in mud. It coated him thickly, like a second skin. He had very little memory of the past few days; there was a great big empty patch between when she found him in the desert and when Dog had come barking into his dreams, pulling him up from the fever. Deathrider's vision was still bad, blurred to hell, but he could see enough to stand and to track people moving. He didn't feel quite so panicked now that he had some visual sense of what was happening around him. The only concern he had now was how to disguise himself once the swelling was gone. The whole point of Micah's stupid plan had been to hide Deathrider's distinctive eyes.

Once Deathrider had realized the swelling had decreased, he'd tied the petticoat strip over his eyes. It was thin cotton, and he could still see through it—just—but it gave him some cover from recognition. He wasn't in any condition to be recognized, and he was feeling all too fallible after the insanity in the Apacheria. He was still weak as a kitten and in no way capable of fighting or fleeing. It still hurt to move, and he was awfully weak. He could only just manage to give himself a sponge bath unaided.

"How in hell did I get so muddy?" he asked, frustrated when he couldn't lift the worst of the filth easily. "What did you do? Dump me down a mine shaft?"

"I beg your pardon?" She sounded outraged. But she always sounded outraged, or irked, or just plain put out. It seemed to be her natural state. She appeared in the doorway, radiating resentment. He wished he could see her face. He'd love to know what she looked like. "I'll have you know you're muddy because I *saved your life*," she sniffed at him.

"I didn't know mud had healing properties."

She didn't deign to answer that.

It didn't matter how much he scrubbed at himself, he

didn't feel any cleaner. "Is this even coming off?" he asked, exasperated. "I can't see to tell."

"Don't go thinking that I'll help you." She was still in the doorway though, and he had the sense that his clumsy mopping at himself was annoying her. Dog was barking madly in the background. She turned and let loose with a scolding worthy of a seasoned cowhand. "You leave those chickens alone! You got a whole thighbone to chew on. You don't need to eat those birds too!"

Dog fell silent. Deathrider didn't blame him.

"How am I supposed to reach my back?" he complained when he almost lost his balance trying to scrape the filth off. "How did I even *get* mud back there?"

"It's your own fault."

"I'm sure. I have a history of wallowing in mud when I'm dying of fever."

"The water in that pail is filthy. You're just making yourself dirtier," she scolded him.

"It's filthy because I used it to clean myself."

He heard her sigh. "Let me get you some fresh water." She muttered under her breath as she snatched the cloth out of his hands and stalked off with the water pail. When she returned, she thumped the pail down by his feet, sending water sloshing. "Turn around," she snapped. "Let's get this over with."

"I thought you weren't going to help me?"

"It's either that or watch you spread the muck all over yourself for the next few hours. At the rate you were moving, I wasn't going to get a chance to bathe until the wee hours."

She was so tall. He'd not met a woman close to his height before.

She grabbed him by the shoulders and turned him roughly. He heard her muttering again as she swiped at his back with the cloth. He groaned in pleasure. He didn't mean to; it just slipped out.

"Am I hurting you?" She paused, concerned. For all of her prickliness, she could be mighty considerate.

"No," he reassured her, and then clamped his mouth shut. If he told her it had been a groan of sheer pleasure at the firm pressure on his sore muscles, she might stop. She was that contrary. She wiped circles on his back, scrubbing the mud away with movements that sent spirals of bliss curling through him. It felt so damn good. His body had taken a hell of a beating these past weeks, and it sure appreciated her attentions. Maybe a little too much.

"Don't you go getting ideas," she snapped at him, clearly reading his mind.

Although until she had said that his ideas had been amorphous. Now they twisted into concrete images. He was aware of his bare skin, of the flimsiness of the cloth tied around his hips, of her closeness as she cleaned him. His sheer helplessness was weirdly arousing.

Somehow not being able to see her made the moment even more loaded. As she ran the cloth over his neck and shoulders, she fell silent. The air between them grew charged, and he broke out in gooseflesh.

"I'll do your arms and legs," she said, and maybe he imagined it, but he thought her voice sounded a little unsteady. "But that's all, you hear? The rest is up to you."

He shivered as the cloth wound its way over his body. Down each arm, over his hands, between his fingers, tracing his spine, ending abruptly above the cloth at his buttocks, resuming at his thighs, running down the back of his legs. Here and there she seemed to linger—and he held his breath.

Hell. Two days ago he had been on the threshold of death, and now here he was horny as a bull buffalo in spring, just because some woman was wiping mud off him. And he'd never even properly *seen* the woman.

He felt a wave of crushing disappointment when she stopped. He turned to face her, and he heard her breath catch. He could well imagine what she was seeing. He was as hard as hell, and the bit of cloth he had wrapped around his waist was hardly going to disguise it.

"I told you not to go getting any ideas," she warned him. "I'll shoot you if you try anything."

"You're the one rubbing me down," he pointed out.

"Cleaning you," she corrected.

"Don't blow it out of proportion. It's just an instinctive reaction." Strangely, he wasn't at all embarrassed. Partly because he couldn't see properly, and partly because he was crawling out of his skin with lust. He wished she'd touch him again.

"That design on your chest," she said abruptly, referring to his tattoo. "What does it mean?"

"It's private," he said, his voice husky.

"Oh." There was a brief silence. The word "private" hung between them like a cast spell. He heard the cloth fall into the pail of water. "I'll leave you to finish yourself off," she said. He heard an intake of breath as she realized what she'd said. "I mean, finish cleaning yourself!"

"Don't you need to bathe too?" he asked. Through the gauze of the material bandaged across his vision, he saw her shadowy form grab the clothes the village woman had left for him and drop them on the hay next to him.

"No!" she snapped.

"I'd be happy to do your back for you," he suggested. He bit his tongue when he realized she was all but running for the door.

"Let me know when you're dressed!" she ordered, disappearing outside.

Hell. None of that had been what he'd expected. How had he gone from weak and listless to randy in the blink of an eye? He stripped the mud-crusted cloth from his waist, tossing it aside. He cleaned himself as quickly as he could, marveling at how the mud had found its way into every single nook of his body. By the time he was dressed in the peasant clothes the village woman had found for him, his legs were trembling. He had no stamina at all.

"It's safe to come back," he called once he'd settled himself in the hay. He pulled clumps of hay over his lap to hide the fact that his cock was still standing at attention. It didn't seem to care how exhausted he was.

Deathrider saw a blurry figure appear warily in the doorway. He heard her sigh of relief when she saw that he was dressed and docile. She must have expected to find him still naked and ready to ravish her. He wasn't the type, but she wasn't to know that. He knew that women had a hell of a time in these parts. Even tall, energetic women who had no compunction about threatening to shoot a man if he so much as moved in her direction. He imagined she'd survived this long only by exercising extreme caution. He thought back to the day she'd found him in the desert. She'd been plenty cautious then too, and he'd had to argue like hell to get her to help him.

"Apache," she said brusquely as she came into the barn, "I need you to do exactly what I tell you."

He sat up, concerned by her tone of voice. Maybe she wasn't quite as convinced of his docility as he'd thought.

"I need to bathe myself," she said tightly, "and I'm not spending the whole time worried that you're going to poke me with your stick."

He gave a startled laugh. Poke her with his *stick*?

Although, to be honest, his stick *was* in a poking kind of mood. It was still hard and throbbing. So who could blame her for her caution?

"Hold your hands out," she instructed.

"Why?"

She held up a rope. "I'm tying you up."

"You can't be serious?"

"Look, Apache. I'm *tired*. I've walked the soles of my feet off, nursed you, skinned and plucked and cooked a bunch of dead animals, made and remade that goddamn travois and brought us safely across miles of waterless wasteland. Now I want to bathe. And I don't want to be worried about getting raped while I do it."

"I'm not a rapist."

"And I'm not a fool. I don't know you from Adam. All I know is that you're a dangerous enough character that *three* lots of people knocked you black-and-blue and left you to die in the desert. It was one thing to have you loose when you were semiconscious from fever. It's a whole other thing when you're capable of standing on your own two feet and getting . . . you know . . . *that*." She gestured in the general direction of his groin, which was still covered in hay.

She was deadly serious. He sighed. He couldn't blame her. He'd have done the same in her position, he supposed.

"Tomorrow we'll go our separate ways," she told him firmly. "And you won't have to be tied up anymore. But for tonight, I want you where I know you can't hurt me."

"Fine." He was a lunatic to agree to this.

But he could see her point of view. He wasn't a rapist, but he wasn't a paragon of virtue either. She was a woman alone, and he was a strange man with a clearly violent past (as far as she was concerned). He surrendered and held his hands up. He supposed it was his own fault anyway, for not controlling his arousal. What did he think would happen?

But hell, the feel of her hand sliding down his body had been hard to resist. . . .

He winced. He shouldn't have thought about her hands. If possible, he was growing even stiffer. At least he was wearing the loose peasant shirt and had a lapful of hay. It would have been awkward trying to argue against her if she saw he was still hard as hell.

She roped him up and tied him to the post so he couldn't move far. Typically, though, she was cautious of his comfort, and it wasn't at all unpleasant.

"You get some sleep," she ordered. She was a shadowy shape as she moved in front of the lantern.

She took a fresh pail of water and disappeared into a stall, out of view. She was taking every precaution to keep her privacy, even though he couldn't see anything more than shadows and blurs.

Deathrider closed his eyes, intending to leave her to it. But he was keenly aware of the sound of her clothes rustling as they fell to the ground. And then the splashing of water as she wrung out the cloth. And then she started singing quietly under her breath, not loud enough for him to make out the words, but plenty loud enough to keep him awake. His cock twitched at the sound of her. He sighed and stretched.

Idly, he wondered what she looked like. He bet she had long legs. A woman that tall would have to. And he bet they were muscular, firm and curved from ankle to ass. He imagined her running that soapy cloth down one hard thigh and then the other, sliding it over her round calf muscles. He imagined the swell of her ass as she bent over. . . .

Hell. He was so hard, it hurt. He shifted so his cock lay flat against his belly. The ropes chafed at him as he moved. The whole situation felt as erotic as hell. Being tied up in the hush of the barn, alone, blindfolded, listening to a naked woman soap her body.

He'd have to try this again some time when he could actually enjoy it. . . .

Visions ran through his head of ways the scenario could have played out. If he'd been healthy, and she'd been willing . . .

He wished he knew what she looked like. Were her breasts high and round? Pointy? Pouty? Small and hard? Did she have large pale nipples or pebbly dark ones? Were they hardening under her hand as she soaped them?

Goddamn.

He must have still been suffering from fever, because these were mad thoughts. He should have been getting rest, strengthening himself to go rescue Micah, not fantasizing about a complete stranger.

Although she wasn't a complete stranger, was she? They'd been through quite an ordeal together. She'd saved his life. In some ways, he belonged to her now . . .

Although he didn't really know anything about her.

"Hey, Cleopatra," he called out, wanting to break the rising tension. It felt grotesque to cast her in his personal fantasies when she was just trying to get the mud off herself.

Don't think about how *she's getting the mud off herself . . .*

He heard the singing stop. "What's wrong?" she called, sounding impatient.

"What's your real name?"

"What makes you think Cleopatra isn't my real name?"

"Intuition," he said.

"Well, your intuition is an idiot, because it *is* my real name."

The soft sound of splashing water started up again, and his cock was still hot and hard against his stomach. He wondered about *her* stomach. He bet it was as firm as hell. A woman as active as she was, who spent so much time in the saddle, would be all velvety strength. He loved a hard stomach on a woman. And strong legs, the kind that could squeeze the breath right out of you when they wrapped around you . . .

Damn it. Look at him. He hadn't been this out-of-control randy since before he was a warrior.

"Where are you from, Cleopatra?" He had to distract himself.

"Not here," she said tersely.

"Where are you headed?"

"Can't a girl have five minutes of peace?" she complained.

"I'm just curious about you." She had no idea *how* curious.

"Curiosity won't kill you. Now hush up while I wash my hair."

He wondered what color her hair was. It could be gray for all he knew. He listened to her vigorously soaping and splashing.

He had no one to blame but himself for what happened next. He was so drowsy with stupid lust that his senses were dull. It didn't help that he couldn't see. But he should have noticed Dog barking and not simply assumed he was still terrorizing the chickens.

"Well, honey, it looks like you've been busy since we parted." A stranger's voice came out of the darkness at the stable door. Deathrider felt his hair stand on end. He had a bad feeling about this. There was blatant menace in the stranger's voice.

At the sound of the intruder's voice Cleopatra shrieked from behind the stall, and Deathrider heard the sound of her kicking the pail over. Deathrider couldn't see anything except the golden glow of the lantern light through his blindfold; he twisted in his bindings, trying to catch sight of a shadow, a movement, *anything.* Why the hell had he agreed to be tied up? What a stupid goddamn thing to have done. He tried to work free.

Dog was barking fit to split the night open. How in the *hell* had Deathrider not noticed it? Because he'd been too busy having fantasies about the naked woman over there in the stall.

Adding to the chaos, Deathrider heard the village woman calling in Spanish from the house: "That dog had better not be at my chickens!"

"You might want to tell her not to come out here, honey," the intruder told Cleopatra, speaking in a lazy drawl. Deathrider strained to see him, but there was nothing but light and shade.

The intruder kept talking, lazy as hell. "If she comes out here, I might be liable to shoot her."

"Don't you dare!" Cleopatra gasped. Deathrider could

hear her hastily throwing clothes on. "If you kill her, I'll kill *you*."

Now a shadowy form slipped into the circle of lamp-light. "I don't think you will though. I think if you had it in you to kill me, you would have done it last time. Instead of just drugging me."

Drugging him . . . Who the hell *was* this?

They heard the door to the house slam.

And then there was the unmistakable sound of the hammer being pulled back on a gun.

"Wait!" Cleopatra shrieked. Deathrider saw a shadow pass across his blindfold as she went dashing to save the village woman. "He's tied up!" she burst out in Spanish, standing in the doorway to the barn and hollering into the night. "No need to bother yourself! See? All tied up. He's just barking."

"Well, stop him," the woman said, sounding irritated. "Or we'll never get any sleep."

Deathrider kept wrestling with his ropes as he strained to hear what was happening. But then a shadow stepped directly between him and the light, and he froze.

"Well, well, well," the intruder drawled. "Look at this. You've gone and hooked yourself a fish . . ."

"He's not a fish. He's an Apache. And I need him to shut the dog up." A second shadow joined the first, as Cleopatra moved to untie Deathrider.

"Uh-huh, honey. I ain't that dumb." The intruder's shadow grabbed Cleopatra's shadow and hauled her back against him.

"But the dog!"

"Let it bark. She'll just get irritated. The worst she'll do is come yell at you again. And if she comes into the barn, I'll just shoot her." The intruder said it so casually that it turned Deathrider's blood cold.

"So you got yourself an Indian after all," the man said, sounding approving. "Good for you." He laughed. "San

Francisco's going to be lousy with Indians by the time we get there. I ran into old Sweet Boy Beau, and he had one too. Yours looks a little worse for wear. You do that to him?"

"No," Cleopatra snapped, yanking away from the man.

"He speak English, this one?"

"No," she said hastily before Deathrider could answer.

"No one's going to believe he's the Plague of the West," the man laughed.

Deathrider's breath stopped. *The Plague of the West.*

God*damn.* Why hadn't it occurred to him that she might be tangled up in the stupid Hunt . . . ? She'd known about Pete Hamble. She'd told him Bruno Ortiz had Deathrider (or rather some poor bastard he thought was Deathrider). She'd known all the details. . . .

Why hadn't he twigged?

Because he'd been sick with dehydration and stupid with heatstroke—that was why. And because he hadn't suspected that a *woman* could be one of the Hunters. The only woman he knew who . . .

Oh no. No. *No no no no.*

No goddamn way. It couldn't be.

It *couldn't.*

But it was. Five seconds later the intruder called her by name.

And that was how Deathrider learned that the woman who'd saved him, the woman who'd bathed him, the woman he'd been fantasizing about was the one and only *Ava Archer.* And the intruder was none other than Kennedy goddamn Voss.

Deathrider had met his enemies—when he was blind, weak and trussed up like a prize turkey.

Micah was right—he was definitely cursed.

❧ 17 ❧

DEATHRIDER CONSIDERED ESCAPING. That first night, as he listened to Ava Archer and Kennedy Voss bicker and bait each other, he made plans. Most of them involved violence. He wasn't at full strength, so he'd need help to get out of this mess. Luckily Dog was trained to attack on command; Dog would destroy Voss before he even knew what had happened. And then Deathrider would have Ava Archer to himself. . . .

Ava Archer. It was a surreal thought, that he'd been with her all this time. That the woman who'd soothed him, fed him, bathed him and hauled him for miles across the desert was the very woman who was the instigator of all his misery.

But he had her now. The thought filled him with savage satisfaction. That woman had ruined his life. And now she was his.

Or at least she would be. Soon.

For now *she* had *him*. The bitch actually had him tied up. Just wait until he was out of these ropes. She'd find out why he was called Rides with Death.

With one whistle, Dog could turn the tables on this whole situation. Deathrider just needed to find a way to get Dog untethered. Or to get Kennedy Voss close to the animal . . .

That hideous sense of impotence struck him again, this time with even greater force. He *hated* being helpless.

He fell into a black rage as he sat roped to the pole, listening to two of the most hateful pests on the frontier sniping at each other. Both he and Dog were restrained while Kennedy Voss and Ava Archer were free. It was unfair, unbearable and *unjust*.

He comforted himself with visions of what he'd do to them once he was free of the restraints. He ignored the fact that he was still weak and blind, and indulged in every possible daydream of vengeance. As he did, he squirmed, trying to writhe out of the ropes. But she'd tied him too well.

"We don't want to take a *fake* Deathrider to San Francisco," Voss bitched at Ava Archer. "When I said that, I was talking about what the other idiots would do. I wasn't giving *you* ideas."

Deathrider could see their shadows moving. He wondered what their history was. Hamble had said they were traveling together. Were they lovers?

If they were, they were in the middle of a nasty lovers' spat, because she radiated dislike. Even blind, Deathrider could tell.

"We want the *real* one," Voss said disdainfully.

"There is no *we*," she told Voss stiffly. She was scared of him. It showed in the brittleness of her voice. "And I was going to leave him behind anyway. He wasn't meant to be a fake Deathrider. He's just some Apache I found in the desert."

"Now, don't be hasty. Let me think it over. He might come in useful . . ."

"I'll be whatever the hell I want," she snapped. "He's my Apache, and if I want to leave him, I'll leave him."

"Old Deathrider ain't even an Apache," Voss mused. "It'd never work to take him to LeFoy. He'll never believe that an Apache is the Plague of the West. This is just the complete wrong kind of Indian."

Deathrider snorted at the sheer idiocy of that statement.

They were too stupid to even know that they had the real Deathrider chained to a post. . . .

"Ha! See, there!" Voss leapt at the fact Deathrider had given away that he understood them. "He may not speak English, but he definitely *understands* it. They're crafty buggers."

"What does it matter?" Ava Archer snapped. "He's staying here, whether he understands English or not."

Deathrider saw a shadow loom, and then Voss was crouching in front of him. "You speak English, buddy?"

What the hell? Deathrider thought. He didn't appreciate being mute as well as blind. "Yeah," he said, matching Voss's lazy drawl, "I do."

Voss laughed. "Told you, honey. They're crafty buggers."

"Jesus wept," Ava Archer muttered.

Voss gave a horsey laugh. "I reckon we take him with us."

"There's no *us*, Voss," Ava Archer snarled.

It reminded Deathrider of when she'd found him in the desert. She was fond of saying *There's no us*. It must have reminded her too, because she set to muttering again. "What is it with you people and all this *us* business? First Becky, and then this Apache, and now you."

The hawk is the best of hunters, Deathrider's father always said, *because he stays above and sees the way things are before he attacks.* As he listened to Ava Archer muttering, Deathrider remembered his father's words. He'd been caught up in his rage. It wasn't serving him well. He'd lost sight of what was important. He needed to find Micah—*that* was his ultimate goal. Hamble was taking Micah to San Francisco, intending to pass Micah off as Deathrider. And judging from what Voss was saying, it wasn't a new idea. So Deathrider needed to get to San Francisco . . . or men would be dying in his place.

But Deathrider was still mostly blind and very weak—he wouldn't make it on his own, not in time to save Micah or anyone else.

But Voss and Ava could take him there. . . . Why not use them to get what he wanted?

It wouldn't be easy keeping a lid on his fury, but it would be wise. Voss and Ava Archer could escort him north, and he could use the time to get well and strong. By the time they reached Micah, his eyes would have healed. And these two would be used to thinking of him as weak . . . which would give him the advantage.

Whereas right now he *was* weak. And he had no advantage whatsoever.

"I reckon we can use him as bait," Voss said thoughtfully. "The others aren't to know he ain't the Plague of the West, are they? It helps he's got his eyes bandaged too. What happened to him?"

"I was born blind," Deathrider lied. He didn't want Voss trying to snoop behind the blindfold. The swelling was going down rapidly, and his pale eyes were too distinctive. But the minute he spoke, he could have kicked himself. Ava Archer knew he hadn't been born blind. She was liable to tell Voss about the stinging nettle . . . maybe. But she was clearly mad at him . . . so maybe she wouldn't.

It was nerve-racking navigating this situation blind. He wondered what expression she was wearing.

What was she going to do? He waited to see if Ava Archer would call him out as a liar.

She didn't.

"Bullshit you were born blind," Voss snorted. "You look like a warrior. No blind man is as strong as you. And what were you doing out in the desert if you're blind? Ain't that where you said you found him: in the desert?"

"Spirit quest," Deathrider improvised. "I'm a holy man." He might as well take advantage of their complete ignorance. "I am blind to the world of man, but I have vision in the spirit world." The rubbish he spouted in the name of survival.

Voss went quiet for a minute. "I don't believe you."

"He's not completely blind," Ava said. "He can see light

and shade. He wears the blindfold because his eyes are sensitive to light."

Voss grunted thoughtfully. "That makes more sense." He grunted again as he rose to his feet. "It'll work in our favor anyway. We'll tell everyone old Deathrider here got injured. Who's to say he isn't the Plague of the West?"

"Ortiz and the *real* Plague of the West," Ava said sourly. "They'll have something to say about it."

Voss let out that horsey laugh again. "Honey, we've been over this before. *You're* the one who's going to tell them who is and who isn't the Plague of the West. But I ain't thinking we hand this Indian to LeFoy. We're just going to trick Ortiz into swapping with us."

Hell. Deathrider didn't like the sound of that.

"You aren't serious." Clearly Ava Archer didn't like the sound of it either.

"Oh, but I am, honey."

"Stop calling me that."

"What? Honey? Would you rather I called you darlin'?" She swore at him then, but he merely laughed.

"You got anymore rope?" he asked.

"No." A spike of fear had entered her voice.

"That's all right, darlin,' I got some spare. Why don't you sit yourself down on the other side of the post to that Indian?"

"I beg your pardon?"

"Well, darlin', that laudanum gave me a mighty headache. I reckon I still got traces of it hammering away up there. And I got no desire to be feeling that bad again. So I figure I'll just tie you up for the night, so I can get some rest without worrying about what you'll do to me."

If that wasn't poetic justice, Deathrider didn't know what was. She was getting a taste of how she'd treated Deathrider earlier tonight.

Deathrider heard a scuffle break out. It sounded like she'd tried to run for it. There was the sound of bodies hitting the ground, and he heard hissing and spitting and swearing, then a grunt as Voss took a kick or two, and then a dragging sound.

"You goddamn bastard," she yelled, and then she was muffled. It sounded like Voss's hand had landed over her mouth.

"Hush it," Voss ordered her, "or that woman'll come out to see what the fuss is, and then I'll have to shoot her. And if we end up with a posse after us because I shot some stupid woman, that'll really slow things down."

She kept struggling as Voss hauled her to the post. Deathrider winced as her flailing boots caught him in the ribs. As though he needed *more* bruises.

She gave a squeal, and Deathrider felt a pang of sympathy.

"Hey," Deathrider snapped, "don't hurt her." Although why he should care what happened to Ava Archer was beyond him. The woman was the bane of his existence.

Voss ignored him and shoved Ava Archer hard against the pole. "You're only making this harder for yourself, darlin'."

There was the sound of more struggling. Ava Archer didn't say anything more, so Deathrider assumed she'd been gagged. He could hear her breathing heavily through her nose. He could also hear a disturbing hitch in Voss's heavy breathing. . . . If he wasn't wrong, the bastard was getting off on fighting with her.

"God*damn* you're strong," Voss said admiringly when he'd finally subdued her and lashed her to the pole. Deathrider and she were touching. It wasn't a wide pole.

There was a muffled sound as Ava Archer cursed Voss.

"When all this is over, you and me have an appointment to keep," Voss told her thickly. There was a wet sound and then a grunt. Voss snickered. "Good night, darlin'. I'll wake you up a couple of hours before dawn. I want to be out of here before the villagers wake up. And we've got to ride hard to get to San Francisco before Ortiz rides off with the money."

"Go to hell," Ava Archer hissed as he walked away.

"You can count on it."

Deathrider cocked his head and listened closely to hear what Voss was up to next. It sounded like he was bringing his horses in and getting them settled.

"Did he just kiss you?" Deathrider asked Ava softly. "Was that what that wet sound was?"

"He's got a tongue like a damn lizard," she said in disgust. He heard her rub her mouth on her shoulder.

"Old friend of yours?" Now that they were alone together— or alone-ish, as Voss wasn't far away—he felt a surge of anger. It was stupid, but he felt *betrayed*.

"Kennedy Voss? Are you insane? Voss isn't a friend to any woman. You know what he likes to do to them, don't you?"

"Yes," he said tightly, unable to keep the anger out of his voice, "I've read your books."

She went silent at that.

"I thought you said your name was Cleopatra," he needled her.

"You knew it wasn't," she sniffed. "And I was hardly going to tell you my real name."

"Why not? You must have worked hard to get as famous as you are." He really couldn't keep the rage out of his voice now.

"I did," she snapped, "but you've seen what happens when people know who I am. Look at me."

"I can't, remember? I'm blind. And I think you mean look at *us*."

"There is no *us*, Apache. Get it through your head."

"Yes, there is, Miss Archer. Get that through yours. Until you can get me away from this lunatic, I'm your responsibility."

❧ 18 ❧

THREE DAYS OUT of the village, they ran into some of the other Hunters. The famous ones weren't among them. This was just a bunch of trailhounds, but it was the first sign that Ava and Voss were catching up to the pack.

Ava was beyond surprise these days, so she couldn't say she was shocked to see that they had an Indian captive. It looked like Voss had been right when he said people would be rounding up random Indians and trying to pass them off as the Plague of the West. There was so much money involved, people were trying to scam their way to winning it. Scamming was certainly safer and easier than trying to catch the *real* Plague of the West. She could only imagine LeFoy's face when the Hunters rode in carting all these men. He'd know in an instant who the fakes were—but none of these fools knew that yet.

Still . . . At least there was a bonus if people brought the Plague of the West in alive. It was a relief these idiots were bringing captives to San Francisco and not dead men.

"Look, Voss! Miss Archer!" the Hunters cried merrily when they spied them. "We found him! We caught the Plague of the West!"

"Fancy that," Voss drawled in his hick-farm-boy way, "so did we."

The trailhounds looked put out at that. They inspected the Apache, who was sitting limply on one of Voss's packhorses. He was still tied up. So was Dog; Voss had hooked the animal's rope to Ava's saddle. "Keep him away from me. I don't like the way he looks at me," Voss had instructed her.

The Apache had been more docile than Dog. Ava thought he must be ailing again.

"Your Indian don't look a patch on ours," one of the trailhounds observed.

"That's because we subdued ours." Voss grinned, happily taking credit for the Apache's sorry state. "Look at the beating we gave him. The poor bastard can't even sit up straight."

Ava glanced at the Apache. He wasn't looking good, it was true. He wasn't fevered anymore, but he'd barely said a word for days, and he was listless and limp.

"That just goes to show it's not him," the trailhound argued. "There's no way the Plague of the West would let himself be beaten like that."

Voss flared up at the perceived insult. "The Plague of the West ain't never met *me* before."

The trailhound seemed to remember who he was talking to. He mumbled an apology. But then couldn't resist adding, "I still reckon ours is the real deal."

"Well, let's ask Miss Archer about that, shall we?" Voss suggested. "After all, she's the expert on him."

They all turned to look at her. Ava sighed. She knew what Voss wanted of her. She also knew her assessment would save the poor man the other Hunters had captured— but it would doom her Apache.

She could hardly call Voss a liar. Not in front of all of these men. He'd shoot her. Or rape her and torture her, then shoot her. And maybe shoot the Apache too. So it wouldn't help anyone to take that route.

She'd have to perform. For now. Until she could get herself and the Apache out of this freak show.

She rode close to the trailhounds' captive, who was wide-eyed and lassoed to the back of a horse. She didn't even think he was an Indian. He looked Mexican.

"Do you speak English?" she asked him. He frowned and shook his head. "Spanish?" She switched to Spanish and he lit up. "What's your name?" she asked.

"Hernández. Jorge Hernández."

"This isn't the Plague of the West," she told Voss and the trailhounds. But of course they all knew that already.

"How can you tell?" the trailhound demanded. "He's a known liar! Of course he's not going to say it's him."

"She *knows*," Voss snapped. "She's Ava Archer. She's *met* him, you idiot. She's the reason *you* know about him."

"The man you've caught doesn't even have blue eyes," Ava said dismissively. "LeFoy will laugh you out of San Francisco if you turn up with him, and so will everyone else. You might as well let him go."

"Does *your* Indian have blue eyes?"

"What do you think?" Voss rolled his eyes. "Of course he does."

Ava couldn't believe the nerve of him, lying through his teeth like that. He'd better hope no one ripped the Apache's blindfold off to check.

"We heard Ortiz had him." The trailhound was more sullen than suspicious. He just wanted to vent his displeasure at having his "Indian" taken away from him.

"Didn't stop you from catching him, did it?" Voss said pointedly.

"If you don't let him go, I will," Ava told them. She dismounted and untied Jorge Hernández. Nobody stopped her. "We'll have to bring him with us to the next town."

"Like hell we will," the trailhound snapped. "If we ain't taking him to San Francisco, we can leave him here."

"He'll die," Ava said impatiently. Damn it. She was picking up more and more responsibilities as she went, and she didn't like it.

"Sounds like a solution to me," the trailhound grunted.

"C'mon, Hackett, if we don't have the Indian, we might as well get back to Frisco before everyone else. We can put a bet on Voss here. At least then we can cover our losses."

"He's *my* Indian," Ava snapped. "If you bet on anyone, you should bet on me."

The trailhounds considered that for a moment before erupting in laughter. "That's a good one." The group galloped off, kicking dust in Ava's face. She and Jorge Hernández coughed as the cloud enveloped them.

"You got some nerve, lady," Voss said when they were gone, but once again he sounded admiring. "He ain't your Indian anymore. In case you forgot, you're *both* my prisoners now. And we ain't taking their Indian with us neither. We got no call for him."

"He's not an Indian," Ava corrected him. "And his name is Jorge."

"I don't care if his name is Petunia. You're leaving him here."

"You can ride one of the packhorses," Ava told Jorge Hernández, completely disregarding Voss.

"No, he cain't," Voss disagreed. "They're mine. He can ride on your packhorse with old Deathrider there."

Ava stared dubiously at her packhorse, the one Voss had brought along with him. It was even more pathetic-looking than Freckles used to be. Freckles, on the other hand, had grown perkier since they'd found the creek. It was like her near-death experience had given her a new lease on life.

Hell. She didn't want to ride the packhorse and give her horse to the Apache and Jorge Hernández. She stalked over to where the Apache was slumped on the swayback old packhorse. "Apache, get off that packhorse. You can ride with me."

"You best start calling him Deathrider," Voss advised. "You'll wreck everything if you keep calling him Apache."

Ava rolled her eyes. "No one is around to hear me."

"But they will be. You start practicing, you hear."

"Fine. *Deathrider*, get off that packhorse. You can ride with me."

"That don't seem like a good idea," Voss observed.

"We've done it before. I know he can behave himself. Unlike some." Ava helped "Deathrider" down from the packhorse. He slid bonelessly from the saddle, looking like he could barely stand. Ava slung an arm around him to help him. She frowned at his inability to walk unaided. She'd been *sure* he was getting better the other night. He'd certainly been well enough to . . . enjoy his bath. . . .

She flushed, remembering the sight of his arousal.

It seemed like forever ago, but it had been only a few days since she'd scrubbed the mud from him. She felt the flush spread through her as she remembered rubbing the cloth over those incredible muscles, revealing inch after inch of shining rosewood skin as the mud slid away. She'd felt the charge building between them, an energy like before one of those plains storms: a shimmer, a pulse, a rising *thrum*.

It was just because he was mostly naked, and bathing a grown man was a mighty intimate act, that was all.

Although that wasn't all, was it? That wasn't even close to all.

The *truth*, Ava thought wryly, as she led the still blind and weak Apache to her horse, was that he had a body that made her mind melt. The lean perfection of him would make any woman's knees go weak. Being alone with him in the hushed lamplight, on a sultry night, running a cloth over every inch of his hard-packed body . . . she'd felt the slow uncurling of desire the minute she laid hands on him. *Before*, if she was honest with herself.

And then to see evidence of his own desire . . .

The memory of the hard thrust of him against the transparent cotton of her petticoat made her stomach loosen and that slow, hot feeling uncurl through her all over again. The way the cotton had clung damply to the thickness of him, to the swollen head of his cock . . .

Jesus wept, what was wrong with her?

She shook her head to dislodge the vision. So even his cock was perfect. . . . It didn't mean anything.

She yanked him harder than she meant to toward the horse. Dog whined excitedly to see his owner so close, nudging him with his wet nose.

"Here's the stirrup." As she led his hand to the stirrup so he'd know where to place his foot, she tried to ignore the bolt of lightning that traveled through his fingers and up her arm, straight to . . . places she shouldn't be thinking about right now. "Up you get, Apache."

"Deathrider," Voss corrected impatiently. "You'd better get that through your thick head by the time we get to Frisco."

Ava wished she had some laudanum left. Or any bullets for her gun. She was mighty sick of Voss and his bullying.

She swung into the saddle behind the Apache, who was slumped forward. His long black hair hung in a sheet over his face. Ava pulled him gently upright and reached around him to take the reins.

"You ready to go, Jorge?" she called over her shoulder. Poor Jorge Hernández looked utterly bewildered. She bet he'd just been some poor farmer going about his own business when the trailhounds had captured him. "Don't worry," she reassured him in her clumsy Spanish. "We'll make sure you get home again."

To her astonishment, Jorge Hernández went running at the packhorse and vaulted into the saddle. He lashed the swayback old animal into a gallop and went tearing off through the chaparral.

"Goddamn it!" Voss yelled. He fired a couple of shots, but Jorge Hernández was gone. "I ain't chasing him," Voss growled. "It'd be a pure waste of energy. Looks like you've lost your packhorse."

"Again," Ava corrected. "I've lost my packhorse *again*." At least all the water was on Freckles. Everything else could be replaced. And she couldn't help but feel glad for poor old Jorge Hernández. She hoped he got home safe.

"C'mon, Miss Archer. Ortiz is liable to be there already," Voss said impatiently. "Ride ahead of me so I can keep an eye on you."

Ava rolled her eyes. As if she'd forgotten. He was a stickler for keeping a close eye on her since she'd drugged him with the laudanum. At least he wasn't interested in talking to her. He tended to go shooting small game, keeping her in his sights while he entertained himself killing things. If she tried to run for it, he'd catch her in no time.

Ava kicked Freckles into a trot and scrambled to keep hold of the Apache, who was jolting around like a rag doll.

"Are you feeling all right, Apache?" she asked, hauling him hard against her and wrapping her arm right around him. His hands were roped together in front of him.

"Head hurts," he mumbled.

"You don't feel like you've got a fever anymore." He was warm against her, but he didn't have that furnace heat that he'd had when he was sick. It was just normal human warmth. "You'd best perk up if you want to make a convincing Deathrider," she said dryly.

She felt him tense in her arms. As well he might. It was a mad plan, and it didn't bode well for him. If Voss went through with this, the Apache was liable to get lynched—either by the other Hunters or in San Francisco at the end of the trail.

"Don't worry," she said softly. "I'll get us away from him before you get mistaken for Deathrider."

"So you can take me in all by yourself and win the bet?" he asked, and there was more than a little bitterness in his inflection.

He'd perked up at least. She supposed the threat of a lynching would do that to a man. Especially if he was going to be lynched for something he hadn't even done, mistaken for another man.

"Are you catching Voss's idiocy?" she sighed. "If you haven't noticed, I've been trying to get rid of you since I met you. I don't have the slightest interest in taking you one step farther than I have to; *I* wanted to leave you back in that village." But despite her words, she was oddly comforted by being close to him. His body felt familiar after their time alone together in the desert. She nestled against him in the saddle, and the solidness of him in front of her was reassuring.

"So, you've met this Deathrider character, have you?" the Apache asked her. He was getting livelier by the minute. She began to suspect that he wasn't quite as sick as he seemed. Maybe it was just a ruse to lull Voss into a false sense of security. Which would be smart, as Voss was a mean son of a bitch. The Apache had seemed so weak that Voss hadn't bothered him much so far. He wasn't a threat. Maybe, Ava thought, that was the Apache's intent . . . because if there was one thing she'd observed about the Apache since they'd been together, it was that he was no fool. The man was quick-witted and sharp-tongued. And distractingly attractive . . .

"You know Deathrider well?" the Apache kept prodding her.

"Of course," Ava lied. She didn't know why she bothered, as what did it matter if this beat-up Apache knew that she'd never met the man she had spent her life writing about?

But it was point of pride. Or rather, shame. It would probably ruin her reputation if people knew she hadn't so much as seen the Plague of the West. . . .

"What's he like?" the Apache asked, sitting up straighter.

"Terrifying." She was being glib.

"That so?" He didn't sound like he believed her. "Terrifying enough to deserve this Hunt?"

Ava pulled a face. "No one deserves this Hunt. Except maybe Voss. He should be the one they're hunting."

"But they're not. They're hunting the Indian instead." He sounded even more bitter now.

"Because he's a legend," Ava countered.

"And he's a legend because of you."

"Yes, I suppose so." She didn't like talking about this. It made her feel . . . a big mess of feelings, chief amongst them guilt. "I've got nothing to feel guilty about," she said abruptly.

"If you say so."

"I *don't*. Deathrider is a cold-blooded killer."

"Is he?"

"Yes."

"You've seen him kill people?"

"Of course not. I haven't seen Voss kill people either, but I know he's a killer."

"He admits to it. Does Deathrider?"

"I don't know. I—" She stopped midsentence. She'd been about to say *I don't know. I've never met him.* Jesus wept, she couldn't keep her story straight for even a minute. That was dangerous.

It was definitely time to retire. The thought broke over her like a wave: a revelation. She was going to retire. Now. The decision happened instantaneously. She broke out in chills at the sweet, honest force of it. She'd lost any enthusiasm for her work. Her notebooks were still packed away in her saddlebags, and she had no desire to pull them out. At some point she'd stopped thinking of this in terms of a story—she'd been too busy just trying to survive.

She didn't want to live like this anymore. Not for another minute.

"'I don't know. I *what* . . . ?'" the Apache echoed her, wanting to know how she'd meant to finish the sentence.

"Apache," she interrupted him, "we need to get out of here."

"What?"

"We need to get out of here. Now. I don't want to go to San Francisco. Not with Voss. Not at all. I don't care if they ever catch the Plague of the West . . ." She paused. "No. That's not true. I still care. But I don't *want* to care anymore. I want to stop." The words tumbled out of her, and they were followed by an intense swell of relief. How long had she wanted to stop and not been able to admit it to herself? Because now that she was saying the words aloud, they felt right; they felt true. And they felt *good*.

She laughed, feeling tears well up. "I want to stop."

"*Now* you want to stop?" He didn't sound pleased. He clearly didn't understand the importance of what had just happened. By why would he? He was just an Apache who'd been caught up in events he had no part in. He had his own events.

"You didn't want to stop *before* you got everyone tangled up in this insane Hunt?" he growled.

She blinked, startled by his vehemence. And then she got irked. "Oh no, you don't. You're not blaming me for this Hunt. This is all LeFoy's doing, not mine." She was feeling so much zestier since she'd made her decision. Zesty enough to enjoy bickering with the Apache again. She'd get a ship to New York, she decided. She didn't fancy taking the California Trail east, going against the flow of immigrants, over all of those miles and months of hard traveling. She could rest on the ship, maybe write up the last of her notes into the final books A.A. Archer would ever publish. And then she'd collect her final paychecks and retire. Not to needlepoint though. She hated sewing. . . .

Maybe eventually she'd come back west, she mused. If she found New York wasn't for her . . . she could return to these parts as an independently wealthy woman. She could buy a patch of land all her own and forge a life for herself.

Or maybe not. Maybe New York would suit her. She'd see. She didn't have to make any concrete decisions. She could just see which way the winds blew. . . .

"This is *all* your fault," the Apache said, and she realized that while she'd been daydreaming, he'd been seething. "Every last bit of this is your fault."

"I don't see what you're so het up about," she observed, frowning. Sure, he was tangled up in this, but it wasn't *personal*. It wasn't like they couldn't untangle him. Somehow . . .

"Oh, you don't?" He sounded plenty steamed now. "You don't understand why I'm *het up*? Look at me: I'm beat-up and blind, hijacked by a fame-hungry lady writer and Kennedy goddamn Voss, being dragged to San Francisco, where I'm going to be presented as some kind of prize . . . and you don't understand why I'm *het up*?"

"Calm down, Apache; I know this is bad, but it could be worse." The last time she'd seen him this cantankerous was back in the desert, right before he went down hard with the fever. Maybe he *was* sick again.

Although, to be fair, he had plenty of good reasons to be angry.

"Worse?" he sounded absolutely astonished.

"Yes. It could be much worse."

"How?"

"You could actually *be* Deathrider. Imagine how he must be feeling. The Hunt is about him, not about *you*. And I don't appreciate you blaming me for Voss. *He* hijacked you, not me. If you're going to be angry at anyone, it should be him."

"You're the one who wrote all those books and got everyone stirred up about the Plague of the West—which is a terrible name by the way—and you're the one who told the world Deathrider was a murderer and a child rapist and a kidnapper and a *drinker of blood* . . .". He was so furious now that he was speaking through clenched teeth.

"It's *not* a terrible name," Ava told him, all the while giving him soothing pats. At first she didn't realize she was doing it, but even once she realized she was, she continued. He was clearly unwell. She needed to get him settled down. "Here, have some water." She reached for the canteen.

"I don't want water."

"Of course you do." She shoved the canteen into his hand. "Drink up." She kept patting him. Her palm grazed his nipple through the shirt, and she felt it pucker. That unleashed the slow uncurling in her belly again, which made no sense, as they were in the middle of an *argument*.

"Stop that," he snapped, meaning the patting. She'd felt him jump at her touch. She wondered if he was getting hard again. . . .

What a ridiculous thing to think in the middle of an argument, and with Kennedy Voss only a few yards away.

"You need to calm down, Apache. You're getting yourself into a state." It was good advice. Advice she needed to take herself, considering she was thinking about the hard lengths of his body again. . . .

"If you hadn't written all those books, there wouldn't *be* a Hunt," the Apache continued, still fixated on the whole Hunt business.

"There might be." She sighed and closed her eyes, leaning into him. He smelled good. Like sun-warmed cotton and something else . . . a nice sweaty smell. Masculine. She guessed it was just the smell of *him*.

"Stop hugging me," he snapped.

"I'm not hugging you." But she was. "I can't help it. I'm just glad this is over."

"It's not over," he all but shouted.

Voss turned to look at them. "What's going on over there?" he called.

"He got stung by a wasp," Ava called back, lying without batting an eye. "It seemed safer to say wasp than bee," she told the Apache when Voss had gone back to shooting small animals. "I don't even know if they have bees out here."

"How do you know they have wasps?" he asked, completely exasperated.

"I guess I don't."

"You're impossible," he muttered.

"Thank you."

"It wasn't a compliment."

She'd hoped he'd moved on from the Hunt nonsense, but he only waited a couple of moments before he returned to the topic.

"Nothing is over," he said brusquely. "As far as I can see, we're right in the thick of it. That maniac is going to get me killed."

"He's going to try."

"So how is it over?"

"I didn't mean *that* was over," she clarified. "I meant my career was over."

She was met with stunned silence.

"I know," she commiserated. "It's a shock."

"What do you mean, your career is over?"

"I mean, I don't want to do this anymore. Traipsing around the wilderness with maniacs. I don't want to sleep rough, and almost die of thirst, and find lawyer-Apaches in the desert."

"What Apaches?" He sounded bewildered.

"I don't want to deal with men like Kennedy Voss anymore," she said fiercely. "I don't want to carry a gun, or worry about getting raped, or have to check my bedroll for scorpions. I *hate* scorpions."

"Everyone hates scorpions."

"I hate them more."

"So what you're saying is: now that you've successfully ruined all these lives, you're going to give up ruining lives?"

"I do *not* ruin lives." She was offended by that. But not enough to loosen her grip on him. Freckles had relaxed into a lazy gait, and the afternoon sun was making Ava somnolent. She leaned her cheek against the Apache's back.

"Stop hugging me," he said through gritted teeth.

"I'm not hugging you. I'm just holding on, so I don't fall off." She yawned.

"*You* get to walk away," he said tightly, "but your victims don't."

"I don't have victims," she said sleepily. "I have *subjects*. And I only write about people who do things to get written about."

There was a hoot as Voss managed to shoot himself a critter.

"Like *him*," she said. "I only wrote about him because he did all those foul things. But not everyone I wrote about did foul things. Some of my books are about *nice* people. Like the widow Dell."

"Look what I got! Ain't that the biggest jackrabbit you've ever seen?" Voss was as excited as a boy by his catch.

Ava pulled away from the Apache as Voss came trotting toward them. She sighed. "I bet he's going to make me skin that thing."

She was right. He was.

"This is something else I'm not going to miss when I'm retired."

✦ 19 ✦

"WHY DO YOU do it?" the Apache asked her huskily.

It was late. Voss had roped them both up and staked them to the ground so they couldn't get away while he slept. Dog had flopped by the Apache's feet and was chasing rabbits in his sleep; he twitched and made soft growling sounds. They'd eaten their fill of the jackrabbit that Ava had cooked (badly) over the campfire and now had to sit there in their ropes and listen to Voss snore while he slept.

The stars filled the sky, so many glittering shards that there was hardly any darkness left between them. Ava was staring at the cloudy swirl of the constellations, wondering if she'd miss it when she was back in New York, when the Apache spoke.

"Why do you write the things you do?"

She turned her head to look at him. He wasn't staring at the sky. He was blindfolded with the now-grimy strip of petticoat, his face as blank as a statue's.

She felt a stab of melancholy as she looked at him. He was so battered and so far from home. She assumed he was far from home anyway. . . . She didn't really know where his home was.

"I write about them because they're interesting," she told

him. "People want to read about them." She sighed. "Originally, though, I just wrote whatever people would pay me to write." She shifted her weight, wishing Voss hadn't tied her quite so tightly. Her hands were going numb. "I ran away from home when I was seventeen," she told him and, oh my, didn't that open a box of memories. "I needed to do something to support myself. And I was always good at telling stories." Her education was the most valuable thing her father had ever given her—because of him she could write, and write well, and because she could write well, she could earn a living.

"Why did you run away?" he asked.

He had such a pretty mouth, she thought idly. It really did look like an archer's bow turned on its side. Long, pointed, supple.

"How old are you?" she asked, curious. It was so hard to tell, considering the state of him.

"You haven't answered my question." He did that thing he did, where he talked right over her. It was incredibly annoying.

"I don't know *anything* about you," she said slowly. It was startling really. She felt connected to him after their ordeal—but actually she didn't know anything about him at all. Not even his name. Which was her own fault; she was the one who'd said she didn't want to know it. She wanted to know it now, she decided. Since they were stuck with each other. "What's your name?"

"Why did you run away?" he repeated stubbornly, still talking over her.

"What's your name?" Two could do stubbornness.

"I asked you first."

She pulled a face at him. Not that he could see it. "I was young. I felt trapped." That was skating around the truth though, wasn't it? But what did it matter if this Apache knew? What did it matter if anyone knew?

Ava was surprised to find tears filling her eyes. Her nose

prickled. Ah, she hated to cry. Especially tears of self-pity. But when was the last time anyone had asked her about herself? When was the last time she'd felt like *telling* anyone about herself? She could have died out here, and no one would have missed her or mourned her. . . .

Not even her own mother, who was three thousand miles away. Yvonne had been relieved to have Ava off her hands, and they'd never really seen eye to eye.

When you got right down to it, there was no one in the whole world who would miss Ava if anything happened to her. No one who really *knew her.*

She didn't even have a dog. Even the Apache had a dog.

A thousand trivial things flooded her thoughts—all of the things nobody knew about her. Her favorite food, her favorite color, the fact that she loved the smell of coffee more than anything in the world. Nobody knew that she hated milk or that the she was allergic to cats. Nobody knew that babies made her feel deeply sad or that she loved rainy days. And nobody knew that having her feet rubbed made her melt into the floor with joy.

All of a sudden it mattered terribly that nobody knew any of these things about her. And it made her more willing to talk than she would have been otherwise.

"My mother had organized an arrangement for me," she blurted. "With a man." Ava remembered her rage at her mother. *I'm not you,* she'd shrieked at her, slamming doors and allowing herself to give into incandescent fury. *And I don't want to live like you. EVER!*

"You didn't want to get married?" the Apache asked.

"Did I say 'marriage'? Not marriage. She'd organized an . . . arrangement . . . a . . . situation . . . for me."

He'll treat you kindly, her mother had said. She'd been genuinely astonished by Ava's reaction. She'd been expecting gratitude. That was how little Yvonne Archer knew or understood her daughter. *And he'll buy you a house.*

A house! What would she have wanted with a house?

She was *seventeen*. She hadn't wanted to keep house with an old man.

"As a servant?" the Apache prodded. "Is that what you mean by 'situation'?"

"No, Apache. Not as a servant. As a mistress." Ava felt the old heaviness in her stomach. "You know, a kept woman." Time rolled back, and she felt seventeen again, full of the old disgust, the sinking fear. "He was thirty-five years older than me. He was a friend of my father's." She'd called him Uncle Geoffrey when she was a child. It was all too disgusting for words.

"Your father let this happen?" The Apache sounded appalled. Maybe they didn't have mistresses in his tribe.

"He didn't know. He'd stopped keeping my mother by then. He'd paid for the house and settled a bit of money on her, for her future. Not much. I guess he assumed she'd find someone else to keep her, even though she was in her forties by then, and he didn't want to finance another man's fun. His responsibilities to us were done." She could feel the Apache's confusion. "My parents weren't married," she told him bluntly. "I'm a bastard."

There was a pause.

"My parents weren't married either," he said with a shrug.

Was he making fun of her? She examined him. He was still inscrutable. It was the blindfold. It made him near impossible to read.

"My father had two wives," the Apache told her. His voice was deep, slow and smooth and calm. "But he never married my mother. He would have, but she wasn't interested in being a third wife. And I don't think she ever got over her husband—he died before she met my father."

Ava didn't know anything at all about Apaches, so she didn't know if it was normal to have two wives plus a mistress. Because it sure sounded like the Apache's mother had been a mistress. "Were they together a long time?" He'd used the past tense, so she assumed they weren't together anymore.

"Until she died."

"Oh." She winced. "I'm sorry. About your mother."

"It was a long time ago." He sounded pragmatic. "So you ran away because of the old man? The one your mother tried to sell you to?"

"She didn't try to *sell* me," Ava laughed. "It wasn't like that."

"It sounds like that."

"She wasn't getting any money. She honestly thought it was best for me."

"Better than marriage?"

Ava pulled a face. "No decent man would want a bastard like me. Not one of any consequence anyway. And Mother wasn't interested in me marrying down." Ava sighed. "She thought I'd have a better life being kept by a rich man than being married to a workingman. She always said that would wear me out. Nothing but babies and work. She didn't raise me to scrub floors, she said. My mother was scared of poverty. She'd grown up terribly poor. It was only her beauty that got her out of it." Ava had a vision of her mother sitting in front of the fire, brushing her thick brassy hair. She was like a classical painting come to life. A Titian. All white skin and dreamy expressions, her hair a blazing corona.

"But you didn't want to be a mistress? Was it because he was old?"

"I don't know," she said honestly. "I just didn't want it. The thought of it made me feel sick. I wanted . . . to be free." She'd been so young. When she looked back, it was kind of astonishing how confident she'd been, how independent. She'd been so stupidly courageous—the kind of courage that belonged to the young and naïve. She'd had no idea how rough things could get. Well, she had an idea now.

"I answered your question," she told the Apache. "Now you have to answer one of mine. What's your name?"

"You said you didn't care."

"No, I said I wasn't going to know you long enough to need to know it. Which has clearly not been true. If I'm stuck with you, I might as well know your name."

A half smile crossed those archer's bow lips. "My mother called me Nathaniel."

"Nathaniel? That doesn't sound like an Apache name."

"It's not. It's white."

"Would you two shut up?" Voss barked from across the dying campfire. "I'm trying to sleep, and your yapping is keeping me up. I don't give a shit about your names or who your mothers were sleeping with. Shut the hell up."

"Apache," she whispered after Voss had rolled over, "I'm sorry you got dragged into this mess."

"Me too."

"Shut the hell up!" Voss shouted. A handful of gravelly dirt came flying at them across the camp. Ava managed to dodge it, but it hit the Apache in the chest.

Dog barked.

"And shut that dog up, or I'll shoot him!"

Ava heard the Apache say something to the dog in his own language. Dog settled again.

Ava maneuvered onto her side so she could watch the Apache.

Nathaniel. She wondered what his Apache name was. The firelight shivered on his implacable features. The swelling had gone down so much, she could really see the architecture of his face now. His nose had a wide bridge, and there were deep hollows under his high cheekbones. He was a striking-looking man. Not young but not old. Maybe thirty? Maybe older? She wished she could ask him more questions. Was *he* married? If so, did he have one wife, or two? Did *he* have a mistress?

They'd be lucky women . . .

Oh, listen to her. What on earth was she basing that on? His *looks*? The man was a near-total stranger. So he was

quick-witted and lawyerly. So he'd shown her a little kind-
ness. He'd also been surly and difficult, and he'd clearly annoyed people enough that they'd wanted to kill him. He
could be as bad as Deathrider for all she knew. Honestly.
Since when did a pretty face make her lose her judgment?

Since now.

It was just one more reason she needed to retire.

TWO DAYS LATER, they ran into more of the Hunters. They
came upon them while the group had stopped to fill their
canteens by a spring. It was a big group. Cactus Joe was
there, and so were a few of the other more famous varmints. Ava was surprised to see Becky and Lord Whatsit
were among their number. She dismounted, leaving the
Apache tied up on Freckles, and went to greet them.

"Ava!" Becky lit up at the sight of her. "Thank God!"
She flung herself at Ava and hugged her until Ava thought
her ribs might crack. Even though she barely knew the girl,
she was moved. It looked like there *was* someone in the
world who cared what happened to her.

"We thought Kennedy Voss had kidnapped you!" Becky
exclaimed.

"He did."

Becky looked horrified. "Did he . . . ?" Her eyes were as
wide as saucers.

"He tied me up with ropes every night," Ava told her,
knowing it would only make her eyes get wider. They went
from saucers to dinner plates. Ava laughed. "Don't worry. He
didn't touch me. Not in that way. He's ghastly, but at this
point, he's more interested in the Hunt than in his old habits."

"If he harmed you, I would be more than happy to shoot
him for you," Lord Whatsit interjected. He was looking
rumpled and dusty and was no longer clean-shaven. But he
was his same old haughty self.

"Thank you, Your Majesty," Ava said. "That's very
kind."

"She looks well enough, Jussy. I don't think you'll need to shoot anyone yet."

Jussy? Ava looked back and forth between them. What was going on here?

"Did you hear Pete Hamble caught Deathrider?" Becky said excitedly. "He's about a day ahead of us. We might catch up to him before he reaches San Francisco."

"I thought Ortiz had Deathrider."

"So did we. But now . . . who knows?" Becky shrugged.

"Well, lookit here. If it ain't the King of England and the bar girl." Voss was cheerful as he ambled over. "Joe was just telling me San Francisco is going to be lousy with Deathriders." He grinned. "But I told him ours was the only true one. Ain't that right, Miss Archer?" He winked at her.

Oh hell. Becky actually *knew* Deathrider, Ava remembered. She'd take one look at the Apache and know he was a fake. Ava met Becky's gaze and gave her a pleading look. She could only hope the girl would get the message and play along.

"That's right," Ava said carefully. "Ours is the real Deathrider, no doubt about it."

Becky lit up, and Lord Whatsit craned to see, curious as hell.

Cactus Joe looked dubious. "Well, let's take a look at him, then."

Ava managed to step close to Becky as Voss hauled Nathaniel down from Freckles so everyone could get a look at him. "Becky," she hissed into the girl's ear, "whatever happens, don't let on that you know who the real one is . . . *please*." She had a horrid fear that if Becky called out their lie in public that Voss would shoot the Apache on the spot. He kept the Apache alive only because he was useful.

She needn't have worried; the girl played along beautifully. A little too beautifully, Ava realized later.

"You've got the wrong man," Cactus Joe said in disgust. "This one's a disgrace. He don't look capable of shooting up a molehill, let alone a mining town."

"Are you calling Miss Archer a liar?" Lord Whatsit roared.

Ava noted the way Becky put her hand on Lord Whatsit's arm to calm him.

"Let's look at the evidence, shall we?" Lord Whatsit pulled something from his pocket. Ava winced when she saw that it was one of her books.

She stepped closer to the Apache and put a hand on his back so he'd know she was there.

"It's definitely him," he heard one of the Hunters whispering. "Look how she hovers. She don't want anyone stealing him out from under her."

She felt the Apache take a deep breath. The poor man. She gave him a pat.

"Here we are, a description of the villain," Lord Whatsit announced. "'The ice-eyed killer of the plains came out of the darkness like a shadow brought to life, large but lithe, like a hunting cat; he prowled the camp while the Fullers slept, looking for easy prey. His hair was drawn back, and he wore the single eagle feather, but no war paint. This was no act of war. This was kidnapping, pure and simple. The Plague of the West had taken a liking to the girl, and he meant to have her.'"

Ava felt the Apache thrumming with tension. She kept up the patting. That always seemed to help. She heard him mutter under his breath in his own language.

"You know," Lord Whatsit mused, putting the book down, "now that you think about it, there isn't much description." He flipped through the book. "That's about as much detail of him as I can find."

"Of course there's *description*," Voss said scornfully, snatching the book off his lordship. He squinted at the pages, his lips moving as he read. It was clearly difficult for him. "It says he looks like a cat."

"Your Indian looks nothing like a cat," Cactus Joe said in disgust.

"It doesn't mean he *literally* looks like a cat." Ava couldn't help but weigh in. Because *honestly*.

"It says he's large," one of the Hunters Ava didn't know said helpfully.

"And *he* is large." Voss pointed at the Apache with the book.

"It also says lithe," Lord Whatsit said, his lips pursing in disappointment as he took in the Apache's battered state, which was less visible in the peasant clothes, but still obvious enough to make him seem a sorry figure. "And this man is clearly not."

"You can't judge him on the way he looks now," Ava said defensively. "He may well have been lithe before his misfortunes." Because her poor Apache had been through a lot. More than a normal man could probably have survived.

"He hasn't got an eagle feather in his hair."

"He didn't have anything when I found him," Ava said hotly. "He was completely naked."

"What are you doing?" the Apache hissed at her, turning his head and keeping his voice low.

Whoops. She wasn't supposed to convince them *too* hard that he was Deathrider. Or she'd get him killed.

"What the hell would the Plague of the West be doing out here *naked*?" Cactus Joe was utterly unconvinced. "She's tricking you, Voss. It's Hamble who has the real one. Mark my words."

"It's the eyes that will tell us," Lord Whatsit interrupted. "*The ice-eyed killer of the plains.* It's his eyes that make him stand out." He considered the Apache's blindfold. "Why is he wearing that?"

"Don't touch him," Ava snapped when Lord Whatsit stepped forward. "You leave that blindfold alone."

"Why?" Lord Whatsit looked suspicious. "Surely you want to convince us this *is* the Plague of the West."

"We got no interest in convincing *you*," Voss said. He

was grinning from ear to ear. He was a man who liked to find himself in the middle of a good conflict. "You keep your hands off my Indian."

"*My* Indian." Ava scowled at him.

Voss laughed. "She caught him, and I caught *her*. So as I see it, he's my Indian now." He pulled the Apache away from Ava and led him back to Freckles. "How far ahead is Hamble? Close enough to catch?"

"We're coming with you," Becky blurted.

"It's definitely him," Ava heard someone telling Cactus Joe as she ran after Voss and the Apache. "Look at her. She don't want to let the Indian go without a fight. Why would she do that if it weren't him?"

Good question. Ava slapped Voss's hands away from the Apache and helped him onto Freckles herself. Why *wasn't* she letting him go without a fight?

Because they were friends.

She'd picked up a blind and battered stranger in the desert, and over the course of their time together, they'd become friends. It didn't make sense, but it was true. And she wasn't about to abandon her friend to these vultures.

❧ 20 ❧

EVEN WHEN SHE didn't know who he was, she caused him unholy misery. The woman was a danger to herself and others.

Deathrider sighed as he felt her settle behind him in the saddle. Because even with the fact that she kept endangering his life, she *still* wasn't what he expected. He'd been expecting . . . well, a female Voss, he supposed. A woman without conscience, devoid of sympathy, shallow of character and mercenary of spirit. But what he found was something else entirely.

Ava Archer was all too human.

She was painfully softhearted, more than she cared to admit, prone to taking care of others even when she wasn't aware that she was doing it. It grated on her, but she did it. She always made sure Dog was fed and that the horse was watered, and she'd worked like hell to keep Deathrider alive, even though he was a complete stranger. Not just a complete stranger, but a possible threat to her. She was a terrible cook. She talked constantly. She patted him all the time—because she seemed to think he needed comforting. When she talked about her past, he could hear the sad, lonely, angry girl she'd been.

It was disconcerting, to say the least, to realize that she wasn't a monster.

Annoying too.

After spending so much time with her, literally in her arms, he didn't feel animosity toward her. Not as much as he should have, anyway. She was frustrating as all hell, but he didn't hate her. He wished he did. It would make what was ahead much easier.

And now she was patting him again.

"Stop that," he said shortly.

She didn't. "You keep sighing. You need to trust me. I'll get you out of this."

He doubted it. She only seemed to get him in deeper. But at least they were getting closer to Micah, who was clearly the "Deathrider" Pete Hamble was dragging to San Francisco. According to Voss and the other Hunters, Hamble was less than a day ahead of them now. The plan was to accost him in the morning. And then to compare Hamble's "Deathrider" with Voss's "Deathrider." Deathrider assumed they'd be ripping his blindfold off in the course of the comparison, and then things would get very interesting indeed.

He tried to relax as they rode—it wasn't easy, surrounded by all these men who were out to kill him—but he needed to gather his strength for the ordeal ahead. The first step would be to rescue Micah. The second would be to rescue himself.

At least his vision was almost back. Very gradually the blurriness had faded, and the detail had crept back into the world. If he kept the blindfold high on his nose, he could peer out beneath the lower hem; he could see only his hands and the horse's shoulders, and the blur of the ground below, but at least he could *see*. That boded well for his escape.

"We need to find a way to get some bullets," Ava Archer told him. She was still patting him; it was driving him insane. As was the heat of her against his back and the feel of her against his ass and legs. She was strong. He couldn't wait to see what she looked like . . .

"Becky will probably give me some if I ask . . ."

Deathrider let her plan aloud without interjecting. It kept her busy. That and the patting, which was doing distracting things to his body. She'd slipped from actual patting into rubbing circles on his chest. It was supposed to be calming but in actual fact it was sexy as hell. Tantalizing. Especially the way her fingertips were less than half an inch from his left nipple, and there was the constant threat of her rubbing over it. He'd always had sensitive nipples. When her hand grazed them, he just about came off the horse with the shocking pleasure of it.

If his hands hadn't been roped up, he would have stopped her.

Probably.

"Nathaniel?" Her breath was warm against his neck when she spoke.

"What?"

"Do you think you can see enough now to shoot? If you took the blindfold off? I know you can only see shadows, but would that be enough? Because—I'm going to come clean with you—I'm a terrible shot."

Wait a minute. He'd been so drugged by the feel of her hand rubbing at him, he hadn't really been listening to a word she'd said. Now his brain caught up. "Hold on. What? What do you mean, you need to find a way to get bullets? Are you telling me you *don't have any bullets*?"

"Not a one. But, like I said, I'm sure Becky won't mind giving me some."

"Wait. Are you telling me you haven't had any bullets this whole time? Or did Voss take them away from you?"

"Both," she admitted. "He took them away from me when he kidnapped me in Mariposa, and I haven't had any since."

"In Mariposa? You mean, *before* you found me in the Apacheria?"

"Yes." She'd gone from rubbing to patting again. Quite vigorously. She'd picked up on his mood and was frantically trying to calm him. It wasn't working.

"Are you telling me that you've been threatening people with an *empty gun*?" He felt light-headed at the horror of it. The damn woman could have gotten herself killed.

"Of course. Even an empty gun is better than *no* gun. Not that it worked. Voss got me anyway. I didn't even have the empty gun on me when he caught us this time. I was naked, remember?"

He tried not to remember. He needed to stay on topic and not get caught up in those thoughts again.

"You're completely insane." He was beginning to get a picture of the woman who'd ruined his life. She cannonballed through life, on her own mad trajectory, smashing through walls and blowing up other people's lives. But that wasn't her aim. She was just a destructive force. "You need to learn about *consequences*," he told her. "You can't go around threatening people without having the ability to back up your threats. You'll get yourself killed."

"I haven't yet," she said cheerfully.

"No, you just get *other people* killed."

"I do not. Name one."

"Deathrider."

That silenced her. He felt her hands claw into him. He'd hit a nerve with that name. He frowned. It wasn't quite the reaction he was expecting.

She let out a shaky breath. "You don't think he's dead, do you?"

Definitely not the reaction he was expecting.

"I think Ortiz probably has the real one." She was off talking again. "Voss thinks so anyway. I'm not so sure. Pete Hamble might have him too."

"He doesn't," Deathrider said shortly.

"He *might*."

"He doesn't."

"He *might*." She gave him a gentle slap on the chest. "You have a nasty habit of disagreeing with me."

"Only when you're wrong."

"I think the money will keep Deathrider alive," she said, and he heard the worry in her voice. "The extra money. Le-Foy's offering a bonus if he's brought in alive, and I think that will probably save his life."

For how long? Deathrider wondered. The aim might be to *get* him to San Francisco alive, but what, then? A public lynching?

"I thought you wanted him dead." Talking about this was stirring up the old toxic feelings. Maybe he *could* hate her after all.

"No."

"I thought you said he was just like Voss? A killer."

"Stop talking now." She'd turned sour on him in the blink of an eye. That was interesting. She even pulled her hands away and deprived him of pats. Her hands settled stiffly on his sides instead, motionless.

"No." He wasn't about to stop talking now, not when they were getting to the interesting stuff. "How is he different from Voss?"

He could practically hear her thinking as she struggled to answer him. "I don't know," she admitted finally. "He just is."

"That's not an answer."

"He saved my life," she blurted.

"What?" He knew for a fact that wasn't true. He'd never met her before in his life. He heard a weird sound. "Are you *crying*?"

"No," she said fiercely. She thumped him on the shoulder. "Shut up."

"What do you mean, Deathrider saved your life?"

There was a tortured silence. He waited it out. She was a talker; she wouldn't be able to keep the words bottled up for long.

And he was right. She didn't.

"I told you I ran away from home," she said. "I didn't want to be some man's toy. His glorified bed servant."

She certainly had a way with words. They conjured up some images. But the bitterness in her voice made him imagine it from her point of view, and it left a sick feeling in his stomach and a bad taste in his mouth.

"I didn't want to spend my life pleasing older men, never being allowed to show how I really felt or speak my mind."

That surely would have been impossible for her.

"I didn't want to get tossed aside every few years and each time have to get a slightly poorer man to keep me. To work harder because I was losing my looks, to be more guarded and less myself. I didn't want to have to hand my body over to someone else and to pretend I wasn't feeling disgusted and violated."

"And writing about Deathrider saved you from this?" He followed the trajectory of her story straight to the point.

"When I ran away, I got a job writing for a periodical. They wanted stories of the frontier. But my stories didn't sell very well . . ."

"Until you wrote about the Plague of the West . . . ?" he guessed.

"He was the first. I wrote a serial for a ladies' journal, and it sold so well, it was reserialized in a national paper and then collected into a book. That was when I managed to make enough money to live on. And because of it, I got to keep writing, about all kinds of people. If it hadn't been for Deathrider, I might have starved to death . . ."

"Or got another job," he said dryly.

"Doing what?"

"Doing one of the jobs regular people do."

"It's that easy, is it?" she snapped. He'd really touched a nerve now. She was smoldering with fury. "Do you know what kinds of jobs there are for women? Cooking? Doing laundry? Being a maid? Or whoring? As a wife, a mistress or a cut-rate whore—taking care of a man is one of those jobs *regular people* do," she said angrily, "when they're *women*. And I don't see why I have to do it." She managed to get her anger under control. "And I *don't* have to do it. Because of Deathrider. Because of him, I've been able to support myself and put money away for my future."

"Because of him . . . ?" Deathrider felt a bolt of fury. "Because you made up stories up *about him.*"

"Everything I wrote was based in fact." She sounded absolutely sincere. It was infuriating. Either she was a consummate liar, or she was willfully naïve.

"He didn't rape that Fuller girl," Deathrider told her firmly. "And he never kidnapped a child. Or shot up a town."

"Yes, he did," she snapped. "I was in Mariposa. I saw the bullet holes. I heard all about it."

"Other than Mariposa," he amended.

"How do you know?" she asked suspiciously. "Have *you* met him?"

"Have *you*?" He waited for her to lie to him.

"Fordham Fuller told me himself about how Deathrider raped his daughter."

"Maybe Fordham Fuller was a liar," Deathrider said, struggling to keep his voice calm. He'd never so much as *met* Fordham Fuller. At least so far as he knew. And he'd never raped a human being in his life, let alone a *child*. The fact that this daft woman had written a book about it, smearing his name, made his blood boil.

"He didn't seem like a liar," Ava said, but there was a thread of doubt in there. "But Matt Slater . . . he said the same as you. He said Fordham wasn't telling the truth . . . and that Deathrider was innocent."

Thank you, Matt.

"But I don't see how Matt Slater would know," she snapped. "He wasn't there. And why would Fuller have lied about something like that? A man's not likely to make up a story about his daughter being raped . . ."

"But he might be mistaken about *who* did it."

Ava sighed. He wondered if she'd start patting herself the way she patted him when he was upset. "I have had my doubts since talking to Slater," she admitted quietly. "And about a few other things too . . ."

He frowned. "What other things?"

"I don't know. Small things. Things that never quite added up. It's just . . . what if I've been wrong?"

"You *are* wrong."

"You don't *know* that."

Yes, he did.

"I got all those stories from reliable sources," she insisted. "I tried to check them, as best as I was able . . . mostly."

"Mostly?"

"Well," she said defensively, "sometimes I just need to get a book in on time, and there isn't quite enough information and so I have to . . ."

"Lie?"

"Fill in the gaps."

"With lies."

"If something is clearly a lie, I don't tell the story," she snapped. "I only write things that happened."

"You *think* you do." He didn't know if that made the whole situation better or worse. She seemed utterly sincere. Even conflicted. Confused. Troubled.

"Yes. I *think* I do . . ." She sighed again. "But sometimes I have doubts. After Matt Slater . . . I have doubts about Fordham Fuller's story."

"But you went on to write about Slater too," he reminded her. "You made the Slaters' lives a misery with that book. And none of it was true."

"Yes, it was! I was *there* for most of that one. I witnessed it firsthand. He *was* a mail-order groom. He *did* marry the widow Smith. And she *was* notorious. And Deathrider *did* go by the name Tom Slater—they said they were brothers."

In retrospect, that had been one of Matt's dumber ideas. It had put his brother Tom in danger. Effectively, he now faced all the same dangers as Deathrider did—because people now thought they were the same person. Deathrider wondered how Tom and Seline were coping, out there on the run, and whether they'd had the misfortune of running into any of these Hunters on their way to Mexico.

"Lady, you have one poison pen," he said, thinking about the ripple effect of her books and the number of people whose lives they had upended.

She went quiet again. It was a heavy kind of quiet, loaded. Brooding.

Against his better judgment, he found himself feeling sorry for her.

❧ 21 ❧

AVA WAS A light sleeper on the trail, especially when the likes of Kennedy Voss were about, so it didn't take much to wake her. Becky barely touched her, and she jerked awake.

"Hush," Becky hissed, putting a hand over her mouth to silence her. "We're getting you out of here."

Ava couldn't pull the hand away from her mouth because Voss had roped her up again, much to the merriment of their traveling party. The Hunters thought it was hilarious that she was tied up every night. Especially after Voss had told them about the laudanum.

"Drugged me near about to death," he said, grinning at their hilarity. He was as amused as the rest of them. He was one strange man. "And those trailhounds too. All of us drooling idiots, and the damn *dreams* we all had! One of those boys thought he was flying, kept saying he was an eagle or some nonsense. I wouldn't have minded being an eagle, but I just nodded off like a fool. Must have slept two whole days straight through." He gave Ava a pat on the cheek after he finished tying her up. "She's a tricky one, this one. Gotta keep a tight rein on her."

Well, he had a tight rein on her now, she'd thought morosely as her hands went numb. She hated being tied up. It

was demeaning. And the sense of powerlessness was horrific. How in the hell could she protect herself, tied up like
this? She didn't sleep well and was on such a hair trigger
that she kicked out hard when Becky woke her.

"It's just me," Becky hissed.

It was deep night. The fire had fallen to ashes, and most
of the group were silent in their canvas tents. Ava had a
clear view of Voss, who had his back to her. He seemed to
be fast asleep. When it was clear that Ava wasn't going to
scream, Becky took her hand away from Ava's mouth and
fussed with her ropes. She couldn't get the knots undone.

"Leave them," Lord Whatsit whispered. "I'll carry her
to the horse, and we'll sort her out once we're away."

Of course he was involved too. The two of them were as
thick as thieves.

"I'm not leaving without my Indian," Ava hissed at
them.

"As if we'd leave him behind!" Becky told her in a whisper. She sounded like she was enjoying herself.

Ava was strung as tight as fencing wire when Lord
Whatsit carried her to the horses. To her astonishment, the
Apache was already there. But he was up on Lord Whatsit's
horse, instead of on Freckles. And he was gagged as well
as blindfolded. She bet he wasn't happy about it either.

"You can ride with Becky," Lord Whatsit whispered,
"until we get you untied." He plonked her on Becky's
sturdy little mare.

They slunk out of the camp, and Ava winced at every
clink of a bridle or snort of a horse.

"Don't worry. They won't wake up," Becky laughed.
"We stole your idea and drugged them. Jussy had a bottle
of laudanum in his baggage, and when Voss kept going on
and on about how you'd tricked him, I thought *Why not?*
Voss was so busy worrying about *you*, he never stopped to
think *I* might be a threat to him." She sounded deeply
proud of herself. "People always underestimate me."

"It's because you're such a little thing, petal," Lord Whatsit said admiringly.

Petal?

"Are you two a couple now?" Ava asked in astonishment. She knew they should probably save talking until they were well away, but her curiosity got the best of her. And now that she knew the Hunters were all drugged, she felt a little calmer. Calm enough to want to know if Becky and his lordship were lovers. Becky was such a stringy, rough sort of girl, and Lord Whatsit was . . . well, he was *Lord Whatsit.*

"Oh no," Becky giggled, sounding very young. "I'm not stupid. After Pete, I know men aren't to be trusted. But we're having fun together, aren't we, Jussy?"

"You are the moon in my sky, petal."

Becky laughed. "Pete used to say things like that too before I gave in to him. I've learned my lesson though. I ain't never giving in to a man again."

Becky let Lord Whatsit ride ahead on his Arab, which had a faster gait than her little mare. The moon was sickle thin and riding low. They didn't have long until dawn.

"I don't reckon he's too interested in women anyway, to be honest," Becky told Ava cheerfully, as they put some distance between themselves and the camp. "He's never once got handsy or tried to kiss me."

"He's English," Ava pointed out. "Maybe they do things differently?"

"Maybe. But he's a lord, and I'm . . . well, me. There ain't no future in it." She paused and then giggled again. "But he sure is a hoot to travel with."

"I bet," Ava said dryly.

"And he's a crack shot! You've never seen anyone shoot like him. He'll manage to keep the other Hunters away from Deathrider, no problems."

Ava frowned. "What do you mean?"

"I mean Jussy will be able to shoot anyone before they get within ten feet of him."

Something wasn't adding up. "Shoot who?" Ava asked, confused.

"Voss and those maniacs! With Jussy with us, we'll be able to get Deathrider to San Francisco easily. And then we can claim the prize!" Becky sounded giddy with excitement.

Ava felt a shock go right through her. *Deathrider.* Things fell into place. "Pete Hamble *does* have him. I knew it! Have you seen them already?" Her mind was racing. "And he's still alive? Do you think we'll catch up to him in the next few hours? Untie me!"

"Pete Hamble?" Becky sounded confused. "What do you mean, Pete Hamble? Why would we want to catch up to Pete Hamble?"

For a moment it was like Becky was speaking a foreign language; Ava couldn't find the meaning in the words.

"You said we'd be taking Deathrider to San Francisco . . . ," she said slowly.

"Yes," Becky agreed, and now she was sounding a bit annoyed. "*We* will. Jussy and I got you free from Voss, so I think we've got every right to share in the prize."

"But . . ." Ava couldn't find the logic. "I don't understand."

"I know you think you caught him fair and square, and of course you did, but Voss had both of you trapped. So it's only fair now that we've rescued you that we split the profits three ways."

Voss had both of you . . .

Both *of you . . .*

"Wait. *What?*"

"I can leave you tied up too, you know, and Jussy and I can haul you both into San Francisco and keep *all* the money for ourselves." Becky clearly thought Ava was being greedy; she'd missed the fact that Ava was reeling.

"Becky," Ava said sharply, "slow down. I'm lost. When you say . . ." Jesus wept, it couldn't be true. Both *of you* . . . "When you say '*both* of us,' you mean me and . . . and . . ." Her voice trembled as she spoke. "And . . ."

"And Deathrider," Becky snapped. "Obviously."

Obviously. Ava felt faint; the world spun around her. *Both of you* . . . Ava and . . . Oh my God, her Apache . . . her *Apache* . . . Her mind flashed back to finding him in the desert. He'd been beaten and bruised and naked . . . because . . . Jesus wept, *of course.* Because he was the most wanted man in the west!

She felt like a complete fool. All of this time . . .

She hadn't even wanted to know his name, not until recently.

My mother called me Nathaniel. . . .

She'd never seen his eyes, she realized. Because of the swelling and then the blindfold, she had no idea what color they were—they could very well be as pale as ice. And she'd only *assumed* he was an Apache because she found him in the Apacheria. What she thought was the Apacheria. Maybe.

But how was she to know what kind of Indian he was? Especially when he was naked . . .

She remembered the silvery white scars and the old bullet holes in his beautiful rosewood skin.

Why hadn't it occurred to her that he might be Deathrider?

Because she'd been blinded by the story that Ortiz already had Deathrider . . . She'd made a rookie mistake. She hadn't questioned things; she'd taken them for granted. She'd made assumptions. And because her Apache—*Nathaniel*—didn't look at all like she imagined Deathrider would, it hadn't even occurred to her. He'd been weak and battered: defeated. And she'd been picturing . . .

Oh my God. She remembered bathing him. The strength of him, the incredible musculature of a warrior in peak condition. The tattoos. *That* was what she pictured when she thought of Deathrider. She'd been staring the truth in the face all along. . . .

"Becky," she said numbly. "Just give me a minute here. You're saying that my Apache is . . . is . . . the Plague of the West . . . ?"

Becky was puzzled. "What?"

"Just *tell* me."

"Of course he is. You know he is. You and Voss told *us* he is."

Oh. Ava deflated. Becky had believed Voss's lies. That was all. For a moment, she felt utterly ridiculous for even considering that the Apache was . . . But then Ava remembered something. "Hold on," she said abruptly. "Becky . . . you've met Deathrider before. You *know* him . . ."

"I traveled with him in Matt Slater's wagon train, from Independence," Becky reminded her. "I must have gone almost five hundred miles or more with him, before he disappeared. Back when he was going by the name Tom Slater. I'd know him anywhere," Becky said with satisfaction. "And so will Pete. When we turn up at the Palladium with him, we'll win the prize for sure." Becky sounded a bit breathless. "And then Pete will see what I'm worth."

Ava's head hurt. "Are you telling me I've been traveling with the Plague of the West this whole time?"

Becky finally seemed to catch up. "Wait. Are you telling me you didn't *know*?"

"Get these ropes off me." Ava held her wrists up. *"Now."*

Once she was untied, she took over the reins and drove the mare hard after Lord Whatsit and the Apache. Becky squealed and hung on for dear life. By the time they caught up to the Arab, a screamingly pink-and-orange sunrise was breaking, flooding the world with light. All the better to see him with . . .

"Stop!" Ava called to Lord Whatsit.

Confused, he slowed his animal.

"Don't let her snatch him off us, Jussy!" Becky ordered. "Get your gun out!"

"I'm not shooting a woman," he said, appalled.

"You don't have to shoot her—just stop her from stealing him."

Ava ignored them. She slid off the mare as soon as they'd all stopped, and she yanked on the Apache's—*Deathrider's*—bound hands, pulling him off Lord Whatsit's Arab. Lord Whatsit let him go, much to Becky's displeasure. Ava yanked the gag out of his mouth. She needed to talk to him.

"He's *ours* now. Don't go letting her just take him!" Becky complained to Lord Whatsit. She stayed mounted so she could give chase if they ran for it.

"Now, petal, be sporting. To be fair, she's the one who caught him."

Ava ignored them. She ripped the Apache's blindfold off.

Her knees just about gave way beneath her. It was *true*.

The swelling around his eyes had gone down completely, and staring back at her were the palest, most striking ice blue eyes she'd ever seen. They were thickly fringed with black lashes, which only made them seem paler.

"Apache," she said weakly. "You're . . . you're . . ." She felt unsteady, like she was trying to keep her balance in the middle of an earthquake. "You're *him*."

He showed no sign of unsteadiness at all. He was even *regal* as he stared her down. Then his gaze flicked up to Becky. "Seems like bad luck you were in the group," he said mildly. "You're one of the few people who could have known."

"Not *bad* luck," Becky contradicted him. "Not at all. You're about to make my fortune."

The ghost of a chilly smile crossed his archer's bow lips. "Is that so?"

"You're Deathrider," Ava burst out, still not quite able to believe it. She felt shocked to her core. And more than a little betrayed. "Why didn't you tell me?"

"I can't imagine why," he said sourly. He met her gaze, and she felt lightning chase through her. "And from memory," he told her, "you didn't *want* to know my name."

It was true. She was such an idiot.

Now that she knew who he was, she looked at him afresh. She saw his height and the power in his body. The proud look. This was the man she'd been writing about all of these years. She shivered. It was like finding out a fairy tale had come to life. . . .

"It's a pleasure to meet you," she said numbly. Because what else was there to say?

"I wish I could say the same," he replied. His pale eyes were as cold as ice as he swept her with his gaze. "But you, I'm afraid, have been a crushing disappointment."

❧ 22 ❧

H E KEPT REMEMBERING the look of hurt on her face. It
was ridiculous to care about her feelings when she'd
almost caused his death a thousand times over. But Deathrider found he did care. He kept replaying her look of shock
and the way her face drained of color before she flushed,
turning red from the tip of one ear all the way to the tip of
the other; she'd winced like a child being scolded by her
mother, crestfallen, ashamed; and then her chin had jerked
up and she'd fought to give him a haughty look. She'd stared
him down. Like a queen. Even her battered brown hat
seemed like a crown, considering the imperious way she held
her head. But there'd still been a look of hurt in her eyes.

She had deep brown eyes. He'd been distracted by that
at the time. They were a velvety dark brown, much softer
than he'd been expecting. Although he didn't know what
he'd been expecting. Something pale and steely maybe. Not
those doe eyes. There were darker ripples in their chocolaty
depths. They pulled him in and almost made him forget
where he was and what he was doing.

"*I'm* a disappointment," she echoed eventually, and he
could hear the slight wounded tremor in her voice. "*Me?*
That's interesting. Because for a legend, you're a sad sight."

That was true enough. But it was working in his favor,

because none of them was watching him closely. Even knowing who he was, they weren't on their guard. They assumed the ropes were enough to hold him.

They were wrong.

As he'd ridden with the Englishman in the darkness, he'd managed to work a small knife free from the Englishman's belt without him noticing. Deathrider was an experienced hunter and could move without causing a ripple in his wake. It wasn't too hard to palm the knife, considering the pace at which they were galloping and that he was jolting all over the place. The Englishman was too busy trying to keep Deathrider in the saddle to notice small movements. Deathrider made holding on to him harder than it needed to be for the Englishman, flopping bonelessly, to give cover to his theft of the knife.

Then he had managed to work the knife through the ropes as they bumped along. He'd been sure when Ava had hauled him from the horse that he'd be given away, that the ropes would pull free in her hands, but somehow he'd managed to keep hold of them tightly enough that she didn't notice. None of them did. They were too busy watching Ava's show. Deathrider played along, glad of the distraction.

Once Ava had ripped his blindfold off, he'd played for time, to give his eyes time to adjust. And the miracle was, he could *see*. It felt mighty odd, after being blindfolded for so long, and his eyes were sensitive to the spreading sunrise, but he drank in the color of it all with an explosion of relief. He wasn't blind!

He took in the woman in front of him with avid curiosity. He'd been wondering about her all this time. She was rumpled and stained and looked tired as hell; she had dark circles under her eyes and hollow cheeks. But she was striking as hell. She had a long, straight nose, slashing cheekbones, big dark eyes and a downturned mouth that was sexy beyond belief. He drank in his first sight of her. She looked better than he'd imagined. His gaze lingered on the collar-bone visible between the open neck of her peasant shirt, and on her long limbs. She looked strong. Powerful. Supple.

And hurt. He'd genuinely hurt her feelings with that crack about her being a disappointment.

Which made him feel about an inch tall, but had the advantage of making her easy prey right now.

Despite Becky's admonition, the Englishman hadn't pulled his gun. He was merely sitting loosely in his saddle, watching events unfold, confident he was in charge of the situation. Deathrider liked his odds.

Even though he was bruised and weak, they were no match for him. They just didn't know it yet. Dog did. He'd picked up on Deathrider's body language and crept forward, ready to spring. He was still tethered by a rope to Freckles, but Deathrider figured he could probably drag the horse with him a few steps—and that would be all he'd need.

Deathrider calculated how many steps there were between him and Becky. Ava's gun had no bullets, so it was only the Englishman he had to worry about. And the Englishman had a soft spot for Becky, so he'd be easy to neutralize. Deathrider gathered his energy. He'd have only one shot at this.

He inhaled and gave a sharp whistle and then leapt sideways. Dog surged forward, barking like a wild creature, his lips curled back to reveal his fangs. Ava screamed, and the Arab reared beneath the Englishman. Deathrider flicked the ropes from his wrists and leapt onto the mare behind Becky. He had the knife to her throat before she could even scream.

"Hush," he cautioned her. "You don't want to hurt yourself, do you? Dog!" He called his animal off. Dog pulled Freckles closer to Deathrider and turned to face Ava and the Englishman, growling low in his chest.

On the ground, Ava Archer's mouth had dropped open.

"What are you *doing*?" Her battered brown hat had fallen off, and Deathrider saw she had red hair. Beautiful dark red hair that glinted in the sun. It fell over her shoulder in a thick braid, which shot sparks in the sunlight.

He ignored her. "Why don't you pass me your gun, mister?" he said lazily to the Englishman.

"I don't think so." The Englishman pulled his weapon and aimed it at Deathrider's head. Deathrider moved so Becky was between him and the weapon. He pulled Becky's gun from its holster. He'd shoot the weapon from the Englishman's hand—he just needed to be careful that the man's weapon didn't fire in the process and accidentally shoot one of the women.

"I know you're fond of her," he warned the Englishman. "Be sensible."

"I'm not in this for the money, you savage," the Englishman told him. "I don't need to keep you alive for the bonus. I'm quite content to shoot you now and simply take your head to LeFoy."

"No!"

To Deathrider's shock, Ava launched herself at the Englishman, pushing him off the horse. The gun went off, firing straight up into the sky. As the bullet came back to earth, it hit Ava in the leg. Deathrider's heart stopped. And then she screamed bloody murder, which shocked it into beating again. The banshee screeching made Dog whine and wriggle backward. He looked up at Deathrider, concerned.

"You shot me, you idiot!" Ava yelled at the Englishman, who was tangled up in his stirrup and hanging upside down.

"Jussy!"

"Ava!"

Becky and Deathrider fought free of each other as they dove from the mare and ran for the Englishman and Ava.

"How bad is it?" Deathrider asked, shoving Ava's hands

away from her wound. It looked like the bullet had gone clear through her calf, but it had pulled threads from her skirt and stockings with it, embedding them in the wound. He didn't like the look of it.

"How bad is it? It's bad!" she yelled, howling when he touched it.

"Stop yelling, you big baby, and let me look at it."

"Baby!" she was outraged. "I just got *shot*!"

"I've been shot plenty of times," he told her, trying to keep her distracted. "This is nothing."

He pulled his shirt over his head and used it to bandage her wound. "We need to get you cleaned up." He glanced up at Becky, who was trying to wrestle the Englishman out of his stirrup. "You got any of that laudanum left, or did you use it all on Voss and the Hunters?"

"If you've hurt him, I'll shoot you!" Becky threatened him.

"He's fine. Give me the laudanum." He sighed as he realized Ava Archer was crying. She was white with pain and trembling. Her hand had found his arm and was patting it.

There went his freedom.

THE ENGLISHMAN HOLSTERED his gun only after Ava threatened to shoot him. She'd snatched Becky's pistol off Deathrider and waved it threateningly at the Englishman. She'd taken a dose of laudanum and wasn't to be trusted with the weapon, so Deathrider wrestled it off her.

"You said he was a crack shot," Ava slurred at Becky, "and look at him: shooting me by accident."

"It was hardly his fault," Becky protested. "And go easy on him. The poor love has broken his ankle."

"Stop bickering," Deathrider told them. "Save it until we get to safety." He was the only one able to move under his own power. Ava was shot; the Englishman had broken his ankle when he got tangled in the stirrup; and Becky had gone and pulled something in her back, trying to get the

Englishman untangled. She was hunched over and in incredible pain.

They were possibly the most incompetent Hunters of all time.

"You're lucky I'm not a marauding killer," he sighed. "Or you'd all be dead by now."

"Why *aren't* you marauding?" Ava asked suspiciously. "It makes no sense." She was slurring her words something awful, and her eyelids were very heavy. In a minute she'd be nodding off. He didn't have much time.

"I've never been one for marauding," he said, leaving her to go and help the Englishman into the saddle. "Seems a messy, pointless business."

"Unhand me," the Englishman protested. Deathrider ignored him and boosted him onto his Arab. The man was deathly pale and sweating in pain.

"Becky, can you ride?" Deathrider considered her contorted body. "You probably need some laudanum too."

"I don't believe in it," she said stiffly. "I like my wits about me."

"Me too," Ava slurred, "but no one gave me a choice."

"Becky can ride with me," the Englishman offered. "I'll take care of you, petal."

Deathrider saw the tears well in Becky's eyes when she heard the tenderness in the Englishman's voice. He sighed. Amateurs. Deathrider helped her up and watched as she was cocooned in the Englishman's arms. She burrowed into his chest.

"No shooting me, you hear?" Deathrider warned the Englishman. "I'll get you all to a town and make sure you're cared for, but you're not to shoot me. I won't shoot you either. Deal?"

The Englishman didn't look happy about it but gave a jerky nod.

"I guess you look like an honorable man," Deathrider said dubiously. "Shake on it?" He held his hand out. The

Englishman looked down his nose at it but swallowed his pride and shook it.

"Why are you helping us?" he asked Deathrider. He looked deeply confused.

"Because I owe her one," Deathrider sighed, jerking his head in Ava's direction. "She saved my life." She'd also endangered his life, and worse, but now probably wasn't the time to carp on about it.

"C'mon Cleopatra," he said, bending to help her up. She was barely conscious. "I'd carry you, but I'm still not far from being one of the walking wounded myself." He pulled her arm around his neck. "Can you hop to the horse?"

"You couldn't carry me anyway," she slurred. "I'm too big."

"Is that a challenge?" She couldn't walk anyway. She could barely stand. He scooped her into his arms and carried her to the horse. She was deadweight but nothing he couldn't manage, even in his sorry state.

"Show-off."

"Don't you know who I am?" he drawled, helping her astride the horse. "I'm the Ghost of the Trails, White Wolf, the Plague of the West." He swung up behind her in the saddle. "I carry women like you off on a daily basis."

"There's no need to be sarcastic."

"Sure, there is." He turned to the Englishman. "Follow me," he said. "There's a settlement just northeast of here." He glanced westward, knowing that was where Micah was. Hell. He'd have to ride hard to catch Pete Hamble and Micah now. After he'd sorted these three.

Dog barked and Deathrider realized he hadn't untethered him. He whistled and Dog jumped up, resting his paws on the saddle. The mare grew skittish, and Ava gasped.

"It's just Dog," Deathrider soothed her as he untied Dog. "You two are friends, remember?"

"He looked like he was going to kill me before," she said in her laudanum-slow way. Then she sighed. "I'm scared of dogs."

Deathrider kicked Becky's mare into a trot. Dog barked happily and ran alongside with Freckles and the packhorses. "Keep your leg up, sweetheart," he told Ava. He pulled the leg that had been shot up in front of them, hooking it around the pommel of the saddle. The shirt he'd bandaged her leg with was sodden with blood. They needed to get her some help pretty quick. Deathrider clamped his hand on the wound. Ava had slid off into a laudanum haze; she didn't even flinch when he touched her calf. He rearranged her so her head was against his chest, and held her tight against himself. At least she wouldn't feel pain while they rode. Unlike poor Becky, whom he could hear moaning and whimpering. He hoped the Englishman could talk her into taking the laudanum—or she was going to have a horrific ride. The Englishman probably needed it too, but one of them had to be clearheaded enough to ride.

It was good to have that blindfold off. Deathrider drank in the rolling landscape, which was crystal clear in the morning light. He would never take his sight for granted again. Or his body. He was feeling closer to his normal self. He could ride easier, and breathe easier, and he didn't ache from head to toe.

Before they reached the settlement, Deathrider stopped to get himself ready. He could hardly go riding in with his long hair flying, bare chested, his tattoos visible. He'd be liable to get shot, considering the whole territory was on the lookout for him. He borrowed a shirt from the Englishman. It was tight on him, but it buttoned up. And he stole Ava Archer's hat. He pulled his hair into a knot and jammed it under the hat.

"You almost look white," the Englishman observed, saying it as though it was a compliment. "Almost."

He'd do well enough. People saw what they wanted to see, and the folks at this place would see a white man. Especially because he was riding in with other whites.

The settlement was a collection of modest Spanish

ranches, not huge aristocratic haciendas, just a farming community dating back to Spanish settlement. Deathrider hedged his bets and made for the small whitewashed church. They were greeted by a wiry padre who shaded his eyes with his hand as he watched them ride up.

"My friends need a doctor," Deathrider said in Spanish as he explained their sorry state. "We were set on by those menaces out of San Francisco. The ones chasing that Indian," he said. He was hazarding a guess that the padre had at least heard of the Hunt.

He had. "It's a sorry state of affairs when honest travelers aren't safe," the padre commiserated. "We have no doctors here, but Señora Torres is a capable healer. She can set bones."

"How is she with gunshot wounds and bad backs?" Deathrider asked, lifting Ava down from the mare.

"We'll see," the padre said mildly.

It turned out that Señora Torres was better than Deathrider could have hoped for. He carried Ava to a bed inside the señora's house and then carried Becky to a couch and the Englishman to a bench. The Englishman had fainted the moment he climbed down from the Arab.

"Leave them with me and the girls," the señora said, shooing Deathrider away. She sent her daughters scurrying for water and soap, sheets to cut into bandages and various bits and pieces.

"I will help you with your animals," the padre said, ushering Deathrider away from the chaos.

Now that they were safe, Deathrider was overcome with exhaustion. It was an effort to get the horses stabled and fed and their saddlebags unbuckled.

"We had one of those Hunters through just last night," the padre told Deathrider, as he filled the troughs with water for the horses.

Deathrider felt a wild stab of hope. How many of them would have been this close?

"Not a man by the name of Hamble by any chance?" Deathrider asked, trying to keep his voice even.

The padre gave him a sharp look. "Yes. Is he a friend of yours?"

"Quite the opposite," Deathrider said grimly. "Did he have an Indian with him? Because *that* man is a friend of mine."

"He did." The padre looked worried now. "You're friends with the Plague of the West? Is that why you're all injured? Because we want no trouble here."

"He's not the Plague of the West," Deathrider assured the Padre. "He's just an innocent caught up in this nightmare. Just like us."

Not that Ava Archer was innocent. He looked at the house. To save Micah, he'd have to leave her here. And who knew what would happen to her—if Voss would find her again . . . ?

It was none of his business.

But, if it was none of his business, why did he feel so responsible?

✦ 23 ✦

THE BEST THING to do would have been to slip away. But Deathrider couldn't bring himself to do it. The padre said Hamble had left less than two hours before, so it would be no trouble to catch him up. According to the priest, Micah was not only alive, but was also his usual mouthy self. That was reassuring. If Deathrider borrowed the Englishman's Arab, he and Dog would have no trouble tracking them down quickly. The ground was parched from a long summer, and so there'd been no rain to wash the tracks away; the devil winds weren't blowing either, so any tracks they'd left would be as clear as day.

It was time to save Micah.

But he couldn't leave without saying goodbye. He *should* have, but he couldn't.

He stood on the veranda for a while, watching through the lace curtains as the señora and her daughters finished bandaging Ava Archer's wound, wondering what was *wrong* with him. The woman was a nightmare. He should have been glad to leave her. To be free of her.

"Come in, señor," Señora Torres called when she spied him through the open door. The double doors to the bedroom opened directly onto the veranda; the señora held back the lace curtain and beckoned him to enter. "Come and see. Your wife will be as good as new."

He opened his mouth to tell the señora that Ava wasn't his wife, but stopped himself. What did it matter? Instead, he gave her a smile and stepped inside. He saw the señora give a disapproving look at his hat, which remained on his head, but he wasn't about to take it off.

"I will give you some privacy," the señora told him. "We'll go set your friend's ankle now. Come on, girls."

"Thank you." He watched them go. They smiled at him and closed the door to give Ava and him privacy.

Ava herself was still asleep. Deathrider crept closer and sat awkwardly on the wooden chair next to the bed. The señora and her daughters had cleaned her up and dressed her in a white nightgown. Her leg was bandaged and propped up on a pillow.

She sure was pretty. Deathrider felt odd as he looked at her. The sun streamed through the lace curtains and fell in sweet patterns across her face. She had freckles, he saw, constellations of them. There was a sprinkling of dark moles too. He hadn't noticed the freckles before—he guessed he'd been too distracted. Sitting here, in the morning stillness, he took the chance to study her. He'd been dying to know what she looked like; here was a chance to drink his fill. Wisps of flame-bright hair curled around her temples, and her eyebrows were a foxy red-brown, as were her eyelashes. Her skin seemed almost translucent, violet and shadowy under her eyes, and flushed with palest pink elsewhere. She was a unique blend of ethereal and earthy.

She looked younger as she slept, more vulnerable. He could imagine the girl she'd been at seventeen: a beauty packaged up to be passed off to some old man. A plaything, she'd said.

He took her hand, which rested on the quilt. It was rough and sun browned. Not the hand of a plaything. Her fingers curled around his when he touched her, and her eyes fluttered open. Her pupils were tiny.

"Hey," he said softly. "How's the leg?"

"What leg?"

She was still deep in a laudanum haze. He squeezed her hand.

"Your eyes are so . . . *beautiful*," she breathed.

He flushed. How did she always manage to take him by surprise? He never knew what she was going to say. It was disconcerting.

"I didn't know," she said. "Isn't that silly? I knew your eyes were pale, but no one ever said how beautiful they are."

"Maybe most people don't think they're beautiful," he said, embarrassed.

She made a dismissive noise. "It's not an opinion. It's a *fact*." She let out a dreamy sigh. "I've wanted to meet you for the longest time."

He felt awkward as hell. "You should probably stop talking now," he said. "You're drugged up. When you come to your senses you might regret saying all this."

"No," she said vehemently, "I won't."

Her eyes were so dark against her freckled skin. Fierce and soft all at once.

"I was scared you'd be killed before I met you," she admitted, and to his horror, her eyes filled with tears.

"Now that you've met me, I guess it doesn't matter if I get killed," he joked. Then he watched, even more horrified, as she started sobbing.

"You didn't do any of those things, did you?" she cried.

"Hey," he protested. "Don't cry." He didn't know what to do with crying women. He didn't have much experience with them. What did you do? He took a leaf out of her book and started patting her.

But she just cried harder. "I don't think you raped Susannah Fuller," she said.

"I didn't," he agreed. "I told you that."

"Or kidnapped that boy."

"I *rescued* that boy," he told her. "His mother is one of my greatest admirers. Which she certainly wouldn't be if I'd kidnapped him."

"And the shoot-out in Fort Kearney?"

"Wasn't my fault. Some kid took into his head to kill me. He wanted me as some kind of trophy."

"Was that because of my books?" she asked miserably.

Hell, Deathrider thought. He'd wanted to find A.A. Archer and punish her—now he'd found her, and she was taking all of the pleasure out of things by *punishing herself.*

"Yes, sweetheart," he sighed, "it was because of your books. As was the idiot in Independence who wanted to kill me, and the one in the Sierras, and the pair on the Siskiyou Trail. And all the other idiots over all the years—they all wanted to kill me because of your books."

"I saw all your scars," she whispered. "Those were all because of me too, weren't they?"

Deathrider's stomach clenched as he remembered her bathing him. She *had* seen all his scars. Up close.

He reached out and ran a finger down her cheek. "It's a shame we didn't get to meet in other circumstances, sweetheart," he said softly. "I reckon we could have had some fun, you and me." Because she was some kind of woman. Nothing like he'd expected. And like no other woman he'd ever met before. And he would have damn well liked to have tried that bath again . . . albeit with a different ending this time. . . .

"The thing is, you're so . . . *nice,*" she marveled. Her big dark eyes searched his. "I didn't expect that. For you to be so nice."

"No one's ever called me nice before," he admitted. "I'm not sure I like it. Nice isn't manly."

"It *is,*" she disagreed. And then she was sobbing again, in earnest.

He brushed her hair back from her forehead. "Don't cry,

sweetheart. You're fine. It's just the pain and the medicine and all the excitement. A good night's sleep will fix everything."

She shook her head. "No, it won't. I've made a horrible mess of things." She pulled his hand toward her, pressing it to her cheek. Her gaze was full of misery.

"You have," he agreed. "A god-awful mess. The worst mess I've ever seen firsthand."

She frowned. "That doesn't make me feel better."

"No, I imagine it wouldn't."

"I want to fix it," she whispered.

It was the oddest thing, but every word she spoke was like an arrow shooting straight into him. He'd never thought to hear Ava Archer say those words. It never occurred to him that she would *want* to say those words.

It was probably the laudanum talking. That was all. Tomorrow she'd wake up and be straight back to the bloodless wielder of a poison pen. She'd write an account of the past few weeks that would include him ravishing some damsels, kidnapping some innocents, shooting up a town or two and maybe terrorizing some kittens.

"Nathaniel?" she said, and there were still fat tears rolling down her freckled cheeks. "I'm so very sorry. For all of it. I didn't know . . . I never thought of you as a real person. Not until I met you."

That seemed true enough.

"Please tell me how to fix it," she begged.

He gave a startled laugh, and there was more than a little bitterness in it. "No, sweetheart. You broke it; you fix it. It's not my job to find a solution to this mess. You clean up your own mess."

She bit her lip. Then she nodded. "I will." A fierce look came over her face. "I *will*. I promise."

He pulled his hand out of her grasp.

"Please don't go," she hiccuped. For a moment he thought she knew he was planning to ride out, but then he realized she just meant don't leave the bedroom. "Stay with me for a bit?" she asked.

He nodded. "Just for a bit."

Goddamn, it was hard to leave her. It didn't make any sense at all.

"I'll wait until you go to sleep," he said hoarsely.

"Thank you." She startled him then by trying to sit up.

"What are you doing? You're supposed to be sleeping."

"I will. There's just something I want to do first."

"What?"

"This." She threw her arms around him and pulled him into a tight embrace. He felt the press of her breasts against his chest and the feel of her cheek against his neck. "I'm sorry, Nathaniel," she whispered into his ear. "I'm so, so sorry."

He didn't know what to do. Her body felt wonderful; her words even more so. "Sorry" didn't fix anything at all, but it still felt good to hear. He wrapped his arms around her in return, dropping his chin against her head.

"I'm sorry too," he sighed. He didn't know what for. Just for the whole sorry mess of life, really. For the fact that things could never be simple. For the way her body felt against his, and the way she made him laugh; and for the fact that they'd saved each other and doomed each other, and saved each other again; and because this had to be an ending and not a beginning.

She pulled back and stared up at him, her eyes liquid and her downturned mouth pouty from crying. She gave a hitching sigh. He watched hypnotized as she slid toward him and pressed her mouth to his.

He shouldn't let her. She wasn't in her right mind; she couldn't know what she was doing. He froze, knowing he should push her away. But she felt so good. Her mouth was warm on his, and she melted into him, her hand sliding up the nape of his neck, under the hat, and into his hair. He fell into her kiss headlong, surrendering to her. She led the kiss, deepening it, her tongue slipping against his lips, teasing them open. His hands curled into fists against the small of her back as her tongue slid into his mouth gently. Desire curled through him slowly, like a summer breeze. It was lazy and sweet and like nothing he'd felt before. There was no ferocity. It was a slow drowning. Lethal in its subtlety. Too gentle to fight against, too intense to resist.

When she finally pulled away, he was dazed.

She fell back against the pillows, her brown eyes hazy, and her lips swollen. She looked rumpled and sexy as hell—it took every ounce of his self-control not to climb into that bed with her.

He was breathing hard, like he'd run a mile.

She smiled, a dreamy, sleepy smile. "I'll see you in the morning," she murmured. Her eyes were slipping closed.

It *was* morning, he thought dumbly.

"Nathaniel Rides with Death," she sighed. "Magnificent." And then she slid off into slumber, leaving him sitting alone on the hard wooden chair next to the bed, reeling.

She was incandescently beautiful against the white sheets, her hair aflame in the morning sun, a smile on her pouty mouth, the tracks of her tears still visible on her pink-flushed cheeks.

That was his last memory of her. A few minutes later he crept out, knowing he would never see her again. By the time she woke, he would have rescued Micah, and the two of them would have left this whole sorry mess behind. And Ava Archer would be part of his past, someone he'd known in another time and place.

Someone he would never, ever forget.

❖ 24 ❖

Fort Laramie, Wyoming, ten months later

Ava arrived in Fort Laramie at the height of summer, riding in with the cavalry reinforcements. By then she was one of the boys, and she'd managed to crawl out of the worst of her black mood. She and Freckles had ambled along with the column for months on the way out from California, watching the winds chase through the prairie grasses, marveling at the herds of buffalo, listening to the boyish banter of the men. Ava had come to Laramie to see the greatest gathering of Indian tribes in human history, and the signing of their treaty with the United States government. *If* the Indians signed the treaty, which no one was at all sure would happen.

Ava had been in San Diego when word of the Great Treaty had gone around, and she hadn't been able to resist tagging along with the army reinforcements. It was a long journey to Fort Laramie, but what else was she going to do? She was avoiding San Francisco, because that ridiculous Hunt was still on, even though it had lost its urgency. It had all been a bit of a disappointment in the end. A lot of showmanship with no show at the end of it. Once Ortiz had turned up in October with his false Deathrider, only to meet with LeFoy's scorn, people realized that the game wasn't going to be easily cheated. Word went out fast that LeFoy *knew* the Plague of the West and could spot a fake a mile off. That stopped the trade in false Deathriders in its tracks. And no one could seem to catch the real one. There were plenty of rumors about both him and his redheaded whore, but no one could find either one of them.

"Do you think there ever *was* a whore?" Ava had asked Becky when they'd first reached San Diego, where they planned to lie low for a while. She'd been starting to have her doubts. Deathrider had never mentioned the whore, and she'd seen no sign of the woman in her time on the Hunt. The woman seemed more myth than reality.

"Of course there was a whore," Becky scoffed. "Everyone in Mariposa saw her." Becky launched eagerly into the subject. She could talk endlessly about the Hunt and all of the characters connected to it. It was her raging obsession. "Besides, I knew Seline. She was with us in Matt Slater's wagon train. She and Deathrider were great friends."

"What?" Ava had been astonished. "You never told me that!" She was horrified. That meant Deathrider— *Nathaniel*—had known the whore for years. It meant that it wasn't a casual relationship . . . which meant . . . Oh hell, who knew what it meant, except that it hurt like blazes to think about?

Was that where he'd gone after he'd left Ava? To find the whore? The thought made Ava sick with jealousy.

"Seline was nice," Becky said. "She had orange hair. Not red like yours, actual orange. I think she dyed it. She was the most amazing cook."

Ava scowled. She herself was a terrible cook.

"She was the type men fall all over themselves for. You know the kind. Tall. Striking. Big boobs. *Obvious.*"

Ava looked down at her own chest, which was modest. Becky's words haunted her. Visions of a big-breasted redhead draped all over Deathrider tortured her for months.

She'd stopped asking Becky questions about the whore, and about Deathrider; she'd discovered the details were just too painful.

She left Becky and Lord Whatsit back in San Diego when she headed out with the cavalry. The pair of them was still hatching plans to win the Hunt, with or without Deathrider, and had no interest in joining her on her new adventure.

"I didn't like Laramie the first time around," Becky sniffed, "and I don't see any reason to go confirm my dislike of the place. Besides, Jussy and I have a plan."

The latest plan seemed to include LeFoy. Becky thought he'd be open to throwing the competition Becky's way, so long as he got a cut of the winnings.

"All we need is for *him* to say we got the right Indian," Becky said. "Which I reckon he'd do, if he could make a profit out of it. He's not pure."

He certainly wasn't.

Ava was tired of talking about the Hunt. She'd lain low since Deathrider had run off, and she didn't fancy being caught up with Voss and those killers again. The whole thing made her feel tired and dirty. And as guilty as all hell.

Ava had left Becky and Lord Whatsit to their planning and decided to go and see the spectacle of the treaty instead. It would get her away from California and the Hunt, and it would save her from her indecision. What else was she going to do? Catch a ship back to New York?

She'd tried that. It hadn't worked. She'd bought a ticket, twice, on two separate ships, but when the day came to board, she couldn't make herself go. The thought of going back east filled her with dread. Both times she'd stayed in her hotel room, watching out the window as the ship she was supposed to be on pulled anchor and sailed away without her. There was nothing for her back east. Nothing she wanted.

Now and then she thought of her mother with a vague

sense of unease. There was unfinished business there. One day she would have to return . . . but she couldn't face it just yet.

But Ava didn't know *what* she wanted anymore. She'd fallen into a deep dark hole in the months following her adventures with Deathrider. Her gunshot wound had festered, and she'd succumbed to infection and raging fevers. She'd been laid up at the Torres ranch for more than three months. A couple of times they'd even thought she was going to die. Becky had stayed with her through it all, helping Señora Torres to nurse her and talking her through the worst of her delirium. When Ava had finally surfaced, she'd been weak and shaken. And she hadn't quite found her feet since. She was thinner, paler and more uncertain.

Not least of all because while she was sick, *he'd* left her. She wasn't sure when . . . Her illness had been long and disorienting. But according to Becky he'd been out the door the day they got to the ranch.

Hearing that cut Ava to the quick.

She often woke from her dreams, reaching for Deathrider. *Nathaniel.* But he was never there. And after a while, she had the oddest feeling that perhaps she'd dreamed him up . . . that perhaps he'd never really been there at all. . . .

The Ghost of the Trails . . .

While Ava had been sick, Lord Whatsit had ridden off a few times, looking for Deathrider. He never found him, although he did find his Arab not far from the ranch. That soothed his fury at "the damn Indian," as he'd taken to calling him. Lord Whatsit loved that horse. He'd been hanging mad when he'd discovered it was gone from the padre's stable; Becky had been sure he would shoot Deathrider for a horse thief if he ever found him.

By the time Ava was finally healing, it was early winter, and the Hunt had well and truly moved on. The Hunters were up north, according to the rumors, sweeping through the gold towns, following whispers about the whore being seen back in Moke Hill. They thought wherever the whore was, Deathrider was sure to follow. The thought made Ava irritable.

Laramie was a way to escape the constant rumors, to try to leave the past behind her. It was a distraction, one that required long days in the saddle and a lot of physical exertion that wore her out. She figured that maybe if she got herself tired enough, she'd be able to sleep peacefully and not dream about him.

The farther she got from California, the more the past year seemed like a fever dream. The trail was as hard to ride as she remembered, but it was slightly more pleasant than last time because of the pretty spring weather. Last time this stretch had come at the end of the trail, when she was already exhausted, and it had been searing late summer; the travails of the Lava Lands and the other desolate stretches of trail had been nightmarish. This time the slightly cooler days and nights helped enormously, as did being fresher in the saddle.

The cavalry officers and men she traveled with were a civil enough bunch, as rough as you'd expect from soldiers, but they tried their best to behave around her, which was rather endearing. Their captain had taken a shine to Ava and made sure she was well cared for. He had his second lieutenant pitch her tent for her every night and he lent her a bed frame, which could be assembled inside the tent. It even came with a striped mattress.

"I can't steal someone's bed," she'd protested.

"It's my bed," Captain Scott had told her gallantly. "And I won't hear of you refusing it."

She'd never traveled so well in her life. The smell of wildflowers filled the tent at night, and sometimes she slept with the flaps pulled back so she could see the heavy moon rising over the sea of grasses. By the time they'd reached the plains, it was full summer, and the grasslands were sweet meadows of flowering yarrow and hyssop, windflowers and columbines. The sage smudged the waving grasses with patches of silvery blue, and the air was fragrant with the scent of flowering milkweed.

Ava was cosseted like a princess by the troops. They cooked for her and brought coffee to her tent in the morning. Most of them were sweet boys, barely old enough to shave; the rest were grizzled old soldiers, glad of a woman's company. None of them stepped so much as a toe out of line. That was mostly because of Captain Scott, who led by impeccable example.

Ava should have enjoyed herself. . . . It was a pleasant adventure, during a mild and sunny summer. But she didn't. She was still low-spirited and prone to bouts of melancholy. As she lay on her iron camp bed, staring at the milky moon casting its light over the waving grasses, her thoughts drifted inevitably to the summer before. To the Hunt. To *him*.

Deathrider.

Where was he now? Was he close by or back in California with his whore? Would he be coming to the treaty meeting at Laramie, or had he turned his back on his people?

Just like he'd turned his back on her . . .

That was unfair. He didn't owe her anything.

It didn't seem to matter how unfair it was, though, she couldn't control her feelings, and she *felt* abandoned. Worse, betrayed. He'd left her, wounded and all alone. Well, not all alone. She'd had Becky and Lord Whatsit, but she'd *felt* alone. And then she'd almost died, and he hadn't been there. He hadn't even said goodbye. . . .

He didn't owe her anything, she reminded herself tersely, again and again, as she lay there in the milky moonlight on the vast prairie. It wasn't his fault she'd gone and developed all these silly feelings for him. And they *were* silly. Great big, wet, girlie feelings that flooded over her at the dumbest times. Like the day they reached the Sierra Nevada and it hit her that she was leaving California behind, and leaving California meant leaving *him*. She was leaving behind her

time with him. It felt like a kind of death. And she'd wept
like a baby as they rode through the mountains. Tears that
just wouldn't stop. Captain Scott had been mighty concerned about her, but she'd hinted that it was some kind of
woman's problem, and he'd steered well clear of the topic
after that. He had sisters, he told her, as though that meant
he could possibly understand.

Everything made her think of Deathrider: rivers, trees,
trading posts, sunsets, sunrises, dogs. . . . He was everywhere. Everywhere they rode, she wondered if he'd ridden
this way before. Had he camped here where they pitched
tent for the night? Had he drunk from this river? Had he
bought flour or sugar or tobacco from this trading post? Not
tobacco. She'd never seen him chew it or smoke it . . . but
what if he'd taken it up since she'd last seen him? That felt
even worse, like another small death. Because it was true—
he *would* do things she didn't know about. Thousands of
them. Millions of them. He would travel to places she'd
never see, meet people she'd never know, even one day
probably fall in love with a woman . . . a woman who
wouldn't be Ava. . . .

Oh, there went the tears again. It was abominable.

And things got only worse when they reached the Great
Plains. This was where his people were. She didn't know
exactly where, but somewhere on these plains. Somewhere,
over this stretch of hundreds of miles, he had grown up. Or
so she'd heard. Some said he'd been adopted, which considering the paleness of his eyes seemed probable. But who
knew? She couldn't rely on anything anymore.

Was *this* stretch his? Had he bathed in these streams?
Had he watched these butterflies flit through the coneflow-
ers and bergamot? Had he lain on his back in the feathery
grasses and watched the herds of white clouds cross the
pure blue skies? Had he hunted these buffalo? Made adorn-
ments from the quills of porcupines just like the ones ambling along through the grass?

She saw him wherever she looked, even though he was nowhere to be seen.

It was a relief to finally get to Fort Laramie in mid-August. This wasn't a place she could imagine him, although deep in her heart she harbored a desperate hope that he would turn up to the Great Treaty with his people. It wasn't likely, but she was happy to grasp at straws. It was all she had left.

✦ 25 ✦

THE HUT SAT low to the ground, a sod affair flanked by wind-blasted trees. The windows had no glass, but there were wooden shutters to keep out the wind and rain, and there was a makeshift chimney. Deathrider paused outside, watching the thin thread of blue smoke curl from the chimney. The sight of smoke from that chimney never ceased to make his heart pound harder, as though she was still alive and waiting inside for him. But of course she wasn't; it was just Two Bears visiting with his memories.

Deathrider didn't knock. He simply pushed the door open and stepped through.

His father was sitting in her rocking chair, with her blanket over his shoulders, even though it was midsummer and hot. He was staring into the flames in the fireplace, rocking, his expression contemplative.

"I knew I'd find you here," Deathrider sighed. He took in the modest one-room hut. It was exactly as Deathrider's mother had left it, right down to the mug full of flowers in the middle of the table. The wildflowers had dried out years ago, their colors faded, their petals as stiff as straw. Her bed was neatly made in the corner, with her crocheted blanket tucked in at the corners and her patchwork cushion plumped up and ready for her return. Only she'd never return; she'd been dead for years.

In fact, she was buried outside, right under one of the wind-blasted trees. There was a wooden cross with charms hanging from it, marking her last resting place. Now and then Two Bears added another charm to the collection. When the wind blew, you could hear the beads and quills and small bones clicking together. Spirits talking.

Deathrider had walked from the summer camp, bringing Dog with him. It was a long walk, but he enjoyed the solitary time. The camp was busy, and he needed some time alone. He never did well among large groups of people. The old restlessness was rising—worse than ever. He tried to focus on the prairie as he walked and to push the restlessness aside; to enjoy the day for what it was. But he had a lot on his mind. There were big decisions brewing for his people.

The sky was delphinium blue, the sunshine golden on the nodding heads of the meadow flowers. Dog bounded through the grasslands, chasing small animals, as bouncy as a puppy. Deathrider envied him his joy. His spirit was unquiet and his thoughts troubled.

"It's morbid the way you sit in here in the dark," he told his father once he'd entered the hut and observed Two Bears for a few moments.

Two Bears gave him a disgruntled look. "Don't disrespect your elders."

"It just makes you sad coming here; I don't know why you do it."

"No, I'm always sad. This place simply makes my sadness appropriate."

Deathrider grunted. He pulled a chair out from the kitchen table and dragged it next to the rocking chair. He sat down beside his father and looked around the room. "You've been coming here a lot," he observed. "There's no dust. You've been cleaning."

"Your mother has been coming to me in dreams."

Deathrider put his head in his hands. "Don't start this again."

"She's worried about you. I come here to keep her company, to put her spirit at ease. It's the least I can do, since I can't put her at ease about *you*."

"I came home, didn't I?"

"Did you? Part of you still seems a very long way away."

Deathrider ignored that. He hadn't told his father anything about the Hunt or about a certain redhead who had haunted him ever since. His father just liked to guess, in the hope that he'd find something out by accident.

"What's my mother's spirit fretting about now?" But Deathrider knew exactly what Two Bears was going to say. The man was stubborn as a buffalo.

"She wants you to get married."

Deathrider groaned. "She does, does she?"

"Her spirit won't rest until you are settled."

"That's funny because she's been coming to me in dreams too," Deathrider said sarcastically, "and she tells me *you* should get married again. She says if you were busy with a new wife, you'd be less of a pain in the ass to your son."

The wind rattled the charms outside.

"That's her," Two Bears sniffed. "She's scolding me for your bad manners."

Deathrider laughed. "You're impossible."

Two Bears sighed and drew the blanket tighter around himself, even though it was like a sweat lodge in the hut, with the fire roaring. "I'm getting old," he said.

"Are you? You managed to bring that buffalo down in the hunt just fine the other day. You look stronger than me."

"I *am* stronger than you." His pride got the best of him there. He frowned as he realized that he'd bragged himself out of his own argument.

"Such an old man," Deathrider teased.

"I worry about you," his father said bluntly.

"Well, don't. I'm here. Like you wanted. But instead of enjoying my return, you're sitting in here with the spirit of a dead woman, brooding."

Two Bears shot him a sharp look. "I'm not brooding. I was thinking about Broken Hand's invitation."

Deathrider rubbed his face. "That would make *me* brood. What are you going to do?"

Before the buffalo hunt, the Indian agent they all knew as Broken Hand had come with an invitation for Two Bears and his people. Broken Hand was visiting all the tribes of the plains, and had been at it for months, inviting them to treat with the whites at Fort Laramie.

Broken Hand was a former trapper by the name of Fitzpatrick, a tall, thin white man who'd won his Indian name when he broke his hand fighting the Sihásapa, the Lakota tribe the whites called Blackfeet. The fact that he'd survived with only a broken hand told you he wasn't someone you wanted to get on the wrong side of.

"The Great Father in Washington sent me," Broken Hand had told Two Bears and the eight bands of warriors. "He wants peace on the plains."

Two Bears had remained impassive, but Deathrider knew him well enough to detect the faint amusement. "Peace with whom?"

"He wants peace between whites and Indians, and peace between all of the tribes." Broken Hand knew them well enough to read their frank disbelief. "I know," he sighed. "He's asking the impossible. But it's not a bad idea . . . in theory." Broken Hand met Deathrider's gaze. "Your son will tell you there are more and more wagoners every year, a plague of them. Last year alone they were like locusts. Tens of thousands of them, riding through Lakota territories, risking life and limb."

"They killed a lot of buffalo," Two Bears said mildly.

"Yes, they did. And they fouled waterways and spread disease . . . I tell you, Two Bears, it's in your best interests to meet with the whites and negotiate terms, to stop these wagoners invading your lands."

Their lands. The Arapaho had only been on these plains since Two Bears' father had been headman. The Lakota had pushed them out of the Black Hills, and the Cheyenne had pushed them out of the northeastern plains. The Arapaho were currently defending themselves against the Crow, the Ute and the Pawnee. It wasn't just the whites who invaded their lands; the Arapaho were constantly under pressure. And they in turn pressured the Kiowa and the Comanche. The plains were a seething war zone of nomadic tribes who had mostly been pushed west by the eastern tribes. Which was one reason why the whites wanted a treaty; so long as the tribes were at war, the white wagoners were in constant danger.

"Who has agreed to go to Fort Laramie to meet with the Great Father?" Two Bears asked curiously.

"The Great Father won't be there himself; he'll be sending his representative, Colonel Mitchell. He's the superintendent of Indian Affairs."

Deathrider saw his father's disquiet. "You haven't answered me. Who has agreed to go?"

"The Lakota."

There were murmurs at that.

"The Lakota are our allies," Two Bears said approvingly, but he was clearly surprised. "Which of the bands? The Oglála?"

"All of them."

"Including Red Cloud?" he asked Broken Hand, and there was a further flicker of unease.

"Yes."

There were more murmurs.

"Is anyone *else* going?"

The Lakota were the most powerful tribe on the plains, and they were at war with almost everyone. Who would be brave enough to turn up and face the Lakota?

But then again, who would want to leave the treaty to their mercies, without being able to represent their own interests?

"The Crow."

Everyone hated the Crow.

"The Shoshone, the Rees, the Cheyenne."

The Arapaho were closely allied to the Cheyenne. But the Lakota hated the Shoshone; the Shoshone hated the Cheyenne; and the Rees hated the Lakota.

Deathrider wondered if Micah would be there with the Shoshone. He hadn't seen his friend since they'd returned from their ordeal last winter.

"The Pawnee?" Two Bears asked.

"Not the Pawnee," Broken Hand admitted. "They're too afraid of the Lakota. But the Assiniboine, the Mandan, the Hidatsa and the Arikara are all possibly coming."

"Is there room for them all?"

Broken Hand almost smiled at that. "Barely. The plains are straining under the weight of you all."

"And how is the Great Father planning to prevent bloodshed during this Great Treaty," Two Bears asked dryly, "with so many blood feuds in one place . . . ?"

"The U.S. government asks that all feuds be suspended while we pass the pipe and work out terms."

"Terms about what?"

"Borders." Broken Hand knew them all well enough to register their concern.

Deathrider could read the tension in his father's shoulders. *Borders.*

"I think this is an opportunity," Broken Hand told them quickly before their concern could grow. "A chance for you to take some control. If you don't, the tide of immigrants is just going to keep pouring through—and you'll lose everything."

"The Lakota might have other ideas about that," Two Bears said dryly.

Broken Hand nodded, looking grim. "But if the Lakota shed white blood, the Great Father will send in the army. And that will lead to nothing good, not for any of you."

Deathrider remembered his experience with the U.S. Army, and he could well believe it.

The day after Broken Hand left, there was a messenger from the Lakota and, two days after that, a messenger from the Southern Arapaho. It was after all the messengers had left that Two Bears had taken himself off to the hut.

"What are you going to do?" Deathrider pressed his father now, sitting beside him in the hut. "Are we going to Fort Laramie?"

"I don't see that we have much choice," Two Bears said softly. "Our allies have asked us to go, and we are people who stand by our allies."

Deathrider nodded.

"We will have never seen so many people in one place," Two Bears mused. "Broken Hand said everyone is bringing their people. There will be trading and competitions and opportunities to visit old friends." He gave Deathrider a sideways look. "I imagine among so many people, it won't be too hard to find you a wife."

Deathrider groaned. "Don't you ever give up?"

"I will. Once I have you settled."

"I'm not sure who's more frightening. You or the Lakota."

❖ 26 ❖

THE BARRACKS AT Fort Laramie were kept with military precision. Things had changed since the last time Ava had been through. Back then Fort Laramie had been lousy with hopeful prospectors and wagoners, and the place had been a loose and dusty makeshift trading post and wagon-repair market. Riding in this time, she found the army had whipped the place into shape. The place had been freshly whitewashed and swept: a monument to the United States government, a showpiece for the Great Treaty. Army engineers had even built a wooden amphitheater with a canvas roof.

How many Indians were they expecting? Ava was shocked to even contemplate the numbers who could fit in that thing. She couldn't wait to get over there to examine it closely.

She'd go tomorrow. For now she was having a hard time just staying awake. It had been a long journey.

She was given a private room in the colonel's quarters, along with the honorary guests, including the superintendent of Indian Affairs. Captain Scott and the men were across the beaten-earth parade ground, in the adobe barracks.

"You let me know if any of my men bother you, Miss Archer," the colonel said gruffly when he'd greeted her out on the parade ground. "We don't have many women in these parts, and sometimes those boys forget their manners."

"They've been perfect gentlemen so far," Ava replied politely. She was deathly tired, and she hoped she wouldn't have to perform for too long. When the colonel told her they were throwing a dinner in her honor, for the officers only, she had a hard time not groaning. The last thing she felt like was sitting at a dinner table with a bunch of shiny-buttoned, mustachioed army men. Still. At least she could learn about the treaty. If there was one thing she'd learned, it was that men talked an awful lot when you got them at a dinner table with a glass of liquor in hand.

The colonel was conversant enough with a woman's needs to make sure she had time to change out of her traveling clothes before dinner. Ava had brought a couple of dresses with her this time: a day dress and an evening dress. This was probably an evening-dress occasion, she thought with a sigh, envisioning a long night ahead.

She cleaned herself as best she could with only a washbasin and struggled into the sage purple gown she'd had made up in San Diego. It had a two-tiered skirt and a V-shaped bodice and looked halfway decent, despite being rumpled from her luggage. She brushed her hair out and then hastily pinned it up again. There was no mirror in her room, which was probably a blessing.

Captain Scott was waiting to escort her to dinner, and he made sure he sat next to her. He was a nice sort. Soothing. That probably wasn't much of a compliment, except that after the last year, soothing was about all she could handle. She was grateful the men didn't expect her to speak much. She ate her beefsteak and potatoes and listened to them talking excitedly about the festivities ahead.

"I would imagine you've met an Indian or two in your time, Miss Archer?" the superintendent asked eventually, when the conversation was winding down. By then Ava had squirreled away lots of interesting facts about the treaty they were intending. The colonel was flushed from the bourbon, which they'd been drinking liberally, and he fixed her with a singularly patronizing smile. He used to be a fur trapper, she'd learned, and he still had more than a few of the rough edges you'd expect to find in a trapper.

"Indians? I've met one or two," she replied politely. She was trying to keep her answers to a minimum. If she proved dull company, they might let her slink off to bed early.

No such luck. At her answer the superintendent burst into laughter. "One or two!" he hooted. "I've read your books, Miss Archer, and I happen to know that one or two includes the Plague of the West himself!"

Ava flinched as though a horse had trodden on her foot.

"I met him once!" the man on the other side of Captain Scott exclaimed, leaning forward to smile shyly at Ava. "You write about his eyes in your books, but nothing quite prepares you for them in real life!"

No. Nothing does, she thought wistfully, remembering their clarity, like sunlit ice.

"It's like looking into the eyes of the devil," the man continued.

She had an insane urge to laugh. If that was how the devil looked, she was doomed. She pressed her lips together and made herself nod.

"Do you think he'll come?" Captain Scott wondered. "Fitzpatrick says he's back with the Arapaho, and they're coming."

This time Ava felt like a horse had kicked her in the chest.

He was here.

Not here here. But *here.* On the plains.

And, Jesus wept, maybe *here*, in Laramie.

"If he does come, he'll just be one killer among many," the colonel snorted. "He doesn't hold a candle to some of them."

Ava started to shiver. It was the shock of it. *She might see him again. . . .*

"Oh look, you've scared her," Captain Scott protested. He put an arm around her. "There, there, Miss Archer, you have the United States Army to protect you."

"I do beg your pardon," the colonel apologized. He was flushed with consternation. "But Scott is quite right. You've nothing at all to worry about with our fine men guarding you."

Ava barely restrained herself from rolling her eyes. She wasn't *frightened*. She was . . . She didn't know the word for what she was. Overwhelmed with a mess of feelings, most of which were stunningly foreign to her. She was nervous and excited, anxious and breathless and tingling from top to toe; her heart was racing, and her palms were sweating; and suddenly, madly, she felt like dancing. Twirling in circles and singing at the top of her lungs.

She hadn't realized how gray and flat the world had felt for such a long time. Now, with just the *hope* of seeing him again, all of the color had rushed back in all at once. Everything positively *sang* with delight.

Deathrider was nearby. He was *alive*, and he was close.

And she didn't care what kind of idiot she made of herself, or how many times she had to risk her life, she was going to see him again.

Because they had unfinished business.

THE SIOUX WERE the first to arrive. Or, rather, the Lakota, as Ava quickly learned they called themselves. On her third day at Fort Laramie, she'd discovered the women. She'd been led to believe she was the only woman in camp, but it wasn't true. There weren't many others, but they were there, discreetly hidden from her supposedly delicate eyes. At least until everyone learned that she wasn't that delicate after all. Then the women emerged from the woodwork and went back to their normal lives. Ava followed them, happy to find people to talk to who weren't soldiers.

These women were the camp wives, and each and every one of them was Indian, although they were from different tribes. They'd been given white names by their "husbands" (who all had actual wives at homes, but no one seemed to blink an eye at that), but Ava ferreted out their real names. The colonel's "wife's" name was Laughing Raccoon, which Ava thought was a much better name than "Jane," which is what everybody at Fort Laramie called her.

"It's only one of my names," Laughing Raccoon told Ava cheerfully. "Among my people, names can change. You can have different names at different periods of life."

Laughing Raccoon was a Lakota woman, which is how Ava learned that Sioux was a white name for the tribe.

"And within the Lakota there are seven . . . groups? Families?" Laughing Raccoon struggled to find the right word in English.

"Clans?" Ava suggested. She was taking notes. Meeting Deathrider had thrown her ignorance into sharp relief. She still cringed with shame at remembering that she'd mistaken him for an Apache. . . . She was going to work to remedy her ignorance.

She was zinging with energy since learning he might be coming, and she needed somewhere to put that energy. Interviewing people was the thing she knew how to do best, so that was what she did. The soldiers were all busy, so she turned her attention to the camp wives instead. They were much more interesting anyway.

"My people are the Brulé," Laughing Raccoon said proudly, as she stood with Ava, watching the Lakota come in a tide toward Fort Laramie. "That's them over on the right flank." She beamed with pride as she watched her people approach. "Agnes is Lakota too, but she's Oglála."

Ava was astonished at the sheer number of Lakota heading toward them. She had a feeling the colonel and the superintendent were too. There were some nervous soldiers in Fort Laramie today. The dragoons and the infantry stood on parade, chests puffed out, faces inscrutable, brass buttons shining in the sun. But they looked paltry compared with the sea of Lakota moving their way.

There must have been more than a thousand warriors alone, without counting the women and children. They came parading in full war paint, and the headmen and warriors wore magnificent feathered headdresses. There was a strict order to their assembly; the younger warriors followed their leaders in columns, and at the back came the women and girls, decked out in ornate ceremonial tunics, draped in beads and shells. They were all spectacular, resplendent with ribbons and feathers, and architecturally ornate hairstyles.

"There," Laughing Raccoon said reverently, directing Ava's attention to one warrior in particular, "that's Red Cloud."

"Who?" Ava had never heard of him. She wasn't alone. His fame hadn't spread to the whites yet, but it would. His name was already legendary among the Plains Indians. She made a note.

"Our allies come behind us," Laughing Raccoon told Ava, shining with pride. "The Lakota are the most powerful tribe in all the world; even our allies are fearsome."

Ava didn't have the heart to tell her that the paltry collection of soldiers on the parade ground was just the tip of the iceberg. The United States Army might well be the most powerful tribe in the world. They would be the worst foe the Lakota had ever faced—but if this treaty did its job, perhaps they would never need to come face-to-face, except in friendship.

Knowing what she knew of humans, though, Ava had her doubts.

The other women had joined them on the porch of the colonel's house, craning their necks to see the incredible display of power from the Lakota.

"Who are your allies?" Ava asked, her pencil flying over the pages of her notebook.

"The Cheyenne"—Laughing Raccoon pointed to the next wave of people arriving behind the Lakota—"and the Arapaho."

Ava snapped the tip of her pencil against the page. *Arapaho.*

Deathrider.

There was no way she would ever spot him in that mass of humanity. But she tried. She stood there as the Lakota came to a halt, closest to the fort, and she watched the ripple of movement stall, spreading back through the Cheyenne and the Arapaho, who were at the very farthest edge of the crowd. The superintendent went to welcome the leaders as the army bugler sounded "Boots and Saddles," a tune Ava would forever after associate with a dry mouth and a pounding heart. The three tribes were the only ones to arrive that first day, so the dragoons didn't need to worry about any of the groups fighting, as they were all allies.

Ava stood on the porch long after the other women had dispersed, the Lakota and Cheyenne women off to find their friends and relatives and the others back to their daily chores. She watched, enthralled, as the Lakota, Cheyenne and Arapaho staked their lodges and built their camps, intermingling and talking. There was laughter in the air as the shadows grew long.

"Quite a sight, isn't it?" Captain Scott marveled as he came to join her.

She nodded, not quite able to speak. There was no way Deathrider *wasn't* out there. No one in their right mind would miss this.

But now that she saw the tribes, she felt how alien she was from him. These were his people. This was his life. And it looked nothing like hers.

She didn't care, she thought fiercely. She didn't care how

alien they were from each other. She wanted to see him again. And then . . . and then she'd see what would happen next.

"We won't see the likes of this again in our lifetimes, I'll wager," Captain Scott told her. He unhooked his spyglass from his belt and handed it down to her. "Here. You'll see better." He gave her a concerned look. "But don't go any closer. You stay right here on the porch, in view of the boys. We don't want to go losing you in the crowd. Or to have some brave take a shine to you."

Ava took the spyglass without tearing her gaze away from the scene before her. She was watching entire villages form before her eyes. Temporary lodges were going up in the blink of an eye.

"Miss Archer," Captain Scott said, his voice husky. She finally looked up. He was staring down at her with a puppy-dog expression, which startled her. "You're mighty pretty when you're in a state of wonder."

Oh no. That wasn't something she wanted to deal with. What did you say to that?

"Thanks for the spyglass," she said awkwardly.

That seemed to be enough for him. He grinned at her, tipped his hat and headed back to his work. Jesus wept, she hoped he stayed mild, or she might be in for some trouble.

But Captain Scott faded from her thoughts the moment she lifted the spyglass to her eye. She spent the rest of the day watching the tribes setting up camp; she moved the spyglass ceaselessly, looking for a certain pair of broad shoulders, a single black-tipped eagle's feather, a mouth that looked like an archer's bow turned sideways and a pair of blazing pale eyes, the shade of ice.

By the time the evening had fallen, ashy lavender, and the campfires were flaring orange in the darkness, she still hadn't found him. But there was a slow-burning glow of hope that was rising in her like daybreak.

He was out there somewhere.

❧ 27 ❧

THE NEXT DAY brought tension. Deathrider watched the Shoshone arrive, feeling the thrumming animosity rising in the camps of his allies. That damn army bugler started up again with that honking reveille that rang out over the camp, playing in the arrival of the Shoshone. As they saw the Shoshone warriors, the Lakota women let loose with their blood-chilling death songs, lamenting the sons and fathers, brothers and husbands lost in battle to the Shoshone.

"This could get nasty," Two Bears said mildly.

But it didn't. The army was clearly worried it would, the soldiers moving forward to visibly remind the tribes they had promised peace, but the Shoshone ignored the Lakota women; in fact, they seemed to enjoy the spectacle, treating it as proof of their prowess as warriors. Deathrider saw Micah only from a distance. He was gleaming with armbands; brass disks hung from his headdress like miniature suns; and his neck was draped with so many layered threads of white beads that it was amazing he could hold his head up. He was fit and dark from the summer sun.

Deathrider was glad to see he was looking well. He hadn't seen his friend since they'd returned to the plains. When Deathrider had found Micah and Pete Hamble,

Micah had been in a sorry state. He'd been bruised and sunburned and sullen; he looked like Hamble had barely fed him. He was just a bag of bones. Deathrider had crept up on Hamble easily enough; the idiot was too busy talking to hear Deathrider's near-silent footfalls. Micah had seen him, though. At first he'd lit up, glad to see Deathrider was alive and strong enough to come rescue him. He'd saved the bitching for once they were free and clear.

Deathrider had knocked Hamble unconscious before the bastard had even registered that he'd been ambushed. Hamble had been bent over the fresh-laid campfire, trying to get it lit, yapping about some woman he'd known back in Frisco. One blow and he was down. But not dead. Deathrider figured that honor should go to Micah.

"He's all yours," Deathrider had told his friend as he unknotted Micah's bonds.

"I don't need your help," Micah complained as he tried to shake his hands back to life. "I can take care of myself."

"I can see that," Deathrider had said dryly. "You had him just where you wanted him."

"I did." Micah nudged Hamble with his foot, rolling the man over onto his back.

"Sorry to ruin things for you."

"I'm used to it." Micah reached down and began yanking Hamble's clothes off.

Deathrider watched as he took all Hamble's belongings and left the man naked. "Remind me never to piss you off," he said

"You already pissed me off. Many times."

"You want me to find some stinging nettle for you to rub into *his* eyes too?" Deathrider asked as he watched Micah lash Hamble's body to a Joshua tree.

"You're always so ungrateful," Micah bitched as he saddled up Hamble's horse. "If it weren't for me, you'd be dead. I saved your life with that nettle."

"And now I've saved *your* life, so I figure we're even."

"I didn't ask for you to save me," Micah snorted as he swung into the saddle. "I had him—"

"I know, I know, you had him just where you wanted him." Deathrider eyed Hamble's packhorse. Hell. It was a sorry way to travel.

"Where's your horse?" Micah asked him, surprised to see Deathrider astride the packhorse.

"I had one on loan—I had to give it back." Deathrider had given a longing look over his shoulder, toward where he'd set his lordship's Arab free. He'd much rather be on the Arab than on the packhorse.

"Where in hell have you been anyway?" Micah demanded as they rode into the inky night.

"It's a long story."

"That's fine. We've got a long piece of traveling ahead. And the least you can do, after all you've put me through, is keep me entertained while we travel." He was fumbling through Hamble's saddlebag as he spoke, looking for food.

As they rode home, Deathrider told his friend some of what had happened—but not all. Some of it was too tangled up and sore for him to tell. The bits of it with red hair and sloe-dark eyes . . .

"Traveling with you was blasted misery," Micah told him, sounding cheerful enough when they finally parted ways on the plains, pausing to watch the grass heads flick and wave in the winds.

"Back at you," Deathrider agreed. He was going to miss his friend. "Stay safe."

"I will—you won't be anywhere near me."

Deathrider had laughed. But the laughter had faded as he'd watched Micah ride off into the sea of grass. He'd had a bittersweet feeling that things had changed forever.

Now as he saw Micah with his people here at Fort Laramie, Deathrider knew for sure they had. Micah had changed. Hell, *he* had changed.

Jim Bridger came in with the Shoshone, escorting them

with his head held high. The trapper had married into the Snake band, and he came as a full-fledged member of the tribe. The army seemed more than a little startled to find a white man among the leadership group accepting their welcome.

The Shoshone were armed to the teeth, Deathrider noted. Just as he was, just as the Cheyenne and Arapaho and Lakota were. Everyone had come prepared for this meeting to go terribly wrong. And no one was particularly hopeful.

"You brought the white man, I see." Running Elk joined Two Bears and Deathrider as they watched the Shoshone set up camp. "Just like the Snake. Bringing white men where they don't belong."

Neither Two Bears nor Deathrider rose to the bait. The Lakota chief seemed disappointed.

"Good to see you, old friend," Two Bears greeted him. "Did you bring any of your daughters?"

Deathrider shot him a warning look. He was incorrigible.

"They're all married now," Running Elk said with great satisfaction. "So there's no risk of losing one to your white man."

Two Bears grunted. He should really have complimented Running Elk's good fortune then, but he couldn't find it in him today by the looks of it, because he stayed silent.

"There *is* something your white man could come in handy for," Running Elk suggested. "He could go and talk to the whites and find out how this will unfold."

"My *son* will be happy to."

"Will I?" Deathrider asked.

His father didn't deign to answer that; he just gave Deathrider a shove in the direction of the fort.

"My daughters married men of great honor," Running Elk was telling a morose Two Bears as Deathrider moved off.

The whole place had a carnival air. He threaded through the Lakota camp toward Fort Laramie proper. He'd been here more times than he could count, but it was difficult to recognize the place today. The ground behind the fort fell away, down to the confluence of the two rivers. People were heading down to fill their pails with fresh water. Where once there had been wooden palisades and a rough structure, there was now a neatly organized army barracks. Off to one side, Deathrider could see the bluecoats building something; there was the sound of hammering. It was a wooden structure, like nothing he'd seen before.

He hunted for someone to get answers out of, glad he hadn't gone for full face paint. It would have probably scared the whites witless. When he reached the parade ground, he stopped to stare at the soldiers standing on display. They were getting sunburned. None of them looked in a position to answer his questions.

He heard voices coming from around the corner of a small building. It was a square whitewashed adobe house, with a porch that wrapped around two sides, one side facing the camped Indians, the other looking down over the river. The voices were coming from the riverside, away from the sight line of the parade ground.

"I know this is a sudden," a man was saying in English, his voice pulsing with barely suppressed emotion. "But I'm in love with you. You stole my heart the moment I saw you, but I didn't know it until much later. This summer we've spent together, on the trail here, has been the greatest of my life."

Deathrider pulled a face. Really? Surely if the man's heart had been stolen, he would have known immediately?

Deathrider was just being sour because his own heart was beat-up these days. Just like the rest of him.

This was private. He probably shouldn't intrude. He should let the lovers enjoy their vaguely silly moment and take his sourness off somewhere else.

"You are the most perfect woman in the world," the overly dramatic suitor declared. That was clearly untrue. Because Deathrider had met the most perfect woman in the world, and she most certainly wasn't *here*. She was off causing havoc more than a thousand miles away.

"I'm asking you to marry me!" the poor lovesick idiot proclaimed.

Deathrider sighed. He'd have to go and find someone else to ask about the process of the treaty—these two were clearly busy. And clearly not the right people to ask.

But then a voice came ringing, clear as a bell, setting the lovelorn suitor in his place. And it was a voice Deathrider would have known anywhere.

"Get up off the ground. You're getting your trousers dirty," she said, her very practicality harsh beyond words.

It couldn't be . . .

But it was. Deathrider didn't even need to see her to know. He'd spent most of his time with her *not* seeing her, and he could have picked out her voice anywhere.

"I love you," her lovesick suitor repeated, sounding truly desperate.

"It's probably just sunstroke, Captain," she said, and damn if she didn't sound like she'd be patting him. That was what she did when she thought people were about to crumble in front of her.

Deathrider felt a bolt of joy so powerful, it almost felled him. *Ava Archer.*

"Or it might be the pressure of this treaty," she soothed him mercilessly, not giving him so much as the slightest sense of hope. "It's bound to get to a man, an event like this, with all of these people. All of it your responsibility. It's bound to make you a bit daft in the head. You're just imagining that you love me. You don't even know me."

Ouch. The poor man. Whoever he was.

"It's you that's made me daft, Miss Archer."

Although Deathrider knew it was her—knew it down deep in his body and soul—the sound of her name was like the sun coming out, blinding him. It *was* her.

"You've taken my wits, and my will, and rendered me helpless."

"Funny, you don't seem terribly helpless. In fact, you seem quite handsy."

Deathrider scowled at that. *Handsy?*

He rounded the corner of the house and saw her. She was hard up against the porch railing, bending so far backward, she looked like she might go tumbling. Pressing his suit was one of the bluecoats; he was on one knee, but he'd had the nerve to grip her hips in his hands and try to pull her toward him.

"Let go of her," Deathrider barked before he could think better of it.

Her head whipped up, and her big dark eyes went even bigger. Her sexy-as-hell downturned mouth popped open. "Nathaniel!"

He had competing urges. Part of him wanted to laugh with the sheer joy of seeing her; the other part of him wanted to thump the bluecoat who was yanking on her hips.

"I *knew* you'd be here," she said as a smile broke over her face, one that was so startling that he almost forgot what he was doing. He'd never seen her smile before, he realized stupidly. It was astonishing. She went from being striking to being absolutely breathtaking. Like when a pretty afternoon broke into a blazing sunset.

The bluecoat stumbled to his feet, blushing scarlet. He was quite young, Deathrider saw, for all his rank.

"I beg your pardon," the bluecoat said, sounding irritated. "But we're in the middle of something."

"No, we aren't." With characteristic bluntness, Ava Archer pushed past him. "We were done."

The color drained from the man's face.

"That was cold, sweetheart," Deathrider told her. He couldn't seem to stop smiling. It was because *she* was smiling. It was catching, like a disease. The two of them were grinning at each other like a pair of idiots.

"I missed you," Ava Archer blurted.

"I missed you too." He hadn't meant to say that. And hell, of all the people to miss, the woman who ruined his life was a stupid one to pick. But goddamn, he *had* missed her. So much it was like he'd lost a limb.

"He's an *Indian*," the bluecoat told her like she was blind and hadn't noticed.

"Not just any Indian," she corrected him. "This is *my* Indian." She was still grinning that sunset-bright grin.

The bluecoat looked appalled. He dusted his knees as he backed away from them. Deathrider spared him a sympathetic glance. "You don't want her," he told the man. "She's nothing but trouble."

"It's true," Ava agreed. "I am."

The bluecoat slunk away, looking absolutely miserable.

"You seem to have that effect on men."

"*You're* smiling."

"I'm not normal." Deathrider looked her up and down. He'd never seen her dressed up before. She was in a white gown sprigged with ivy leaves. The green of the leaves brought out her coloring. The skirt made her waist look tiny. "You look nice in a dress."

She looked down at herself, flushing. "What, this old thing?"

"Cleopatra," he said, his voice growing husky, "I'm going to kiss you now. Unless you tell me not to."

"If you don't hurry up, I'm going to kiss *you*."

"Me first." He pulled her into his arms and fell hungrily into her mouth. All of the long months of longing were unleashed as he kissed her. He'd thought of nothing but her, dreamed of nothing but her, wanted nothing but her. It was madness. Because he hadn't been lying to that poor bluecoat. She *was* nothing but trouble. Complete and utter trouble.

He pushed her against the wall of the cottage, pressing his body into her. He ran his hands down her long muscular arms as his tongue traced the plump sulkiness of her lips.

She opened under him, her mouth hot and wet. He slid his tongue into her as his hands plunged into her hair. Hairpins fell, tinkling on the brickwork. He felt her hands find his hips, hauling him harder against her.

"Ava," he moaned.

"Wait." She pulled back. She was smiling, her mouth red and puffy from his kisses. Her brown eyes were glazed with desire.

"No," he said, dropping kisses against her neck. He opened his mouth and swirled his tongue against her throat. "I've been waiting for months."

"Stop talking," she said thickly, "and come with me."

SHE LED HIM inside the cottage, walking backward as she pulled him by the hand. He didn't even stop to think what would have happened if they ran into anyone. Luckily for him they didn't. She opened a door and led him into a bedroom.

He couldn't look away from her. She moved slowly, lazily, half-drunk with desire. Her eyes were heavy lidded. She let go of his hand and skipped out of reach as he grabbed for her.

"Patience is a virtue," she scolded. She pulled the blind and closed the door, turning the key in the lock.

He'd lost his mind, he thought as he watched her lean against the door, head back, her gaze sweeping his body. Outside, thousands had gathered to decide the future of the Great Plains, and he was in here . . . behind locked doors . . . surrendering to his basest animal urges. . . .

Ava Archer bit her lip as she examined him, and the gesture was so sexy, he was hurting. *Who gave a damn about the Great Plains?* he thought with a groan, diving for her. He pinned her to the door, reclaiming her mouth. She laughed and kissed him back with equal fervor. Her hands ran up the front of his body; he could feel them through the buckskin of his shirt, the shock of them as they ran over his hard nipples.

Her tongue thrust into his mouth. He curled his arm around her body, reaching for her ass.

"I can't feel anything through this damn dress," he growled.

"I thought you liked it," she laughed breathlessly.

"I'd like it off."

She stretched her arms up above her head. "So take it off." She looked up at him teasingly.

Hell. He'd had no idea. The woman was wildfire.

He put his shaky hands on her shoulders and turned her. She spread her hands against the wooden door, fingers splayed. He ran his hand down the length of her back and felt her shiver. He bent close and kissed her neck. Her skin was hot. He licked her and felt her shivers become shudders. "Feel good?"

"Yes," she breathed.

"Want more?"

"Yes."

He took her earlobe in his mouth and gave it a firm suck. He heard her moan. As he traced her ear with his tongue, he undid the buttons down the back of her dress, exposing a very sexy muscular back. The tan line between her neck and her shoulders turned him on beyond belief. Beneath the line, her skin was creamy white. He traced the line with his finger, over her shoulders. Then he parted the gown, revealing a simple corset and some very transparent muslin underthings. He could see her moles through the cotton. He peeled the dress off her, letting it drop to the floor. He untied her petticoats, letting them fall too.

This was what he'd wanted to see. She was left in just her corset, chemise and pantalets. The pantalets were stretched tight over a magnificently firm round ass. She was spectacular. And those legs. They went on forever, long and curvaceous as hell. Deathrider ran the flat of his hand down her. She arched her back and her ass rose, rounder than ever. He ran his hand over her cheeks. So firm, so warm.

He was so hard, he felt like he could come without her ever touching him.

She looked over her shoulder at him, her smile almost his undoing.

"Vixen," he said thickly.

She turned around and he *ached*. Her breasts were small and perky, thrusting at the whisper-thin muslin. Her nipples were large and dark, hardening as he looked at them. He reached out to rub them with his thumbs. She groaned and arched into him. Hell, her tits were incredible. He wanted to taste her.

He lowered his head to suck her through the chemise. Her nipple swelled in his mouth, filling it. He squeezed her other breast in his hand. Sucking and squeezing, sucking and squeezing until he felt her begin to melt against the door. He pulled back, enjoying the look of mindless bliss on her face.

She was wet for him. He could see her pantalets were damp. The shadow of her was tantalizing.

"I want you naked," he told her, pressing a kiss against her mouth. Licking the inside corners of her lips. She mewled against his kisses. He took that for a yes.

When she was naked, he lowered her to the bed. She was sheer perfection. He kissed every last inch of her, while she writhed beneath him. He rubbed his hands over her round hip bones and her firm stomach. He lowered his head into the wet heat between her thighs as he cupped her ass. He drove her to the edge and back a dozen times. And he was still fully clothed.

That needed to be remedied.

She stretched languorously when he pulled away to yank his shirt off. Fuck, she was beautiful. Her breasts seemed all jutting nipple.

"I love your body," she purred as she stared at his chest.

His body loved her back. His nipples were tingling, and she wasn't even touching him.

"Take your leggings off," she ordered.

He didn't need to be asked twice. As he peeled them off, his cock leapt free. It was hard as hell, the head already slick with precum. Her finger slid over its swollen tip, and he thought for a moment he'd come right then and there.

"Don't you dare," she warned.

He sat on the bed and yanked her toward him. "Ride me," he begged.

Her eyes widened. And then she grinned. "Yes, please."

She swung one long, muscular leg over his hips, hovering over his twitching, hungry cock. He cupped her luscious ass in his hands, loving the feel of her. His gaze was full of her dark nipples, pointy and hard, their long tips aching for his mouth. He obliged, flicking his tongue over them, one after the other. She moaned. And then she slid onto his cock, and he couldn't think anymore. He was at her mercy.

He buried his face in her tits and held on to her ass as she rode him. She was strong, and she fucked him near senseless. Just when he thought the pleasure couldn't get more intense, it did. She clenched around him. He sucked on her tits as she came, and as he felt the intensity of her shudders pulling him deeper inside of her, he surrendered to the violent pleasure of his release.

❧ 28 ❧

AFTERWARD, THEY LAY in the dim room, stunned. Naked, they were pressed flesh to flesh for a long time without speaking. And it felt as natural as breathing. Neither of them had ever experienced anything as uninhibited, as wild and free or as tender.

"So, you missed me, huh?" she said eventually, and she sounded so self-satisfied that he gave her a smack on the ass.

Which she didn't mind at all.

One thing led to another, and they lost another hour or more.

When they surfaced, the day was growing late. Ava was aware of Deathrider's uneasy quiet. He was brooding again. She felt a stabbing disquiet and lifted her head to regard him.

When he met her gaze, his was solemn. It sent fear cascading through her. She couldn't have articulated why, but some deep part of her was waiting for him to leave her.

Then she saw a glint of amusement.

"What so funny?" she asked.

"You're patting me."

"I'm not." She curled her hands into fists.

He pulled her closer. "You always pat me when you're worried about something."

Always. It made them sound . . . permanent. Which she knew they weren't.

She didn't know what they were yet. But none of it was certain.

"I need to get back to my father," he said, capturing her hand in his as it started patting him again.

"Your father," she said, startled. "Your father is here?"

"He is," Deathrider sighed. "And if he finds out about you, my life is going to get complicated, fast."

She felt a stab of hurt. He noticed.

"I just mean he's trying to marry me off," he clarified, "and if he saw us like this, he'd have you married to me before you even got introduced to him." He grimaced.

Ava wasn't sure how to take that.

"I need to go, sweetheart. There's a treaty to sign . . ." He disentangled himself and sat up.

"I barely know anything about you," she said, holding the sheet to herself and feeling painfully vulnerable as she watched him getting dressed. "Are you one of the leaders invited into the amphitheater?"

"No, but my father is. I said I'd find out whatever I could about the way this is going to play out."

Ava pushed her hair out of her face and knelt up on the bed. "*That* I can help you with. What do you need to know?"

He paused and considered her, half in and half out of his shirt. "How do you know about it?"

She rolled her eyes. "I'm Ava Archer," she said, as though it was painfully self-evident. "It's what I *do.*"

He sat back down on the side of the bed and pulled his shirt on. "Of course it is," he said dryly. "Go on, then, Ava Archer. Tell me what you know."

"Only on one condition . . ."

His eyes narrowed suspiciously. "What?"

"I want to see everything. The colonel won't let me leave the fort, because they can't protect me. But I could go with *you.*" She gave him a sunny smile.

"Oh no." He shook his head. "It's not safe."

She rolled her eyes. "Nothing is ever safe. If I can survive Kennedy Voss, I can survive this. And I want to see the competitions. I want to see the markets. I want to be part of the feasting and watch the courtships. I want to see it *all*."

"Of course you do."

"And I want to meet your father."

"Oh no, you don't. That's one step too far." But he sounded lighthearted enough.

"Shake on it." She held out her hand.

He looked at it in disdain. "We're past the shaking stage, sweetheart." He leaned across and kissed her instead. And once they started kissing, they couldn't stop.

THE NEXT FEW days were the most joyful of Ava's entire life. She knew they couldn't last. She and Deathrider were from two different worlds, and the circumstances were so surreal; it was like a strange and beautiful dream. Sometimes she wondered if she wasn't still back in Señora Torres's house in California, dying of infection from her gunshot wound, having one last vivid fever dream. Because if she had to have one last dream before she died, this would be the one she'd want.

She and Deathrider spent a delirious week. Between the tense and astonishing events of the treaty during the days and their delirious nights together, they existed in a haze. The week blurred into a bright, loud, overwhelming shimmer of feelings.

It was hard to focus on anything that wasn't *him*. Which caused a few problems.

"Miss Archer!" Captain Scott had detained her that first morning after Deathrider had slipped away, back to his people. He left her with a kiss that was so tender, it brought tears to her eyes. She was turning into a complete sap.

Ava had braided her hair and pulled on her traveling clothes and headed for the porch, where she planned to watch the happenings in the camp while she waited for Deathrider to return. She wasn't really interested in soothing Scott's wounded ego before she'd even had her coffee, so she was shorter with him than she should have been.

What a disappointment he'd been, she thought as she watched him approach. She'd thought he was nice. But for all Scott's sentiment the other day, he'd been handsy as all hell, touching her in places he had no right to touch.

"I wanted to talk to you. About yesterday."

Of course he did. His behavior had been abominable. She waited for his apology.

But it didn't come. To her astonishment, he had the nerve to *scold her*.

"It's against army regulations for Indians to be in the barracks proper," he said stiffly.

He wasn't serious? Especially as how Laughing Raccoon was emerging from the colonel's house right at the instant he spoke, carrying a pot of coffee and a handful of tin mugs.

"I'm afraid I'll have to report you to the authorities." Two bright spots of color burned high on his cheeks, and his eyes glittered with animosity.

"You mean, you'll report me to the *colonel*?" She stared pointedly at Laughing Raccoon, but he didn't seem to get the hint. Bluntness was in order then. "Are you saying, Captain, that's what's good for the gander isn't good for the goose?" she asked briskly.

"This has nothing to do with geese," he said stiffly, "and everything to do with decorum."

"Coffee?" Laughing Raccoon interrupted them, holding out her hand for them to unhook a tin mug from one of her fingers.

"Not for me." Captain Scott's chin went up.

Ava stared him down and took a mug, holding it out for Laughing Raccoon to fill. "Thank you," she said.

"I'll be going down to the Brulé camp in a moment, if you want to come along," Laughing Raccoon offered.

"I can't. I'm sorry," Ava apologized, not breaking eye contact with the captain. "I'm meeting someone."

Captain Scott flushed a deep and angry red. "You're a disgrace to your race," he said viciously before stalking off.

"What's wrong with him?" Laughing Raccoon asked.

Ava didn't even know where to begin. She shrugged and drank her coffee.

As the morning aged, the tribes kept pouring into Fort Laramie, until there were campsites as far as the eye could see. The supply train with all the gifts from the government to the Indians was late, held up in St. Louis, and the superintendent and the colonel were conferring furiously with Fitzpatrick, the man Deathrider called Broken Hand. From where she stood on the porch, Ava had a good view of their comings and goings. They seemed panicked that the Indians would leave when they discovered there were no gifts of sugar, or tobacco, or any of the other treasures the army had organized.

"This may end before it even begins," the colonel confided in Ava when he and Fitzpatrick emerged from the cottage to smoke their pipes on the porch. The superintendent had gone to send messengers to St. Louis. "Or it may even erupt in open bloodshed."

"Over some sugar and tobacco?" she asked dubiously.

"And blankets," he said defensively. "Knives, cloth, coffee, beads. A fortune worth of materials, Miss Archer. Signs of good faith."

Ava was still dubious. But she held her tongue.

"Deathrider!" Fitzpatrick lit up when he saw Ava's lover ambling through the fort toward the cottage. He waved Deathrider over, not realizing he was already headed in their direction. Ava could see Captain Scott across the square, glowering. She gave him a jaunty little wave.

"I'm glad to see you," Fitzpatrick said, "we have a problem."

Deathrider listened to his problem but didn't look concerned. "Now that they're here, I doubt they'll turn around and leave." His gaze was on Ava. He couldn't seem to look away. She suppressed a smile, feeling a surge of desire. That look in his eyes was intoxicating.

"Besides," he told the men, "the Lakota have asked the Shoshone to a feast tonight."

Fitzpatrick looked shocked. "But they're enemies . . ."

"It's like finding night has become day," Deathrider agreed. "Everyone is in an uproar."

"How do you know the Lakota won't kill the Shoshone midfeast?" the colonel interrupted.

"We don't," Deathrider said with a shrug.

That sent them into another frenzy. "We'll need to arm the men, have them ready." The colonel summoned Captain Scott and gave a series of staccato orders. Scott stared sullenly at Ava and Deathrider as he received them.

"The Cheyenne and the Arapaho have been invited after the feast," Deathrider told them. "It will be a mighty celebration."

"Over the bodies of your enemies?" Scott snapped.

"Scott!" the colonel barked. "You speak out of turn." Then he turned to Deathrider and repeated Scott's words, but without the vitriol: "Over the bodies of your enemies?"

Deathrider shrugged. "Who knows how events will play out? The Oglála are fierce warriors, and there is much bad blood with the Shoshone. But the Brulé are keen to treat. So we shall see."

"Scott! Spread the word to our guests that there's a total alcohol ban for this week. No one is to touch a drop.

That includes our men. The last thing we need is to add drunkenness to this tinderbox." He mopped at his damp forehead with his sleeve. "This week will see the end of me, I swear."

"I don't envy you, Colonel." Deathrider put his hand on Ava's back. "Now, if you'll excuse me, I promised to show Miss Archer the camp."

"It's the damnedest thing," Ava heard the colonel saying to Fitzpatrick as they walked away, "but I always imagined those two would be mortal enemies. Have you read her books?"

"Fiction," Fitzpatrick said dismissively.

"Total fiction," Deathrider agreed, grinning down at her.

"Not *total*," Ava protested. "Just . . . incomplete."

He took her hand and pulled her down the slope toward the camps. The feel of his big hand closing around hers sent shivers through her. He felt it and smiled at her, his eyes chips of pale winter sky.

She still couldn't believe he was here. In the flesh. And that he was *smiling* at her. Maybe she'd died of that infection . . . or even way back in the desert of thirst. . . . Maybe none of this was real. . . .

But who *cared* if it was real? It felt magnificent to walk in the sun with him, hand in hand, as he pointed out the tribes and their leaders; she peppered him with questions, and he answered. His thumb stroked the back of her hand, and she just about melted. He turned her into a wanton. She just wanted to drag him into the nearest tent and ravish him. Last night and this morning, he'd spent endless hours torturing her with pleasure, but she hadn't had a chance to return the favor yet. And the things she'd like to *do* to him.

"Where are we going?" she asked as he changed direction abruptly, almost yanking her arm out of its socket.

"To find some privacy. Your patting is driving me wild."

She hadn't even been aware she *was* patting him, but it

was true. Her hand was curled around his biceps, patting it in soft strokes.

"Where can we find privacy out here?" she laughed, looking around at the teeming people. There were make-shift lodges, tents and teepees in every direction; cook fires were burning, animals were grazing and children were running wild.

"My place," he growled, pulling her so fast, her feet barely touched the ground.

❖ 29 ❖

H IS PLACE" WAS a teepee in the Arapaho encampment.
Right in the *middle* of the Arapaho encampment. Ava
blushed scarlet as he spirited her through the makeshift village of teepees, not introducing her to anyone. She looked
around, wondering if his father was here, but there seemed
only to be women and children. They were all staring at
Ava curiously.

Deathrider pushed her gently through the opening, and
then they were in their own private cocoon, away from everybody's prying eyes.

The moment they were alone, he was kissing her, and
she fell into him hungrily, pulling at his clothes. She
couldn't get close enough, fast enough. They were naked
and down on his furs before she could draw breath. And
that was where they spent the rest of the day.

The first time was hard and fast, the second slow. She
traced every tattoo on his body with her fingertips, enjoying
the way he shivered at her touch. And then she kissed his
old scars, one by one, starting at his ankles and working all
the way up to his face. She made it take an age, until he was
mindless with desire.

The third time was sleepy. They were spooning, with her
back pressed against his chest. She rose through layers of

sleep as she felt his mouth on her neck, his hands on her breasts and the hard length of him pressing against her buttocks. She rubbed against him, arching her back. He had only to touch her, and she was wet. She reached behind to guide him into her. It was slow, tender, a series of long thrusts as his breath swirled warm and sugary against her neck. When she came, she found she was crying. When he came, he breathed her name. That only made her weep more.

"Don't cry, Cleopatra," he whispered, pulling her close and pressing a kiss on her temple.

"I'm just happy," she said stupidly, brushing the tears away.

He pulled the furs over them, and they drifted back to sleep.

The next time Ava woke, she shrieked to find herself looking at a man. Or rather *he* was looking at *her*. It was growing dark, and the man had a lantern in front of him. He was sitting cross-legged in the middle of the teepee and staring at her intently.

Her shriek woke Deathrider, who sat up, pulling the furs with him. She scrambled to grab them, to keep herself covered.

Deathrider groaned. Then he said something in his native language. He sounded snappy but not alarmed. Ava looked back and forth as the two men had a conversation she couldn't understand. She couldn't read the other man's face. Was he angry? He had a very stern look about him.

She kicked Deathrider under the covers. Why wasn't he telling her what was happening?

He glanced at her and sighed. "Ava," he said grudgingly, "this is my father."

She could have died. Of course it was. And here she was naked, in his teepee. She blushed again. "Nice to meet you, Mr. . . . ?"

"Two Bears," the old man grunted in heavily accented English.

"I thought you were with Running Elk," Deathrider complained, flopping back into the furs and pressing the heels of his hands into his eyes. At least he was speaking English now, so she didn't feel quite so anxious about what was happening. Deathrider's father was still watching her with that intense gaze. It made her nervous.

"I *was* with Running Elk," his father said, also switching to English. "But he has the feast with the Shoshone, so I had to leave. We have a couple of hours until we have to go back."

Ava inched her hand toward her chemise, which was on the ground nearby. She thought she saw Two Bears's lips twitch in amusement. He didn't move to help her. Or to turn his back so she could dress in peace.

"I see you haven't prepared any food," Two Bears told his son dryly. "There is nothing for me to eat."

"Get a wife if you want food waiting for you." Deathrider didn't remove his hands from his eyes.

"You see how he disrespects his father?" Two Bears told Ava sorrowfully as she contorted herself to try to slip into her chemise under the furs. "Can you cook?" he asked Ava.

"No," Deathrider said shortly. "She's a terrible cook."

"Hey," Ava protested.

He lowered his hands and gave her a look.

"It's rude to say it, even if it's true," she muttered.

"That's a shame," Two Bears sighed; then he rose. "I will see if Spotted Owl has something to share with us. I assume you'll stay for dinner, Woman in the Furs?"

"Her name is Ava." Deathrider sounded completely exasperated. "I'm sorry about him," he apologized after Two Bears had left. "You'd best get dressed. He won't be long. He's clearly dying of curiosity."

"He is?" Ava wondered how Deathrider could tell.

By the time Two Bears came back with food, they were

both dressed. Two Bears sat opposite her and watched her closely while they ate. He made her nervous as all hell, and she kept dropping things.

"You can stay here," Two Bears said decisively. "We have room."

"She has a room," Deathrider said impatiently. "Back at the fort."

Two Bears ignored him. He met Ava's gaze. His dark eyes had the vaguest of twinkles in their depths. "You can stay here," he repeated firmly. "I will take my son to the Lakota camp now. There will be some goings-on late into the night, I imagine, and I don't want him shot climbing into a window later at the fort. White men are not known for their tolerance when it comes to visiting their women late at night."

Ava pressed her lips together so she wouldn't laugh.

"I won't be long," Deathrider promised Ava when he kissed her goodbye, leaving her sitting cross-legged in the furs.

"That is a lie," Two Bears told her. "He will be as long as he needs to be for the sake of decency. Our allies need to be appeased.

"Don't lie to women," she heard Two Bears scolding his son as the flap closed behind them. "It never ends well."

AFTER TWO DAYS of staying with Deathrider, Two Bears told her to gather her things from the fort.

"Don't get ideas," Deathrider warned his father again. By then, Two Bears had dropped so many hints about marriage that Ava knew very well what ideas Deathrider was talking about.

Deathrider himself wasn't talking marriage. Anytime they weren't discussing the treaty negotiations, which were moving slowly, they were . . . not talking at all. The moment they were alone, they were making love. It was impossible to think, let alone speak.

Ava felt an odd pang whenever he warned his father off the topic. Not that she was thinking marriage . . .

Was she?

What would that even look like? As she stared at the hide of the teepee walls, she imagined living with him, with his people. Would she be happy? Would *he*? He never seemed to stay in one place for long. What if he wandered off and left her . . . ? What then?

No, it was best not to think about the future. She had *now*, and that was all that mattered.

"You don't want to leave your belongings unattended," Two Bears told her on her third morning with them. He was preparing to go off to the amphitheater with the chiefs again. "It's a waste of time," he'd said of the treaty the evening before, when he'd come back from a day of talking. His voice was rough from smoking. "You might as well put rain back in the clouds as talk to a white man." He'd given Ava a sideways look. "No offense."

"No offense taken," she'd said cheerfully. "I quite agree. White men are a pain in the ass."

She startled Two Bears into a laugh.

"I like her," he told Deathrider the next morning as he left for another day's talking. "Help her go get her things."

"You don't have to," she said awkwardly once Two Bears had gone.

"You're here all the time anyway." Deathrider finished his breakfast and pulled his moccasins on.

"I don't have to be," she bristled. She felt suddenly exposed. Like she'd been forcing herself on him. It was because . . . because she liked him so much . . . and she wasn't sure how he felt about her in return.

Oh, he liked her well enough in bed. But what did that mean? Men liked to play in bed. It was *out* of bed where you learned how a man really felt about you.

"Come on, Cleopatra, no brooding today. Today we're

going to watch the competitions." He pulled her out of the teepee and into the sunshine. "And then we'll get your things and bring them back here."

Ava pushed all her broody thoughts aside and followed him out of the sprawling camps and onto the prairie beyond, where the younger warriors were staging horse races and competitions that included knife throwing, archery, ax tossing and wrestling. Flocked in chatty groups around the men were young women from all the tribes, preening and flirting, looking for husbands.

"You can't be serious?" a horrified voice broke into Ava's thoughts, and she turned to see a warrior in a heavily beaded and quilled tunic. His hair had been braided into an ornate style, the ends of his braids wrapped in rabbit fur and the fringe teased above his face. "That redhead had better not be who I think it is," the stranger snapped, glaring at Ava. "I heard she was here."

Ava had never seen him before, but he seemed to know her. And he didn't like her one bit.

"Are you *mad*?" the warrior railed at Deathrider in perfect English. "I mean, I knew you were, but I never thought you were *this* mad."

"Ava," Deathrider said calmly, "this is my friend Micah. Who appears to be out courting." He looked Micah up and down. "I can only assume your mother made you wear this."

"Ava . . . ?" Deathrider's friend put his hands on his hips and gave a disbelieving laugh, his head nodding up and down in numb astonishment. "What the hell is wrong with you?"

"Should I leave you two alone?" Ava asked, taking a cautious step back. He was a big warrior, and he looked mighty angry.

"Lady, you should have left us alone a *long* time ago." He turned his anger on Ava. Deathrider stepped quickly between them.

"She's not what you think," he soothed his angry friend, holding his hands up in a gesture of peace.

Micah gave a bitter laugh. "She's *exactly* what I think. How in the hell can you bring her here after everything that happened last year? Pete Hamble almost got me *lynched*."

Ava gasped as something clicked. *This* was Deathrider's friend, the one who'd left him in the desert.

"You left him to die!" she said furiously.

"What?" Micah blinked at her, shocked.

"How dare you rage at me when you're the one who blinded him and left him to die in the desert? *I'm* the one who saved him." Ava pushed Deathrider out of her way. She could fight her own battles.

"The hell you are," Micah growled. "*You're* the reason he was in the desert in the first place. And for the record, lady, I didn't *leave* him. That maniac Pete Hamble dragged me off."

"What?" Ava frowned.

"That's right, lady. Hamble was going to march me right into San Francisco and hand them my head. *He's* the one who left Nate to die in the desert, not me. And he did that because of *you*."

"You didn't tell me that," Ava accused Deathrider. "Why didn't you tell me Pete Hamble had your friend?"

"Because you were his *enemy*, you madwoman," Micah snapped at her. "As soon as he could see again, he came and got me."

Ava was having the oddest sensation of double vision. It was like being two people at once. She could remember clearly how it felt to be in the desert with Nathaniel, when she thought he was an Apache; she could see him in her mind's eye, weak, battered and blind. But then she felt all the swirling lust and happiness and . . . oh, Jesus wept, surely not . . . *love* of the past few days . . . and she struggled to make the Apache and Deathrider come together in her head as the same person.

It was all so confusing.

He'd been Deathrider all along. That was hard enough to understand, but now to learn that the whole time she'd known him, he'd been trying to rescue his friend . . . She remembered their struggle to find water, his fevers, his compliance when Voss had kidnapped them, his further compliance when Becky and Lord Whatsit had kidnapped them. . . . The whole time he'd been trying to get closer to Hamble so he could save Micah.

"That's why you left me at Señora Torres's," she said numbly.

"She's not what you think, Micah," Deathrider told his friend again. He put his hand on Micah's shoulder.

"She *is*, you idiot." Micah shook his hand off. "Think about all the years we've been through hell because of her. Think of the times we've had to run. Think of the gunslingers. Think of *all of it*. Because of *her* and those stupid books. That damn Hunt is still on, and here you are mooning over the woman behind it all."

"I'm not mooning," Deathrider snapped.

"Don't let her pretty face fool you," Micah warned. "I guarantee she's only with you for the story. You just wait. In a year or so, there'll be a book about all this." He flung his hand out at the vivid scene behind them. *"The Gathering of Bloody Fools Who Let a Redheaded Viper into Their Midst."*

"She apologized, Micah," Deathrider told him. "She's sorry."

"Is she?" Micah was steely with disbelief. "That's nice. I'm sure she'll be sorry again after the next book comes out. And the one after that." He shook his head. "I want nothing to do with her. Once she's ripped your heart out and used the blood to write her next book, you'll see that I was right."

They watched him go, stalking off into the crowd. Ava felt shaken.

"Do you mind if we don't watch the competitions?" she asked. "I might just go back and pack my things . . ." She searched his face. "If you still want me to come . . ."

He nodded, but he was looking tense. "Of course."

They were silent as they headed for the fort. And he didn't hold her hand.

❧ 30 ❧

ON MONDAY, SEPTEMBER 8, the treaty ceremony drew the negotiations to a close. Deathrider remembered the date, because it was also the day that he discovered Micah had been right. He should never have trusted Ava Archer.

Things hadn't been easy between them since they'd run into Micah, but when Deathrider actually stopped to think about it, when had it *ever* been easy between him and Ava Archer? Sex didn't erase the past. Just because she drove him wild didn't mean there weren't years of bad blood between them.

Micah had made him nervous, raking up the past like that; Deathrider had fallen headlong into a love affair with a woman who had wreaked havoc on his life, and it made no sense when you stood back and looked at it. The shock on Micah's face had sent a cold arrow into Deathrider's heart.

He'd trusted Ava for no other reason than he wanted to. Because he wanted *her*. But what had she done to earn his trust, really?

Nothing.

The thoughts tumbled through his head as they'd moved her into the teepee, and he felt himself withdrawing from her, watching her carefully. Suspiciously. Who was she, this woman? Was she Cleopatra, the softhearted, sharp-tongued woman who'd saved him from thirst, from Voss, from death? Or was she A.A. Archer, the merciless author of bald-faced lies about him? Or was she someone else entirely?

He was so confused.

His father clearly picked up on his mood, because he stopped hinting at marriage. They rode together to Horse Creek, where the treaty ceremony was to occur, flanked by the other warriors of their tribe. Ava wasn't with them; she wasn't one of them. She was riding along with the other whites, the only one not in uniform or heavily armed.

The clearing by Horse Creek was the only place big enough to hold everyone: man, woman and child. When the tribes had gathered in a circle, Deathrider found he had a clear view of Ava. As he watched her, he felt a chill. She was pulling something from the pocket of her riding skirt.

A notebook.

His blood turned cold as he watched her open it to a fresh page, lick the tip of a pencil and start taking notes. There was a lot to take in, and she wrote furiously.

Micah had been right. . . .

The treaty ceremonies began with every nation performing as part of the welcoming ceremony. When their turn came, the Arapaho sang as one nation, but Deathrider struggled to find his voice. He was fixated on the way her pencil danced over page after page of her notebook, recording every tiny detail. . . .

She'd never said she *wasn't* writing another book, he realized numbly. . . .

After all, why else was she in Fort Laramie in the first place? His stomach fell. How had that never occurred to him before? Why *else* would she be here? Why hadn't he questioned it? He'd seen her that day at the fort and lost his goddamn mind. Grinning witlessly at her, falling into bed with her . . . never once thinking to ask *why she was here*.

Micah was right. She was here to write a book about the

treaty. About the greatest gathering of Indians in the history of the nations.

And she'd lucked into a bonus story by finding Deathrider. . . .

He burned with rage. He was a fool. Worse than a fool. He'd never felt so humiliated in all his life.

Two Bears was giving him a concerned look. Deathrider realized he'd stopped singing. He lifted his voice, throwing the weight of his rage into the song. Damn her, and damn these whites. They all knew this treaty was nothing but a show.

The Cheyenne display suited Deathrider's mood more than his own people's song had. Their Dog Soldiers tore into the center of the circle, in war paint and mounted on their horses. The animals had been dusted and decorated with ribbons, with red ocher symbols painted on their flanks to show off their coups. The Dog Soldiers put on a terrifying show; their cavalry put the whites to shame.

Deathrider saw the colonel's face drain of color. The Cheyenne weren't even the most terrifying soldiers here today—that honor went to the Lakota, who had beaten these Dog Soldiers scores of times. Ava hadn't paled, Deathrider saw; in fact, she was scribbling faster than ever.

Once the welcome ceremonies had drawn to a close, Broken Hand stood in the center of the circle, introducing the nations to the superintendent, Colonel Mitchell. Broken Hand looked nervous. As well he might.

Deathrider saw Red Cloud at the head of the Oglála Lakota. He was brooding as he listened to Colonel Mitchell offer "restitution."

"What does he mean?" Two Bears asked Deathrider quietly. There was similar muttering around the first circle of warriors.

"He'll give us gifts because the wagoners have eaten our buffalo and let their animals eat all our grasslands."

"Restitution means gifts," he heard his father murmur to the others.

Gifts. Deathrider was scornful as Mitchell listed the foodstuffs, farming equipment, livestock and hardware.

"And this will not be a one-off gift," Mitchell told them, talking to them all like they were children. "This will be paid *every year.*"

"Is he simple?" Two Bears asked Deathrider.

"In exchange for these yearly gifts," Mitchell continued, "you will allow white travelers rights of passage across your lands."

Here it came. The sting in the tail. Deathrider stole a glance at Ava. She was in the act of pulling a second notebook from her pocket. He felt a lick of hate.

"You will also allow us to erect way stations along the trail, for the white travelers," Mitchell continued. "In return we will help you to define your own borders. Sovereign boundaries. And then we will help you to learn to respect those boundaries."

"Can you call it a gift if you expect things in return?" Two Bears said mildly.

"Civilization is upon you," Mitchell declared, "whether you like it or not. And civilization means the cessation of wholesale slaughter and warfare. You must stop killing one another."

Most of the tribes didn't speak English, so interpreters were translating Mitchell's speech, and whispers spread through the crowd as the meaning of his words sank in.

Red Cloud was stone-faced. In the conferrals Deathrider had attended, Red Cloud had been vocal that the whites were liars who were not to be trusted. Deathrider's gaze went to Ava again.

"They will do to us like they did to the peoples beyond the Mississippi," Red Cloud had said dismissively. "Put us in one of those 'Indian Territories.' Living like starving dogs."

"In exchange for our gifts," Mitchell said in closing, "we expect you to nominate *one* headman, who will speak for all of you."

That was when Deathrider recognized the whole affair for the farce it was. It would be impossible for these diverse and fractious nations to elect one man to represent all of them. He could see the incomprehension in the faces of the Lakota and on the faces of his own people. The whites didn't understand his people. Or any of the other nations gathered here today.

The clannish Lakota would never agree to this treaty. Red Cloud had come only to gauge his enemies and to take the gifts. He would play along and then do exactly as he pleased.

"If you cannot elect a headman, we will choose one for you," Mitchell told the murmuring crowd. Deathrider saw the dragoons were growing nervous and were fingering their weapons. It was time to end this nonsense.

But they couldn't. Because the "gifts" were still en route. They had days to kill.

"What are you going to do?" Deathrider asked his father as they left the Horse Creek site.

"The same as everybody else," Two Bears said. "Talk endless circles, watch the competitions, take their gifts and then go home."

"Are you going to sign the treaty?"

"Does it matter?" Two Bears said philosophically.

DEATHRIDER MADE IT back to the teepee before Ava. He was agitated, his mind racing. *You just wait. In a year or so, there'll be a book about all this* . . .

Why had he thought she had stopped writing? She'd never *said* she had. . . .

His gaze drifted to her belongings. She'd been scribbling in those notebooks. . . . Were there more notebooks in there . . . ? Did they contain the seeds of future books? Hell, did she have *manuscripts* in there? Books written about *him*?

She'd certainly have a lot of material by now. . . . The

urge to look was almost too strong to bear. He'd never violated anyone's privacy before and wasn't about to start now.

But then his mind flooded with those dime novels she'd written over the years. The stories of rape and murder, of kidnapping and *drinking blood*. His heart thundered in his ears, and a red fog rolled through him. She'd ruined his damn life; she'd risked the lives of his friends, and she'd *still* been out there today, scribbling away in that damn notebook.

And against all his better judgment, he gave into his raging curiosity and went through her belongings. Even though he'd been afraid of what he'd find, he was shocked by the extent of it.

Manuscripts. Lots of them. More books to be, with the name A.A. Archer scrawled across the top in a confident slashing hand.

She came in as he pulled another manuscript from her bags and threw it on a teetering pile.

"What are you doing?" The color had drained from her face. As well it might.

He stood.

She took a step back. "It's not what it looks like," she said.

He didn't dignify that with an answer. "I want you out of here by the time I get back," he told her flatly.

"You don't understand."

"I think I do. I want you out."

She grabbed his arm. "Please, Nathaniel."

"My name is Rides with Death," he growled, shaking her off. "Not White Wolf, not the Plague of the West and not any of those other lies you peddle. I have no interest in being your *specimen*."

"I never . . ." She caught herself. "No, I did. I know I did. And I'm sorry for it. Desperately sorry."

"No, you're not." He was so angry, he felt like hitting things. Like ripping the teepee apart from its poles. "If you were sorry, you wouldn't still be doing it."

"I'm not!"

Unable to believe that she'd dare utter such a bald-faced lie, he pointed to the manuscripts.

"None of that is made-up!" she told him. He was disgusted to see her defending that rubbish. She was just like Mitchell this afternoon, standing there lying to their faces. "I *won't* make the same mistakes again," Ava begged. "I promise you."

He couldn't stay. He wouldn't be able to hold his temper in check.

"We have different ideas of what that mistake was," he snapped. "You seem to think it's *what* you write, but as far as I can see, everything you write is poison."

"Stop," she said furiously, blocking his way as he tried to leave. "Maybe I've made mistakes, huge mistakes, but I *own them.* And I'm trying to do better. But if you love me, you have to love all of me. These books are part of who I am, for better or for worse." She held her chin high, her eyes glittering with tears.

He recoiled. Her words ripped something open inside of him, something painful. "I never said I loved you."

She staggered, as though he'd hit her. If he'd thought she was pale before, now she was positively bloodless. Her chin lifted even higher, and she gave him a brittle, regal look of disdain. "No," she said. Her voice was flat and cold. "I guess you didn't." Silently, she gathered her belongings, cramming the manuscripts back in her bag.

Except for one. That one she dropped on the furs, where they'd woken just this morning, tangled in each other's arms.

"Read it," she suggested tightly. And then she left.

He wasn't going to read the goddamn thing. He picked it up and threw it against the hide shell of the teepee.

And then he sat in the furs, with his head in his hands. He felt ten years old again. Bereft.

❧ 31 ❧

Ava was crying by the river when he found her. He was the last person she wanted to see. Well, maybe the second-to-last person. But, unperturbed, he came and sat down beside her. He stared at the confluence of the two rivers and the ways their waters flowed together, causing ripples of silver, like the fins of many fish.

"Did he ever tell you about his mother?" Two Bears asked thoughtfully.

"What?" Ava frowned.

"My son. Did he ever tell you about his mother?"

Ava scrubbed the tears from her face. She didn't want to cry in front of *him* or anyone related to him. "No," she said sulkily, wishing he'd go away so she could just cry herself into a puddle. Maybe she could flow with the rivers out to sea and just disappear. "We didn't have that kind of relationship." That set the tears off again. It turned out they didn't have *any* kind of relationship. She didn't mean anything to him except, oh God, as a sexual *plaything*.

She let out a hiccupping sob, and Two Bears gave her a startled look.

"I never had daughters," he told her gingerly. "I don't know quite what to do . . ."

"You don't need to do *anything*. Just leave me alone."

He made a thoughtful noise. "Well, I have had wives. So I *do* know enough to know that's not true." He simply sat there with her, watching the river slide by, while she cried.

"What about his mother?" Ava asked eventually as her curiosity got the better of her.

A smile flickered across Two Bears' lips. His lips, which looked remarkably like a bow turned on its side. "Brings Death," he said, his voice warm.

"Pardon?"

"That was her name. Brings Death."

"Oh." It was a name that conjured up all sorts of unpleasant things. It was no wonder she'd had such a heartless son, with a name like that, Ava thought ungraciously.

"She came one winter, during a snowstorm," Two Bears said. "I was out checking traps; I remember I wasn't having much luck, and I didn't want to go home to a scolding from my wives. We all felt like fresh meat by that time of the winter, and they'd been giving me hell. So I stayed out later than I normally did. And then I saw a shape through the snow. I thought it was a bear. Bear meat is a treat beyond measure in the depths of winter."

"Wouldn't a bear be hibernating?" Ava interrupted. She was so caught up that she'd stopped crying.

"Mostly they do. But this one wasn't." He gave her a quick smile. "But of course it wasn't a bear. It was Brings Death." Two Bears stared into space as he remembered. "Her white name was Gail Woodruff. She'd been traveling with her husband and children when the Lakota set on them."

"Traveling in winter?" Ava was horrified. Winters on the plains were brutal. The drifts could be twenty feet deep.

"They were green," he said with a shrug. "And they suffered for it. By the time she staggered toward me, she was the only one left. I took her in, and my wives nursed her. Unfortunately for us, she brought white plague with her. The tribe sickened and people died, and I was forced to cast her out." A shadow crossed his face.

"You loved her," Ava guessed.

"We never said the words," Two Bears said, "but I suppose I did. She wanted a house, like the whites live in, so I built her one, not far from the winter village. She lived there until she died. Rides with Death was born there."

"Rides with Death," she blurted. "Because he was the son of Brings Death?"

Not because he was a terrifying killer . . .

"Why are you telling me all this?" she asked.

Two Bears shrugged. "Because life is messy. And then it ends."

She didn't find either thought particularly cheering. He patted her on the knee. "You're young. You'll understand one day."

"Understand what?"

"That it will always be messy. You'll never understand each other. You'll be at cross-purposes. And then one day you won't have them anymore, and you'll wish you could argue just one more time. Misunderstand each other just one more time. Never say 'I love you' just one more time."

I never said I loved you.

"It's not the same," she said miserably.

"It never is." He stood up. "I'm sorry you're sad, Woman in the Furs." He put his hand on the top of her head. "My son has made me sad many times. And happy many times." He gave her a pat. "If you ever decide you want to get married, I will be waiting for your offer. I have a son who is in desperate need of a wife. Do you have a mother?" he asked abruptly. "Marriage is a job for mothers."

"I do, but she's thousands of miles away, and I haven't seen her in years."

"Humph," he said. "That might make things difficult."

Ava watched him amble off, back up the slope, toward his people.

She had no people to go to, she thought as she looked at

the sea of humanity spread across the plains. Not even one person. There was just her.

What on earth was she going to do now? Where could she go?

RETURNING TO THE fort had been a searing humiliation. The superintendent and the colonel were too busy to have paid much attention to her comings and goings, but Captain Scott noticed. He gave her a gloating look that boiled her blood. She wasn't going to stay, she decided. She had enough for a book—and she *was* going to write a book, no matter what Deathrider thought of it—so she didn't need to stay.

In the morning she would ride out. Where, she wasn't sure yet. St. Louis wasn't far. Maybe she could take a steamboat upriver. She was tired of being in the saddle. Maybe some time in a cabin on a boat was just what she needed. She bet there were all kinds of characters on a steamboat.

Through her window she could see the teepees glowing in the dusk. They were like lightning bugs in the darkness. Some were painted with designs that shivered and danced as the light moved inside the teepee.

Because life is messy. And then it ends.

She sat on the bed, the same bed where she and Deathrider had first made love.

He was such an *idiot*. And so was his friend, that Micah fellow. Both of them such *idiots*.

She sat in the dark, brooding, staring out at the lightning-bug teepees. The thing was, they weren't idiots. Not really. She was feeling so horrid precisely because they *weren't* idiots. Because everything they said was true. Their lives had been in jeopardy because of the books she'd written.

But everything *she'd* said was true too.

Because life was messy.

She didn't want to go to St. Louis. Or New York. She wanted to stay here. With *him*. Because she loved him.

Him. Not the legend, not the character in her books, not the larger-than-life figure who cast a long shadow from here to California. She didn't know *that* man.

She loved the droll Apache she'd picked up in the desert, the man who never lost his wits, even after being blinded and left for dead. She loved the man who was too kind to leave her or Becky or Lord Whatsit to suffer, even though it meant putting his own safety at risk. She loved the man who had a mouth like an archer's bow turned on its side, who had eyes like sunlit ice; the man who could kiss her until she couldn't remember her own name and love her until she wanted to die from the pleasure of it. The man who listened to her chatter and who soothed her when she fretted. She loved *him*.

Even though it was messy. Even though she didn't know the hidden depths of him. Even though he'd never said he loved her. She loved *him*.

Ava prided herself on her independence, on her courage and on her ability to survive just about anything. Well, here was one more thing she had to survive, that was all. So her heart hurt? Didn't everybody's?

She didn't want to give up yet, she thought fiercely. She remembered the black hole of the past months, before she'd found him again. Her life had felt like a wasteland.

Him being angry at her was still a damn sight better than not being near him at all.

It was infuriating but true.

Because life was *messy*.

❧ 32 ❧

"WHAT IN HELL are you talking about, 'life is messy'? What kind of nonsense is that?" Deathrider snapped. He stopped dead when he stepped through into the teepee. Ava's manuscript was sitting on his furs, propped up so he couldn't miss it. It was still crumpled, but his father had done his best to smooth it out.

"Stop meddling," he warned his father, snatching the manuscript and tossing it to Two Bears. "I'm not in the mood."

"You haven't read it," his father said.

"Of course I haven't damn well read it. I have no interest in reading it."

"Did you hear they're making Cut Nose the headman of all the nations?" Two Bears said.

Deathrider blinked at the abrupt change in topic. Cut Nose was Arapaho. It didn't bode well for their relationship with Red Cloud's Oglála.

"Our emissaries will go into that amphitheater and sign the treaty tomorrow," Two Bears continued. "Or not. But none of the headmen is allowed to represent the nations. The emissaries will be named 'chiefs.' As headman, I will not be one of them."

Deathrider was shocked by the heavy-handed crookedness of it. And he didn't think the U.S. Army could have shocked him any more than they already had.

"Red Cloud will not allow the Oglála to sign," Two Bears told him pragmatically. "Of the Lakota, I think only the Brulé will sign it. The treaty demands the Lakota hand over the lands by the Powder River to the Crow—Red Cloud will never stand for that."

"It will mean war," Deathrider said.

"There is always war."

"But this whole stupid process was meant to *stop* the killing. What was all that talk of 'lasting peace'?"

"There is no such thing."

"What are you going to do?" Deathrider asked his father. He felt stunned.

"Me? I'm going to help myself to all of their gifts, and then I'm going to go home. I think the more relevant question is, what are *you* going to do?"

"About what?"

Two Bears handed him the manuscript.

Deathrider refused to take it. "She's a liar."

"Or she's just a person who told a lie or two."

Deathrider scowled at him.

"Haven't you been listening to a word I've said?"

"Yeah," Deathrider said sarcastically. "Life is messy."

"It is." Two Bears nodded, pleased.

Sometimes Deathrider thought age might be getting to his father.

"People lie," Two Bears told him sagely. "Nobody agrees. Wars will be fought. Land will be lost. People will die. It's just constant mess. None of it seems like a good reason to kick a woman out of your furs. Especially a woman who loves you."

"She doesn't love me." Deathrider scowled. "She was only sleeping with me to get information for her damn books."

"You're only saying that because you haven't read this." Two Bears put the manuscript in his hand.

"How do you know? You can't even read."

"I'm your elder. I'm wise." He reached out and took Deathrider's face in both his hands and pressed his forehead to his son's. "Sometimes you are so much like your mother."

Deathrider couldn't stay mad at him after that. The man was a weasel.

WHILE TWO BEARS fussed about, packing up so they could leave after the treaty was signed and the gifts collected (although who knew when *that* would be), Deathrider started reading the damn manuscript. The title alone caught him off guard. *The Redemption of Ava Archer: A Setting Straight of Many Things*. He read it all the way through without getting up from his furs. The thing made him mad as hell. Maybe madder than he'd ever been in his life.

Now and then he read bits out to Two Bears, who agreed that he had every right to be mad. When Deathrider was done, he dropped the manuscript and glared at the teepee wall.

"Well, hell," he said.

"I've laid out your ceremonial clothes," Two Bears told him.

"What the hell for?" He wanted to kick things. She'd not only made up lies about him and ruined his life, and the lives of his friends, now she was depriving him of being *mad* at her. That book she'd gone and written was a thorough accounting of each and every exaggeration, fabrication and out-and-out lie she'd ever written. But she'd gone further than that. . . . She'd put *herself* in the book. It was the story of her life, warts and all. She had written about her childhood, her parents, her lovers, her travels, her loneliness, her greed, her desperate longing to meet the Plague of the West. . . .

And she'd ended it in the Apacheria, long before she'd ever met Deathrider, when she was alone and scared and at risk of dying of thirst. It was a book about consequences. And about the longings of a lonely girl . . . to have people listen to her; to be an adventurer, rather than a decoration or a plaything; to *matter*.

"Courting requires nice clothes," Two Bears said, brushing down the fringed tunic.

"Courting?" Deathrider looked up.

"I've asked her to dinner. That seems like a good first step."

"You *what*?" Deathrider's heart seemed to jump in his chest.

"You're a slow reader. I thought you'd be done well before now. She won't be long."

"Have you cooked anything?" Deathrider asked him. It was a stupid question, but he was so abruptly overcome with nerves that he couldn't think what else to say.

"Buffalo," Two Bears said proudly.

"Where did you get buffalo from?"

"I traded for it. Now, get dressed. I have things to do."

"What things?"

But Two Bears didn't answer.

DEATHRIDER'S HANDS WERE shaking as he laced his shirt. He shook them, trying to get rid of the tremor. Why was he so goddamn *nervous*?

Because he loved her.

He loved that madwoman. She was a fast-talking, quick-tempered, no-good, lying, sexy-as-all-hell harridan. She brought him nothing but trouble. But, as his father said, life was messy.

And he was a stone-cold idiot.

Micah was right too. What kind of idiot fell in love with the woman who'd ruined his life?

A lucky one.

He remembered watching Alex torture herself over Luke Slater, and Matt Slater torture himself over Georgiana—and his father torture himself over his mother. So, this was what it felt like. . . .

It was an upside-down, painful, horrid, flat-out *wonderful* way to feel.

AVA WAS SITTING in bed writing up her notes when Two Bears came knocking at the window. She frowned when she saw him there.

"Why didn't you come to the door?" she asked after she'd lifted the sash.

"Because I wanted to talk to *you*," he said, like that made perfect sense.

"Oh." She peered down at him. "Do you want to come in?"

"I've come to ask you to dinner."

Ava narrowed her eyes. "Does Deathrider know about this?"

"Yes," Two Bears said cheerfully. "He's getting dressed now."

"And he's fine with it?" Ava didn't trust him. "Are you matchmaking again? Because you know he hates that."

"He won't hate it this time."

"He will," she sighed. She hated herself for getting her hopes up. For a moment, she'd thought Deathrider really *had* invited her to dinner. But of course he hadn't. Because he hated her. "He will most certainly hate it this time. And next time. And all the times after that. You need to accept that he doesn't want to get married, not now, not ever."

"Why are you still here?" Two Bears asked her bluntly.

"I . . . the treaty . . ."

"Because you love my son."

Ava flushed. It was true. But she didn't like other people knowing it was true.

"And *he* loves *you*."

Ouch. "No," Ava hastened to correct him. "He *doesn't*. In fact, he told me he doesn't himself."

"He's read your book," Two Bears told her, "the one you

left for him. Now you're asked for dinner. And he's wearing his ceremonial robes."

Ava couldn't take it all in. "What does that mean, he's wearing his ceremonial robes?"

"It means he loves you." Two Bears tugged on her wrist. "Come on. You don't have time to change."

Ava didn't know how to feel. She was tingling with hope, but also sure this was a mistake. Two Bears was meddling again, and Deathrider was bound to lose his temper.

But at least if she went, she'd *see* him. And if she *saw* him, she might be able to *talk* to him.

"Hurry," Two Bears urged her. "We need to find some buffalo meat on the way."

"We what?"

"Don't worry. We'll find some. Have you seen how many people are out there? Someone is bound to have cooked buffalo."

❊ 33 ❊

TWO BEARS ABANDONED Ava at the entrance to the tee-pee. He lugged the pot of roast buffalo meat to the cook fire, muttering about how he'd been cheated by the person who'd sold it to him.

What did she do now? How did you knock on a teepee? There was no door.

"Hello?" she called nervously. Her palms were sweating. She rubbed them down her thighs.

The hide pulled back, and there he was. He looked even better than she remembered. For a moment, she was so glad to see him that she grinned. But then she saw his solemn expression, and her grin faltered.

"Your father asked me to dinner," she said, gesturing to Two Bears, who was standing over the fire, looking for all the world like he'd been cooking buffalo for hours.

"I love you," Deathrider blurted.

"What?"

He winced. "Hell. I meant, hello. I meant to say hello."

Her mouth fell open. "You *what*?"

"You're the most annoying woman I've ever met." His eyes were shining like quicksilver.

"That's more what I expected you to say," she said. She was reeling.

"You pose a serious threat to my life and liberty."

"I said I was sorry for that!" She bristled. How many times was he going to punish her? Admittedly, it was a big one . . . so maybe he had a few years left of making her wear that one.

"But I can't be happy unless you're around," he said. He looked flustered. "I'm mad at everyone all the time."

"He is," Two Bears agreed from his position by the cook fire.

"Apparently I don't care that you're a liar."

"I'm *not* a liar!" she disagreed, slapping him in the chest. "They were all—mostly—honest mistakes."

"I don't care that you talk all the time . . ."

"I do not!"

"You do," Two Bears told her regretfully.

"I don't care about anything but being with you. Because I love you." He took a deep breath, steadying himself after that unexpected outburst. "Well?" he said.

"Well, what?" Ava still didn't know what to make of any of it. She was offended, but she was also trying not to cry with sheer joy.

"You're supposed to tell me you love me too."

"Am I?"

He scowled.

She lifted on tiptoe and kissed him.

"That's not saying it," he muttered against her lips.

"I love you," she whispered. And then she kissed him again, and this time he kissed her back.

"The buffalo is ready!" Two Bears sang. He shoved between them. "Everybody sit down. I've been slaving over this for hours."

"He didn't, did he?" Deathrider asked Ava.

"No, he picked it up on the way here, from some Cheyenne woman."

"I knew it." He held her back when she went to follow Two Bears into the teepee. "We need to talk later."

"I thought you said I talked too much?"

"*I* need to talk," he admitted. "I owe you an apology."

"No, you don't," she said honestly. "You have every right to be furious with me. But I'm still going to keep writing."

He rolled his eyes. "Of course you are."

"What can I say? Life is messy."

"You've been meddling again," Deathrider complained to his father as they joined him in the teepee. "*Life is messy.*"

Two Bears ignored him and changed the subject. "I've been thinking about your mother," he told Ava. "I don't think it's right you haven't seen her in so long. Where does she live? St. Louis?"

"New York."

"You'll need to go to New York, then. It's important that your mother knows your husband."

"What husband?" Ava asked, rolling her eyes. He really was impossible.

"I've never been to New York," Deathrider said.

"What are you suggesting?" Her heart had lodged in her throat.

"It's not his place to suggest anything," Two Bears broke in. "It's his father's place."

Deathrider's clear blue gaze met hers. His eyes were twinkling. She couldn't breathe. *I love you* was one thing. . . . This was something else entirely.

"Do your job, then, old man," Deathrider told his father without once looking away from Ava.

Ava's heart was thundering. The sound of it filled her body and seemed loud enough to echo across the plains.

"By rights, his mother should talk to your mother. But we have no mothers here. So then I should talk to your father," Two Bears suggested.

"I haven't seen my father for almost fifteen years," Ava told him faintly. "He isn't part of my life."

Two Bears grunted.

"He doesn't like things being out of order," Deathrider observed, amused. "Or so he says. It seems to me though that he's always lived his life in a disorderly fashion. Loving women he shouldn't, fathering children who make his life a misery."

"Not a misery," Two Bears disagreed. "Just difficult." He licked buffalo grease off his fingers. "Ordinarily," he told Ava, "I would start with an offer of two ponies, and your father would push for a dozen. Then I would tell him that you wouldn't make much of a wife unless you had a husband with as many skills and talents as my son, and I would offer three ponies. Or sometimes only one, if he had offended me by not demanding enough ponies."

"By not demanding *enough*?"

"It would suggest my father is not wealthy enough to be able to pay a high dowry," Deathrider told her, amused.

"And I can certainly afford a dozen ponies," Two Bears said grumpily, as though Ava's imaginary father had actually insulted him by suggesting he couldn't. "Not that I would pay that."

"You don't think I'm worth a dozen ponies," Ava said, offended.

"You're too old."

Ava's mouth fell open, and Deathrider laughed.

"It's not funny," she snapped.

"Four ponies is my final offer," Two Bears said firmly. "You don't have many childbearing years left, and four ponies is generous."

"It *is* generous," Deathrider told Ava. "Most mothers only get two for their daughters."

But Ava was looking mutinous. "I might not be young, but I come with *experience*."

Two Bears looked shocked.

"Not *that* kind of experience," she gasped, blushing as she realized where his mind had gone.

Deathrider grinned at her, knowing that was a stone-cold lie. "I'd pay more ponies for that kind of experience."

She gave him a dark look. "I don't need your ponies. I'm wealthy in my own right."

"One pony," Two Bears snapped. "You lose one for being a loose woman and one for shaming my son by suggesting you bring more wealth than he does."

"I *do* bring more wealth than he does," Ava snapped back at him. "And I won't be bought and sold for ponies. If anyone's doing the buying, it's *me*."

Deathrider sat back to enjoy the show. His father had definitely met his match.

"I'll give you two ponies for your son," she offered. "He's not in the first flush of youth anymore, and he's a beat-up specimen."

"A beat-up specimen! He's an experienced warrior!" Two Bears protested. "Every scar is a mark of honor."

"Every scar is a *dent*."

Deathrider helped himself to another serve of buffalo. This looked like it might go on a while.

"And you want to talk about *looseness*," she raged. "He used to consort with *whores*."

"What's a whore?"

Deathrider choked on his buffalo meat. Then he had to explain to his father what a whore was.

Two Bears nodded. "This is proof of his virility. Very important in a husband. Six ponies."

"Proof of . . . ," Ava sputtered, outraged. "You called *me* loose and took away a pony!"

Two Bears narrowed his eyes. "You're right. It should have been two ponies."

Ava gasped, outraged. "That would have left *none*."

"Maybe still one. But not a very good quality one." Two Bears was enjoying himself.

So was Ava. "I'll give you two ponies for your son, and that's my final offer."

"His hunting skills alone are worth three." Two Bears sat back, as obstinate as a mountain.

"I'll give you three, but only if he never takes another wife."

Two Bears erupted in mock outrage, lapsing into Algonquin, but Deathrider could tell he was enjoying himself mightily.

"No second wife, no third wife. And no mistresses," she insisted.

"For a man this virile?" Two Bears cried. Deathrider just about choked on his buffalo again at that. "Five ponies!" Two Bears insisted.

"Five ponies?" She narrowed her eyes. "And I get him all to myself, for the rest of his life? No other wives, no other women at all?" Her gaze drifted to Deathrider.

"Don't look at me," he said, grinning. "This is his decision."

"Since when have you ever done what I told you?" Two Bears asked him in Algonquin.

"There's always a first time."

"Is this what you want? This woman? Even though she's old and talks a lot?"

Deathrider nodded. "Yes, Father. This is what I want." He paused. "But I still think you could get seven ponies."

In the end, he got six. Ava brought them to Two Bears' teepee the next morning and tied them nearby. Then she sat, as Deathrider had told her to do, and waited. The tribe watched, askance. Who paid a dowry for a *man*? What nonsense was this?

Two Bears made her wait for most of the day, for the sake of appearances. And then he came out and inspected the ponies. She'd brought good ones. She figured Deathrider was worth it. Approving of the ponies, Two Bears untied them and led them to the other side of the teepee, where he tied them up again. Then he invited her in.

Deathrider was waiting for her, grinning from ear to ear

like a fool. He was dressed in his ceremonial buckskins again, with a chest-plate necklace of porcupine quills and beads. His shining dark hair was in two braids, decorated with his usual black-tipped eagle feather, and his pale eyes were impish with delight.

Ava was glad she'd dressed up too, in her ivy-sprigged morning gown, or he would have put her to shame. She'd tied her green ribbon in her hair and tucked some late-flowering asters into its knot. Brides needed a flower or two, didn't they?

"This is when you would wait for the mother to fall asleep," Two Bears told Ava, taking her hands. "Once the mother is asleep, you both may leave—as husband and wife."

"That's it?" she said, astonished. "There are no vows?"

Two Bears shook his head. "No vows. You came in here a single woman. You leave a wife." He squeezed her hand. "Welcome to the tribe, daughter."

Ava found herself overcome with tears. *Daughter*. She met Deathrider's gaze. It was gentle. He held his arms open, and she fell into them, laughing and crying all at once.

"Hi, wife," he said huskily, lowering his head to kiss her.

"Wait!" Two Bears snapped. "You need to wait until I'm asleep."

"But it's only afternoon," Deathrider said, annoyed.

"Lucky for you I need a nap." He lowered himself onto his furs, muttering to himself about the ingratitude of children. He pulled the furs up over his head. A moment or so later, they heard some very unconvincing snores.

Deathrider rolled his eyes, and Ava giggled.

"Shall we?" he asked, holding the teepee flap back for her to exit.

"We shall," she said happily, stepping through. There were people milling about, waiting for them. Ava blushed at the knowing smiles.

"Isn't there some tradition among the whites about carrying a bride over the threshold?" Deathrider asked.

She squealed as he swept her off her feet and carried her off. But he only got a few steps, and then he stopped. "Hold on," he said. "We don't have anywhere to go."

He turned back around and carried her back into the tee-pee. "Out," he ordered his father. "It's our wedding day. I want to be alone with my wife."

His wife.

Finally. She belonged to somebody.

EPILOGUE

Utopia, Oregon, 1853

"L OOK WHAT I got," Matt Slater said. He came in from the snow like a bear, his dark hair and beard spotted with snowflakes. He was carrying a package wrapped in brown paper.

"Matt," Emma wailed, snapping a tea cloth at him. "Leave your boots out on the porch! I only just bought that rug, and I don't want your great big boot prints on it!"

"Why didn't you come in the back door like a normal person?" his wife asked him, lifting on tiptoe to greet him. "You know Emma makes everyone come in through the kitchen."

They were all at Tom and Emma's for a not-so-quiet wedding celebration. It was deep in December, close to Christmas, and already thin on light, even though it was the middle of the day. The wedding was being held in the house, rather than down in the small church in town, because of the bride's checkered past. The groom would have fought like a lion if anyone had questioned his bride's right to a church wedding, but the bride preferred a private family affair, surrounded by people who loved her.

There were so many of them there that they wouldn't fit

at a dinner table, so it was a stand-up affair. Emma had turned the front two rooms into a wonderland; there were festoons and bunting and candles galore to brighten up the dull day. She'd moved all the furniture to the edges of the room. "So there's room for dancing," she said. "It's not a wedding without dancing!"

"Matt wouldn't dance at our wedding," Georgiana had sighed.

"Good thing too," her sister-in-law, Alex, had laughed. "He's all left feet."

"He danced with me once," Georgiana said, "out on the trail. But he'd had a lot to drink."

"Well, there'll be dancing today!" Emma exclaimed.

The three of them had spent the day decorating the house, hanging the festoons of weeping spruce and the lacy ribbons. Emma and Anna had cooked up a storm, and they'd brought the wedding cake up from Seline's, their bakery in town. In the afternoon, the men ambled in, bringing the hordes of children with them. It was a fight to keep them away from the food.

"After the wedding!" Emma scolded, shooing them away. "Go do backflips off the stairs or something. But if you break anything, you'll be washing dishes all night!"

Outside, the bitter winter winds rattled the windows and blew gusts of snow into drifts against the side of the house, but inside the fireplaces were cheery with dancing flames and snapping with pinecones, and the candles flickered merrily. There were ale and cider, lemonade and ginger beer, and even two bottles of champagne on ice, which Emma had ordered especially for the occasion.

The house was full to bursting with people and ringing with the sound of children's laughter.

"This is *exactly* what I pictured when I bought this place," Emma said happily as she sailed past Tom. He snagged her by the hand and pulled her into the kitchen, where he kissed the life out of her.

"Not in the kitchen!" Anna scolded, whacking them with a wooden spoon. "There'll be enough time for that nonsense later." She pushed them back out into the chaos.

Emma shrieked when she saw Matt was still standing on her rug in his outside boots. "Out!" she yelled, pushing him out onto the porch.

He was unperturbed. "You were much friendlier when you were a whore," he said mildly.

Georgiana scowled at him from the doorway.

"You deserve everything you get after that," Emma told him. "Now, get your shoes off and hurry up! We've been waiting for you!"

"Victoria and Ned still aren't here either," Alex called. "You can't start without them!"

"Don't you people know that you can't be late for a wedding," Emma grumbled, heading back inside.

"Doesn't anyone care what I've got here?" Matt asked his wife, holding up the brown paper package.

"A wedding present, I presume?"

"I'm so sorry we're late!" They were interrupted by Alex's sister and her husband and their brood, who came tumbling out of the weather and up the porch stairs. "The baby needed feeding."

"There's always a baby that needs feeding in this family," Matt said.

"No!" Emma blocked the doorway with her body. "No one comes in until they've taken their shoes off."

"She has a new carpet," Georgiana explained to Victoria, reaching out to take the baby so Victoria could take her boots off.

Now that Victoria and Ned had arrived, the rooms were full.

"Doesn't anyone care about my package?" Matt asked.

"After the wedding," his wife soothed him, leaning into him and jiggling Victoria's son on her hip. "If we don't get this done soon, Emma's liable to explode."

"You'd think it was *her* getting married."

Georgiana laughed. "That will be the day. Tom keeps asking and she keeps saying no."

"That's because she's smart. Look at him. The more she says no, the more he's under her spell."

"Is that so? I should have said no to you, then?"

Matt looked horrified. "Bite your tongue. It was bad enough waiting all those years! I would have died if I'd had to wait any longer."

"She says no because they're already married," Luke told them, appearing with a glass of ale for Matt.

Matt rolled his eyes. "Sure they are."

"They are. I did it myself."

"You what?"

Luke grinned. "It was my first task as mayor. Seline . . . I mean, Emma . . . came barreling into the room the minute I'd taken my oath, dragging Tom with her, telling me to get the damn thing over with because she was sick of him pestering her."

"She didn't drag me," Tom corrected, joining them. "I wanted to be there."

"Why wasn't I invited?" Matt was outraged. He thumped Tom. "How come Luke got to go?"

"Because he officiated." Tom scowled and thumped him back.

"Fight!" Georgiana's twins shouted, leading the children in a chorus. "Fight! Fight! Fight! Fight!"

"You two always leave me out," Matt sulked.

"It was *private*," Emma said, rolling her eyes. "None of you needed to be involved."

"Only Luke," Matt grumbled.

"He was the only one who could do it. Stephen was off down in Amory to officiate the funeral of that old trapper."

"I'll never forgive you for this," Matt told his brothers.

"We'll add it to the list of things you'll never forgive us for," Luke said dryly.

"Don't drag me into this," Tom told him. "You mean, he'll never forgive *you* for. He likes *me* just fine."

"I used to. I don't anymore. And I'm not sharing the package with you now."

"No one cares about your package."

"I do," Georgiana reassured him.

"Me too." Alex thumped her husband on the arm. "I can't believe you didn't tell me you married them."

Matt brightened. Good. Alex would sort Luke out for him.

"Everyone *hush*. Get in place and behave yourselves! Alex, go get the groom!" Emma was in a state.

"Where is he?" Alex looked around, suddenly realizing he wasn't there.

"Through here," Anna called from the kitchen. "The poor love isn't feeling very well! He's overcome with nerves. And you might want to get your brother Adam in from the stables."

"Oh glory." Alex went flying through to the kitchen.

"You've got your job cut out, getting this lot to behave," Tom told his wife, taking the opportunity to nuzzle her as she passed.

"I've handled worse," Emma said, heading for the stairs. "I'll get the bride. Luke, you go stand over there, under the mistletoe. And this time, don't forget to say, 'You may kiss the bride.' Honestly, who forgets that part?"

"You did it deliberately at our wedding, didn't you?" Tom asked his brother.

Luke grinned. "I got no interest in watching you two slobber all over each other."

"Well, you heard her. Don't forget it this time."

"Do you think this'll be the first time they've ever kissed?" Luke asked.

"Yes," everyone chorused, rolling their eyes.

It had been quite a courtship.

"What *is* in that package?" Georgiana whispered to Matt. "I assume you've already opened it?"

He grinned. "You know me too well."

She leaned over and read the address. "It's addressed to 'the Slaters.' It might not have been yours to open."

"I'm a Slater, ain't I?" Impishly, he twitched the brown paper open, giving her a glimpse of its contents. Her eyes widened.

"Oh my," she breathed. "There's one for each of us . . . ?"

"And an extra."

"Do you think that means . . . ?" She frowned. "*What* does that mean?"

He grinned. "You'll have to wait until this nonsense is over to find out."

Alex came out of the kitchen in a swirl of blue skirts, all but carrying a tall, slender man. She poured him a stiff drink from the selection on the buffet. "Here," she ordered, "drink this. It will stiffen your nerves."

The poor man was shaking something fierce as he drank it.

"Maybe he's too sick to get married today, Alex," Adam said as he followed them. He still had snowflakes in his hair. He looked plenty worried about his older brother.

"Nonsense. He just needs to pull himself together." Alex hauled the man over to Luke. The thin man made a soft mewling noise at the sight of the mistletoe.

"You all right there, Stephen?" Luke asked kindly.

Stephen nodded, but he was very pale.

Alex straightened his collar and gave him a smacking great kiss on his cheek. "This is the best decision you ever made, and you know it." She was welling up.

Stephen looked appalled. He'd never been good with his sister's tears.

"Ma and Pa would be so proud of you," Victoria agreed. Oh no, now *both* his sisters were weeping. He shot Luke a panicked look.

"Women," Luke said with a helpless shrug.

Alex elbowed him in the stomach. "Don't you 'women' him. Not now. Say something nice."

"At least you're not married to *her*," he told Stephen with a grin, nodding in Alex's direction. Then he winked at his wife. "Was that what you meant by 'nice'?"

"Wait till I get you home," she muttered.

"Is that a promise?"

She blushed. "You are the *worst* flirt."

"I think you mean I'm very good at it."

"Can we start this wedding yet?" Emma hollered from the head of the stairs.

"Yes!" Alex hollered back.

"My mother would be rolling in her grave at the sight of this wedding," Georgiana sighed. "No one around here has any manners."

"Which is just the way you like it." Matt's arm dropped around her shoulders, and he hauled her close.

She couldn't argue with that.

"All right, Susannah, start playing!" Emma came dashing down the stairs and joined Tom in the crowd. She pulled her handkerchief out as Susannah started playing the piano in the corner of the room. Emma was crying before the first chord had sounded. Across the room she saw Anna and Winnie standing by the kitchen door, crying just as hard. She gestured for them both to join her and Tom. Family belonged together at weddings. She only cried all the harder when she saw how Tom put his hands on Winnie's shoulders, to comfort her. He was a good, good man.

The room was hushed except for Susannah's sweet playing and the loud sniffles coming from Emma and Anna. Poor old Stephen Sparrow was looking so peaky that Alex moved to stand behind him, to catch him in case he fainted. And then the bride appeared at the head of the stairs, and Alex realized that her older brother would be just fine.

Calla was a vision in lace. Thanks to Georgiana, her glossy dark hair was caught in cascades of ringlets above her ears; thanks to Emma, she was swathed head to toe in a gown fit for a princess; thanks to Alex, she was wearing a borrowed hair comb that had belonged to the groom's mother. Her dark eyes shone as she stared down at her husband-to-be. The groom himself appeared mesmerized, his mouth half-open at the vision before him.

They made quite a couple, the painfully shy preacher and the exotic ex-whore. As Luke led them through their vows, no one in the room doubted that it was a match well made, and by the time he reached the end, there wasn't a dry eye in the house.

"Wait!" Luke exclaimed after he'd pronounced them husband and wife. "I forgot! I'm supposed to ask you to kiss the bride."

There was laughter, and a few cheers. But Stephen Sparrow looked fit to faint again.

"Not here," Calla said firmly. She took his hand and led him out of the room. "This bit is just for us."

There was whooping as the door closed behind them.

"He's in for quite a time of it tonight!" Luke grinned.

"Didn't our girl look beautiful?" Anna asked, mopping her face. She gave Winnie a fierce hug. "It'll be you next."

Emma noticed the way Winnie's gaze drifted to Georgiana's eldest, Leo. "Not until you're twenty-one," she said firmly.

"You're being very patient," Georgiana told her husband as he waited through the food and the cake and the speeches. It was only once they'd cheered the bride and groom off, watching as their sleigh wound down the hill into town, the lanterns glowing through the snow, that Matt brought his package up again.

"Stop clearing up," he told Emma. "We're not done yet."

"Oh yes, we are," she disagreed. "There're still all the dishes to do."

"We'll help you," Alex sighed. "This family sure makes a mountain of dishes."

"No, sit back down." Matt glowered at her. "I've been mighty patient, but it's *my* turn now. Why is it no one ever listens to me?"

"Poor Matt." Luke rolled his eyes. "Everyone sit down. He's clearly got a bee in his bonnet about something."

To Matt's annoyance they all sat. Everyone always did what Luke said. It was infuriating. "Kids," he said, clicking his fingers at his lot and Luke's girls, "go and do the dishes for your aunt Emma."

They groaned.

"Do it."

"But we want to see what's in the package too!" Phin protested.

"Get along," Luke told them all. "Aunt Emma and Anna worked hard all day. You go and help them out by doing the dishes."

Matt could have kicked something. Look at that. Luke told them what to do, and they all did it, not a grumble to be heard.

"It's not funny," he snapped at Tom, who was smirking.

"The package," Georgiana reminded him, patting him on the behind, none too gently. She didn't have much patience with his bickering with his brothers. It was because she was an only child. Poor thing. He couldn't imagine not having brothers to fight with.

Matt took center stage.

"What is it?" Alex demanded.

"Patience, big sister, patience." Slowly, teasingly, he crinkled the paper back, inch by inch.

Luke threw a crust of bread at him. It whacked him full in the face and dropped onto the package. "Stop being an ass," he told Matt.

Matt went to hurl the bread back at him, but Emma got in the way. "Give me that," she snapped. "If you break any of my new things, I'll skin you alive."

"I hate being the youngest," Matt muttered. "Fine. Ruin the suspense. Here." He pulled the paper away.

"Books?" Tom said. "All this over some books?"

Matt rolled his eyes. "Yeah, idiot, all this over some books." He tossed one to Luke. "This one's for you and Alex."

Luke caught it and Alex peered over his shoulder. "It's that old book. That one about us. *The Gruesome Grady Gang* by A.A. Archer."

"It's signed," Matt told them. "And there's a letter in there for you, from Deathrider."

"He's alive!" Alex gasped. "Oh, thank God! All the rumors said he was dead . . ."

"Well, he was alive when he wrote this," Luke said. He and Alex fell into silence as they read their letter.

"This one's yours and Emma's." Matt tossed another book to Tom.

Tom caught it and stared down at the cover in surprise.

"Well?" Emma demanded. "What is it?"

"The Outlaw and the Whore," he said slowly. "By A.A. Archer."

"The story of Deathrider's last ride," Matt said solemnly, "and the death of the redheaded whore Seline."

"How do you know that?"

"He opened the package earlier," Georgiana sighed.

"Read the last page," Matt encouraged his brother.

Tom flicked to the last page, and his eyes widened.

Matt grinned.

"Honey," Tom said to his wife, "apparently you were killed by Apaches. And then I was killed by someone called 'Bad Becky' and her lover, 'the Lord of Justice.' I mean, Deathrider/Tom Slater was . . . Apparently as I died, I called your name with my final breath."

"Of course you did." Emma took the book off him. "Does that mean . . . it's all over? For him? And for us?"

"I guess so. Looks like Bad Becky and the Lord of Justice collected on the bets in San Francisco. Bet they were the toast of town." Tom turned the final page and took in an advertisement at the back of the book. "There's a sequel coming about their exploits apparently."

"Is there a letter for us in there from Deathrider?" Emma asked. "I'll be put out if he's not written to me too."

"I have them here. One for each of you," Matt said. He passed them over.

"I know which book is *ours*," Georgiana said with a grin, reaching over Matt to pull a book out of the package.

"No, sweetheart. That one isn't for me." He dropped a kiss on her forehead. "That one's for you and Emma to share. Although I reckon Leo might be interested in it too." Matt met his stepson's eyes across the room. Leo was practically an adult and had remained when the little kids went to watch the dishes. His gaze was solemn.

Emma's head snapped up. "Why? What is it?"

"The Hog of Moke Hill," Georgiana said gleefully, holding up the book.

"It tells the story of a filthy tyrant named Hec Boehm . . . ," Matt said. Leo went pale and Emma's eyes glinted.

"And what happens to him?" Emma asked, sounding greedy for information.

Matt laughed. "I don't want to spoil the story for you, but according to our friend Miss Archer, he meets a mighty bad end . . ."

"Thank goodness," Georgiana sighed, flipping to the end of the book. "Is this one true? Or is it made up like *The Outlaw and the Whore*?"

"Read your letter," Matt suggested, "and I'll think you'll learn which bits are true."

"He got *married*!" Alex squealed, ripping their letter out of Luke's hand. She'd been reading over his shoulder, but now she took the letter away from him. "Rides like a Dolt actually got married! *Deathrider* got married!"

"He did not!" Emma snatched the letter out of her hand. "Who to?"

"Who to?" Georgiana demanded when Emma stayed silent, tearing the letter from her sister-in-law's hand. *"He did not!"*

"He *did*!" Alex laughed, and twirled in a circle. "It's too perfect for words."

"Would you three witches stop speaking in riddles and *tell us*?" Tom demanded.

"Rides with Death," Emma announced dramatically, "went and got himself married to . . ."

"Tell me, you harridan!"

"Ava. Addison. Archer. *Herself.*"

Tom groaned. "Does that mean we have to go and rescue him?"

"Don't you *dare*." Emma plonked herself in his lap. "We only just finished fixing up the house and got ourselves properly settled. You're not going anywhere."

"Well, *someone* needs to rescue him."

"He's a big boy," Luke drawled. "He can take care of himself."

"Yes," Georgiana laughed, "haven't you read the books?"

"What did you get, little brother?" Luke asked, wandering over to Matt.

Matt looked down at the last book. *The Redemption of Ava Archer: A Setting Straight of Many Things.* He flipped open to the inscription. *For Matt Slater. Who was right all along.*

"I got an apology."

Luke tousled his hair. "That's a first."

"Tell me about it." Matt met his brother's gaze. "You reckon they'll be happy together?"

"I think they'll enjoy making each other miserable."

They turned to look at their wives, who were gleefully hugging Emma. Tom was watching with a goofy smile.

"Just like us, huh?"

"Yeah, little brother. Just like us."

Turn the page for an excerpt from
the first Frontiers of the Heart Novel

BOUND FOR EDEN

Available now from Jove

Grady's Point, Mississippi, 1843

ALEXANDRA BARRATT WASN'T a violent woman. Most times she couldn't even crush a house spider. But Silas Grady was no spider. Silas Grady was a blackhearted, lily-livered, weak-kneed swamp rat. If anything, death was too good for him.

She couldn't believe the nerve of him, knocking on her door like nothing had happened. He was swaying on his feet and there was still dried blood stuck to his neck.

"It's your only hope," he said thickly. "Marry me, Alex."

If Sheriff Deveraux hadn't been standing right there she might have forgotten she wasn't a violent woman and reached for the ax. But Sheriff Deveraux *was* standing right there.

"Marry me, Alex. I can keep you safe."

"Safe!" White fury licked at her. He was mighty lucky that ax was out of arm's reach. "And who will keep me safe from *you*?"

"Alex—"

"It's Miss Barratt to you, and how *dare* you come here after what you did today?"

"What I did . . .?" He swayed, confused.

Alex said a silent prayer. With any luck she could carry this off and get out of here before Gideon showed up. Silas was a lecherous, scheming idiot, but his brother was something much, much worse. "You arrest him," Alex demanded, turning to the sheriff.

The fat old man looked startled. He made a gruff *harrumphing* noise and hiked his pants up. "Now, Miss Barratt, you know I can't do that."

"I know no such thing. Every week since Ma and Pa died I've come to you with a complaint about this man." She pointed a fierce finger at Silas's face. "He and his brothers have terrorized us. They've tried to starve us out. And you've done nothing!"

The sheriff grew red-faced, but didn't manage more than a mutter. It was all Alex expected from him, bloated excuse for a lawman that he was. "If you won't do anything I'll send for a federal marshal."

"Now, really, Miss Barratt, this isn't the frontier."

"It might as well be, for all the law there is around here." She lifted her nose in the air and tried to look imperious, which wasn't easy considering her rising panic. She had to get out of here before Gideon came. He'd probably made it home by now and found the mess she'd left . . . Oh glory, the thought was almost her undoing. Gideon was a maniac. Who knew what he'd do to her if he caught her?

"If you aren't going to arrest him, I don't see what choice you leave me." She kept brazening her way through it. Thank the Lord Silas was still concussed from that blow to the head. If he had half a brain he'd be demanding that the sheriff arrest *her*. He had fair cause: over the course of the afternoon she'd knocked him out cold, stolen his brother's property and assaulted his evil witch of a mother.

And it was entirely his own fault, she thought, fixing him with a black glare. He flinched and fingered the wound on the back of his head.

"I've told you at least twenty times in no uncertain terms

that I won't marry you," she snapped at him. "But you won't take no for an answer, will you? Well, I didn't say yes when you starved us, and I won't say yes now. So get off my property! It *is* still my property, you know." She turned her black glare on the sheriff, who at least had the good grace to look shamefaced. "If you won't arrest him, you could at the very least escort him off my land! Trespassing *is* still illegal, isn't it?"

"Come on, Grady," Sheriff Deveraux mumbled. "You'd best try your luck another day." He took Silas by the elbow.

"I'm your last hope," Silas said miserably. "He won't hurt you if you're my wife."

"Get out!" The edge of hysteria in her voice was quite real. She slammed the door behind them and yanked up the trapdoor to the root cellar, where her foster siblings were hiding. "Up!" she ordered. "Quick!"

"Give the gold back," her foster sister moaned as she struggled up the ladder. "Now, while the sheriff is still here."

"Are you mad?" Alex raced through the small house, throwing what precious little they still had into a sheet and tying it into a bundle. She tossed it to her foster brother, who was sitting on the lip of the cellar, looking despondent. "Don't worry, Adam," she soothed, running her fingers through his tousled hair.

"*You're* the mad one!" Victoria snapped. "Gideon will kill you if you don't give that gold back."

"He'll kill me anyway," Alex said grimly.

They heard a shot and Victoria screamed. Alex ran for the front window.

It was too late. Gideon was here. Poor, fat Sheriff Deveraux lay on the squashed dogwood blossoms, slain by Gideon's shotgun. As Alex watched, Gideon took a swing at Silas with the still-smoking gun. Silas managed to duck, but slipped on the fleshy blossoms and fell on his behind. Gideon kicked him.

"This is your fault, Spineless," he snarled. "If you hadn't kept sniffing after that bitch, none of this would have happened." The look on his narrow, ferrety face made the hair rise on the back of Alex's neck. It wasn't the anger that was frightening, it was the glint of barely suppressed glee. Gideon wasn't just going to hurt her, he was going to *enjoy* hurting her.

He looked up and saw her standing in the window. "Evenin', Miss Barratt," he called. Like they were meeting down at the store, or at one of Dyson's dances. She'd be damned before she'd show him fear. Alex yanked the blind down. It was a relief not to look at him, but a little scrap of cloth wasn't going to protect her from him. She bolted the door.

"Well, that ain't a neighborly way to behave," he called. God help them, the bastard was enjoying himself already. "Ain't ya going to ask us in for tea?" He laughed and Victoria started to cry.

"What are we going to do?" Vicky whined. "We don't even have a gun."

No. And the ax was still buried in the block out on the porch. Alex grabbed a couple of kitchen knives. They looked puny in her hands. "Here." She gave one to each of her siblings. "We'll go out the bedroom window. Go!" She grabbed a fire iron for herself.

Victoria looked down at the knife in horror. "What do you expect me to do with this?"

"Be careful," Adam said. "Ma said to be careful with knives. They cut."

Alex closed her eyes. What was she thinking? What good would a knife do Adam? He couldn't hurt anyone. *You were touched by God,* Ma used to tell him when the town children had laughed at him and called him names. The Sparrows had taken him in when no one else would have him. *You're one of His special children.* He was eighteen now, the same age as Vicky, but he was still a child. He would always be a child, and she had no right asking him to wield a knife.

"Don't touch knives," he said firmly as he looked down at the blade in his hand. "Don't touch the stove, it burns; don't touch the fire, it burns."

There was a knock at the door. "Last chance to be neighborly, Miss Barratt!"

"Go to hell!"

"Alex!" Alex heard the raw terror in her sister's voice at the exact moment she smelled the smoke. Victoria had opened the bedroom door to reveal a slow rolling cloud of smoke and the lick of orange flames. The bastard had set fire to the house!

"Oh, little pigs!" Gideon called, his voice bright with laughter. "Open up or I'll huff and I'll puff and I'll blow your house in!"

"We're going to die!" The knife fell from Victoria's fingers and clattered to the floor.

"No, we're not." Alex shoved Victoria and Adam toward the ladder to the loft where Adam slept. "Climb," she snapped. The smoke was rising and they coughed as they scurried upward. As soon as they reached the narrow loft, Alex threw open the window. There was a big old black cherry tree growing close to the house.

"You can't expect us to climb down that!" Victoria gasped.

"Why not? We did it all the time when we were children. Out you go, Adam. Be careful. When you get to the bottom, run for cover in the woods. If we get separated, we'll meet at the old fishing spot." She turned back to Victoria as Adam disappeared down the tree. "Did you hear me?"

"The old fishing spot, I heard." Victoria coughed. "If I die climbing down that tree, I'll never forgive you."

"Fair enough."

"Alex?"

"What?"

"What if Bert and Travis are out there too? They might have circled the house."

It *had* occurred to Alex that there were still two Grady brothers unaccounted for. But what choice did they have? They could hardly stay here and burn, could they? And walking straight into Gideon's arms wasn't an option. "I saw them heading into town earlier. They'll be out drinking all night," she reassured Victoria, although she wasn't sure it was true. Gideon might have fetched them home after all the kerfuffle.

She heard the crackle of wood and winced. "Hurry, before the whole house goes up." The two of them scrambled into the tree. Alex heard Victoria's shallow breathing. "Don't look down," she counseled. By the time they reached the bottom the house was an orange blaze.

"Oh, little pigs!" Gideon was coming around the house, his mad voice high and clear, even over the crackling of the fire.

Alex grabbed Victoria and they went belting toward the woods. And ran smack bang into Silas. Victoria screamed.

"Shut up," he growled, covering her mouth with his hand.

"You let her go!" Alex shrieked, clawing at him.

"Shut up the both of you, or he'll find us." Silas's eyes widened suddenly and he went very still.

"Adam!"

Her brother still had his knife, the tip of which was pricking Silas in the kidney. "Knives are sharp," he said, "knives cut."

"Spineless?" Gideon's voice was coming closer. "Have you caught a little pig?"

"Let her go," Alex hissed at Silas.

"Let me help you," he begged.

"You?" she scoffed. "I'd sooner trust an alligator than a Grady." Alex took the knife off Adam.

Silas regarded it with disdain. "That won't be any match for his shotgun."

"Run, Victoria. Take Adam and run."

"Where?" Victoria was wild-eyed with panic. "And what about you?"

"If we leave him, he'll only come after us. Get away. I'll

meet you at that place I mentioned." She shooed them with her hand. "Go!"

She couldn't risk looking away from Silas. She was afraid he'd make a lunge for her. She could hear the crunch of bracken under her siblings' feet as they ran, and then they were gone and she was alone with Silas Grady.

"What are you going to do now?" He sounded smug. He had her. She couldn't run; he would throw her to the ground the minute she turned her back.

"I'll tell you where the gold is if you promise to let me go."

He shrugged. "Gideon will make you tell us where the gold is anyway."

"Spineless!"

She jumped. Gideon was so close.

"I can protect you, Alex," Silas whispered. "Your brother and sister are free. They can stay free. I can keep you safe."

Like hell. Alex's fingers tightened around both the knife and the fire iron. She would rather die than give herself to Silas Grady. But she couldn't die, she thought desperately. Victoria and Adam would never survive without her. They needed her.

"You promise you can keep me safe from Gideon?" She crept closer to him, playing for time. The longer she kept him occupied, the better the chance of Victoria and Adam getting away safe. The hilt of the knife was slippery in her sweaty palm. Did she have it in her to use it?

"I'd do anything for you," he said. It was hard to see his face in the falling darkness, and the glow from her burning home backlit him, rimming him with orange light. It was a mercy not to see his expression. She didn't want to see his stupid look of adoration, or the uncompromising lust in his eyes. She shuddered.

"Anything?" She crept closer, until they were almost touching. One thrust would send the knife sinking into his belly. Her fingers tightened around the hilt.

She broke out in a cold sweat and the knife trembled in

her hand. She couldn't do it. She just didn't have it in her to murder a man. She pictured Vicky and Adam waiting for her at the fishing hole, huddling together in the darkness as the bullfrogs sang and the mosquitoes whined. If she didn't kill him now, she would have to sacrifice herself. She clenched her teeth. One thrust and it would be over . . .

No. She couldn't. The knife fell from her fingers and she tasted ash. "You win," she said softly.

"Oh, Alex." Silas's foul mouth crushed down on hers and his disgusting tongue jabbed at her lips. The minute she felt that thick, hot slug of a tongue she came to her senses. Revolted, she spun around and struck out. The fire iron whistled through the air and came down hard on the back of his head. Silas made a grunting sound and then slumped to the ground.

She heard Gideon closing in, still mocking her with a sound like a squealing pig. Panicked, she ran. Behind her, the black cherry tree had caught and blazed like a roman candle, and there was an almighty crunching noise as the house collapsed in on itself. Sparks flew skyward into the night. There went home.

Alex ran like the devil himself was after her. She had to find Adam and Victoria and get out of Grady's Point before Gideon caught up to them. She heard a gunshot echoing through the firelit woods. Never mind getting out of Grady's Point, they had to get out of the state, maybe even the South. She wouldn't rest safe until she'd put a thousand miles between herself and Gideon Grady.